UNDER THE JAVA MOON

BASED ON A TRUE STORY

HEATHER B. MOORE

SHADOW
MOUNTAIN
PUBLISHING

Image credits: page i, design element by mmalkani/Shutterstock; pages vi and vii, maps designed by Sheryl Dickert Smith; original camp map from *Tjideng Reunion*; all interior photos provided by the author.

Visit us at shadowmountain.com

This is a work of historical fiction. Although based on the real-life experiences of Marie Vischer Elliott, additional characters, interactions, and dialogue are fictitious and products of the author's imagination.

Library of Congress Cataloging-in-Publication Data

Names: Moore, Heather B., author.
Title: Under the Java Moon: based on a true story / Heather B. Moore.
Description: Salt Lake City: Shadow Mountain, [2023] | Includes bibliographical references. | Summary: "A World War II novel about a Dutch family who is separated during the war when the Japanese occupy the Dutch East Indies"—Provided by publisher.
Identifiers: LCCN 2023006865 | ISBN 9781639931538 (hardback)
Subjects: LCSH: World War, 1939–1945—Concentration camps—Indonesia—Java—Fiction. | World War, 1939–1945—Prisoners and prisons, Japanese—Fiction. | Prisoners of war—Indonesia—Java—Fiction. | Dutch—Indonesia—Java—Fiction. | Java (Indonesia)—Fiction. | BISAC: FICTION / Historical / 20th Century / World War II | LCGFT: Novels. | Historical fiction. | Biographical fiction. | War fiction.
Classification: LCC PS3613. O5589 U53 2023 | DDC 813/.6—dc23/eng/20230313
LC record available at https://lccn.loc.gov/2023006865

Printed in the United States of America
Publishers Printing

10 9 8 7 6 5 4 3 2 1

Dedicated to Marie Vischer Elliott,
a woman of grace, strength, and faith.
With all my heart, thank you for letting me tell your story.

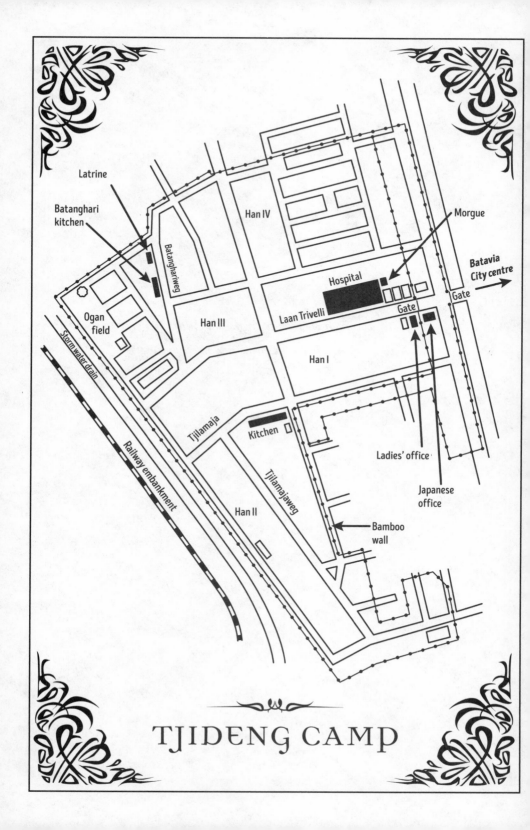

TJIDENG CAMP

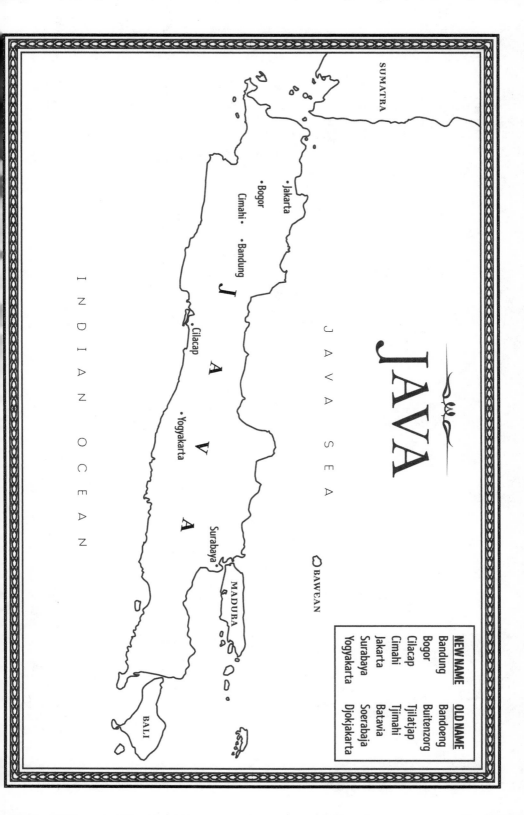

SUMATRA

INDIAN OCEAN

JAVA SEA

JAVA

·Jakarta
·Bogor
Cimahi· ·Bandung

·Cilacap

·Yogyakarta

Surabaya·

MADURA

BALI

◌ BAWEAN

NEW NAME	OLD NAME
Bandung	Bandoeng
Bogor	Buitenzorg
Cilacap	Tjilatjap
Cimahi	Tjimahi
Jakarta	Batavia
Surabaya	Soerabaja
Yogyakarta	Djokjakarta

INTRODUCTION

In August 2021, I had the privilege of meeting Marie (Rita) Vischer Elliott for the first time when she traveled to my home state. My husband and I visited with her for a couple of hours, and she told us stories about her remarkable life in her lovely South African accent. Marie is now called Mary by family and friends, but for clarity, I'll refer to her as Marie in this introduction and as Rita—a childhood nickname—in the main story. During our first meeting, Marie and I were both vetting each other. I wondered if I'd be able to do justice to a story that Marie had kept to herself for so many decades. She wondered if she was truly ready to share such private and difficult memories.

Marie told me that her family never spoke of the war after it ended. Her parents had wanted to fully move on. Years later, Marie ventured to ask her mother some questions, but her mother gave precious few answers. The topic was still considered a closed book to the past. Because of all that she'd endured, Marie never wanted to watch war movies or read about wars. She especially stayed away from stories about concentration or prison camps and their victims. Like her parents, she was keeping her past firmly behind her.

Yet, a change came over Marie in recent years, and she was surprised to realize that she wanted to share her past. She wrote up a brief summary of her experiences, and she began to tell her family and friends about what had happened to her. The lock she'd kept on her memories and fears was slowly turned, then opened.

Marie's remarkable story begins when she was a child, living in Indonesia (then called the Netherlands East Indies or Dutch East Indies).

Both her parents were originally from the Netherlands. Her father, George Vischer, who worked for the Royal Packet Navigation Company (KPM), was stationed on Java Island.

During World War II, after Japan invaded, conquered, and then occupied Indonesia, Marie's family was divided up and sent to live in Japanese prisoner-of-war camps. Marie, her mother, grandmother, and younger brother Georgie were sent to the Tjideng camp, which interned women and young children. Men and older boys were sent to their own camps. This began a period in Marie's life that would shape her childhood, her future, and her beliefs.

Although I had read dozens of books about World War II over the years, I hadn't ever read anything about the Dutch people's experience in Indonesia. When I searched for books or films about the subject matter, I found only self-published memoirs. I bought everything I could find and began to read.

I was already excited to write a historical novel about Marie's early life just from what she'd shared with me in our first meeting, but I knew nothing of the war's impact on Indonesia and its people until I dove deeper into research. Story after story shared by former POWs revealed experiences long buried. At the end of this novel is a list of the memoirs and other historical sources that helped frame this book.

As a backdrop to Marie's story, it's important to understand why Indonesia became a strategic asset to the Axis power of Japan during the war. Due to oil embargos against the Axis powers, the oil fields that spanned the Netherlands East Indies (NEI) drew Japan to the islands, searching for mineral resources to fuel its war effort. To Japan, the Dutch colonies were a diamond in the Pacific.

In the early 1600s, the Dutch had joined other traders, such as the Spanish, Portuguese, British, Ottomans, etc., bent on securing trade routes and trade posts throughout southeastern Asia and the Americas. In 1602, in order to establish a dynasty over other traders, the Dutch founded the world's first multinational trading empire called the Vereenigde Oost-Indische Compagnie (VOC) or Dutch East India

Company. This began two centuries of the VOC running trading posts. When the VOC declared bankruptcy in 1796, the Netherlands government took over, and Dutch colonization of the East Indies went into full effect. Over the next several decades, Dutch families moved to Java and Sumatra, seeking opportunities in private enterprise.

On the day that the Japanese military bombed Pearl Harbor (December 7, 1941, in the States, but December 8 in the NEI), the NEI was spurred into action, and they declared war on Japan. Every Dutchman age eighteen or older was conscripted into one of the royal military branches to undergo accelerated military training. Overall, the Dutch relied mostly on the western Allied powers for help. But the Allies were busy defending other Pacific Rim countries, such as the Philippines and Singapore, leaving the NEI vulnerable to attack.

Battles raged between Japan and the Dutch, on land and on sea, ending with the Battle of the Java Sea, in which the NEI and Allied fleet was soundly defeated. Three days later, Japanese forces landed on Java Island, and one week later, on March 8, 1942, the NEI governing body officially capitulated to Japan.

As a result, more than one hundred thousand Dutch men, women, and children were funneled into prison camps. An additional forty thousand Dutch men became prisoners of war, many of them shipped to work camps in Burma, Japan, and Thailand.

The Dutch-Indonesians, or Indos, were caught in the middle. Descended from Dutch and Indonesian marriages, due to decades of intermarriage from Dutch colonization, the Indos were given a choice: live in the prison camps or serve the new Japanese regime.

Earlier, the Netherlands had imposed its culture on that of the native Indonesians, and now, with the takeover of the NEI by Japan, everything related to Dutch culture was replaced by Japanese culture. Even Batavia, the capital of the NEI, was renamed to Jakarta. The Japanese language was taught in schools, the Japanese calendar implemented, and local time became Tokyo time.

Around 6,000 of the 18,110 islands of the Indonesia archipelago are inhabited. In 1941, the total population of the NEI was around sixty million. By the end of the war, thirty thousand European POWs, the majority of them Dutch, had died. In total, four million civilians, including Indonesians and Indo-Europeans, perished as a result of malnutrition and forced labor.

Under the Java Moon follows the story of Marie and her family, as they endured the hardships of living in a POW camp during World War II. At the end of February 1942, Marie's father, George Vischer, fled for his life with a group of naval officers in order to join up with Australian Allied forces. On a fateful day in March 1942, Marie Vischer was ushered out of her home. Marie, her elderly grandmother, her mother, and her toddler brother were forced into a women's prison camp run by the notoriously cruel Japanese commander Captain Kenichi Sonei.

This is Marie's story.

HISTORICAL TIMELINE

May 15, 1940
The Netherlands surrenders to Germany

December 7, 1941
Japan attacks Pearl Harbor

December 8, 1941
Netherlands East Indies government declares war on Japan

December 11, 1941
Japan occupies Malaya

December 25, 1941
Hong Kong surrenders to Japan

January 10, 1942
Japanese forces invade Netherlands East Indies

February 15, 1942
Fall of Singapore

February 27, 1942
Battle of the Java Sea, lost by Dutch and Allies

March 1, 1942
Japanese forces land on Java Island

March 5, 1942
Batavia (Jakarta) fully occupied by Japanese forces

March 8, 1942
Dutch forces decide to capitulate to Japan

CHARACTER CHART

HISTORICAL CHARACTERS

Vischer Family

George Vischer

Maria Johanna (Mary) Vischer

Marie (Rita) Vischer

George (Georgie) Vischer

Robert (Robbie) Vischer

Maria Van Benten (oma, grandmother)

Dientje (Tie) Jansen (aunt)

Jacques Gouverneur

Eduard (Ed) Gouverneur

Olga Slingerland

Corrie Van der Hurk

Mrs. Venema

Ina Venema

Dr. Ada Starreveld

Kemala (name changed)

Anja (name changed)

Bima (name changed)

Dea (name changed)

Tjideng Camp Guards

Captain Kenichi Sonei   Lieutenant Sakai   Kano   Noda

Officers of Auxiliary Minesweeper *Endeh*

Commander P. Rouwenhorst

Lieutenant Commander J. F. W. de Jong Van Beek en Donk

Lieutenant Commander First Class B. Hessing

Lieutenant Commander Second Class M. J. Arnoldus

Marine Steam Service (Msd) Officer Second Class, Lieutenant P. Hooft

First Lieutenant George Vischer

Second Officer Government Navy, Lieutenant D. H. Poelman

Second Officer Government Navy, Lieutenant Third Class H. Rutgers

Third Officer Government Navy, Lieutenant Third Class D. P. C. Feij

Third Engineer Government Navy, Lieutenant Third Class G. M. J. Van Wijnmalen

Recruit Quartermaster J. J. Ter Pelkwijk

Recruit Quartermaster H. T. Jaden

Crew of Auxiliary Minesweeper *Endeh*

Sailor First Class P. Castricum

Sailor First Class W. O. Mackintosh

Sailor First Class W. A. T. Mulder

Sailor First Class A. M. Buys

Sailor First Class C. Chatelain

Sailor First Class J. Jens

Sailor First Class W. Bakker

Recruit Sailor A. W. Pesch

Recruit Sailor F. C. Loeffen

Recruit Sailor H. J. Hijmans

Sailor Third Class J. F. Franken

Hospital Attendant's Mate J. F. Van Beek

FICTIONAL CHARACTERS

Vos Family

Willem	Claudia	Greta	Johan
Hetty	Elly	Petra	Hilda

PROLOGUE

"The history of these Japanese camps threatens to be forgotten,
because those who were there have kept silent about them
and those who have broken the silence have done so too late,
after their indignation and their hate had softened or faded,
and they had already died the death that is called mildness."

—JEROEN BROUWERS, TJIDENG CAMP

September, 1945

RITA

Rita Vischer never thought she'd see her father again. Not because they'd received a notice at Tjideng camp that something had happened to him at the Glodok prison camp. But because of the other children in the camp who'd lost their fathers. The news of death came in every day, and there were so many of them. Who was Rita to not share in their fate?

The children's grief over the news of losing their fathers, their brothers, their opas, was just another in a long list of losses. They'd lost their homes, their schooling, their bikes, their toys . . . but it was the unknown that hurt so much.

Three years. It had been over three years since Rita had seen Papa. She remembered his brown eyes but couldn't picture his face. Every day she checked the list that the British Red Cross sent to prison camps throughout the island of Java.

His name had yet to be on it.

As eight-year-old Rita perched on the wilting fence in front of the house she'd been sharing with more than a hundred other women and children, she examined the faces of the men and boys walking into camp. She couldn't look away from the joyous reunions that didn't include her family. Her heart had lodged in her throat, and her eyes burned hot, but still, she watched. And still, she hoped that out of the limping, hobbling men with gaunt faces mapped with three years of war, she'd see her father's familiar brown eyes.

He was not here. He wasn't among the scarecrow-thin men and boys arriving at Tjideng. These men looked nothing like the men or boys Rita had known before the war. Before Japan invaded the Netherlands East Indies and took over Java Island. Before the Dutch surrendered.

Perhaps Papa would never return. Perhaps he'd been among those who'd died of malnutrition, disease, torture, or exposure to the relentless tropical sun.

Rita had witnessed all of these in the women's camp.

To live or to die. That was the question she faced each day. Each hour. Rita had seen sheer willpower drive a woman to live another day, defying all odds against diseases like malaria, mumps, dysentery, measles, whooping cough, beriberi, and tropical sores, when another woman might simply collapse during roll call. The weight of the merciless sun and suffocating heat becoming the breaking point that sent a woman or girl to her knees. Never to rise again.

Even now, the joyous reunions playing out at Tjideng didn't erase the burden of the past. The heaviness sat upon Rita's shoulders like a metal box full of memories waiting to be opened again.

Her heart thumped as, only meters away, a teenaged boy—lean and lanky with sharp edges for cheekbones—embraced his petite mother.

They each wept. Reunited at last. The mother and son had both survived their internments. What would the future bring now?

All will be well, her mother's voice echoed in Rita's mind. Would it ever be well? The human heart was on its own timetable it seemed. To continue beating, or to stop. She didn't know if all would be truly well, for her, or for anyone. But she had to believe in something, so she chose to believe and let her mother's words imprint themselves on her skin.

PART ONE
1941–1943

CHAPTER ONE

"Pray for us."

—JEROEN BROUWERS, TJIDENG CAMP

Four Years Earlier: December 9, 1941

RITA

"What are they digging, Ita?" Georgie asked, pointing his stubby finger in the direction of their neighbor's house, where a group of men dug a trench between the properties.

Rita looked up from where she'd carefully laid out the set of new clothing for her teddy bear on the veranda. Oma had sewn them this past week, and it was time to try them on. Rita especially liked the little white shirt with its stitched-on Dutch flag.

"It's a bomb shelter," Johan cut in.

Rita narrowed her eyes. Johan was always about, joining in, and then playing with Georgie so that Rita was left on her own. At nine, Johan was a know-it-all. And his scruffy dog, a black retriever, was never far behind. Kells trotted across the yard, bounded up the veranda steps, and nudged his head against Rita's arm.

"Don't say that, Johan," Rita said, giving the dog a scratch. She didn't want her little brother upset or scared about why they had to build bomb shelters along Laan Trivelli.

"He's going to know soon enough," Johan said in that superior tone of his.

A sliver of sunlight bounced off Georgie's blond curls as he looked from Johan to Rita. "What's a bomb shelter, Ita?"

Rita's real name was Marie. She wasn't sure when her parents had started calling her Rita, but it had stuck since her mother's name was Mary—very close to Marie's own given name. Since her little brother couldn't say the "R" when he'd learned to talk, he'd started calling her Ita.

"It's a place that will protect us from bombs, I think." Rita said this with a sigh, a little uncertain herself about what was truly happening across the yard, though she'd been told many times that she was wise for her age. She shot Johan a glare, as if silently telling him not to say more. "There won't be bombs here, though. We'll be safe, Georgie."

Johan leaned his tanned arms against the railing of the veranda. His blue eyes were the same blue as many of her own family's. Instead of the blond hair that was so common among the Dutch, however, Johan's was nearly red. He wore it parted and combed to the side.

"Why are they digging, then?" Georgie pressed.

This was a very good question. The war had always been in Europe. The Netherlands was occupied by Germany. But there were no Germans on Java, and the war wasn't here.

"They are just being safe, but we'll be fine—" Rita started to explain.

"They're digging trenches because of what happened yesterday." Johan's gaze went to Rita. "Don't you know that Japan bombed Pearl Harbor yesterday?"

Rita stiffened, glancing at Georgie. "Of course, I know it." Just because Johan was older didn't mean he was smarter at everything.

"Pearl Harbor is far away," she said. "What does that have to do with us? We're not part of the war."

The war in Europe was always talked about on the radio. Every kid on Java Island, even Georgie at two, knew who Hitler was. Sometimes

Rita would ask Johan questions because she was too curious about the things Mama and Oma wouldn't tell her. Papa was busy with his job at the Netherlands' naval headquarters and only came home at night.

But right now, she didn't want Georgie to be scared about being bombed. He was too young to worry about things that wouldn't happen anyway. Johan waved at a fly that had started pestering him. Then he hopped up on the veranda and sat cross-legged next to Georgie. The dog, Kells, settled next to Georgie, who gave the dog a fierce hug. The black retriever rolled over onto his back to get a belly rub.

"Since Germany conquered the Netherlands last year," Johan continued, reaching over to scratch his dog's soft, floppy ears, "we aren't safe anymore from Japan. They're coming here next."

Rita pulled her knees up to her chest and peered at Johan. "Why does Japan care about us? We're not doing anything wrong."

Johan sighed like her question was silly. "Japan wants our oil fields. The Allies have cut them off, and we have lots of oil."

Biting her lip, Rita gazed at the men clustered around the trench they were digging. Was Johan speaking the truth? She wasn't sure because he liked to tease a lot. Yet something prickled her skin, and it wasn't an insect.

Next, Johan spoke in a low voice as if hoping the adults inside the house wouldn't overhear through the screened windows. "My father said that the bomb shelter is for your family too."

That caught Rita's attention. What would her parents think about that?

"Can we play in it?" Georgie asked in his innocent tone.

Rita wasn't sure how to answer, but she didn't want Johan to, so she hurried to say, "No, we can't play in it because it's going to be muddy with all the rain. We'll only go there if we have to, but I'll hold your hand." Georgie gave a solemn nod, and she reached for his hand and squeezed. "It will be like a game. You can close your eyes, and I'll tell you stories. Like at bedtime."

Johan, for once, didn't counter Rita. But now she was distracted and found herself watching the Javanese men, including their gardener Bima, in their digging. There were other dug-out trenches along Laan Trivelli. Six feet deep and five or six feet long. The roofs were made out of grass turf, held up by bamboo, giving an opening to see the sky at least.

Even though the December weather was warm and humid as usual, a shiver skated across Rita's arms. She didn't want to get inside a trench that was the size of a grave. Even if there were bombs coming. Maybe she could hide in her bedroom under her bed.

Johan's mother called him from their veranda, and he hurried off, Kells loping behind him.

By the time the sun had shifted against the horizon, Rita didn't feel like playing with her teddy bear anymore. "Come on, Georgie," she said. "Let's help Kemala in the kitchen."

They found their cook, Kemala, making egg rolls, which she called *loempia*—a favorite food of the family's. They usually bought them from a Chinese man at the market, but he hadn't been around the past week. Kemala was a Javanese woman, native to the island of Java. She wore a peach-colored sarong and her long dark hair in a braid. Rita often helped their cook with whatever needed to be done.

Most of the Dutch families living in their neighborhood on Laan Trivelli had servants. Rita's family had a gardener, a cook, a maid, and a nanny. Mama told Rita to always help whenever she could. Mama didn't like housework much, so she spent most of her time sewing the children's clothing, making dresses for herself and the servants, and working on embroidery, crocheting, and knitting. She even made carpets and tapestries. Since Papa was so busy, their gardener worked in the gardens and made repairs around the house and yard.

Now, Kemala was making the egg rolls.

"Where's Mama?" Georgie climbed up on a chair.

Rita moved close to him so he wouldn't fall off.

"Your mama is resting," Kemala said. She spoke Malay, but she'd learned some Dutch, and Rita had learned some Malay. Their conversations were always a mixture of both.

Rita frowned over Mama, though. She had been resting almost every day. Midafternoon was always the hottest part of the day, and that was when Georgie had to take a nap, but it was almost sundown. Was Mama sick?

"Can we help you make the egg rolls?" Rita asked.

"Of course," Kemala said with a smile, showing the small chip on one of her front teeth. She'd once told Rita it happened when she'd crashed on her bicycle.

Rita had been fascinated with the story because when she was Georgie's age, she'd almost been run over by a bike when she'd been with their nanny, or *baboe*, on their way to the market. Rita had pulled away from their nanny, Anja, and run straight into the bicycle. The pain was so terrible that she'd cried the whole way home.

"Can I help?" Georgie asked in an eager voice.

Her easy smile still in place, Kemala slid over the bowl of rice, bits of egg, and chopped vegetables for Georgie to stir.

"Very slowly," Rita said as she scooped out a spoonful and set it in the middle of a wrapper. Then she began to roll—it was her favorite part of making egg rolls.

Next Kemala asked Rita to stir the *pecel*—a sauce made with peanuts and spices, while Kemala began to fry the egg rolls.

Georgie said he wanted to watch for Papa to come home. One of his favorite activities.

"I'll come," Rita said, finished with her mixing. Then she could see the progress on the trench too.

Just as they reached the veranda, Georgie called out suddenly, "Papa's here!"

Sure enough, Papa had wheeled his bicycle into the front yard. He strode up the long walkway to the house, carrying the newspaper. He wore his naval officer uniform, but his sleeves were pushed up, and the collar of his shirt was stained with perspiration. Rita felt proud when she saw Papa in uniform. Mama had said he was a very hard worker and everyone respected him. He'd become a chief engineer officer with a

Diploma C, which meant he could serve on Dutch submarines and any size ship.

"Papa!" Rita called, hurrying down the steps.

Georgie scurried behind her.

Papa scooped off his hat. The orange of the setting sun gleamed against the black waves of his hair. His brown eyes crinkled at the corners as Rita hugged him around the waist. He smelled as he always did, of starched cotton and pine and the sea air. He pulled her close for an instant.

Georgie's arms clamped around Papa's leg.

"Let's get inside." Papa said, his tone stern. "I'm burning up."

His tone sent Rita on alert, and she released her father. Was he worried about what had happened at Pearl Harbor? Perspiration darkened the back of his shirt as he strode up the steps to the veranda.

Rita grasped Georgie's hand and followed Papa into the house.

Mama walked into the front room just as they arrived. Her blonde hair was wispy about her face from her nap, but her fair skin was paler than usual. Was she sick? Or maybe she was worried like Papa?

"George," Mama said in her soft voice.

Papa stepped close and kissed her cheek. "How are you feeling, Mary?"

Mama was nearly six feet tall, making her a couple of centimeters taller than Papa, but she still wore heels when she dressed up. Her blonde hair contrasted with Papa's neat dark hair. Rita loved the way her mother's eyes sparkled when she looked at Papa. Usually when they greeted each other, he had a smile that he shared only with her.

Right now, no one was smiling.

"What's this?" Mama said as Papa handed her the newspaper.

The headlines on the front page were set in large, bolded type. Rita knew a couple of the words, but Mama whispered the rest: "Netherlands Indies Declares War on Japan." Mama covered her mouth with a hand. "Oh, no."

Rita gazed at the printed words that made her stomach hurt for some reason. What would Johan say about this? Did he know yet?

"Can it be true?" Mama asked, her tone shaky.

Papa scrubbed his fingers through his hair, making it stand up. "Let's sit down. We need to talk."

It was then that her parents must have realized their two children were watching and hearing everything.

"Rita," Papa said. "Take Georgie into the kitchen. Help out Kemala with dinner."

She didn't want to say that they'd already helped. Instead, she grasped Georgie's hand and once again took him into the kitchen. His lower lip was trembling—not because he'd been able to read the newspaper headlines—but because her brother felt the things other people felt. If they were upset, he was too. He didn't need to know why.

"I want Mama," Georgie whispered, his large hazel eyes filling with tears.

Rita looped an arm about him, pulling him close. As she ruffled his blond curls, she said, "She has to speak to Papa. Then we'll be together for dinner."

Georgie bit his lip and nodded.

"Come on," Kemala interrupted. She'd been watching from the doorway. "You can both help wipe off the table."

His eyes brightened then, and with another word of encouragement from Kemala, they wiped down the already clean table.

Even though Rita's hands were busy, and the kitchen had begun to smell delicious, she listened hard to make out the hushed conversation between her parents. Words like *blackout* and *curfew* were spoken by her father.

Rita had heard these words on the radio before. They were always about Europe and Germany. Not Java and Japan.

"What's all this?" Oma said, coming into the kitchen.

Rita turned to see her grandmother. Oma was a tall woman, too, but her hair was more brown than blonde. And her eyes were hazel—which meant they had more than one color in them. This had always fascinated Rita.

"Oma!" Georgie said, dropping the cleaning rag and lifting up his arms.

Oma chuckled and stepped close to hug the little boy. Then she drew away. "Smells delicious, Kemala."

The woman dipped her chin, and next Oma fastened her eyes on Rita. Her smile always calmed Rita's heart—no matter what she was worried about.

"Can I help with anything?" Oma asked, squeezing Rita's shoulder.

Somehow Rita felt better. Her grandmother had come to Java after visiting Uncle Jack in America. Rita hoped that Oma could stay with them forever. She played games with them, bought them trinkets or treats at the market, and told them stories about the Netherlands.

"We need to set the table for dinner," Rita said. "Georgie, you can do the forks."

He slid off one of the chairs and gleefully hurried to the utensil drawer.

The screen door shut, and Rita turned to see her father crossing the yard, tugging on a pair of worn gloves. He'd changed out of his navy uniform and wore a loose tan shirt and shorts.

"Where's Papa going?" Georgie said.

Rita had no idea, but then Mama spoke from the doorway, "He's helping our neighbors dig a trench."

Oma released a long breath. "Has it come to that?"

Mama nodded.

Rita's heart was thumping again like a racing rabbit. She rose from the table. "Can I help him dig, Mama?"

Her gaze seemed about to say *no*, then she glanced outside. "Maybe there is something you can do. Take drinks to the working men. They must be thirsty."

Oma crossed to Mama, and the women clasped hands.

Even though the women weren't speaking, Rita knew they were

both worried. She didn't want to imagine exactly what they were worried about. Rita helped Mama fill up four glasses, three for the Javanese workers, and one for Papa.

Then she headed out of the house, walking slowly to carefully carry the first two glasses to the men. She wanted to get away. Inside the house, the emotions were becoming too heavy. Outside, with her father, there was air, trees, and an orange sky. Maybe she could help dig, or maybe she could help with the roof. Whatever it was, she wanted to stay busy. To drown out her fears that her island was now at war.

CHAPTER TWO

"I was 17 years old then, and all my Dutch teachers were recruited into the military service; as a consequence, the schools
were closed. Every healthy Dutch citizen 18 and over was also
inducted into the navy, army or air force. They had to undergo a
physical. They received their uniform, underwent an accelerated
military training of approximately 30 days, were issued a rifle and
ordered to go 'fight the [Japanese] for Queen and fatherland.'"

—WILLEM H. MAASKAMP, WERFFSTRAAT PRISON

MARY

"Please be a dream," Mary Vischer whispered as a wailing siren split
apart the darkness of the night. But waking up with a jolt screaming
through her whole body was no dream.

Her husband, George, was already moving about the bedroom in
the dimness, pulling on a shirt, then grabbing a flashlight they'd set
aside for air raids. "We need to go, Rie," George said. "I'll get the children up if you fetch Ma."

Mary turned over in bed, squeezing her eyes shut for another half
second. Exhaustion pulsed through her.

"Rie," George said again. He'd started calling her Rie, pronounced
ree, when they'd met in Holland—since her mother's name was Mary,
too.

"Maybe it's a drill," she suggested, her eyes still closed. She felt the warm weight of her husband's hand on her shoulder.

"I'd like to believe it's a drill, but we're not making that bet."

With a groan, Mary opened her eyes and rose to a sitting position. Why was she so tired? It might be the middle of the night, yes, but over the past week or so, she'd been dragging. She picked up her eyeglasses from the bedside table, then pulled on a robe, not for warmth, but because the trench her husband had helped dig days ago wouldn't be all that clean.

By the time Mary reached her mother's bedroom, she was already coming out, carrying her own flashlight. With the blackout order in place, no one was allowed to turn on lights after curfew, and flashlights had become a popular purchase item. Down the hallway, the children's voices echoed with questions. Little Georgie's higher-pitched one asked for his mama and was quickly followed by her husband's lower, rumbling tone of assurance.

"Is everyone ready?" George asked, his deeper voice reaching Mary and her mother.

"Yes," Mary said.

As long as the family was together, they were ready.

George reached the front door and held it open, then motioned for them to step onto the veranda. On his hip, he carried their sturdy, blond-haired son. Grasped in his large hand, he held onto Rita. She'd brought along her teddy bear.

Mary's heart tugged at the sight. Her young children had already been exposed to things they shouldn't have to be, Rita at nearly five years old and Georgie almost three. War half a world away was terrible enough, but with the bombing of Pearl Harbor, the Japanese military had increased their offense, literally arriving at Java Island's doorstep. The Royal Netherlands East Indies Army had mobilized, and every male Dutch citizen, aged eighteen and up, was asked to join the navy, army, or air force to fight for the Queen and their fatherland against Japan.

With so many teachers joining the military forces, schools had been shut down. Every day, the newspapers called for seventeen-year-old volunteers to work in civilian defense jobs. At the fire department, the radio stations and telephone switchboards, the airports and harbors.

How had this all become their world? Arm in arm with her mother, Mary hurried across the lawn to the bomb shelter. Their neighbors, the Vos family, were already inside.

George guided the two children inside, then he held out his hand to aid Oma, and finally Mary.

"Everyone here?" Willem Vos asked. He and his wife, Claudia, were sitting across from them, on the opposite bench. Their son, Johan, sat next to Greta. She was twelve, a petite girl, who kept mostly to herself.

Once everyone was seated on the crude benches, George adjusted the grass turf roof. The first few times they'd had air raid drills, the entire neighborhood of hiding people had kept completely silent, listening for any sound of an approaching plane as the siren wailed from its tower.

Now, Mary could hear chatter from various shelters. The voices were indistinct, yes—but it somehow made her feel less afraid and less alone. The entire neighborhood was in this together. Somehow, they'd make it through, come what may.

"Mama," little Georgie whispered against her neck.

Mary pulled him onto her lap in the near darkness. His small body nestled against hers, and she breathed in his scent of warm sun and leaves. As much as Mary loved both of her children, there was something different about Georgie. He hadn't gone through the terrible twos like most toddlers did. He was eager-to-please, affectionate, quiet, but joyful. Almost too good for this world of harshness and pain and doubts.

Rita sat on the other side of her. Oma kept a firm arm about Rita, while George remained near the entrance of the shelter, peering out into the black night.

"I can't even hear any airplanes," George said, as if it were possible to hear them over the sirens. "Everything will be fine."

"It's a practice drill," Willem added. The man was a few inches taller than her own George, with rusty-brown hair. He also served as a naval officer at the Netherlands' naval headquarters in Batavia.

Next to Willem, his wife Claudia threaded her arm through his. She was a heavyset woman nearing fifty years old. Her skill as a seamstress was unmatched in the neighborhood, and she sewed baby clothing designed with beautiful embroidery.

"At least it didn't rain much today," George said. "Not much water in the trench."

It was monsoon season, so the water in the trenches would only grow worse as the days wore on. Mary wasn't surprised that Claudia wasn't doing any talking; she didn't feel like talking either. She wanted to be back in bed, with the covers pulled tight around her, even if it was too hot for blankets.

"Did you hear about the Dutch submarines from Soerabaja that sunk a couple of Japanese transport ships?" Willem continued, as if he were merely discussing the weather.

"I did."

Yes . . . they had. And it made Mary want to take the first airplane out of Java. Soerabaja was the naval base in East Java. The fact that the Dutch military had begun an offensive attack on Japanese ships wasn't good news in the least. Soerabaja might be hundreds of miles away, but it was still on the same island.

Her stomach twisted hard. *Too close*, Mary thought. Much too close. She pulled Georgie nearer and realized he'd fallen asleep. What a blessed thing. The pain in her stomach eased into something softer, but it lingered, like faint nausea.

Oma whispered a prayer, ignoring the conversation of the men. Mary had been born Catholic, but like her mother, she leaned more toward less-structured Protestant beliefs. George wasn't much for religion. Born Lutheran, he'd been forced to go to church as a child. That might have contributed to him protesting such formality now. She and her husband made a fine pair. Having her mother in their home here on Java had been wonderful in more ways than one. It had reminded Mary of her roots, and of the harsh trials her mother had dealt with in her life, particularly during World War I. She'd endured an alcoholic husband, who she eventually divorced, then raised three children on her own. Only to come out as a giving, loving, faithful woman.

If there was something to be grateful for on this night of blaring sirens, deepening darkness, and growing fear, it was having her family together, gathered safely. Food in the house. A husband with a job. Everyone was healthy. Mary closed her eyes and joined in Oma's prayers, although Mary's were silent pleadings in her heart.

About an hour passed before the sirens stopped. The quiet returned, and no one spoke for a long moment, letting the stillness stretch. Finally, George ushered everyone out of the shelter when the sirens didn't come back on. He took the sleeping boy from Mary's arms, and Rita held onto her father's other hand as everyone walked tiredly back to the house. Mary rotated her shoulders, bringing feeling back into her arms after holding Georgie for so long.

She turned to wave goodbye to their neighbors. The children and Willem had already gone inside, but Claudia stood gazing up at the sky.

"Have a good night," Mary said. "I hope there aren't any more interruptions."

Claudia set her hands on her hips and tilted her head as if she were studying the phases of the waxing moon. "It's been foretold. Did you read the Malay paper from earlier today?"

Mary shook her head. She didn't read Malay, the native tongue of the island, although she could get by with speaking a little at the markets and to their employees. "What did they say? More military attacks?"

Claudia took a few steps until she was on Mary's property. "They printed the story of the Djojobojo legends. Mr. Venema explained it to me."

The neighborhood was full of European contract workers and their families. The Dutch family, the Venemas, lived a few doors down, and they were joint friends. Captain Jan Venema and his wife had three daughters, the youngest fifteen.

"Ah, I know a little about the legends. What did the article say?" Mary had heard about the twelfth-century monarch who'd made predictions that some Javanese believed in. The monarch had ruled over Kediri, one of the Hindu kingdoms.

Claudia smoothed back hair from her face. The moon bathed her in a pale light, making her features look at bit ghostly.

"This one is about how the Javanese were warned centuries ago that their misdeeds would be punished by living under the rule of a seafaring people."

Mary blinked. "The Dutch?"

Claudia shrugged. "Perhaps. The sea-faring people would divide the land up for themselves, but then they'd be driven away by the people coming from the north."

Hairs stood up on Mary's arms. Japan was north.

"The people from the north would remain here for the time it takes for corn to ripen, or however long a rooster lives."

"Which is . . ."

"Three months or three years," Claudia provided. "After that, a Ratu Adil would appear and take over, ruling over the islands and bringing them to independence and prosperity."

Mary released a breath. The legend was hauntingly accurate about the past. Could there be truth in all of it? Regardless . . . it was uncanny that a twelfth-century monarch had revealed such details. "Let's hope that whatever is about to happen with this war, the duration is three months instead of three years."

Claudia rested her hand on Mary's shoulder for a brief moment. "I feel like I'm praying every moment."

Mary nodded, thinking of Oma's prayers and her own inside the bomb shelter.

Claudia's hand dropped. "It's all we can do, eh? Leave God in charge."

She sounded like Oma. "Yes. It's all we can do." Fortunately or unfortunately. Mary couldn't shake the foreboding, along with the feeling of frustrated exhaustion as she walked back into the house.

The clock ticked from the kitchen. Rarely was the house so quiet as to hear it. Everything was still dark, but Mary didn't turn on her flashlight. George must have already put the kids to bed, and Oma would certainly be asleep. Mary had never known someone who could fall asleep so quickly as her mother.

As she stood in the middle of the room, collecting her thoughts on having endured another bombing raid, her stomach surged. She pressed a trembling hand against it, wondering if she was going to be sick. After taking a few steadying breaths, she continued along the hallway, keeping her flashlight off. Her eyes had adjusted to the dark, and besides, the moonlight lit up the curtains in the windows. She paused at the partly open door of the children's bedroom. All was quiet. Peaceful, even.

Another surge of nausea swept through her. The last thing Mary wanted to do was be sick. There wasn't time. She didn't want to pass something to her children, and who knew when the next air-raid siren would blare?

But she had a feeling this wasn't the stomach flu. She might hope that after extra rest and mild food she'd be back to normal. But the doubt was too strong.

When Mary entered her bedroom, George was already in bed, but he wasn't asleep. He sat propped against a couple of pillows, his arms linked behind his head.

"I was about to come looking for you," he said, his voice a quiet rasp. "Are you all right?"

Mary decided not to focus on her nausea, but said instead, "Claudia told me about the Djojobojo legend that was printed in the Malay newspaper."

"Oh?"

Apparently, Claudia knew something that George didn't. That was quite a feat.

Mary climbed into bed and laid her head upon the crook of her husband's shoulder. His arm slipped around her, and she drew in a breath.

He smelled of grass and earth and a faded version of his shaving cream, which should have been long worn off by now.

For the next few minutes, she told her husband about the legend that predicted Java would be under Japan's rule for three months, or three years.

"I know that Claudia believes in these sort of things, but let's hope this one is merely folklore, and the occupation doesn't happen at all," he said, his tone a murmur above her head.

"Let's hope," she echoed.

Another minute passed, and although George didn't move, she felt the tension vibrating through him. "What's wrong?" she asked, even though she didn't want to hear any bad news that he might not have had a chance to share with her yet.

"Besides imminent invasion by Japan?" he asked. "I feel stuck. My wife and children are vulnerable here. Rumors are flying about Allied strategies against Japanese forces, but we are outnumbered and out-gunned. I don't see a good way out, Rie."

Mary tilted her face upward. "Surely the Allies will aid us? Isn't that what you mentioned last night?"

"It's a hope everyone has, but in truth, the Allies have their hands full trying to hold off the Japanese army in Hong Kong and the Philippines. Not to mention Singapore."

Mary curled her fingers into her husband's shirt, thinking about how so many countries in the Pacific Rim were being bombed. It wasn't realistic that her now-military husband could remain on Java in his own bed each night. So she asked the question she'd been avoiding. "Are you going to be called onto a submarine?"

His answer came immediately. "I might be."

Another minute ticked by as Mary let the information sink in. George was a qualified submarine engineer. So far, it seemed that the Dutch submarines had the upper hand, at the moment. What if . . . what if George went down in one of the submarines and never surfaced again?

Tears stung her eyes at the thought, and she blinked rapidly. She didn't need to fall apart. She needed to be strong. To be steady. To be the brave wife her husband needed right now.

Apparently, her stomach didn't agree with her resolve because another surge of nausea welled up inside her. This one stronger than any she could remember. She scrambled off the bed and rushed to the toilet. Bending over the toilet, she purged her stomach, although there wasn't much to purge. She hadn't been very hungry that day and had eaten little.

The sink faucet turned on. George had come in.

"I was hoping this would pass, but it seems . . ." she broke off. The nausea faded somewhat, but her stomach felt like an empty pit.

George helped her stand, then pressed a wet cloth against her face.

Mary took it and wiped her face and neck. Then she took the glass of water, also offered by her husband.

"Thank you," she whispered.

"Feel better?" he asked, one hand at her waist, keeping her steady.

"Yes."

George's palm slipped along her arm, then he threaded her fingers. "You haven't been feeling yourself for a couple of weeks."

He'd noticed. Of course, he had. He noticed most things, even when she didn't want to talk about them. Perhaps it was time to mention what she suspected. Every day their world turned another degree toward upside down. Time was precious, and her husband needed to know. "I think I'm pregnant."

CHAPTER THREE

"Reliable news was hard to come by and was replaced by rumors. To add to the confusion, now and then a Japanese plane would fly over—a bomber on its way back to its base, or a navy Zero, a fighter plane, spewing its ammunition over dirt roads. One of these fighters even made a dive and took a potshot at my brother as he was swimming in our little backyard pool. At the same time, from the vantage point of our bungalow halfway up a hill, we could see troop movements in the distance on the highway."

—BAREND A. VAN NOOTEN, CIHAPIT CAMP

RITA

Rita perched on a branch about halfway up the mango tree in front of their house. It would have been a perfect lazy afternoon, sitting among the cooler leaves of the tree after a soft afternoon rain, fragrance blooming all around her, if she allowed her imagination to wander. But her stomach ached. Oma told her it was worry. And Rita was worried about her Papa. He was later than usual coming home. Yet, Mama said that Papa was fine. He was very busy helping out with the navy, that was all.

Still, Rita wanted to be the first to spot him. She'd asked as many questions as she could think of. "Is he fighting the Japanese?" Rita had asked Mama.

Her face had turned the color of a peeled egg. "No, Rietie, he's working behind the scenes to strengthen Dutch forces."

Rita wasn't exactly sure what "behind the scenes" meant, but she'd overheard Papa saying something about supplying water to submarines. Did he carry barrels of water around?

Her attention was caught by the slam of a screen door coming from the neighbor's house. She peered through the copse of branches to see if it was Johan. But it was one of the neighbor's Javanese workers coming outside to beat dust from a rug.

Rita turned her attention back to the road to watch for Papa. It had been raining all morning, but now that the rain had stopped, the heat began to creep across the yard. It hadn't reached the mango tree yet. That would all change when the clouds raced away.

As the *thump thump* of the beaten rug echoed through the yard, Rita changed her position, moving to a higher branch. She wished she could climb high enough to stop the Japanese planes from flying over Java. It seemed that every day, and sometimes every hour, there was news about Japan taking over another island. Johan told Rita what he'd learned each time he came out in the yard. He listened to the radio a lot since he no longer went to school.

She didn't know if all of Johan's stories were true, but she didn't dare quiz her parents. Mama was feeling sick a lot and took naps during the daytime, and Oma and Mama paced the floors until Papa came home at night.

Other things had changed too. Dea, their housemaid, only stayed half the time she usually did. Kemala came in the afternoons only, prepared dinner, then left. Rita had asked her if she had a bomb shelter at her house, but Kemala had shaken her head then said, "The bombs are for your people, not mine."

It made Rita wonder, *Why did some people hate other people?*

"Where are you, Ita?" Georgie called from the base of the tree.

Rita shifted so that she could see straight down the trunk. "Up here." She rustled a branch and glanced toward the house, where Anja sat on the veranda, keeping an eye on Georgie.

"Help me up," Georgie said.

That wouldn't be a good idea. "I'll come down." Rita glanced down the road a final time. No sign of Papa.

Within moments, she'd climbed down the tree that she scaled almost every day.

"Let's play with the ball," she said, taking her brother's hand. The clouds were still blocking the sun, keeping the air cooler.

Rita fetched the ball from the corner of the yard and tossed it to Georgie. He didn't catch it, but he laughed and ran after it.

She smiled at her brother's laughter. It was good to hear it, since there weren't many things to smile about. Her parents always looked worried. Mama stayed in her bedroom more and more. Even Oma had been quiet lately.

Rita tossed the ball again, and Georgie made a valiant effort to catch it. He missed. "Keep your hands together," she called. "Like this."

Georgie brought his hands together, but when Rita tossed the ball again, he didn't move. The ball bumped his elbow.

"You can still move, Georgie," she said. "But keep your hands together when you catch."

"I can show you," Johan said, suddenly appearing. He must have come out of his house when Rita's back was turned. "Sit," he told his dog, who obeyed.

This time when Rita threw the ball, Georgie caught it with the help of Johan.

"Got it!" Georgie announced in a proud tone. He tossed it back, and it went about a meter, so Rita stepped forward to scoop it from the ground.

Just then, the clouds parted, and the sun's rays settled on Rita's head and shoulders and arms. The temperature notched higher, as if a light had been turned on.

"Come inside," Anja said immediately.

The dispersing clouds meant that the planes could see the island. As if on cue, the air raid sirens went off.

Rita's pulse jumped, and she craned her neck to look at the white-blue sky. She couldn't see planes anywhere. Maybe it was another drill.

Johan took off toward the bomb shelter, his dog loping after him. Then Mama, Oma, and Dea came out of the house, carrying flashlights. Behind them, Kemala carried a sack of fruit. Darkness was hours away, but who knew how long this raid would last. Mama also carried a bag that contained a few supplies, including a pouch of rubber wafers. Everyone took them to the shelters. The rubber pieces were to put in between their teeth and prevent a concussion if a bomb exploded nearby.

"Let's go, Rita," Mama said, her expression one of grim determination. "Come with us, Anja."

Rita dropped the ball and snatched up Georgie's hand. They trudged to the shelter. Their gardener Bima came around the side of the house and ushered everyone inside, much like Papa did when he was home. Rita hated walking through the cold, muddy water that had collected at the bottom of the trench. She sloshed through it, then sat on one of the benches. The dog was at least smart enough to perch on the end of the bench. He didn't bark, but whined a few times.

Through the edges of the shelter's roof, patches of blue sky were visible.

Rita stared at the slice of sky, wondering where the planes were. Johan stayed by the entrance, standing and looking outside, too, like Papa did.

Mrs. Vos started talking to Mama about some of the recent invasions by Japan. The Philippines had been invaded last month, and now New Guinea and a number of islands in the NEI were being, or had already been, overtaken.

"Soon, we'll have nowhere to go," Mrs. Vos fretted.

"The newspaper says that Australia and the NEI are working together to stave off Japan," Mama countered.

Mrs. Vos shook her head, her eyes full of worry. "Japanese battle-ships are outnumbering and outpowering our minesweepers and anti-submarine patrol boats. What are our vessels compared to the world's largest battleships? Did you see this morning's paper?"

Mama shook her head because Papa was the one who collected the newspaper and brought it home in the evenings.

"Japan has declared war on the Dutch government after their inva-sion of Borneo and the Island of Celebes." Mrs. Vos paused. "They're coming after our oil fields, and it looks like they'll get them. They are also promising the Indonesians independence from the Dutch."

"Maybe we should talk about this when the children, and the *others* . . . aren't around," Oma interrupted, whispering.

Mrs. Vos dipped her head. "They need to know what's going on, Mrs. Van Benten. It's no secret why we're all sitting in a bomb shelter with soaking wet feet. Children will understand what they can, but our lives are changing."

Rita looked between the women. She didn't see Oma upset very often, but her face was like immovable stone now.

Mrs. Vos slipped her arm about Greta's shoulder, who kept her head down, her hands clasped in her lap.

A silent moment passed, at least as silent as it could be with a siren wailing down the street.

Oma closed her eyes, and her lips moved in what Rita knew to be a silent prayer. Oma had been praying a lot the past several weeks.

Mama's hand covered Rita's, and despite the cool, dank air, she felt warmer after that.

The sirens howled and wailed, going on and on. How long did they have to stay here? The sun would set soon, and then the bombers couldn't see anything. Right?

Rita felt hungry, but she didn't want to ask for food. Everyone was probably hungry, and she didn't know what Mama had brought in her bag. Johan had told her that she should be grateful she was only hungry. Stories about other islands getting bombed had reached even her ears, mostly through Johan, which meant their food was bombed too, he'd said.

Johan turned from his lookout spot. "I see a plane."

Mrs. Vos stood immediately and sloshed through the water to join Johan.

Rita nestled against her mother as worry tightened her throat.

"Oh, my goodness," Mrs. Vos said quietly. "They're Japanese planes."

Rita's skin rippled with fear.

Oma's silent prayers became urgent whispers.

Then, Rita heard it. A deep rumbling noise. If there had been clouds, she might have thought it was thunder coming before a storm. But the sky was clear, and the sound of a plane moved closer and closer. Rita's stomach turned into a mess of knots. Was the Japanese army going to bomb her house?

Every second that passed felt like an hour.

The plane passed over, and the thunder grew quiet.

Rita waited. Held her breath. Clenched the rubber wafer between her teeth.

No explosions came, though.

Nothing.

One minute passed, then another.

"It's gone," Mrs. Vos said, her voice airy, as if she'd been running back and forth to the house.

"Will it come back?" Johan asked the question they all wanted answered.

"I think the plane was passing over," Mrs. Vos said, but she didn't sound sure. Not at all.

Of course, the adults knew a lot more than Rita did, but every day, life changed more. They were eating simple meals. Oma didn't take her and Georgie to the market anymore in case there was a bomb raid.

Above the shelter roof, the leaves rattled with the wind. A sweet sound especially when it brought clouds along with it. Then the rain came, pelting and swift, dripping its way through the roof above. Soon, the air sirens stopped.

Anja, Dea, and Kemala rushed out, heading to the house. Oma picked up Georgie and followed. Rita was about to leave with her mother when Mrs. Vos said, "Now that we're alone, you need to know that the Japanese army has been making promises that they don't have the power to make, but it looks like they're going to try."

"That would mean a revolution," Mama said, gripping Rita's hand. "In the middle of a war. We can't have the islands in an upheaval from within if Japan is going to help the Indonesians take over the Dutch government. What will become of the Dutch citizens?"

"Time will tell," Mrs. Vos said in a strained voice. "I don't like any of it, and the queen is in no position to give us her attention. She's in exile herself."

Mama nodded, her lips in a tight line.

As they climbed out of the shelter, they were greeted by the wind tugging at the bamboo bushes bordering their yards. Above, the mango tree swayed, and down the road a ways, the palm trees looked like they were dancing. Rita knew the wind would make the palms drop some of their coconuts.

Kells began to bark as Johan ran back to his house. Rita held onto Mama's hand as they pushed through the rain toward the veranda.

Once Rita entered the house, Anja, Dea, and Kemala were already inside, closing all the windows.

Without even bothering to change into dry clothing, Mama went directly to the radio in the dining room, turned it on, then sat at the table to listen.

Rita was surprised because Mama usually waited to listen with Papa when he came home. The announcer was in the middle of a news report, talking about the number of aircraft held by Allied Java Air Command.

"Is that us?" Rita asked, moving to stand near her mother. Rita's hair was damp, her clothing half wet, but no one told her to go change.

Mama looked over at her, and instead of shooing her away, she extended her arm. Rita settled into the chair next to her.

"Yes. We are outnumbered, Rietie," Mama said.

"By how much?" Rita asked. She could count to nearly one hundred even though she wasn't in school yet. One day, Johan had challenged her, and she'd missed only three numbers.

Mama nodded toward the radio, and then Rita heard it.

"Allied Java Air Command has eighty-six operational planes, and the Japanese forces have over three hundred modern aircrafts."

Rita wondered if Johan knew this. Or if his father did? Or *her* father? Papa didn't fly planes, but sometimes planes bombed ships—Johan had told her that too.

"Is what Mrs. Vos said true? We have nowhere to go? We are trapped?"

Mama turned to her then and placed her cool hands on either side of Rita's face. "The most important thing to remember is that we are together. You, Papa, Oma, and little Georgie. That's all that matters. We are alive, we are safe, and we have food in our house."

Rita felt like a lump was moving up her throat, making it hard to swallow. She wanted to believe Mama, and she did, yet . . . Papa hadn't been home for two days.

CHAPTER FOUR

"The Indies had been preparing for war for years but were
not really ready. The Netherlands Eastern Forces Intelligence
Service, comparable to the American CIA, was well informed.
. . . But because there was no state of war, they could do no
better than keep a watchful eye on the many Japanese living in
the country. Japanese merchants, photographers, tailors, dry
cleaners . . . tended to be the best in whatever trade they were
in. . . . After the attack on Pearl Harbor, these people disappeared,
only to resurface as high-ranking officers after the Dutch
surrendered. All those years they had been spying on us."

—JOHANNES VANDENBROEK, SINGAPORE ISLAND

GEORGE

George Vischer climbed back into the truck and settled next to
Lieutenant Hooft. The rain pinged on the roof of the military truck,
a melody to the deeper rumbles of thunder. The world outside was
streaked with gray, cut apart by lightning that shot from the clouds like
muzzle fire. George wasn't driving this time, and for that he was grateful
since the roads were quickly filling up with puddles from the downpour.
He was more comfortable in a ship or submarine than driving a testy
military vehicle.

Hooft started the truck, then shifted gears and pulled back onto
the road that would return them to naval headquarters. They'd been

traveling for days, negotiating purchases with opium factories across Java. In fact, this was the fourth time in the past month and a half that George had been away from his family for days at a time. He was exhausted.

"So that's our only choice, huh?" Hooft asked. He was a dark-haired man, shorter than George, but broader at the shoulders.

"It appears so." George released a sigh. They'd just left an opium factory after securing another agreement to purchase distilled water from the plant. Everything was in a shortage, but enough money would buy what they needed. The shortages compounded by the day. Who would have thought that an opium factory would be the saving grace of the Dutch navy?

Locating distilled water was one of George's recently assigned tasks. At naval headquarters in Batavia, he was in charge of making sure that the naval depots throughout the archipelago were supplied with navy ships and aircrafts. He knew they were outnumbered. Everyone knew it. No one talked about it, though. Would they all be expected to "fight to the death" like Churchill had told his British troops in Singapore to do?

Counter that with dozens of news reports over the past few weeks about the Japanese military's brutality and its unwillingness to follow any rules of war. It was a sobering thought. If the Allies wouldn't back down, and neither would Japan, then the battlegrounds would reap more destruction.

George oversaw the purchase of materials for both fleet and aircraft. Unfortunately, materials were getting harder and harder to come by now that Java was under attack. Airfields near Bogor, Yogyakarta, and Malang had been attacked. Bombed and abandoned. So they had to drive to an opium factory and purchase distilled water for submarines. The distilled water was part of the crucial process of removing salt from seawater and turning it into usable fresh water.

The rain continued to pound on the truck and fill the potholes in the road as they drove toward headquarters. At least they were finished with their assignment, and George could check on his family. George adjusted the AM radio in the truck, piping in a staticky news report, confirming the Japanese bombardment of an airfield near Malang. Although the city was on the east side of the island, and George and his family were on the northwest side, any bombardment of Java had an impact. But the news was old, which surprised George. It was as if the newscaster was trying to fill the time with information, regardless of how old it was, while waiting for updates.

For weeks, the Japanese military had done a number on Java, dropping bombs on airfields throughout East Java. Stories had reached them of Dutch people evacuating the larger city of Surabaya. George had witnessed the destruction with Hooft as they'd been traveling to various factories. And last week, the airfields near Bogor and Bandung were bombed in West Java. The strength of Japan's armed forces was felt every day now, but not everyone was living in fear. Most of the Indonesians in George's acquaintance were continuing business as usual—selling in the markets and shops to the Dutch, and many of them were still working for the Dutch. But political rumblings had started, and groups had formed that were decidedly anti-Dutch.

Not only were the Dutch facing the external enemy of Japan, but an internal conflict was growing as well, as groups of Indonesians similarly longed for independence from the Dutch. Japan had been sending out messages of support to the Indonesians—but Japan also had an agenda. George wasn't necessarily a political man. He loved the sea and loved following his career path as an engineer—it was what had brought him to Java Island in the first place. But he knew that Queen Wilhelmina would not simply turn over islands that the Netherlands had colonized for three hundred years now. Not with centuries of investment and developing infrastructure . . . did this mean it all came down to money?

Still, another side of George would never begrudge a people's desire for independence. He wasn't part of the original colonization centuries ago, but he'd read enough to know that the Dutch had frequently used ruthless methods to take control of various islands. The history between the Dutch and Indonesians wasn't always pretty, but in this modern era, surely peaceful agreements could be made, couldn't they?

George knew he might be fooling himself. The news report currently coming from the blaring radio was anything but peaceful. There would be no easy solution to any of this. The rain stopped, and the northwest wind pushed the clouds across the steely sky. Brushstrokes of blue opened. The sight of the sun might be welcome in some parts of the world, but here, on Java, it meant that bombers would be on their way again.

George exhaled as he thought of his family at home. Were the air raid sirens going off again? Was his pregnant wife rushing to the bomb shelter with their two children and Oma?

Every day was not only an outward battle with invading forces but an inward battle of wanting to be on Laan Trivelli with his family, helping and protecting them. Yet, if he wasn't doing his naval duty, like the others with him, there would be no one to stop Japan's progress. Even if most days the efforts seemed futile. Clearly, Japan had the upper hand.

The majority of Allied forces were going head-to-head with Nazi Germany on the other side of the world. This left other countries basically at the mercy of the determined Japanese imperial army.

"How is your wife doing?" Hooft asked as the radio cut to another program.

George had confessed to a couple of his officer friends that his wife was pregnant with their third child. Both friends were married with children, and they understood the added risk during these perilous times. Schools, churches, and hospitals had turned into air raid shelters. Food was being rationed, and medical supplies were even harder to come by. What if when Mary's time came, she couldn't get good medical care?

"She's been feeling sick most days but is sleeping better at night at least."

Like George, Hooft lived in KPM company housing and had been on Java for several years. KPM was the Royal Packet Navigating Company—or the Koninklijk Paketvaart Maatschappij—that George had been with for over ten years, having arrived in Batavia in 1927. But when the war started in 1939, both George and Hooft had been mobilized into the reserves of the Royal Netherlands Navy. "Kids all right? Mine are going stir crazy without school to keep them busy. Or maybe I should say that my wife is ready for this conflict to be over already."

"Agreed. I don't know how much my mother-in-law can bear. She doesn't need more challenges in her life. Her visit here was supposed to be peaceful. Ironically, we were all happy she was in Batavia rather than Holland when the Nazis took over." George's gaze strayed to the fields they were passing. The peanut fields were soaked with rain. They were still some distance from naval headquarters, and it was nice to be away from the base for a short time.

"This still might be the better place," Hooft said. "Despite everything." But then his fingers tightened on the steering wheel, and he tilted his chin toward the upper part of the window. "Bomber?"

George leaned forward and stared at the plane flying nearly overhead. White smoke streamed from the low-flying plane as it jetted across the clearing sky. It didn't take long to see the red painted circle. "Japanese bomber," he said under his breath. "And it's heading in the same direction we are."

Hooft braked the truck, slowing, then pulled over to the side of the road. He continued into a copse of trees, the branches snapping against the windshield.

"What are you doing?" George said, trying to push back the panic that had started to flicker in his gut.

"It's heading toward the airfields near Tandjong Priok harbor," Hooft said. "This vehicle is a target for the next plane. We'll wait here until the bomber has dropped its load."

"How do you know where it's going?"

"Look at that trajectory. It's flying too low to be passing over."

George wasn't as well versed in aircraft as Hooft—who'd started out in the air force, then transferred to the navy several years ago.

If the bomber let loose on the airfield north of Batavia, it would compromise naval headquarters.

They'd stopped near the peanut fields, beneath a copse of tamarind trees. It wouldn't be any protection if a bomb landed on top of them, but maybe the trees would conceal them.

George scooted on the edge of his seat to peer through the windshield as he crouched down then stared in the direction the bomber had flown. "I think the Dutch are going to have to surrender," George said, drawing in a gulp of air. "If the naval base is evacuated, then what? Join the army or a guerilla force?" There were rumors of civilians taking up arms and forming bands in the mountains, waiting for the Japanese forces to land.

Hooft's expression was grim. "I don't know. We need to be ready for anything."

Rainwater dripped from the tamarind trees above, pelting the windshield. "The Allies have the greatest forces in the world—yet we're getting bombed every day."

"Right. But our mother country is under German occupation, and our queen is in exile in Britain."

Another plane screeched overhead, this one much closer to land. The thundering of the sturdy aircraft seemed to buzz through George's entire body. He gazed after it, prickles rising on his neck. And then he saw them.

Bombs dropping from the plane in the distance. Had the sirens even had time to go off? George hadn't heard them this far out.

Time slowed. The bombs sunk toward the earth, foot by foot, meter by meter, closing in on the airfield.

On impact, the earth sprayed upward where a bomb missed an Allied plane. For a moment, George felt detached from the scene. As if he were watching a film reel. But the brown of the earth and green of the fields around him were no movie. This was happening to him. To his island. To his comrades.

The next bomb hit its target. The fire was almost immediate. Beyond the first fire, another explosion burst the ground apart.

Next to him, Hooft hissed a curse word. The war had literally arrived at their doorstep. There was no strategizing that could turn the tide now. It was just a matter of time before naval headquarters would be compromised.

The fire expanded, deep orange and yellow against the soft blue of the sky. A startling contrast. Although it was impossible, George swore he felt the heat from the flames lapping against his skin. Warmth spread through him, hot and fast. He rocked back on his heels.

Pre-war, if a plane had caught on fire, men and water trucks would have rushed toward it to douse the flames. But now, there was nothing and no one trying to put out the flames. Because they all knew more bombers could very well be on their way.

Sure enough, a handful of moments later, as George and Hooft stayed beneath the grouping of trees, a rumble split the sky.

This time, two bombers, flying close together, zoomed over the fields right toward the airfield.

George's heart galloped as the next set of bombs fell, crashing to the earth and destroying everything in the targeted circumference. It was like watching the world burst apart.

For several long moments, neither George nor Hooft spoke, their gazes focused on the new reality both were facing. Time inched forward, and then it caught up.

Anxiety spiked inside of George. They needed to go. They needed to find out what their orders were. And if there were no orders, George was going to check on his family.

"Let's go," George rasped. "I want to check on my family."

"Me too," Hooft echoed.

Hooft started the engine, then stepped on the gas pedal. They sped along the rutted road, plowing through puddles and skimming potholes.

The men fell into silence once again.

George rolled down his window to let the wind wash over him—a mixture of heat and moisture and the nutty fragrance of the passing peanut fields. His stomach felt like it had been hollowed out with worry. The bombs were still a far cry from the neighborhoods here. But in Europe, residential neighborhoods were being bombed. What was to stop the Japanese military?

It wasn't something that George wanted to admit to his fellow officers, but maybe it would be better if the Netherlands East Indies surrendered. If not, civilian lives would be lost, and the women and children were essentially trapped.

Where could they go? Into the mountains? Out of the predominantly Dutch neighborhoods? Into the Javanese neighborhoods? He'd thought of Java as his home for many years. Yet, now they might soon be refugees.

They couldn't see the damage from the road as they headed to the naval base, but they'd hear a report soon enough. When they arrived at the base, Hooft parked the truck, and they both hurried into the headquarters building to find . . . chaos. Men were on the phones; others were crowded around a radio. George doubted that it was all due to the airfield strike he'd witnessed. Those had become common enough.

"What's happening?" George asked Willem Vos as soon as he spotted him.

"The *Langley* has been sunk."

George's stomach hollowed out. The *Langley* was a United States aircraft carrier transporting thirty military aircraft to the NEI. It took him a moment to comprehend how stunning the loss was.

"There's more," Vos said, his voice barely audible above the chaos. "The ABDA forces have been decimated in a battle on the Java Sea."

George stared at Vos. ABDA stood for American-British-Dutch-Australian, essentially the Allied forces.

"Yesterday, we lost the Royal Netherlands cruisers *Java* and *De Ruyter* as well as the destroyer *Kortenaer*."

Each name that Vos mentioned was like a blow to George's stomach.

"The British destroyers *Electra* and *Jupiter* are also gone. And today,

USS Houston and the Australian cruiser *HMAS Perth* were downed by Japanese gunfire and torpedoes."

George had no words. So much destruction, not to mention the loss of life that must have occurred. "The sailors?" he asked, his throat feeling scraped raw.

Vos swallowed. "We don't have exact numbers yet, but it will be in the thousands."

George reached for a nearby chair and leaned his palm against it for support. The conversations, orders, and stuttering of the radio clanged all around him. But he only thought of the men. The people. The lives lost. Those left behind.

It took several moments for George to collect his thoughts.

The news would grow worse, of that he was certain. Java would soon be under Japanese occupation. That was the only foreseeable outcome. How would that look for him and his family? He needed to get home, to talk to his wife, to prepare for the transition—even though he didn't know what to fully expect.

He turned from Vos and Hooft and headed toward the exit. His assignment had ended for the foreseeable future.

"All officers report to the conference room immediately."

The announcement shouldn't have surprised George, yet he hated any further delay in getting to his family. With the others, he headed to the conference room. They crowded in, twenty-four of them in total.

"Thank you for assembling," Commander P. Rouwenhorst said. "As you can imagine, we are all reeling with the news of such significant loss. We are putting into action our plans to head out to Australia. We'll build up the forces there and create a counterattack." His gaze landed on George, then moved on to the other men. "We leave tonight. Put your affairs in order as soon as possible. I don't know how long we'll be gone."

CHAPTER FIVE

"'Dark clouds above the Pacific, the Netherlands declare war on Japan.' 'It is better to die while standing upright than to live in a kneeling position.' These were some of the headlines in the local Dutch newspapers heralding the grim reality that World War II hovered like a giant bird of prey over the beautiful islands in the Pacific affectionally called 'The Belt of Emeralds.' The Indies was suddenly and unwillingly transformed into a battlefield."

—DENIS DUTRIEUX, CIMAHI CAMP

MARY

Mary paced the yard as Rita watched from her perch in the mango tree. Their nanny, Anja, had gotten Georgie down for a nap, and Oma was likely resting too. The heat had returned, and with the near-daily monsoons, the humidity was almost insufferable.

But worse than the dampness of the air was the smoke they saw every day now. Right now, Mary could smell it in the air. It was only a matter of time before the Japanese armed forces occupied Java. Over the past few days, they'd shopped for dried foods at the market. They couldn't very well store fresh foods for long, so those would be wasted.

But supplies were already running out.

Her neighbors had talked about pooling their resources during the Japanese occupation.

"Do you see them yet?" Claudia Vos asked, coming out of her house, her hair pulled back and tied in a handkerchief.

"I haven't seen any of the military men coming home yet." Mary could only hope they were all safe. Their husbands had both been gone for nearly three days.

Claudia released a sigh and perched her hands on her hips. Perspiration already stood out on her brow from the short walk across the yard. "I've been speaking to some of our neighbors about getting together a neighborhood school until the regular schools open back up. Mrs. Venema said her daughters would be happy to help teach. Do you think the Japanese military will let us run our own schools?"

"Why wouldn't they?" Mary asked.

Claudia pursed her lips for a moment. "I guess it depends on if they are occupying Java for three months or three years."

Mary knew she was referring to Djojobojo legend.

"I want to go to school, too," a small voice called from above them.

"Oh, my goodness." Claudia brought a hand to her chest. She craned her neck to look upward. "I didn't see you there, Rita."

Rita giggled. "I can watch for Papa up here."

"I'm sure you can," Claudia said in a cheerful tone.

"Me too," another voice said.

"Johan, is that you?" Claudia's tone wasn't as cheerful this time.

"We're watching for the men," he called down.

"Let us know when you first see them," Claudia told her son. She looked at Mary with a wry smile. "Every time I give that boy a chore, he finds a way out of it. He listens to the radio obsessively. I think he knows more about what's happening than most of our husbands."

"Come quickly," Oma said, coming out onto the veranda.

Both women turned.

"The newscaster is talking about the battle," Oma continued, then pushed through the door and went inside.

That wasn't anything new, but the urgency in Oma's voice told Mary this was something important. She hurried to the house, Claudia at her side. The two women entered to find Oma bracing her palms on the dining room table while the radio played from the counter.

Mary stopped at the table and clasped her mother's hand as the newscaster announced that the battle for the Java Sea had been lost. Three Allied destroyers had been sunk, as well as two light cruisers. Other ships had been badly damaged, and the loss of life was estimated to be in the thousands.

"No," Claudia whispered, covering her mouth.

If that wasn't bad enough, the newscaster predicted that the Japanese troops would come into Java by the next day.

"Tomorrow," Oma echoed. "What will happen to us?"

Mary blinked. Had they heard right? Was this really happening?

Mary put an arm about her mother's shoulders. "We will stick together, that's all that matters."

Oma leaned her head on Mary's shoulder. The three of them remained quiet as the newscaster droned on. Nothing he said was comforting. Kemala came into the dining room from one of the back rooms, accompanied by Dea.

Claudia updated her.

"Will they make us become Japanese?" Kemala asked.

Mary truthfully didn't have an answer for her. She'd read news articles about the Netherlands under Nazi occupation. Would it be like that?

"Papa's here," Rita said, hurrying into the house.

Mary strode to the door and walked out onto the veranda.

Sure enough, George was riding his bike up the road. His clothing was wet and muddy. Had something happened to him? Was he injured?

Beyond him, Willem rode his own bike.

"Willem!" Claudia said, hurrying across the veranda and down the steps.

George climbed off his bike, his movements short and jerky. Rita rushed up to him. Instead of greeting her with a hug, he held her at arm's length, telling her something Mary couldn't hear.

Rita didn't look happy. She stayed where she stood, staring after her father as he strode toward the house.

What was going on?

Mary assessed George as he approached. He wasn't limping or anything. No injuries, then. Just caught in the rain?

She moved to the edge of the steps as he strode up them, his eyes focused on her.

"Did you hear the news about the Java Sea?" he asked, his voice a rasp, as if he had a sore throat.

"Yes, we heard it just now."

The moment he reached her, he took her hand.

Instead of giving her a hug or a kiss on the cheek, he said, "We need to talk. Immediately."

He looked past her, nodded to Oma, then left his boots on the veranda. He led Mary into the house.

"You're wet and muddy," Mary said, but there wasn't any bite in her tone. Mud could be cleaned up later.

They continued to the hallway, and George walked into their bedroom. Once she was inside, he shut the door behind them.

He didn't speak at first, but crossed to the window and gazed through the screen at the flowering bushes outside their window. The silence stretched, and he scrubbed his fingers through his hair.

Mary finally said in a quiet tone, "What is it, George? You're making me nervous."

He turned slowly then. His brown eyes were darker than she'd ever seen them, full of . . . what? Wariness? Pain?

"Rie . . ." He crossed the room and stopped before her. Taking her hands in his mud-speckled ones, he said, "They're shipping officers out to Australia. News has come in from other locations about Dutch officers being arrested and jailed as prisoners of war. They're sending us to join the Allied forces and plan our next counterattack."

Australia? Mary stared at her husband, hoping this was a false alarm. But his brown eyes were as steady as ever. If George was leaving, that meant she'd have to face Japanese occupation alone. She didn't want him arrested though. Was Australia the only solution? When would she hear from him? How would they communicate?

She ignored the panicked questions running through her mind. Above all else, she wanted her husband safe . . . alive. "Willem too?" she asked.

"Yes," George confirmed. "And Hooft."

Mary hoped this was good news. They were all seasoned navy men. Beyond their bedroom door, noises of the children and Oma could be heard. Georgie must be awake from his nap. But inside the bedroom, the silence grew, and she found herself tightening her grip in George's hands. He was waiting for her answer. She knew it wasn't like he could say no to the orders, but throughout their marriage, he'd never made significant decisions without first consulting her.

And following these orders was certainly significant.

She blinked back the threatening tears and looked down at their linked hands. It was a lot to process . . . the bombing, the approaching Japanese forces, little children and an aging mother to worry about, her new pregnancy . . . "When?"

George's tone was soft, regretful. "Right after midnight."

Mary lifted her gaze as his words rocked through her. "Tonight?"

"Yes, I wish it was different. I wish we had more time."

"Me too," she whispered. There was no use holding back the tears. Mary wasn't much of a crier, but she was pregnant, and this was all . . . too much.

George pulled her in his arms, enveloping her in his warmth. Because she was taller than George, their bodies aligned perfectly, and her current fragility felt supported by his solid strength.

She no longer cared that he was wet and muddy. Would he even stick around for dinner? She knew her George. He was meticulous about his ships. Everything would have to be inspected, likely more than once.

"Are you staying for dinner?" she murmured.

"Yes," he said, his mouth close to her ear. "I'll leave soon after. I think it's better we tell the children and Oma that I'll be on a special assignment. I don't want to worry Oma about me heading out into the sea."

Mary closed her eyes and breathed in her husband's earthy scent. She wanted to be strong, she really did, but she knew herself. "What if you're spotted? Are you going in a submarine?"

"No, a minesweeper," he murmured.

Mary drew back at this and scanned her husband's face. "What else can you tell me? Anything? How will I know that you've arrived safely in Australia?"

"Commander Rouwenhorst will be at the helm," he said in a soft tone. "And . . . the minesweeper is called *Endeh*. We're taking a skeleton crew. I can't tell you more than that."

Mary bit her lip. She had many questions, but it might be good for her not to know too much more. She'd have to be satisfied with this much, she knew. "I want to tell my mother," she said. "It will be hard enough to bear."

George's brows tugged down.

"I don't know what it is," Mary continued. "Perhaps this pregnancy is making me feel more vulnerable." The tears started again, but she quickly wiped them away. She didn't need to appear in front of her children with puffy, red eyes. "I need someone to talk to while you're gone."

George released her, then cradled her face. "All right, Rie. We'll tell your mother." Then he leaned forward and gently kissed her.

Mary wished that this kiss wasn't a goodbye. She wanted her husband home, every night, next to her. She wanted to wake up beside him every day.

The next couple of hours hurt her heart. Watching George with the children, putting on a false bravado for their sakes. After the children were tucked into bed, George started packing.

Mary stood in the doorway, watching him. Her husband had always been a stalwart, driven man. He had no problem doing the hard tasks of a navy man, yet he'd wanted to gain as much education as possible. Back in the Netherlands, he'd gone to trade school for three years to become an engine fitter and turner. Following a couple of years of working in a factory, he'd joined a marine engineering school, becoming a 5th engineer. This had led to his assignment in the Netherlands East Indies.

He'd fallen in love with submarines, but he continued taking courses and moving up in rank. Now he was qualified to serve as the senior engineer on any submarine.

"You're packing light," Mary commented when he filled a smaller duffle.

George shifted his gaze to her. "I can purchase things in Australia if needed. Their rationing isn't so strict. I thought . . ." He paused. "I thought you could sell some of my things if needed."

"We won't need to—" She stopped. The tears were back.

George held out a hand. "Come here."

She walked across the room and stopped in front of him.

George moved a bit of the blonde hair that had escaped her loose bun behind her ear. Then he rested his hand on her shoulder. "You sell anything of mine that you need to. I don't know how long I'll be gone, but our stuff isn't important. Your well-being is."

Mary released a thready breath.

His hand settled at her waist. "Hide any valuables, though. Anything you want preserved. Maybe beneath the floorboards."

Mary nodded. Her throat had tightened, and words failed her.

She imagined husbands and wives saying goodbye to each other all over Batavia. Sailors fleeing to Australia to build up forces and prepare a counterattack.

When George had finally packed, Mary walked with him outside. Oma was in her room, a lamp light on, but she'd already said her goodbyes after the children had gone to bed. So it was the two of them.

"At least the full moon will give you plenty of light," Mary murmured.

"Yes," George said. His answer was one word, but she heard the emotion in his voice. He secured his bag to the back of his bicycle, then turned to her.

"Each night as the moon rises, look up at it, and I'll do the same. Thinking of you and the children. Under the Java moon."

"Of course." Was this really happening? Was her husband going to set off in Japanese-controlled waters with other sailors?

Just then, the creak of their neighbor's door sounded. Willem Vos was coming outside. Their privacy was about to be interrupted.

Mary grasped her husband and kissed him. He pulled her tightly against him, then whispered, "Take care of yourself, Rie, and the children."

"You, too, George," she whispered back. "I love you."

He pressed a last kiss on her forehead. "I love you, too."

Mary stood for a long time, watching the empty Laan Trivelli long after George and Willem had pedaled away. Long after Claudia had gone back into her house.

The breeze was warm tonight, but she stood with her arms wrapped about her as if to ward off a chill. Mary imagined her husband overseeing the inspections of the minesweeper and the commanding officers planning their route through the Soenda Strait—the most direct route to Australia from Batavia. The days ahead as they made their way to Australia. The days ahead that she would be without him.

How many would be on the minesweeper? George had told her it would be a smaller crew.

Hide your valuables, George had told her.

Tonight, she thought. *I must do it tonight.* She didn't know when the Japanese forces would march onto Java, but nothing was stopping them now. Not with so many Allied ships destroyed, and so many sailors dead.

Mary returned to the house and went into her bedroom. There, in the closet, she kept a locked box. She trusted their servants, but she'd always been protective of the precious pieces her husband had given her over the years from his travels to various ports. In the light of a flashlight, she examined the beautiful collection of earrings, bracelets, rings, and necklaces.

The wooden box wouldn't fare so well when buried in the moist earth, saturated time and time again by monsoon rains. So she searched in the kitchen for a metal box that could contain everything. Finally, she decided on a flour tin. She transferred the flour into a bowl, then wiped out the remaining residue.

Next, she loaded the wooden jewelry box into the metal one and headed out to the gardens. After locating one of the gardener's shovels, she began to dig, using the moonlight as her guide.

A low sniffle caught her attention. Panic flared inside of her, but then she saw that the dark form coming toward her was only Johan's dog, Kells. "Hello, boy," she said in a soft voice. "Want to help?"

The dog sat on his haunches next to Mary and tilted his head, as if in question. "All right. You can watch, then." She gave the dog a firm scratch on his head, then set back to work.

As the shovel blade cut into the earth, time and time again, beneath the light of the same moon George could see now, she knew that with each shovelful, each moment, George was moving farther and farther away from her.

CHAPTER SIX

"The Battle of the Java Sea was fought and the Allied navies were made impotent . . . [Our] unit was ordered to a military airfield in West Java, where a squadron of Martin bombers was operating. But as the unit possessed only men and no equipment, it was soon made clear that we were of no use and should leave the next morning. Then came a message from the prime minister, Mr. Churchill himself. All members of the RAF [British Royal Air Force] were to arm themselves and to make for the hills. Here we were to fight as guerrillas in a force to be known as the Blue Army."

—ARTHUR STOCK, YOGYAKARTA CAMP

GEORGE

The full moon was both a blessing and a curse, George decided. The Auxiliary Minesweeper *Endeh*, a 175-ton vessel that typically held sixty crew but currently held only twenty-four, had been forced to change course since Japanese ships were blocking the Soenda Strait.

"Looks like we're heading north," Vos said, coming to stand by George at the railing as the sea breeze tugged at their clothing. Vos spoke in a low voice, as if there were a nearby Japanese vessel listening in.

George nodded, his only answer for now.

Everyone was on edge, and the tension was as thick as tar. Conversation among the men was limited and brief. No one slept, even though it was nearly four in the morning. Although the minesweeper's intended job was to detect and detonate enemy mines, no one was focused on that. The real threat was a Japanese ship spotting them.

Hooft joined them at the rail, his mouth set in a grim line.

"Any news?" George ventured to ask.

"Rouwenhorst is taking us to the South Borneo coast, and from there we'll cruise between the smaller Soenda Islands. We'll make a break for Australia once we're clear."

George heard the roughness in Hooft's voice, and he turned toward him. When they'd been readying for departure, Hooft had taken it upon himself to cut away the main mast of the minesweeper in order to make the silhouette smaller. While pushing the mast overboard, he'd been struck in the abdomen.

He'd brushed it off then, but now, his face twisted in pain as he held an arm against his stomach.

"Are you in pain?" George asked. "Maybe you should lie down? That hit was stronger than we thought."

Hooft grimaced but shook his head. "I think I cracked a rib, but it will heal soon enough."

"I agree, and you should lie down," Vos said.

"Not going to happen," Hooft said. "Not with Japanese all around us."

Vos sighed, then craned his head to examine the skies. "We should have left at first dark. This moon is exposing our path."

George wholeheartedly agreed. But they'd had to do all the inspections first, and with the mission planned last minute, they couldn't have left any earlier. He followed Hooft's gaze and studied the large white sphere in the black sky. Was its brightness keeping Mary awake too? He hoped she had gone to bed after he'd left. She needed all the rest she could get. Before leaving, he'd written down all the information he thought she might need, including a note to the bank manager that Mary should have access to their funds.

He hoped his officer's pay would continue no matter who occupied

Java, and that even if rations were stricter, his family would have plenty of food and supplies for their needs. His consolation was that Oma was in good health at sixty-seven. She was a strong woman and had endured many trials already. Perhaps it was both a blessing and a curse that she'd come to the Netherlands East Indies. She'd missed the breakout of the war in Europe and the subsequent German invasion of the Netherlands, yet now . . .

"It's nearly 04:00 hours," Vos said.

"Right." George headed to the engine room where his shift was about to start. Before he reached the stairs, he saw a dark form about two hundred meters away. The moonlight splashed across a destroyer ship, and since the Allied ships were either sunk or crippled, that could mean only one thing.

The destroyer was Japanese.

Had they spotted the minesweeper yet?

Then, another form emerged . . . a second Japanese destroyer.

George blinked in the moonlight, hoping that his eyes were bleary and playing a trick on him. What were the chances the *Endeh* could slip past undetected? *None* . . . echoed through George's mind.

His breath jerked, and he turned and hurried down the steps to the engine room. At the bottom of the stairs, he shouted, "There are two Japanese destroyers following us."

Lieutenant Van Wijnmalen's eyes rounded, and he sprinted up the stairs.

George turned to the control room, his chest tight with tension. The others had gone silent, staring at him. Then the commander's urgent voice came over the 1MC—or 1 Main Circuit, the ship's main public address system. "This is not a drill. This is not a drill. Two Japanese destroyers have been spotted. God's grace will get us past them undetected, but right now, halve the engine speed."

George and the others set to work immediately. No one spoke as they went about their duties. By the time the engine speed had slowed, perspiration stood out on George's face.

Each moment of waiting passed with agonizing slowness.

Then George heard a popping sound above the engine noise. Guns. Light caliber guns by the sound of it. The Japanese troops were firing at the minesweeper.

Almost instantly, the commander's voice came through the 1MC, "Slow the engine to a crawl."

George set about the task. The engine was at its lowest setting, and for a moment the bullets stopped. He moved to the edge of the engine room, trying to hear better as the other engineers watched him in silence, fear plain in their expressions.

George wiped at the sweat on his face. His throat felt like it had been scratched dry. He needed water. What he really wanted to do was get out of this stuffy engine room and find a lifeboat. Were the Japanese destroyers toying with them? Or had they moved on from the small minesweeper?

"Stop the engines!" the commander said, his tone urgent, even panicked. "This is not a drill. This is not a drill. All engines must cease."

George spun back into the room and followed orders.

Then, the ship's alarm clanged at the same moment Van Wijnmalen came barreling down the stairs. "Life jackets!" he hollered as he grabbed his from the supply along the wall. "Everyone up on deck and to the lifeboat!"

The alarm continued to clang as the commander's voice blared through the 1MC, "This is not a drill. All hands to the lifeboats."

George and the others reached for their life jackets as Van Wijnmalen tugged his on. The man turned back toward the stairs and headed up.

But he didn't get very far.

One second, George was reaching for a life jacket, and the next Lieutenant Van Wijnmalen disappeared. No. Everything disappeared.

The engine room. The men around him. The walls. The floor.

We've been hit, George dimly thought. His ears were throbbing, and his head felt like it had burst, then come back together, only to burst again.

What was that sound?

It was a high-pitched keening, almost mechanical, but louder than anything George had ever heard. He tried to lift his hands to cover his ears, but his arms were so very heavy. The high-pitched sound lowered and separated.

"Vischer, jump!"

Someone was calling his name? Telling him to . . . jump?

George's eyelids felt like sandpaper, but he dragged them open. The first thing he saw was searchlights skating across the minesweeper's deck. He began to remember. The alarm, the commander telling everyone to get in the lifeboat. The sound of gunfire. The searchlights must be from a Japanese ship. And now he was on deck. Wait. How was he on deck? Hadn't he been in the engine room?

Then he smelled it. Smoke. He turned his head to see flames. The ship was on fire, and . . . there were men lying on the deck like he was. Not moving.

With a groan, George pushed up on one elbow. His skin felt like it was on fire, although he couldn't see any flames on his clothing. Rips in his pants revealed gashes from shrapnel.

Nothing hurt, though. How was that possible?

"Van Wijnmalen," George murmured to the man lying a few feet from him. His face wasn't right, though. It was half gone.

At the realization, pain shot through George, and he began to feel his injuries. Like a throbbing, living thing. He couldn't pinpoint where he hurt, though—it was everywhere.

"Jump, Vischer, jump!" someone called to him. But the sound was muted, almost like he was dreaming it.

He turned his face toward the railing, away from the fire. Men bobbed in the water that reflected the glittering stars. The Japanese destroyer's searchlights lit up the men's faces, then moved on. Beyond them, the lifeboat was on fire. The men wouldn't last long in the water, and only a couple of them were wearing life vests. How this realization got through George's murky mind, he didn't know.

With another groan, he moved to his knees. Then slowly, he stood. Pain lanced through his wounds, but at least he was on his feet. Another sweep of searchlights passed over him, and he wondered if the Japanese soldiers saw him staggering. All the men he passed on the way were dead. George was the last one alive on the minesweeper.

His gaze landed on Chatelain and Jens. Neither sailor was moving. Pesch and Pelkwijk were motionless, too. Another sailor, Franken, was also dead.

He tried not to think what these deaths meant, what it would mean for the families these men had left behind.

Another sweep of the searchlights had George gripping the railing. With the lifeboat on fire, he looked toward the dinghy. They could use that. He scanned the sea for his living comrades. Bobbing in the water not too far from the ship was his friend Pieter Hooft, who wore no life jacket. "The dinghy is intact," he rasped to Hooft. "We need to get it freed."

"Toss me a line," Hooft answered.

George scrambled about for a line, moving around the men who'd been alive moments ago. With the strobing of the searchlights, George's gaze skated over their mortal wounds, and he swallowed back the bile that rose in his throat. When he found a line, he tossed it over, then hauled Hooft toward the edge of the minesweeper.

Surely the searchlights revealed their actions, but George couldn't worry about that now. Every part of his body ached, and his strength was ebbing, but somehow he was able to help Hooft climb aboard. Hooft was clearly in pain too—from shrapnel, or from the earlier accident? Regardless, the pair of them worked to launch the dinghy.

Before they could get the dinghy lowered, a new sound reached them. That of a ticking clock combined with the sound of a high-pitched engine. Accelerating. Moving faster and faster. "Hit the deck," Hooft shouted.

The two men flattened themselves just before a torpedo blasted behind them, splintering and rocking the minesweeper.

George groaned as he covered his ears. Waves of shock reverberated through him, and his chest felt like he had a truck parked on top of it.

"Vischer," Hooft said. "Vischer, we need to jump."

Again, George dragged his eyes open.

Hooft was on his feet, hovering over him, a hand on his shoulder. "Let's get off of this thing."

"What about the dinghy?"

Hooft's eyes shifted, and George looked over. One of the davits had broken, and the dinghy hung vertically.

"Maybe we can free it still," George said as he pushed to his knees. His head pounded, and his limbs felt like they were on fire.

"It's too far to reach." Hooft grabbed on to George's arm and hauled him up. "We need to get in the water."

The men limped to the edge of the minesweeper, and they tumbled into the sea.

The water was like a slap to George's senses. He sunk below the surface for a handful of seconds, and saltwater engulfed him. As he surfaced, he grimaced at the sharp pain of the salt seeping into his wounds. At least it would be healing to any abrasions.

The searchlights switched off, bringing more darkness to the glittering water now. Beyond, the ship was still burning, the fire spreading since the second torpedo hit.

George began to take in his surroundings, noting who was floating in the water alongside him. "Vos," he said, when he saw the man bobbing not too far away, his life jacket holding him up. "Are you injured?"

"I don't know," Vos said, his eyes reflecting the orange flames leaping about the burning minesweeper. "We need to find something to float on before the ship goes down."

"The Japanese are moving on," another man said. George couldn't see his face in the dimness.

Without anyone issuing an order, the men swam back to the minesweeper and, through helping each other, they climbed aboard.

Hooft sat where he'd crawled aboard, his breathing labored. George was worried about him, but he had to work to find items that they could float on. He and the other officers and sailors moved around the dead bodies and searched through the rubble. They tossed over life vests and wood planks.

"They're back!" someone called.

No whining of an approaching torpedo this time, but open firing burst toward the minesweeper. Bullets peppered the deck and anything standing.

Like a synchronized drill, George and the other men leapt off board. Before he hit the water, George felt the hit to his foot. A bullet had either gone through his big toe or grazed it. The cold seawater numbed the sensation, but the aching was fierce.

The rain of bullets also dislodged the dinghy once and for all.

"We need to get that cut loose," someone said. Maybe it was Hooft or another man.

George couldn't be sure because his ears were buzzing again. Then he watched as Vos dove below the surface. Moments later, he and the dinghy appeared. He'd cut it loose, although the dinghy was badly damaged. At least it was still floating, and the bullets had stopped.

That had to be good news on a night where there was very little good happening.

George and Vos clung to the dinghy, along with a few other men, while Hooft floated with a long wooden plank.

The destroyers seemed to think all had been lost, and their large bulks edged away from the wreckage.

Dawn was still at least an hour way, but the black sky had shifted to a deep gray. The minesweeper was a sad, smoldering lump in the middle of the sea, soon to be a grave to the men who'd lost their lives. But there was food aboard, and the dinghy was ill-equipped.

"Let's get back on the minesweeper and find food," George said to the men floating about him. "Then maybe we can make it to an island and hide out until we can get help."

The impossibility of his words should have been laughable. But the pale faces gazing back at him were devoid of any humor, or of any better ideas.

"Let's go," Rouwenhorst agreed.

It might be a risk, but they were desperate. They swam to the mine-sweeper again and hefted themselves on board. Again, George helped Hooft, who seemed weaker as time went on.

If only George was a doctor, or they had medical care. Every man was wounded in some way, but Hooft looked like he was a couple of steps from death's door. Without the numbing protection of the seawa-ter, George found it hard to put weight on his injured foot. A bullet had ripped through his boot and his big toe, taking a chunk of flesh with it. The wound needed to be disinfected and stitched, but finding food and drink was more important.

A few of them rummaged for anything to eat or drink in the pale light of dawn, and they made a paltry collection at one end of the sloping deck. Some of the other men transported the dead bodies to the railing, lining them up, as if they were simply in a roll call formation. One by one, they rolled the bodies off the ship. Then the rains started, and in a short time, most of the fire had been extinguished.

No one tried to take cover from the rain, they simply sat in it, let-ting it wash away the seawater.

As George lounged next to Hooft, trying not to think about the damage to his foot, the clouds parted, and the morning sun appeared. Very little was recognizable on the burned and melted deck. How much longer would it stay afloat? Beyond the vessel, the green sea endlessly stretched in all directions, with no ships in sight. The view was decep-tive, this he knew.

Yet, exhaustion took over, and the lulling of the sea waves support-ing the minesweeper almost put him to sleep. Had he accepted his fate that there was probably no way out of this situation alive? The sun's heat intensified, drying the deck and warming the tops of their heads and shoulders.

If the Japanese military didn't finish them off, then the sun would dehydrate them all. Or they'd die of starvation. They'd eaten food from the few surviving tins, and for the moment, George's stomach was satisfied. He knew it wouldn't last, though, and there was no extra food for another meal. His foot and toe were throbbing anew, but he was much better off than Hooft, whose face was a sickly pallor.

The crew's hospital attendant's mate, J. F. Van Beek, had his own injuries, and it seemed futile to try any treatments when all the medical supplies had been obliterated. So they would wait.

How long would it be until they could be rescued? Or would rescue even come?

The rumbling started out faintly, but every living man onboard knew immediately what the sound meant.

Planes.

The flicker of hope that the planes might be Allied aircraft died the moment Vos called out, "They're Japanese bombers."

George squinted to see the approaching Japanese seaborne bombers. The dark green and yellow bodies marked them as torpedo bombers. There was zero chance they'd fly over a Dutch vessel without firing.

"Get into the water!" someone shouted as the planes neared.

Was Vos yelling or someone else? George hoisted Hooft with him until they reached the railing. Once again, he tumbled into the murky, dark depths of the Java Sea.

CHAPTER SEVEN

"The trek to Bogor took eight hours. To avoid attracting attention,
we blackened our faces, arms and legs with soot. Additionally,
we had stained our hair with black dye, and we spoke as little
as possible as we walked slowly along the side of the road. We
children wore pajamas to conceal our white skin, while the
women had simple cotton dresses with long sleeves on."

—BAREND A. VAN NOOTEN, CIHAPIT CAMP

RITA

The buzz of the radio was already coming from the dining room
by the time Rita opened her eyes in the morning. The newscaster's low,
urgent tones filtered through the crack of her bedroom door. What was
he saying? More bad news?

Through the curtains, she saw that it was early enough that Papa
should still be home. Rita scrambled out of bed, careful to not make any
noise and wake up Georgie. She snatched the teddy bear she slept with
so that he could say goodbye to Papa as well.

She padded her way to the dining room, but there was no Papa having breakfast with Mama. Maybe he was still sleeping? Or maybe he had
the day off? And they could do something fun?

But the words on the radio didn't sound cheerful, and Mama sat at
the dining room table alone, her glasses on the table, her head bowed as
she listened.

Rita decided to wait a few minutes before asking Mama all her many questions. She slipped into a chair and clutched her teddy bear to her chest.

The words from the radio sounded rushed and panicked: "The battle for Java has started," the announcer said. "Japanese forces have landed on the western tip of the island. Allied forces are on their way with a planned counterattack."

Rita scrunched up her nose. She could only guess what a counterattack was; she didn't dare ask her Mama.

"Refugees are pouring into Batavia from surrounding bombed areas," the announcer continued. "The Red Cross is searching for locations to set up . . . Reports are coming in on the devastation by Japanese torpedoes to Allied ships in the Java Sea . . ."

Mama turned off the radio, and then she noticed Rita at the table with her.

"You're up early," Mama said, but she didn't seem surprised at all. Her eyelids were droopy, as if she hadn't slept much. She put on her glasses. "Was the radio too loud?"

"I don't know," Rita said. She couldn't remember if she'd been awake before noticing the radio sounds. "Did Papa already leave?"

"Yes, he's helping with the war," she said on a sigh. "He might be gone a while."

Rita was never sure exactly what "a while" meant when adults said it. "Is he on a submarine?" Papa talked about them a lot. Maybe he was fighting the Japanese forces on the Java Sea? If that was true, would his submarine be hit by a torpedo? No, that couldn't happen. No one could see a submarine since it was underwater.

"He's not on a submarine," Mama said, but her lips quivered. She pressed her fingers against her forehead. She sometimes did that when she had a headache.

"Are you sick, Mama?" Rita asked. "I can make you soto."

It was too early for the cook to arrive, but maybe her mother was hungry. And Kemala made big batches of *soto*—a soup made of broth, meat, and vegetables—and it would be easy to heat up on the stove.

Mama gave Rita a soft smile. "Thank you, but I'll lie down for a little while. If Georgie wakes before Oma, can you play with him?"

Rita agreed, but before Mama could go to her bedroom, someone knocked on the front door.

It was so early in the morning that Rita couldn't guess who it might be. Even Johan wouldn't come over before breakfast. And the cook came in the side door, but it was still too early for her to arrive.

Mama's pale face went even paler. "Wait here, Rita," she whispered.

Rita wanted to see who it was, though. She moved to the edge of the dining room where she glimpsed part of the front door. When Mama opened it, a dark-haired woman walked in. Rita recognized her immediately as Aunt Tie, Papa's half-sister.

Aunt Tie looked a lot like Papa, with her dark hair, but instead of golden-brown eyes, they were mud-colored. Unlike Papa, she didn't really seem to like kids, even though she was almost twenty-nine. Whenever Georgie or Rita would try to talk or play with her, she'd shoo them away. She lived somewhere else in Batavia near her job. She usually came over when Papa was home, so why was she here now? And why was she carrying a suitcase?

The women's voices were low, and Rita couldn't make out everything they said. Then Mama turned and saw Rita. "Aunt Tie will be staying with us for a little while."

Aunt Tie moved farther into the house. She glanced at Rita, then back to Mama. "My neighborhood has little water. Some places were bombed, and now we're being told not to come into work."

"You can stay here as long as you need to, certainly," Mama said, although there was no smile in her eyes when she said it.

Aunt Tie's very next question was, "Where's George? Is he at headquarters this early?"

Mama hesitated. "He's on a mission, but I'm not sure where he is or what he's doing."

Aunt Tie narrowed her eyes. "Ah." Her gaze shifted to Rita again, then she pursed her lips.

"This way," Mama said. "You can sleep in the spare bedroom. We'll be having breakfast in about an hour."

Aunt Tie moved past Rita, not greeting her at all. "I'll lie down until then. I had to walk farther than I wanted to."

Rita watched her aunt lumber past with her bulky suitcase. It rattled along the floorboards, and the sound would probably wake up Georgie and Oma.

Somehow, though, both of them stayed asleep. Maybe because sometimes in the middle of the night, sirens awakened everyone, and they'd have to go into the bomb shelters. That had taught them to sleep through other noises.

Rita walked out to the veranda after Mama and Aunt Tie disappeared into their rooms. At least Mama could get some rest and hopefully feel better. Rita sat at the top of the steps and watched the eastern horizon lighten. Laan Trivelli stayed very quiet as the sun came up, since there weren't any children going to school. Men and women weren't heading off to their jobs either, since so many places had been closed down.

Rita pulled her knees up to her chest and rested her chin atop them. The only sounds were the birds announcing the morning and the distant chatter of monkeys. Monkeys didn't come much into the neighborhoods since the residents would drive them off.

The door of Johan's house snapped open, and Kells loped out into the yard. He headed toward a tree to do his business. Moments later, Kells settled on the veranda of the Vos home, tongue hanging out as he surveyed everything with a keen eye. No one else came out of the house.

As the morning awakened and bloomed with heat, Rita saw four people walking along the road. It was their cook, gardener, maid, and nanny—all walking together. It was an unusual sight because the gardener didn't usually come until later in the day.

Something prickled along Rita's neck, as if a spider had been caught in her hair. She brushed at her neck then stood to watch the approaching people. There was something different about their expressions. They looked downcast and very serious. Had something terrible happened? Did they have an injured family member?

By the time they reached the veranda, it was clear that Anja had been crying. Her eyes were red-rimmed, and she kept wiping at tears on her cheeks. Dea kept an arm about Anja. Kemala kept her hands tightly gripped in front of her, and Bima's mournful expression made Rita feel like crying herself.

"Hello, Rita," Anja said. "Is your mama awake yet? We need to speak with her."

"She's in her bedroom," Rita said, not sure if her mom was asleep or awake. She could peek in though. "Come inside." She wasn't used to being a hostess, but this is what Mama would have said.

Bima shook his head. "We will wait out here."

Rita thought that was strange, but she hurried inside. She walked quietly to Mama's room and opened the door with a single creak.

Mama was lying on her side, facing the door, but her eyes were open. She blinked then moved to her elbow when she saw Rita. "Is something the matter?"

Rita guessed it showed on her face. "Nanny, the cook, the maid, and the gardener are all standing on the veranda. They want to talk to you."

Mama sat up fully, then climbed out of bed. She reached for the nightstand and gripped the edge for a moment. After taking two deep breaths, she said, "Wait in the house. I'll speak to them outside."

Rita didn't want to wait in the house. She wanted to know what was happening. She wanted to know when Papa would come back. She wanted to know why Mama hadn't slept well last night. She wanted to know how long Aunt Tie would be staying here.

So Rita moved to the front room after Mama went outside. She could hear a little of the conversation through the screens at the windows. But it didn't make sense. Why was the gardener saying he was going into the army? He wasn't Dutch. And why was Anja crying so hard?

Rita's stomach hurt, and it wasn't because she hadn't eaten breakfast yet. This was a different kind of hurt.

When Mama came back inside, her own eyes were watery. She didn't tell Rita that she shouldn't have listened at the window. No, Mama sat down on the couch next to Rita and pulled her into her arms.

Rita didn't know why Mama was hugging her, but hugs from her parents were always welcome.

"Why was Anja crying?" Rita asked after a few silent moments.

Mama sighed again. She was doing a lot of that this morning. "With the Japanese soldiers invading our island, the local natives don't want to be outside of their neighborhoods. There are many rumors that the Dutch people will have more curfews and rationing."

Mama straightened and pulled away from Rita. "They are very sorry, but they can't come to our house for a while. Probably not until the Japanese troops leave."

Rita knew that Georgie would be very sad about their nanny. Rita felt sad too, but she hoped it wouldn't be very long before her friends could come back. "Why is the gardener joining the army? He's not Dutch."

Mama's brows lifted. "Oh, Rita. He's not joining the Dutch army. Japan is asking for Indonesian volunteers to join its forces, and if they don't . . ."

When Mama didn't finish, Rita was even more curious.

"What happens if they don't?"

Mama looked away, her gaze on something across the room. "There are only rumors. But they are being threatened with imprisonment." She suddenly looked at Rita and grasped her hand. "It's nothing for us to worry about now. This is a lot for you to understand. We will stay here, in our home, safe and sound. We'll pray for all our friends, and for your father, and for the war to be over soon."

Oma was the one who talked about prayer the most, and now Mama was. Rita wanted to ask how exactly did prayer work, but Mama's eyes were watering again. So Rita wrapped her arms about Mama's waist and held her tight.

A moment later, Oma spoke from the front room doorway. "This has happened to all our neighbors," Oma moved across the room, her walking a bit unsteady—something that happened first thing in the morning.

Oma sat on the other side of Rita and reached across her and grasped Mama's hand. "All the native servants are staying in their villages. At least most of them. Some nannies are staying with their employers for now."

"The radio this morning said that the banks are freezing money," Mama said in a quiet voice. Maybe she didn't want Rita to hear.

Rita knew a little about money. But what did Mama mean about "freezing" money? Rita could count and she sometimes was allowed to buy a trinket or treat when out with Oma at the market. She also knew that if they didn't have money, they couldn't buy things. Now, Rita's stomach was hurting again.

"Oh no," Oma murmured. "Is it too late to make a withdrawal?"

"George took everything out he was allowed to yesterday, so we have it hidden in the house," Mama said. "But he said that many people were too late to get their funds."

Oma was silent for a moment, then she said, "We will focus on what we can do, and what blessings we still have." She looked down at Rita. "Now, how about you help me with breakfast? Your mother can rest a bit more."

This all sounded good to Rita. She liked to help in the kitchen when she wasn't busy with something else. She often sampled what Kemala was cooking. Rita's favorite was stealing the hamburger mixture for Dutch round mince balls. Would there be enough money for her favorite foods? If Papa had gotten all their money from the bank, then they would be fine and still have food, right? She moved off the couch, and just then, the sirens went off.

The sound always made Rita jolt inside. Like she'd been pushed in the stomach very hard. Mama would not be resting now.

"I'll fetch Georgie," Oma said, already moving toward the hallway.

Before Oma reached it, Aunt Tie appeared. Her short, dark hair was snarled on one side as if that's where she'd been sleeping.

"Where's the shelter?" she asked in a sharp voice.

Oma stared at her, and Mama said, "Tie is staying with us for a while."

Tie nodded at Oma, then walked toward the front door.

"It's between our property and the Vos place."

Tie headed outside without another word, and soon, Oma had Georgie in hand. They hurried toward the underground shelter. Johan and his mother and sister were already inside by the time Rita stepped down into the water-filled trench. It seemed that Johan's father had left, too, but Rita didn't want to ask her friend in front of everyone.

Tie sat at the far end of the bench, closed her eyes, and kept to herself.

Johan stood at the entrance watching the sky.

It wasn't long before they heard the planes overhead.

Rita nestled against Oma and held her hand as she wondered if bombs would really drop this time and if she'd be able to see the smoke. Sometimes there weren't bombs at all. Just planes flying overhead.

But these planes sounded closer than she'd ever heard them before. She let go of Oma's hand and joined Johan where he stood. At first, she saw only the blue sky and patches of clouds. Then the planes came into view. Her heart rate doubled, then tripled.

"Oh no," Johan whispered, but it was just as loud as the sirens and the engines.

As Rita watched, she saw dark shapes falling from the planes.

Bombs.

She watched them falling, falling, rushing closer to the ground, until she felt someone tug her away from the entrance. It was Mama who pulled her in tight and shielded her, even though they were in a shelter.

Rita bit down on her rubber wafer just as the explosion rocked through her ears. It was close, she knew, but she wasn't sure how close.

No one spoke for a long moment, not even when the acrid smell of smoke stung their eyes and noses. It felt like another entire hour before the sirens stopped. They were free to leave the shelter, but no one seemed to want to leave.

Finally, Aunt Tie said, "We can't stay here all day." She moved past everyone and stepped out.

That seemed to wake everyone else up, and clinging to Mama's hand, Rita followed the rest. Oma carried Georgie, holding him close. The smoke was thicker than Rita could ever remember, and they all looked toward the direction in which the smoke was still climbing to the sky. Had it hit a house? It was still too far to tell, but it was very close, all the same.

"Has Java surrendered?" Mrs. Vos asked Mama in a quiet voice.

But Mama murmured, "I don't know."

Once inside the house, Rita helped Oma with breakfast. She'd told Mama to go lie down with Georgie. Aunt Tie had disappeared as well. Rita and Oma prepared one of Kemala's recipes—maybe in honor of her. Making the nasi kuning, a rice dish cooked with coconut milk and turmeric, Rita realized how much she missed Kemala. She wished she could've given her a hug before she left. She'd been a friend, and Rita hoped she was staying safe.

They'd left the radio on, but there wasn't any news about bombers. Most of it was about the Red Cross.

"They will help us, right, Oma?" Rita asked.

"Of course," Oma said, but the lines about her eyes were tight, and she said nothing after that.

It seemed all the adults were tense today. And no one wanted to talk about how close the bombs were that had dropped.

After breakfast, Rita went outside into the yard. Everything was quiet outside. Besides, she didn't like the worried looks, the grave expressions, and the silence inside. Without their servants, and with Aunt Tie there, everything was different.

Rita didn't even feel like climbing the trees, so she sat on the grass in the shade. The sun was still out, and even though it was getting almost too hot to play outside, Rita felt like being by herself to think about everything.

She stretched on the grass and nestled her teddy bear next to her. Maybe she'd tell him a story or teach him how to count. But before she could decide which one, she heard a rumbling. Or more like a stomping. The noise grew louder and louder, but it wasn't coming from the sky like the bomber planes.

A movement to her right caught her attention. Johan had come out of his house. He walked to the hedges that bordered the road, then he quickly crouched down.

Rita rose to her feet, then she hurried to her own row of hedges. The thundering sound grew louder, but she had to see what it was. She peered around the hedges and there, coming up the cobblestoned Laan Trivelli, were rows and rows of soldiers.

Japanese soldiers.

Rita couldn't move. Was she even breathing? Their boots marched in the same rhythm. Their uniforms were all the same, too. They wore hats that had flapping neck pieces attached. And each of them marched with rifles with long bayonets. The man in front carried a white flag with a large red circle in the middle of it. The soldiers weren't just Japanese, either. Korean men and Indonesian men marched among them. Radio reports had announced that more and more Indonesian soldiers had pledged their loyalty to the emperor. As they neared her house, she crouched even lower, trying to make herself small. What would happen if they saw her?

What if they saw Johan? Would they make the Dutch children join their army too? Like they had the gardener?

As the marching soldiers passed, Rita couldn't take her eyes from them. Their faces were so stern, their dark eyes unblinking, their bodies moving in exact formation. On their backs, they carried bedrolls and canteens, along with their guns. Their footsteps mimicked the pounding of her heart, and it wasn't until they'd passed and had disappeared from view, that Rita felt like she could breathe again.

She didn't know if Johan was still watching, but she wasn't going to stick around to find out. She clutched at her teddy bear and ran to her house, faster than she'd ever run before. There, Mama would keep her safe.

CHAPTER EIGHT

"Looting erupted everywhere, especially around the town's warehouses. It was the end of an illustrious era and the beginning of a tumultuous, never-to-be-forgotten chapter of our lives. A few days later, planes flew overhead so low that the ground trembled beneath our feet, and the house shook on its foundation. Pamphlets were dropped. The nation was informed that the enemy was nearby and closing in."

—RITA LA FONTAINE-DE CLERCQ ZUBLI, JAMBI CAMP

GEORGE

The Japanese seaborne bombers opened fire on the decrepit minesweeper as George floated with his fellow officers in the undulating sea. Many of the men dived under water, but George was focused on supporting Hooft. The man's eyes were closed, and his body trembled in the cool sea. The temperature of the water was mild this time of year, but it was exhausting to stay afloat, even with life vests.

The minesweeper was on fire again, flames cracking and popping in the morning air, and the level of the vessel had become lower. It was going to sink. After the bombers moved on, there was no point trying to climb aboard again. The creaking vessel was doomed.

What did that mean for the surviving men? For him? For Hooft? They'd lost five men to the torpedoes, which left nineteen of them. Five men's families would be forever changed, leaving behind widows and fatherless children . . . and what about the rest of them? What were the chances of survival? Were they just enduring excruciating circumstances, only to face death in the next few hours?

"Come on, man," George said to Hooft. "We're getting you into the dinghy." The men in the water had gravitated to the biggest floating device—the dinghy. They were either swimming alongside of it, or hanging on.

Vos swam closer to them, his red hair darkened from the water. "How is he?"

"He's slipping in an out of consciousness," George said. "He needs to rest and not tread water."

"Let's get him on the dinghy," Vos said.

It took three men pulling at Hooft to get him onto the dinghy. George wondered if the man was even aware of what was going on.

The dinghy was badly damaged, and a couple of men were trying to plug up the holes in the bottom with pieces of cloth or bits of floating wood they'd snatched from the wreckage. George grabbed for a floating plank, using it to create more freeboard space. Other men snatched life belts out of the water to aid as well. George shifted Hooft onto a plank where he could at least lie down as they waited for rescue.

"You can rest now," George murmured to Hooft. There was no response.

"Make room for one more," Vos called from where he'd slipped back into the water.

George turned and helped haul one of the quartermasters, Jaden, onto the dinghy.

Once Jaden was laid out on a plank, there wasn't room for much more. Vos and a couple of men sat on the dinghy. George perched on the edge, his legs dangling in the water as he watched the two injured men, wondering how much they were suffering. Beyond them, the minesweeper continued to creak and groan as it sank deeper into the water.

All of the men stared as the sea finally rose above the vessel, and the minesweeper was sucked downward until nothing was visible anymore.

None of the surviving men spoke for a long time. The only sounds were the movement of the sea and the distant rumble of Japanese planes, dark specs in the blue expanse of sky.

"What are they doing?" Hessing, the lieutenant commander, said.

George looked up at the sky. Four planes were circling, but at quite a distance. Surely the planes knew there were Dutch enemies clinging to a dinghy in the middle of a sea. But they only continued to circle, and none of them approached.

No one was about to signal to the pilots.

The Japanese prisoner-of-war camps were notorious for their torture and starvation methods. George had even heard a few reports of Allied pilots choosing to leap from their battered planes and freefall to their deaths rather than risk capture by the Japanese forces.

Would George and his comrades be captured and taken as political prisoners? Or would they be shot in the water after all—and meet the same fate so many other sailors had in the past few days?

George glanced about at the surviving men. Not far from George, Commander Rouwenhorst was floating in the water, his hands gripping the upper part of his life jacket. His gaze was rooted to the sky, as if he were waiting for more bombs to drop.

"We should do roll call," George said, choking out the words. He hoped he wasn't overstepping command. "We need to get organized and figure out a system of bailing water and taking turns in the dinghy."

The commander nodded, then began the roll call. Everyone called out their name. *Nineteen* were left out of the twenty-four men originally on the minesweeper.

"May their souls rest in peace," Vos murmured.

The men echoed, "Amen."

It was not a fitting memorial for men who'd sacrificed their lives for the Allied cause. But it was all the men could do right now.

When it was George's turn on the dinghy, he worked to bail water with a steel helmet that someone had fished out of the water. It was a daunting process since the stuffed holes in the bottom of the vessel were still leaking.

The day progressed, hot and humid, with the sun beating down upon them without mercy. The life vests were filled with kapok fibers and had become so waterlogged that those who were on the dinghy took them off and tied them upon their heads to dry out.

A croaking voice alerted George, and he paused and turned to see Hooft's eyes opened. George scrambled over to his friend. "How are you?" he asked.

Hooft's gaze shifted past George and then back again. "I don't feel well."

That was certainly an understatement, George mused. Then Hooft jerked onto his side and coughed up blood. George rubbed the man's shoulder, feeling helpless. "Get it out," he said.

The blow to the man's abdomen the night before must have started internal bleeding. Nothing about that was good. Not when they were floating on a crippled dinghy in the middle of the sea, surrounded by enemy planes, and with little hope of being rescued.

At least George's toe had stopped bleeding, for the most part. It hurt to put weight on it, but he was keeping to his knees anyway.

The buzzing of the planes continued high above, like a mosquito that wouldn't go away, staying just out of reach from being swatted.

Hooft's eyes closed again, and he stayed on his side, one hand curled into a fist. The seawater lapped at the sides of the dinghy in a steady rhythm, echoing the dull thud of George's heart. He wondered if the sinking of the minesweeper had been reported to the naval base yet. Was the Japanese military already announcing its conquest? Would the news get back to Mary and the rest of their wives and families?

"They're moving farther away," Rouwenhorst said. He'd hardly taken his gaze from the sky.

George blinked against the sun and looked over at the commander.

He pointed toward the piece of sky where the bombers had been circling.

Sure enough, if George's sight could be trusted, the Japanese had moved off. To refuel and return?

"Not the best strategy," Bakker said in a humorless voice. "Leaving their enemy in the water, to rise up and strike again."

Someone laughed. George was too tired to figure out who. His head buzzed, his body ached, his toe throbbed, and the tips of his ears were burned. He began to bail water again. A few moments later, he spotted something floating.

"Can you reach that tin can, Vos?" George grabbed one of the paddles and tried to tap it closer to the dinghy.

Vos was already in the water, and in a few strokes, he got ahold of the tin. He turned the can. "They're biscuits."

"We'll eat them at sunset," Rouwenhorst announced.

George spent the better part of the next hour scanning for more floating tins, but there was nothing but seawater.

Rotations changed. Men who were floating in the water climbed onto the dinghy to take their turns bailing. And George slipped back into the water since only five or six could fit onto the dinghy. The hours passed, and they continued to rotate. Men floating in the water, paddling on the dinghy, bailing water, or sleeping on the spare planks next to the injured men.

The afternoon wore on, likely the longest day of any of their lives. Most of the men didn't have shirts on since they'd been awakened in the middle of the night by the torpedo. George's shirt at least gave him some protection from the sun. The sun's rays were merciless, like a hot iron pressed directly to the skin. And the sea below offered little relief, the salt only adding to the painful irritation of sunburn.

At least the Japanese bombers had left.

It was time to take action instead of waiting to be acted upon. By consensus, the men decided to set off in a southerly direction, aiming for the Thousand Islands. If they could reach the northern tip, then they could land in unoccupied territory. The islands harbored coconut plantations, and there would be plenty to harvest and eat. But any error in judgment, even a slight one, would send them off course.

Once the sun began to set, Vos used a knife to open the tin of biscuits.

George wished there was more food to share. Although he was surrounded by seawater, his mouth watered in anticipation.

After Vos twisted the metal lid off, he groaned.

"What is it?" George asked. He wasn't currently riding on the dinghy, but he could see Vos's disappointed expression.

"The tin must have a leak in it," Vos said, turning the tin so that the other men could see inside. "The biscuits are damaged by oil and seawater."

Disappointment shot through George. The men needed sustenance, especially the injured men who were not doing well at all. He looked over at Hooft's still form. The only sign of life from him was the rise and fall of his chest.

"Toss out the food, then," Rouwenhorst said. "We can use the tin for bailing water or something else."

Vos did as told, and when the next shift arrived, it was already dark. George hauled himself onto the dinghy. He took one of the paddles this time. They were making very slow progress, but with the heat of the sun abated, that should improve.

Were they paddling into a trap, though?

Would the Japanese bombers be back at dawn, and would all of this effort be for naught?

There was no way for any of them to know. But if the bombers didn't return to finish them off, then perhaps they could make it to land in time to help Hooft.

During one shift, it was George's turn to sleep. He must have been exhausted in both mind and body because, somehow, he fell into a deep nothingness. Hours later, the light of the rising sun awakened him.

That, and Bakker saying, "There's a coconut floating in the water."

George blinked his eyes open, dearly wishing that the last twenty-four hours had been a bad dream and he was about to wake up in his own bed in Batavia, next to his wife. How was she doing? Were the Japanese forces already on the island? Would there be more rationing of food? George pushed up on his elbows, hoping to see something promising. Something to give him hope. But the sight that greeted him was an endless stretch of rippling blue.

Then he heard a splash.

Bakker was swimming in the water, away from the dinghy, heading for the floating coconut. A couple of the men, weak as they were, cheered on the swimmer.

Then, suddenly, Bakker disappeared beneath the water. George scrambled to his knees, wincing at the jolt of pain when his toe brushed the plank. "Where did he go?"

Then Bakker reappeared, his face drained of any color. He began swimming back toward them. "Something's down there," he choked out. "Something bumped my foot."

The men with the paddles lifted them and searched the water about the dinghy.

Two more men climbed onto the dinghy, and the vessel sunk dangerously low in the water.

"How much weight can this hold?" Vos said. "No one else get on, or we'll all sink."

George saw the panic in Bakker's eyes as he swam closer to the dinghy. If one man panicked, it would spread like a flash of lightning, and that could lead to a different death for them all.

"There are no sharks in this part of the sea," George said, although he wasn't sure if that was true. Sharks would have made themselves known by now, right? He needed to quell any panicking.

"Vischer's right," Rouwenhorst said. "Take my place on the dinghy, Bakker."

George watched as the commander slipped into the water. So George did the same, and Bakker scrambled onto the dinghy.

Bakker's face was drained of color. "We're going to die," he whispered as he hugged his knees to his chest and scanned the water. His voice grew louder, more panicked. "If there aren't sharks here, there will be somewhere. Or the Japanese bombers will return, or—"

"Stop," Rouwenhorst said in a sharp tone.

All heads turned to look at him.

"There's no use complaining," the commander continued. "We are in God's care, but we need to do our part. We are staying focused. We are bailing water. We are paddling to the Thousand Islands. We are at the mercy of mother nature. Pray if you must, but the next man who talks about dying will wish he hadn't."

George hadn't heard anything religious from Rouwenhorst before, but if it worked, then it was necessary. A mutiny would do none of them any good. It was several moments before anyone else spoke. And then it was Vos in a quiet tone.

"Hooft is gone."

George floated to the side of the dinghy closest to his friend. Hooft was lying in the same position as the night before, on his side, his hand curled into a fist, as if in slumber. But his chest wasn't moving. There was no sign of breathing.

George's voice choked on his words, "He was a good man. A loyal man. He sacrificed his life to protect us."

"Amen," several others echoed.

Two men slipped off the dinghy as if knowing George would climb on and prepare Hooft to be buried at sea. There was nothing to wrap him with, so George simply untied Hooft's life vest.

Rouwenhorst cleared his throat and said, "We will pray."

The men paused in bailing water and bowed their heads, joined by the others. Rouwenhorst offered a short prayer. When it was finished, George wiped at his face, then lifted his chin. "God rest his soul."

It was finished. Hooft had served his time here on earth.

George blinked back his salty tears, then rested a hand on Hooft's shoulder. "Goodbye, my friend," he whispered. "Rest in peace."

With the help of Vos, they rolled Hooft off the wooden plank. His body soundlessly entered the water.

George closed his eyes, trying to not imagine Hooft sinking lower and lower, down toward his watery grave. All of the men were silent, and the only sounds that could be heard were bailing water and paddling. After several moments, George opened his eyes and scanned the horizon, then the rest of the sky, trying to determine their location and how long would it be until they reached the Thousand Islands.

Was Hooft's death an omen for them all? Would they, one by one, fall prey to this ordeal? At the pace of a couple of men paddling, it would take them days to reach the northernmost tip of the Thousand Islands. The distance was about sixty nautical miles from Tandjong Priok harbor. How long could a man live without fresh water or food?

The commander's voice broke the quiet surrounding them. "We must pray for rain."

CHAPTER NINE

"Every day was the same and yet a little worse than the day before. In the morning, there was the usual roll call, the forced exercises, and then the long wait for kitchen personnel to show up with their buckets of camp 'food,' consisting primarily of a gluelike porridge and some bread or a bowl of cooked rice in ever-decreasing amounts. The portions were made even smaller by putting marbles in the bottom of the measuring cups. This was an ingenious way to slowly starve us to death."

—JOYCE F. KATER-HOEKE, LAMPERSARIE CAMP

GEORGE

George didn't consider himself a religious man. Yet, he held the belief that the church you were born into was where you remained. Mary was the one in their marriage who had faith, who prayed, who consulted with God. A replica of her mother in that way.

Yet, as the sun rose on Wednesday, teasing at distances too far to paddle to in time, George found himself praying for rain along with the other men. Some were vocal about it. Vos frequently prayed aloud. Even the commander prayed aloud more than once. Others closed their eyes, then murmured a quiet *Amen*.

And still the rain didn't come.

None of them had eaten since Sunday.

George began to bargain with God. It might have been humorous in another circumstance, but when the sun was beating down upon wounded bodies hour after hour, and throats were parched, and skin was blistering, and stomachs were hollow, George was happy to bargain with anyone and for anything.

Hooft's death had been a terrible reality that had shaken them all. George was feeling his own physical toll. His movements had slowed, and he began to fantasize about food and fresh water. The dark irony is that talking about favorite meals was somehow comforting.

During the next shift that George paddled, as the conversation ebbed around him, he noticed the shift in the wind. The air cooled around him, and he looked up to see clouds gathering. Almost at that same moment, the other men noticed too.

"It's going to rain," Bakker said.

"Praise God," Lieutenant Arnoldus said.

"Get the tin," another said. It was Lieutenant Feij.

Arnoldus shifted about, tugging off his shirt to act as a rain collector. Feij did the same, as did Lieutenant Rutgers. George held the paddle between his knees as he took off his own shirt, then held it out as the first drops fell. At first, the rain was a sprinkle of random, spaced-out drops, then the clouds raced together, darkening as they churned. And rain dumped.

George lifted his chin and opened his mouth. The water was fresh, sweet, cool, refreshing. He swallowed down what he could. But it wasn't enough.

The storm was over within minutes, and as it dissipated, a few men groaned. There was no way to save the water that would soon seep through the shirts, so everyone drank what little they'd collected. Men sharing with each other.

Vos had caught maybe a cup of water in the tin. That could be saved for later.

The clouds raced past, and the heat returned. Those who weren't bailing or paddling, sat or floated in a world of listlessness.

In the distance, George spotted the tip of the volcano Salak rising from the western portion of Java. And there was the small island Gede with its mangroves and wild perennials. Seeing the small island was both good news and bad news. Good because it meant they were still heading in the right direction. Bad because they'd made little progress.

"Look," Vos said, cutting into the numb void they were all existing in. "Something's floating in the water."

George paused in his paddling to gaze at the floating item. Not one, but three items. "Coconuts," he said. In tandem with the other paddler, they shifted their direction to collect the coconuts. George didn't want anyone trying to swim for them.

Once they were retrieved, they worked to crack one of them open. Vos tried first, but his hands were shaking too badly, so Bakker took over. George was asked to divide the thin milk between the seventeen men, then he broke up the interior meat, which amounted to about three centimeters per person.

Not much, but it was something.

"God is good," Vos whispered as he ate his first morsel of the coconut.

George decided it was the best thing he'd ever tasted. He didn't remember loving coconut as much as he did now. And they still had two left. Unanimously, they decided they'd eat one a day, although it was discouraging to think if that became the case, it meant they'd be on the sea two more days.

"We need to increase our speed," Rouwenhorst said. "We're all exhausted, but we'll shorten our rotations. Now that we've all had some sustenance, we can put in more effort."

Renewed energy throughout the group lasted about two more hours, until the heat of the sun once again began draining life, bit by bit. It wasn't anything new, but a couple of the men were vocal in their complaints.

"We're like sitting targets," Mulder said to no one in particular. It was his turn to rest on one of the wooden planks, and he was worse off with blisters than most of the others. "The sun is baking us alive, and a couple of mouthfuls of water and two bites of coconut aren't going to keep us going for long." He turned on his side and stared at the volcano Salak.

"We've made it this far," Vos said. "Just this morning we were praying for rain and look what happened."

Mulder waved toward the blue expanse of sky. "Where's the rain now?"

"Rest if you can," Vos said. "Think of your family and how happy they'll be to find out you survived."

Mulder closed his eyes, and his hands clenched. "I don't know . . . I feel half dead already. My skin is literally boiling."

"Once we reach the Thousand Islands, we'll have food and fresh water," Vos continued. "This will all be a bad dream."

"Here, take my shirt while you sleep," Bakker offered.

That seemed to appease Mulder, at least for the time being. He finally drifted into sleep. When the shift changed, no one disturbed him. George slipped into the water.

The sun set, bringing much relief from the blistering heat, and they continued their shift changes throughout the night. All conversations had stopped, and the men paddled, swam, or bailed in silence. Even Mulder was silent in his complaints.

When it was George's turn to rest, his mind raced despite his exhaustion. He stared at the waning moon and wondered if Mary was awake. If she was looking at the moon, too. Four days had passed since he'd kissed his wife goodbye. What did Mary think had happened to George? What did all the families of the missing men think? Had they all been declared dead? Some of them would be right, and that knowledge brought fresh pain over his lost comrades.

George couldn't sleep, but he kept his body still, hoping that somehow he was fueling whatever reserves he had left. He wasn't surprised when the sun made its appearance yet again. He groaned as he sat up and found his balance on the plank. With a quick check of his surroundings, he was dismayed to see the little progress they'd made.

Despite the paddling and swimming, the traveling was agonizingly slow. The men in the water clung to planks when they weren't swimming. If they got rid of the planks, George felt they'd travel all that much faster. And every minute, every hour saved, could be the difference between life and death.

George scanned those on the dinghy. Loeffen had his head bowed, his hands listless at his side. Jaden, one of the crew's two recruit quartermasters, seemed to be talking to himself, soft and low. George spotted the commander, who was currently bailing water out of the dinghy. "What do you think of getting rid of the planks we're holding onto? We could swim and paddle faster through the night. We need to shorten our sleeping rotations, too. We need more swimmers."

Rouwenhorst looked over at George. Although his life jacket was tied to the top of his head, to both dry it out and to offer shade from the early morning sun, his face and upper body were as red as a hot poker iron.

It didn't take the commander long to consider. "Yes, let's do it."

The other men followed Rouwenhorst's orders, and George could only hope it was a good move. But they did move faster, or so it seemed.

No one had extra energy. Yet, the men continued to paddle and swim. They called out encouragement to each other. Songs were sung. Terrible jokes were exchanged.

As the morning blended into afternoon, and there was no relief from clouds or rain, George knew they were running out of time. Each and every one of them was beyond exhausted. The sun today might do them all in.

Rouwenhorst kept checking his compass, and he must have read George's mind because he said, "We need energy so that we can keep pushing through the day. Let's open the second coconut."

So Vos cracked open the second coconut while everyone watched him. Then his brows tugged together. *That couldn't be a good sign*, George thought.

Vos bent his head and smelled the coconut. "Diesel fuel," he muttered, then looked up. "This one is bad." He tossed it into the sea, and all the men watched it float away.

Vos looked to the commander, who nodded his assent. And Vos reached for the third, and final, coconut. "Pray the last one is good," he said, cracking the final coconut open.

It was.

Once again, George was asked to divide the milk and the coconut meat evenly among the men. The couple of swallows of coconut milk and small morsel of the meat were not enough. But it was something.

It was the end of their food, George knew. They were racing against time for their very lives. But the men surrounding him, bobbing in the sea, or tending to tasks upon the dinghy, could defy mother nature only so long.

George couldn't remember the last time he'd slept, but he feared if he let himself rest, he'd never wake up. As it was, his vision blurred with the blaring sun, as the yellow spread across the blue waters. Beautiful, yet lethal.

"Look," someone said.

George rotated slowly from where he was bailing water, his body aching, his skin on fire. Dark spots on the horizon . . . That meant one thing. Japanese ships.

The words reverberated through the men as the paddling and swimming slowed. Were they about to paddle straight into their enemies' grasp?

"They're palm trees, not ships," Van Beek said.

Bakker let out a low whistle. "I think you're right. Palm trees! The most beautiful thing I've ever seen!"

George frowned, then he blinked his eyes a few times, and squinted. Those paddling increased their speed, and suddenly those in the water were swimming with stronger strokes. The dinghy shot forward, and George stared as the realization buzzed through him.

They were approaching the northernmost tip of the Thousand Islands.

They'd made it. They'd stayed on course. And they'd only lost two men.

The men used the last of their reserves. Their goal was in sight. They'd have food, fresh water, shade from the sun. Rescue would certainly be imminent. It would be hours yet, but none of that mattered.

When it was George's turn to paddle, he and Bakker were opposite of each other. George met the stronger seaman stroke for stroke.

And then, he stopped.

Everyone stopped.

A ship had come into view, heading directly parallel between the men and the Thousand Islands.

George wanted to throw up at the sight of the Japanese destroyer.

"No . . ." Jaden murmured. "Not again."

"Everyone lie flat," Rouwenhorst barked.

The destroyer was moving quickly in a straight line. Not toward them yet, but that could change at any instant.

"I don't want to be captured," Mulder said. "Anything but that." He covered his head with his hands.

George couldn't blame him. His heart was thundering so hard that he could barely hear the slap of the water against the dinghy. But he couldn't close his eyes, and he couldn't look away from the Japanese destroyer. It was getting closer.

No one on or near the dinghy moved, or paddled, or swam, or bailed.

The destroyer was about four hundred meters away now.

George held absolutely still. Mulder choked on a sob. No one said a thing. They were all locked in their own wells of fear.

"Please, God, spare us," Vos whispered, the only one to break the silence.

The destroyer didn't change course, but plowed through on its original trajectory. Had they been spotted? Or were they being ignored?

Only when the destroyer had passed the outer edge of the islands, did George believe they'd been passed over.

"Unbelievable," Bakker murmured. "I'd shout hallelujah but I don't want them to hear me."

A few men chuckled.

And just like that, their crushing fear lifted. They'd been spared once again.

George knew he'd been witness to a miracle, but that drove him harder, and he put all his weight into paddling.

"Everyone who wants supper on the islands, let's move."

The palm trees were much more distinct now, and George imagined the coconuts that were ready to receive them.

"How many ways can you cook a coconut?" Vos asked.

The men were laughing. Rutgers threw out a series of jokes. George was amazed. He felt grateful. Humbled. How many close calls had each of the men on this voyage endured? What were the chances of them all surviving five days floating in the Java Sea with so few resources?

By the angle of the sun, George estimated it was about 15:00 hours when they first touched land. George was one of the swimmers at that point, so he was one of the first to feel the seabed beneath his feet.

Bakker swam ahead of everyone, his arms somehow finding more strength. Once he reached the sand, he whooped and laughed. Others joined him, running along the shore in a spurt of unforeseen energy.

Vos sank to his knees in the wet sand and wept.

George's legs trembled, and his chest heaved as he helped drag the dinghy onto shore with a couple of the men, then they quickly abandoned it. Stopping next to Vos, George set a hand on his friend's shoulder. "Come, let's eat."

Vos staggered to his feet, and the two men walked toward a group of coconut trees.

"Watch out below!" Bakker hollered. He'd already scaled one of the trees and was tossing down coconuts.

There was no frenzy to grab the coconuts. Rouwenhorst and Hessing picked them up and handed them over. The men took them, grateful and humble.

They'd made it. Somehow, they'd made it. George didn't bother wiping at the tears on his cheeks. He joined the other men in the shade and cracked open a coconut, one he'd have all to himself.

CHAPTER TEN

"Nobody was allowed to listen to radio broadcasts. All radios had to be registered, and foreign stations were sealed off. We could only listen to Japanese broadcasts. A cousin had given us some valuable items to keep before he was imprisoned, and one of these was a radio. But we did not have the documents for it, so we could not prove who owned it. We were afraid that neighbors or others might betray us if they knew that we owned one. In those days, you never knew whom to trust. Some even betrayed their close friends or relatives for money or special favors."

—WILLY RIEMERSMA-PHILIPPI, TAMPINGAN VILLAGE

MARY

Every hour the radio announcer brought new, devastating news into her home on Laan Trivelli. And there was nothing Mary could do to stop it. She could turn off the radio, she supposed, but she needed to stay informed. As much as she wanted to remain in her bed all day with her covers pulled over her face, she was the head of the family now.

Currently, Mary stood at the front windows as a breeze kicked through the screens while she watched Rita play in the grass. A few meters away, the dog Kells, sat in the shade as it thumped its long-haired tail, watching Rita. As if it had taken on the task of watching over the neighborhood children.

The sun was out, and the rains from earlier that morning surely made the grass damp. But Rita never seemed to mind. When they had gone to the mountains in Poentjak for vacations, she'd rolled down the hills into the tropical forests. So wet grass didn't bother her. She loved anything with nature or running or climbing.

Mary smiled at her daughter and her enthusiastic child's play. Georgie usually shadowed his sister, but he was with Oma right now. Mary was grateful that Rita was playing—forgetting about the war, the sirens, the bomb shelters, and where her father might be.

It had been a week since George had kissed Mary goodbye. A week of not knowing where he was or if he'd made it safely to Australia. He might be perfectly fine, or he might be . . . Mary scolded her errant, panicked thoughts. Wouldn't a wife, married to a husband for many years, know if something terrible had happened? Wouldn't she *feel* it?

She felt only the numbness of disbelief that this had become her life. Sirens and bomb shelters and rations and seeing Japanese soldiers marching along the streets of her home.

Oma was a godsend, and Tie should be as well, but she kept to her room more times than not. Mary could only guess that Tie was grieving over being displaced and forced to leave her home.

Rita and Georgie were small children, which gave Mary hope that they would be the least affected, although Rita had been helping in ways that had impressed Mary. With the nanny, cook, maid, and gardener all gone now, Rita had been helpful in the kitchen and with Georgie. Mary wondered if their servants, who were Javanese, sympathized with the Japanese invasion. It had been broadcast on the news as well, how many Javanese—Indonesians who were native to Java—welcomed the Japanese soldiers.

Throughout history, Japan had encouraged Indonesian independence from the Dutch crown. And with the war affecting the global economy, and oil embargos set against Japan, the Japanese government looked to the Netherlands East Indies for oil since they were totally dependent on petroleum imports. It was to their benefit to pledge their support to the Indonesians and a future republic free of the Dutch.

Now, with Japan occupying Java and the other islands, what promises would be made? And which ones would be kept?

Mary watched Rita jump up and run to the tree. She always insisted on wearing rompers instead of dresses so that she could climb better. Kells gave a merry bark as Rita paused to scratch the black curls on his back. Then she scrambled up the tree to her favorite lookout.

Mary had never asked Rita what the game was, but it always consisted of running about the yard, then climbing the mango tree. Sometimes she had her teddy bear with her, and sometimes not.

The radio volume in the dining room, which was always humming low, suddenly turned up. Mary looked over to see Tie hovering by the table, her arms folded as she listened. There was no regular programming on the radio any longer. All radio shows had been canceled. The hourly news reports were interspersed with music.

The familiar voice of General Hein Ter Poorten came on, sounding rough and tired as he announced that the government of the Netherlands East Indies had officially surrendered to Japan.

Mary felt the breath whoosh out of her. From relief or dismay, she wasn't sure. She'd felt like she'd been balancing on a fence for days, for weeks, even months. Always wondering what would happen next. Would Japan invade or not? Would the Dutch surrender?

News in the past few days had been filled with reports of guerrilla warfare between the army and the Japanese military. The British prime minister, Mr. Winston Churchill, had ordered all members of the RAF to arm themselves and head for the hills, calling themselves the Blue Army.

But now . . . Ter Poorten's assurances echoed through the house. *Dutch citizens have nothing to fear . . . Remain calm . . . Carry on as normal.*

Mary walked into the dining room and sat across from Tie at the table. The woman's expression was sullen and frustrated—all things that Mary could well understand.

"What is this?" Oma asked, walking in with little Georgie clinging to her hand.

Ever since Nanny had left, Georgie had been at Oma's side more and more. When Georgie saw Mary, he hurried over to her and climbed into her lap. She drew her son close and inhaled his little boy smell of sunshine and leaves. Georgie didn't say anything, just nestled close. He seemed to understand when another person was struggling, and he'd brought comfort and solace more than once to Mary.

She often wondered if Georgie had been sent to their family as a peace giver. He wasn't rambunctious like the other young boys in the neighborhood. He was a delight. An absolute light in all of their lives.

"The Dutch government has surrendered," Tie informed Oma.

Oma's brows pinched together. "Is this good news? Does that mean the bombing and the fighting will stop?"

None of the women in the dining room had the answer.

"Claudia told me she heard a rooster crow at midnight," Tie said, her brown eyes focused on Mary. "Did you hear it?"

Mary wasn't as superstitious as Claudia was, but she knew her friend believed that a rooster crowing at midnight was bad luck. "I didn't hear it." But that didn't stop the shiver skating across her skin.

Mary held her son close as, more than ever, she wished her husband were here to explain, aside from superstitions, what this would truly mean for all of them. Even from miles away, and through the artificial communication of a radio broadcast, she knew that Ter Poorten's words were platitudes.

"All Dutch army units have been ordered to surrender to Japan," Ter Poorten continued in his raspy voice.

Mary rested her chin atop Georgie's head and closed her eyes. They were truly under Japanese occupation now. Gone was the hope of the Allies retaking Java. The only freedom now would come when the Allies won the war. The reverse was something that Mary wouldn't allow herself to think about.

Another news item came on. This one directed at European residents—all the Dutch people:

"New guidelines have been set forth by the Japanese command," Ter Poorten said. "All European residents are to show deference to the Japanese army. All rules of courtesy must be followed."

Mary opened her eyes and met her mother's gaze. She looked older by ten years it seemed. Tie had begun to pace the room.

"Provocative behavior is unacceptable," Ter Poorten continued. "Europeans are permitted to leave their homes but only for essential errands such as purchasing food and medical care. When you are in public, do not behave noisily or create a commotion. When you see a member of the Japanese army, you are required to express humility and bow to them. Japanese soldiers are personal representatives of the Japanese emperor."

"Mama," a voice cut in through the deeper tone of Ter Poorten. Rita ran into the house, the screen door slamming behind her. "There's . . ." She gulped a breath of air. "Japanese soldiers coming to our house."

Before Mary could react or even ask a question, a rap sounded at the front door. She stood from the table. Oma took Georgie from her arms, and nodded to Tie.

Both Mary and Tie walked to the front door. Neither of them spoke, because on the other side of the screen stood three Japanese soldiers.

Mary rubbed her sweaty palms against her skirt, wishing that she'd thought to keep everything locked down. But would that have stopped these men? No . . . Their crisp, khaki green uniforms had to be sweltering, as well as their hats, with the flaps on each side.

One of the men, the officer, looked familiar. Mary swallowed hard and opened the door. She didn't speak any Japanese, but when the officer spoke Dutch, she couldn't describe her relief.

"Good afternoon," the officer said. "We are the *Kempeitai*—Japanese military police. You might remember shopping at my store? I recognize you as Mrs. Vischer."

Mary was so stunned that all she could do was nod. This man was familiar because he was a shop owner. Had she known he was Japanese and part of their police force? How was that possible? She'd been going to his store for a couple of years. Before the war even started. That meant one thing. This man had been a spy.

"We need to speak to your husband," the officer continued. "George Vischer."

Tie looked at Mary, who finally spoke, "He isn't here." She didn't want to give out any information, but with three Japanese soldiers scrutinizing her, she added, "He hasn't been home for over a week. He reported to naval headquarters and I haven't seen or heard from him since."

She didn't bother to hide the tremble in her voice from the men. They should know that she was worried about her husband and wasn't hiding anything from them.

The officer's eyes narrowed. "We need to search your house."

"Of-of course." Mary held the door open, and the men entered. She moved to the kitchen and pulled Rita close to her.

Georgie was already held by Oma, and Tie joined their huddled group by the table. The soldiers' boots echoed throughout the house as they searched each room. Mary's pulse jumped with every bang of a door or a cupboard and the scrape of furniture over the tiled floors.

"Why are they looking in all the rooms?" Rita asked in a small voice. "Papa's not here."

Mary squeezed her hand. "They are making sure, I guess."

When the soldiers returned to the front room, they appeared empty-handed. Of course they did, and it seemed they hadn't confiscated anything either. She was doubly glad she'd hidden her jewelry, though. Why, she couldn't exactly explain.

The officer folded his arms, his brow furrowed. "There is no sign of George. Have you received any information of where he might be?"

This, Mary could answer truthfully. "I haven't received anything from my husband or from naval headquarters."

The officer glanced at the two soldiers with him, and silent communication seemed to pass between them.

"Wait," Mary ventured. "Have you heard anything? Do you know where he is?" It might be a risk to question the soldiers, but she had to know—for better or for worse.

The officer frowned. "We have not been informed. That is why we are searching here." His gaze scanned their little family. "Within the hour, trucks will be arriving in your neighborhood to take everyone to the police station. Everyone needs to register. Bring your documents to prove your identities."

Mary blinked. "Register for what . . ." Her voice faded as he cut in.

"And if you hear anything about your husband, it needs to be reported immediately to authorities."

By authorities, she knew he meant Japanese authorities . . . because they were now ruled by a different country.

"I will," she managed to say. "And we will be ready to go to the police station with our paperwork." She might be making promises she couldn't keep. George kept the paperwork in a locked box, but she wasn't sure if she knew where the key was.

But the promise got the Japanese soldiers out of her home. And even though Mary prided herself on being strong and positive in front of her children, the moment the soldiers stepped off their property, she sagged onto the couch. The tears came hot and fast, and there was nothing she could do to stop them. Not even when Georgie cried right along with her.

"Come with me," Oma said to the children. "We will play a game of putting everything back in its place."

Thankfully, Georgie sniffled back his tears and went with his grandmother.

"I'm sorry," Mary murmured when it was only Tie left in the room with her. "I don't know where that came from."

Tie sat next to her on the couch. She wasn't an affectionate woman, and they'd never been close, but she touched Mary's hand. "We need to follow orders. The Japanese officer was very reasonable. Things could be much worse."

Mary didn't want to ask what "much worse" might refer to. She cuffed her tears away. "You're right. We need to focus on one thing at a time. I'll go find the paperwork. Do you have yours?"

"I do," Tie said, "but it wasn't until now that I realized how lucky it is that I brought it along with me."

"Good for you." Mary squeezed her sister-in-law's hand. "I should tell you as well, that I'm pregnant. About four months along."

Tie's brows shot up. "Again? This is not the time to have another child."

Mary bit back a half laugh, half cry. "I didn't know that Japan was going to bomb Pearl Harbor and bring the war here."

"None of us did," Tie said in a defensive tone. "How could we know that Japan would rearrange the world?"

But the disapproval over her pregnancy had been spoken, and there was no taking it back. Mary would never regret the life growing inside of her. Never. Even if she did feel weaker, sicker, and more emotional. She would push through, somehow. She rose to her feet. It was time to put herself back together and focus on what needed to be done.

Once in her bedroom, she found the locked box in the corner of their closet. It didn't look like it had been bothered by the soldiers. Sure enough, it was locked. Now, where would George have put the key? He'd told her once, but she didn't remember. She scanned the bedroom and considered looking under the mattress, in the corner of a bureau drawer, or maybe taped behind something?

Mary searched the drawers on her husband's side of the bureau, but it wasn't there. She looked under the bed, reached beneath all the furniture, and sorted through every clothing item. She had to find the key—surely it was somewhere in the bedroom? Sinking onto the corner of the bed, she gazed blankly at the room. Tears started, unbidden and unhelpful. It wasn't just the key that brought tears, it was everything.

"Mama?" Georgie said, pushing through the half-open door of the bedroom.

Mary quickly wiped at her eyes, but he'd already noticed her tears. "Mama crying?"

She nodded but tried to smile. "I'll be all right. Sometimes Mama gets sad."

Georgie climbed onto her lap, and Mary drew him close.

"Why are you sad?"

"I can't find a key," Mary said. "It's a very important key."

Georgie wriggled from her grasp and slid to the floor. With hands on his hips, he looked about the room. Mary had to smile at the image.

"If I was a key I'd hide over there."

"Where?" Mary asked.

Georgie pointed to the bureau that Mary had already searched under. Before she could say that, Georgie had moved to the back leg and knelt down. "Right there. I'd hide under there."

Mary joined Georgie and reached behind the leg. "Nothing's there."

He pressed his stubby finger at the bottom of the leg. "Under there."

Mary frowned, but she tugged the bureau from the wall just enough to reveal a key under the leg.

"Why are you crying again, Mama? Are you still sad?"

Mary scooped up the key, then pulled Georgie into a tight hug. Kissing the top of his head, she said, "These are happy tears. Thank you for helping me."

Georgie grinned, and Mary sent him off in search of Oma. Once Mary had the box open, she leafed through the papers. There was their marriage certificate. They'd been married by proxy . . . That all seemed ages ago now.

She gathered up the birth certificates and paused before heading into the hallway. She could hear Oma's murmured conversation with her children and their replies. What would she do without her mother?

If only she could be reassured that all would be well in the end. Oma, George, her children . . . and of course Tie.

They ate a quick meal of rice and fruit since Mary had no idea how long it would take to register at the police station.

By the time the trucks lumbered along Laan Trivelli, her neighbors had all been informed as well. Claudia hurried over as they waited near the road.

"Did they search your house too?" she asked in a hushed tone. She clasped rosary beads to her chest, and Mary knew it was probably a sign of the woman's distress.

"Yes, looking for George."

"They asked about Willem," Claudia said. "But there was nothing to tell them. I wish I did know, but maybe it's better that we don't."

Maybe, Mary thought. But she really wanted to know where George was and if he was all right. Even if it was something she had to report to the Japanese army. At least if she knew George was doing well, she could face these changes all the better.

Claudia's two children came out of the house and walked across the lawn. Johan waved at Rita, who waved back. But . . . Greta looked . . . different. Her hair had been cut short, and she wore what looked like Johan's shirt and pants. Since Greta was so petite, they were practically the same size.

"Wait, is that Greta? Why—"

"Shh," Claudia said. "Greta is now my son. I've heard about Japanese soldiers setting up bordellos and looking for unmarried women."

Greta was twelve. And although she was petite, she was also developing a womanly figure. But right now, her clothing was boxy and she looked just as much like a boy as nine-year-old Johan.

"But what about the paperwork?" Mary asked. This was a very daring plan.

Claudia held up her rosary beads. "This is why I've been praying for the past hour. I will say that I've lost the birth certificate. But because Greta looks so much like Johan, there will be no doubt they are siblings—brothers."

Mary studied the siblings. Claudia was right. They could be twins if they weren't different in height. "I hope you can pull it off."

Claudia smiled, but her eyes watered.

Mary had to look away, or she might cry too.

CHAPTER ELEVEN

"Little by little things began to change. It was like water
trickling out of a pump. At first there's hardly any water,
and then more comes out, stronger and stronger.
That's kind of how the war entered our lives."

—ANNELEX HOFSTRA LAYSON, GEDANGAN CAMP

GEORGE

From his spot in the shade beneath a ragged palm tree, George
stared at the blue sky as it faded to orange with the setting sun. His
stomach hurt because he'd eaten so much, but he was still craving food.
Things like *gehakt balletjes*—Dutch meatballs. Or the Indonesian food
made by Kemala. *Nasi goreng*—fried rice. And *rawon*—a beef soup that
included the black *keluak* nut as the main seasoning. Or one of his other
favorites, *nasi campur*—a rice dish made up of a scoop of *nasi putih*,
served with added meat, vegetables, peanuts, eggs, and fried-shrimp *krupuk*.

He exhaled. The coconut had been satisfying enough. Bakker had
eaten twelve by himself. It was a wonder that none of them had become
sick from bingeing food so fast.

Around George, his comrades reclined in the shade, although no
one was comfortable sitting in the sand, and everyone's sunburns were
festering. No one was sleeping. It was as if they'd forgotten how to sleep
more than a few minutes at a time. Now that they weren't in constant

motion, it seemed that their minds had caught up with what they'd endured for the past five days and five nights.

George went over the events, one by one, in his mind. From the goodbye with his wife, to Hooft getting injured while stripping the mast. Then the Japanese torpedoes hitting just after four in the morning. And the deaths.

Maybe that's why George wasn't closing his eyes, and why he and the others weren't sleeping off their exhaustion. When his eyes closed, he saw the lifeless bodies. Men who'd been friends and comrades. Men who had families—families who might be grieving over their terrible losses.

What had Mary been told?

What about young Rita? And little Georgie?

I'm alive, he wanted to tell them. *I survived*, and *I'll keep surviving*.

Tomorrow, he knew, they'd need to explore this island. They couldn't survive on coconuts alone for long. Not with seventeen men who needed more than that. A twinge in his foot caused him to raise his head. After five days in constant water, the wound was not healing well. And walking on it was painful. He'd been putting most of his weight on his heel, which stressed his other muscles.

He closed his eyes, wishing for sleep without images or nightmares.

Yet, as the sun set, sleep remained elusive.

Some of the men ate more coconuts, but George didn't. He contented himself with listening to the conversation floating around him. Most of it was jovial, and it was nice to have Mulder in good spirits. There were moments when George had feared Mulder would bring all of them down with his despondency.

As the evening descended, the clouds gathered above in a tight knot. Rain would be refreshing, and George shifted to prop up the coconut shells he'd used.

The rain burst a few minutes later.

Bakker whooped. "Let it pour!" he called to the heavens.

Other men shouted, but then they began to groan.

The rain pelting their sensitive, sunburned skin felt like nails pricking them over and over. George moved to the trunk of a palm tree to take more shelter, but it didn't provide much protection.

His solution was to go back into the sea. "I'm going into the water until the rain passes," he called out.

All the men followed him out into the sea. They could run for cover under the trees back on the island if they sighted enemy boats or planes. In the sea, they sank down until the water was at their chins. Even though the seawater stung their skin anew, it was better than the pelting drops of rain.

Waiting out the storm took a couple of hours. It was dark by the time the rain stopped, and when the skies cleared to reveal a bright moon and thousands of stars, the men moved back to their places in the sand.

Only then did George's mind finally allow him to sleep. For a short time, he forgot all that he'd endured the past five days as the murky nothing of sleep blocked everything out.

The blessed relief was short, and his memories came roaring back with the dawn. Dragging his eyes open, he blinked against the grittiness. His throat felt raw, and his mouth tasted of sand. As he sorted through the events once again of the past several days, the first thing George concluded was that no rescue was coming.

No one knew they were alive.

Not even that Japanese destroyer they'd seen the day before.

This meant no one would be coming for them.

They had to help themselves.

George moved to his feet. Pain, tried and true, darted up his shin. He winced but hobbled to the trunk of the palm. There, he leaned against it and scanned the sleeping men. Many were wounded. Their burned and raw skin was hard to look at, yet his was no better.

Next, he turned his attention to the expanse of island and the shoreline and water beyond.

By the time Rouwenhorst had awakened, George had a plan to

run past the commander. "What do you think about dividing into two groups and exploring the island?"

"That was my thought as well," Rouwenhorst said. He scanned the men who were still asleep. "Do you think we are recovered enough for such a task? How's your foot?"

"It's manageable, but I don't think we have much choice. We need to explore."

Rouwenhorst nodded. Once all the men had awakened and eaten more coconuts, he told the group of George's suggestion, then added, "Bakker, can you take this half of the group? Look for fresh water and other food sources. George will lead the second group. I'll stay here with Mulder. His blisters are festering. We'll keep watch out for any Japanese vessels."

"Yes, sir," Bakker said.

George looked over at Vos and the other men assigned to his group, which included Hessing and Van Beek. "Let's go."

The sun promised to be a scorcher today, and George kept to as much of the shade as the island would allow. They'd walked several hundred meters when the adjacent island came into view. Only a few dozen meters separated them.

George scanned the shore of the opposite island as they walked. He paused when he saw a lifeboat half submerged in the water, only partially washed up on the shore of the other island. If someone had survived in it, surely they would have pulled it fully onto shore. "Is that what I think it is?"

Vos came to a stop beside him and shaded his eyes from the sun. "A lifeboat?"

"Yeah."

"I wonder which ship it's from," Hessing said.

Everyone fell silent because a damaged and washed-up lifeboat could mean only one thing. The men who'd launched it were no longer alive.

"Think we can swim for it?" Vos asked.

Van Beek scoffed.

"We can try," George said. "We spent five days in the water, what's another hour of swimming? It's less than a hundred meters."

"Let's go, boys," Vos said.

George waded into the warm water, and soon the group of them were swimming. It was worth the trek to see what they could salvage. Also, he was as curious as everyone else to learn where the lifeboat had come from.

When he saw the words *Marula* printed on the side of the raft, he knew it had come from one of the sunken shell tankers. Lost in the Battle of the Java Sea. If they'd been wearing hats, they would have taken them off. As it was, George stood before the raft and bowed his head with the others for a moment.

No one knew the exact events that had led to this lifeboat washing up here, but they could all guess the death and terror that had preceded it.

"Let's get it higher up on shore," Hessing suggested, "and see what supplies are left."

Vos and the others moved the raft with minimal effort.

The lifeboat was in no shape to float back to the other island, so George began to take everything out of it.

"Whoa," Vos said. "This is loaded."

George handed out tins of biscuits and condensed milk. This was a very good start. His stomach rumbled in response to just thinking about it. He hoped there were no leaks in the tins.

"Scotch," Van Beek said.

There were twelve bottles of scotch, in fact. As well as sea charts, masts, sails, oars, and lamps.

"We'll take as much as we can carry," George said.

Among the eight men, they were able to carry quite a few of their findings, and they swam together back to the original island.

As they approached their landing site, George saw Bakker and the others gathered beneath the palms with the commander. Rouwenhorst turned the same time as Bakker.

"You found supplies?" Rouwenhorst called to them.

"Sure did," Vos responded. "We discovered an abandoned lifeboat."

"Whoa," Bakker said, rushing toward them in the hot sand. He grabbed a load from Van Beek. "Where did you find it?"

Once George reached the shady area, he explained about the lifeboat from the *Marula*. Although the men were elated at the supplies retrieved, they were somber about the sunken tanker.

"There are more supplies," George said. "We only brought what we could carry."

"We'll make another trip there to retrieve the rest," Rouwenhorst said. "But first, Bakker's group found something you'll want to see."

"Another lifeboat?" George asked.

"No, a small settlement of huts."

Even though the heat of the day made it almost unbearable to be anywhere but the shade and the water, they trudged along, with Bakker leading the way deeper into the island. The activity of the day so far was aggravating his foot, and George found himself limping significantly again.

He wasn't the only one. Most of the other men's wounds had started to fester. They needed disinfectant and antibiotics, but there were none to be had.

They moved around coconut trees and found narrow paths between vines and bushes. When they reached a small clearing, Bakker paused. "There."

In the middle of a clearing sat a *pondok*—a bamboo hut.

"Is someone living in it?" George asked, incredulous to see this in the middle of the otherwise empty island. The island had been evacuated after the Netherlands East Indies had ordered civilians to leave so that there wouldn't be any lights or fires coming from the land that could direct Japanese planes to the coconut plantations.

"Not now," Bakker said. "I don't know who might have lived here before, but there's some things to use. Besides, there's a freshwater pond out back. Might have been a well?"

That interested George the most. They all headed around the pon-dok. The men circled the pond, and everyone drank their fill.

Then Vos splashed water on his face. Next, he cupped water and dribbled it over his arms.

Hessing took it one step further and walked right into the water. He threw up his arms and cheered. "It's glorious."

Next, the commander walked into the water.

This quieted George's warning about contaminating the drinking water source. The men piled in, one after another. Swimming and wash-ing off the days of salt and sand.

"Anyone have soap?" Bakker called out with a laugh.

There was no preserving the fresh water now, so George joined them, relishing in the sweet relief of the water. The thing that might have made it better was if it was cool water, but even this, the sun had baked warm.

George floated on his back for several moments, closing his eyes to the looming sun overhead. The weightlessness of his body, combined with the simple joy and hope coursing through him, reminded him of the first time he saw Mary in Holland. He'd approached the house where she lived to inquire about renting a room from the Van Benten family. He'd just completed his four-year onboard service, and had returned to Holland to study for his next level of marine engineering certification.

The city of Utrecht was one of the largest cities in the Netherlands, and one of his shipmates had told him that many homes rented out rooms. When he passed by a house with a notice in the front window, he paused. With the spring, tulips had pushed through the flower beds beyond the gate. The fence needed painting, otherwise, the small yard was in good shape.

He headed through the gate, latching it behind him.

The woman who'd opened the door was tall, nearly six feet, George guessed. Her blonde hair was like a halo about her face, and her blue eyes seemed to gaze straight into his heart. He estimated her age to be a few years younger than he, and he wondered which lucky man was her husband.

Why that thought had crossed his mind was anyone's guess. For some reason, he'd forgotten what he'd come to say.

So she'd spoken first. "Are you here to inquire about the room for rent?"

"Yes. Mrs. Van Benten? I'm George Vischer. How long is the room available for?"

At this, she paused, her gaze running over him, likely taking in his KPM uniform. This confirmed him as a member of the KPM company. He thought it would be a good recommendation. After what seemed like an eternal moment, she said, "Wait here."

The door shut promptly in his face, and he stood on the front stoop, wondering if that door would open again.

She hadn't told him to leave, so that was a good omen. Perhaps she was fetching her husband, and they'd interview him and inquire about his financial situation.

George rotated on his heels and surveyed the quaint neighborhood of multistory housing in various colors. He had enjoyed what little he'd seen of Utrecht so far. The tree-lined canals were beautiful, and there were several churches and monasteries. The history went back to medieval ages, and structures such as the Domtoren—a fourteenth century bell tower that was part of the Cathedral of St. Martin—still stood.

The door opened, and George spun to face the door. But there was no husband. An older woman stood there, her hair a mix of blonde and brown, her eyes a pretty hazel. She shared some facial features with the younger woman. Were they mother and daughter?

"Hello," the woman said in a strident tone. "I'm Mrs. Maria Van Benten. My daughter tells me you're here to inquire about the room for rent?"

George's mind swirled with this new information. Perhaps the younger woman wasn't married. What that thought should signify, he didn't know. But when she appeared behind her mother, this time with a soft smile on her face, suddenly George felt like he was suspended a few centimeters above the ground. Warmth flooded his chest, and he smiled back.

"Vischer." Vos's voice interrupted George's memories.

He blinked his eyes open. He was back on a deserted island, in a pond, floating in the water.

"We're going to return to the beach and eat some of the rations," Vos continued.

George righted himself and pushed his way out of the pond. His stomach grumbled in anticipation. It had been nearly a week since he'd last eaten any sort of meal. He wished he was with his family, facing the changes that Japanese occupation would bring, together.

CHAPTER TWELVE

"Riding our bicycles with friends of Vincentius, we saw our first Japanese soldiers. They stood guard in front of the telephone company and at the palace of the governor-general. They were wearing 'sun rags,' strips of cloth attached to the back of their caps. Their helmets were covered with webbing and had leaves stuck to them. Small Japanese flags displaying the words of well-wishers painted in black were attached to their long bayonets which were fixed to their rifles."

—JAN VOS, KEDUNGBADAK CAMP

RITA

"My new name is Willy," Greta said, peering up from the base of the tree where Rita sat perched on the branches. "Can you remember that? It's after my papa, Willem."

Rita squinted down at Greta, trying to decide if she really looked like a boy. Her hair was cut short, and she wore boys' clothing. Maybe to someone who didn't know her, Greta looked like a boy. "I can remember."

Greta nodded. "You and Johan have to make sure you don't accidentally call me by the wrong name."

"I won't," Rita said, hoping she could really remember. When Mrs. Vos took her children to the registration office, everyone was nervous they'd get caught. But they didn't. In fact, Mama said that their own family's registration went very smoothly—probably because the Japanese soldiers were overworked and just trying to get everyone "processed." But when Mama returned, she didn't know anything more about where Papa was.

"Willy," Rita whispered. The name sounded strange to say, but she would have to get used to it. Then her attention was caught by people walking down the road—lots of people.

"Oh," Greta said. "Here come the refugees." Without saying anything else, she hurried across the yard to her own house.

Dutch refugees walked along the cobblestones of Laan Trivelli, carrying suitcases and other bundles. Sometimes it was just women and children. Other times, full families. The refugees seemed to be everywhere now, coming from villages and towns outside of Batavia. They were staying in places like the school, the churches, and sharing houses.

A family had even knocked on Mama's door, and she'd directed them to the nearest shelter.

"What are you doing?" Johan called to her a moment before he began to climb up the tree. "Watching for your papa?"

Rita was always waiting for Papa, it seemed.

Kells whined as Johan abandoned the dog for higher ground. Then the dog circled the tree and finally plopped down, resting his chin on his front paws. Patiently waiting for his best friend.

"Mama says our fathers might not come back home for a while." This wasn't really new information, and it seemed she and Johan had this same conversation every day.

Neither of them knew where their fathers were. And either their mothers also didn't know, or they weren't saying anything.

Johan settled on a branch not far from Rita. His red hair stuck out every which way this morning, as if he'd rubbed a pillow over his head. It might be funny to look at, but Rita didn't feel like laughing. She'd heard on the radio that there had been a run on the banks, and now there wasn't any money left for anyone.

Mama had acted worried, and Rita knew it couldn't be good if people didn't have money anymore. How would they buy their food?

Oma had been working in the garden all week, and Rita had been helping her too. But it took a long time for things to grow, and there couldn't be enough for everyone all of the time.

"Did you read the newspaper last night?" Johan asked, picking off a mango leaf and shredding it between his fingers.

Johan knew she couldn't read, but he often said things to her like a grown-up, and she liked that. "No, I only listened to the radio."

"General Ter Poorten listed the Japanese military's demands," Johan said.

This had Rita curious. Maybe she'd gone to bed before it was talked about on the radio. Everyone was sleeping longer at night because there were no more air raids and no more wading through water to hide in the bomb shelters.

"Ter Poorten said that Japan has demanded the relinquishment of all arms."

Rita scrunched up her face. "Weapons?"

"Yes," Johan confirmed. "It makes sense. Japan is in control now. They are the law and the police. They also asked for self-internment of all military personnel."

When Rita didn't say anything, Johan added, "They're telling all Dutch and Allied military people to turn themselves in."

"So, when our fathers come back, they will have to turn themselves in?" It wasn't good news. When her father came back, Rita wanted him living at their house. Not in some other place.

Johan let the torn bits of leaf float down to the ground. "I hope they are hiding good," he whispered. "Maybe they're going to come back with a big battleship and beat the Japanese forces."

There was no way anyone could hear the conversation unless they were standing directly below the tree, but Rita whispered back, "We could hide them and feed them secretly."

Johan nodded at this.

"What else did Ter Poorten say?" So far, the demands didn't mean that Rita had to do anything differently herself.

"All dead Japanese troops have to be delivered to the Japanese command center."

Rita frowned at this. She didn't want to think about anyone being dead.

"And," Johan continued, "any Japanese who were imprisoned by the Allies have to be released. The Allies have to stop destroying military equipment, roads, and buildings."

"Why would the Allies destroy all of that?"

Johan leaned back against the branch behind him and scratched at his head. "It makes things harder for the Japanese army. That's what my mother said."

Below their perch, Kells rose to his feet and barked.

"Quiet, Kells," Johan said. "Sit, boy, sit." The dog obeyed.

A lady carrying a suitcase was coming up the road. The woman looked about Oma's age. Didn't she have any family?

After the woman passed, and things were quiet again, Johan said, "The Japanese military said that we have to cease all communication with the outside world."

At this information, Rita stared at her friend. "Why?"

"So we don't know what's going on, I guess," Johan said. "But we're going to hide our radio."

Would Mama hide their radio? Should Rita go and tell her?

She peered down the street. Another person was coming up it—no, it was multiple people. Men. Japanese soldiers. Their cloth hats with neck flaps made it easy to distinguish they were soldiers, especially since they carried swords or rifles with bayonets.

"What's going on?" Rita blurted.

Just then trucks came into view. Most of the trucks she saw had been taken from the Dutch and were being driven by Japanese soldiers. Not all of the soldiers were Japanese though. Some were Indonesian—having joined the Japanese ranks.

Kells leapt up and ran toward the hedge dividing the yard from the road and began to bark wildly.

"Quiet, Kells!" Johan demanded.

Kells stopped barking, but every bit of his body was tense. On alert.

Instead of continuing their march, the soldiers stopped at a house several places down. It was the home of Captain Jan Venema and his family of three daughters. The youngest daughter, Ina, was fifteen, and she'd babysat Rita and Georgie before. A couple of the soldiers went to the front veranda of the Venema house. Rita didn't know what was being said or what was happening, but the ache in her stomach told her that they'd be coming to her house as well.

She looked over at Johan, and their gazes connected. His bright blue eyes were filled with intensity she hadn't seen before. "We need to get to our houses. Hide your radio."

Rita swallowed against her suddenly scratchy throat. Then, as if on cue, they both scrambled down from the tree. "Let's go, Kells," Johan said, then took off running.

Rita fled to her own house. Bursting inside, she found her mother and Aunt Tie watching from the front window. From somewhere in the back of the house, she could hear Oma talking to Georgie.

"The soldiers are knocking on people's doors, and there are a lot of them. They're at the Venema house."

Mama opened her arms. "Come here, Rietie."

Rita hurried into them and wrapped her arms about her mother's waist. Her belly was soft, and Rita knew it was because she was growing another baby. Maybe a sister this time?

"Johan said we need to hide our radio."

Mama sighed. "What would we do without Johan?" Her tone sounded light, and Rita looked up, confused. Wasn't Mama worried about the soldiers?

"He said that General Ter Poorten gave a list of instructions from the Japanese army," Rita added. "No more communication with the outside world."

"That's the least of our worries," Aunt Tie proclaimed and walked into the dining room. She turned off the radio and moved it to the sideboard. "If we hide the radio, they'll search everywhere for it."

Rita looked at her mother, who had knelt before her. "Listen to me, Rietie," Mama said as she placed both hands on Rita's shoulders. "If anyone asks you about your father, you must tell them that you haven't seen him and you don't know where he is."

What was Mama talking about? Rita *hadn't* seen her father and she *didn't* know where he was. Then she realized . . . maybe Mama did know something. Did Papa write a letter? Maybe he had come back in the middle of the night, and he was hiding somewhere. But before she could ask Mama about it, a knock sounded on the door.

Brisk and loud.

Mama straightened and, with measured steps, she walked to the door and opened it.

There, on the veranda were three soldiers, reminding Rita of when they'd had a previous visit looking for Papa.

It was the same officer who was a shop owner. In Dutch, he said, "Mrs. Vischer, your family is ordered to evacuate. Pack up what you can transport with you. All the residents of Laan Trivelli are moving into a protected area."

From where Rita stood near the window, she saw her mother visibly flinch.

Aunt Tie stood rooted in place in the middle of the living room as she stared at the officer. "Where is this place?"

"Tjideng. You have one hour," the officer said, glancing about the room, but not really focusing on anything. "Pack your papers and anything essential. You'll not be returning here for some time."

Mama had frozen. It seemed that all of her words were stuck in her throat.

The door shut behind the Japanese soldiers, and their boots tramped down the steps of the veranda.

Rita stared after them through the screen window as they crossed their yard, their footprints quickly swallowed up by the lush grass. They passed the bomb shelter—no one even looked at it—and continued to the Vos home. Soon, Johan would get the same news.

"Tie," Mama said, in a faint voice, her hand pressing against her stomach. "Tell Oma that we need to pack."

Tie said nothing but headed into the hallway.

Rita pushed out a breath and held in the tears that burned her eyes. "Mama, why do we have to leave our house? How will Papa find us?"

Mama blinked and looked over at Rita.

Was she crying?

"Papa will find us," Mama said with determination in her tone. "We are all registered, remember? This will be an adventure, that's all." She smiled again, this time it was more real.

Rita still had more questions, but Mama said, "We don't have much time. We need to pack the most important things to take with us in case we need something. Can you help Oma and Georgie?"

By the time Rita reached the hallway, Oma was in action, finding suitcases for everyone. Georgie couldn't carry one, so he would share with Rita. Over and over in her mind, Rita thought about what was the most important. She gazed at her teddy bear for a long time and then, finally, she kissed it and put it on her bed. Her teddy bear could watch over their house for them.

Rita could hear Mama and Oma in the other room, discussing what things they could bring. One thing they decided on was a portable cot. It could be folded up and it had wheels.

"It won't be hard to transport," Mama told Oma. "You can use it for a bed since we might have to sleep on the ground."

"I don't want any fuss," Oma said. "I can sleep anywhere."

Would it be like camping, Rita wondered. That wouldn't be too bad. It might actually be fun. Maybe they could come back to their house in a few days, and then Rita could tell her teddy bear all about it.

But when Rita went into the front room with her suitcase, she found Mama putting seeds into a box.

"What are those for?" Rita asked.

"So we can plant another garden," Mama said. She looped an arm about Rita's shoulders and squeezed. "We'll have plenty of food at the camp, but it might be fun to grow some of our own."

Maybe they'd be gone longer than a few days, then. Or maybe Mama wanted to have two gardens?

"Can you help Aunt Tie move our things onto the veranda?" Mama said.

It wasn't hard work, Rita decided. Mama and Oma's suitcases were too heavy to carry, but Rita was still strong enough to drag them. Aunt Tie had rolled out the folded cot, and then she sat on her own suitcase after securing the two leather straps. She seemed to be done helping.

Rita had once asked her aunt why she didn't have any children. Mama had shushed her, but Aunt Tie had laughed. It wasn't a very nice laugh, though.

"I'm not married," Aunt Tie had said. "Maybe someday, though. But right now, I like to travel too much, and children would only slow me down."

Rita had wanted to ask her where she traveled to, because she hadn't heard any traveling stories. But Mama had given that shake of her head which meant to keep her questions to herself. Or that something wasn't her business.

There were a lot of things that weren't her business, Rita knew, so it was nice when Johan told her things anyway.

Rita went back inside to see if she needed to help with something else, but Mama said, "You can wait on the veranda. I'm almost finished here."

So Rita returned to the veranda and the silent Aunt Tie. There was plenty of action out on Laan Trivelli to watch, though.

A truck rattled along the road outside their hedges. In the back sat a Dutch family. Maybe two families. No men were with them, only women and children. Suitcases were piled around the families. Japanese soldiers drove the truck. Were they going to the protected place too?

Across the yard, Johan walked onto his veranda, lugging a suitcase behind him. No, it was Greta, her hair cut short. From this distance, they looked almost the same. Greta waved, and Rita waved back.

If everyone was going to the camp, maybe it wouldn't be so different than their neighborhood, after all.

Next, Oma and Georgie came out hand in hand.

"Where's Mama?" Rita asked.

"She's taking one last look around," Oma said.

At this comment, Aunt Tie rose to her feet and headed down the steps, her suitcase thumping after her. She walked to the edge of the yard, then stood, with fists on hips. Waiting for the Japanese soldiers.

Rita wanted to go back inside to look around with Mama. Maybe they'd forgotten something. But just then, Mama came out, pushing the pram that used to be Georgie's. Rita guessed that Mama wanted to bring it for the new baby.

"Are we allowed to take that?" Oma asked.

"We'll find out," Mama said. "You can push it, right, Rita?"

Rita nodded. Maybe she'd put her suitcase in it, too.

"I want to push it," Georgie declared.

"All right, Georgie," Mama said, "you push first, and when you get tired, Rita will help."

Oma said, "Let us help with the cot first."

Rita hurried up the steps with Oma and picked up one side of the cot. Together, they lifted it down the steps, then Oma told Mama, "Don't overdo it."

Mama wiped a bit of blonde hair from her face. "It's too late for that."

"Are you hurting?" Oma asked.

Were the women talking about Mama's pregnancy? Or was something else wrong?

"I'm fine." Mama moved up the steps again, took out a key from her pocket, and locked the door.

"Will it make a difference?" Oma said in a soft voice.

Rita frowned. Why shouldn't they lock the door?

"Maybe not to the Japanese troops," Mama said, "but to me it does."

Oma simply nodded. Mama fetched her bicycle, and although Rita was too small to ride it, she was happy to have it along. With Georgie trailing after them, his pillowcase that contained some of his favorite things now stuffed in the pram, they joined Aunt Tie at the edge of the yard.

That's when Rita saw it. A parade—no, a procession—of people and soldiers. Pushing carts of stacked suitcases as they rattled on the cobblestones, carrying boxes and bags, and walking along with their families. The Japanese soldiers walked the perimeter of the road, carrying their rifles.

Rita recognized some of the people—neighbors and friends of theirs. Olga Slingerland, who was Georgie's age, walked along with her mother. And Corrie Van der Hurk, who was a year older than Rita. Corrie's gaze met Rita's. She'd recently gone to her friend's birthday party.

"*Everyone* has to move?" Georgie said in his innocent voice.

Rita might have known this somewhere in the back of her mind, but to see such a large group of people moving together, made her realize that this wasn't going to be a simple adventure. Where would everyone sleep? What would they eat? Where were all the fathers and the men?

Johan had said the men needed to go, too. So, were they already gone now?

Rita looked up at her mother. Her face was expressionless as she watched the approaching group. Was she worried? Scared? What should Rita feel?

Oma's expression was somber, and Aunt Tie's mouth was pulled into a frown.

The Vos family moved over to Rita's yard, and the group of them stood together. They watched the procession pass by them—the women, the boys, the girls, the babies . . . all moving forward together.

"Is everyone with you?" one of the Japanese officers asked in Dutch. It was the same man who'd come to their house.

"Everyone's here," Mama said.

The officer eyed their suitcases and cot. "Time to go."

Sweat had gathered at Rita's neck. She wanted to sit in the shade, or better yet, climb the mango tree and sit among the cool, fragrant leaves. She didn't want to walk in a crowd of people with the hot sun beating on their heads and backs.

But she would go where her family went. Her gaze cut to Johan. For once, he didn't look like he had all the answers. He stared at the crowd of people in wonder. Greta was keeping her eyes averted. Maybe she was worried about being caught as a twelve-year-old girl pretending to be a ten-year-old boy?

Rita wanted to ask her, but now wasn't the time.

When Mama saw Mrs. Venema and her girls nearing them, she said, "Let's go."

So Rita hoisted her suitcase and followed her family out onto the road.

CHAPTER THIRTEEN

"There were men with tropical ulcers. This condition is unstoppable, and it eats away at the flesh until the bones are exposed. Victims had open wounds, crawling with maggots, which had to be scraped out, washed, and bound with clean rags. That was just about the best care available for this disease, apart from amputations, which were done only as a last resort."

—ANDREW A. VAN DYK, CIHAPIT CAMP

GEORGE

After seeing the deaths of his comrades, a torpedoed minesweeper, and days of endless sea, George shouldn't have been disturbed by the sight of festering wounds. But he felt so helpless, for his own wounds and his comrades'. Even though Van Beek—a hospital attendant's mate—was with their group and had plenty of medical knowledge, they didn't have any medications to treat their wounds, many of which had turned septic and were maggot-infested.

Mulder had taken to groaning in his sleep. The wounds on his back had turned septic, and the only real treatment was dipping in the sea again to drown the maggots. Other men were in equally bad shape. George knew that their group couldn't continue on like this, day after day.

They'd returned to the adjacent island and pilfered the rest of the goods on the *Marula* lifeboat, so at least they had more supplies.

Those wouldn't last long. Vos had discovered an underwater trap full of fish, which they ate some of. But their fish drying experiment hadn't worked—the humidity was too high—and they'd had to throw the rest out.

The men relocated to the small bamboo hut where they could at least take shelter from the sun—although there wasn't enough room for them to be in there all together.

So Rouwenhorst organized another expedition to discover if there were any other food or supply sources. George took part, even though he had to use a walking stick to take some of the pressure off his injured foot. As they scoured the island, they looked for signs of previous occupation. Bakker stopped when they could see the most southerly island, named Peoloe Sebaroe. "I think there's a boat over there—a lifeboat."

"Another one?" Vos said.

Swimming actually brought relief to George's foot, although it was temporary. The lifeboat turned out to be from the *Marula* as well. And this one was fully stocked. They once again hauled supplies back to their original island.

The search party spread out after that, more confident now. They'd been on the island for several days, and there'd been no sign of rescue from the Allies or any Indonesians; but also, they hadn't been spotted by the Japanese military either. Whenever a plane passed overhead, they took shelter beneath the nearest palm trees. Every time, the plane had been Japanese.

When they discovered a large, abandoned bamboo hut that was part of a coconut plantation, Rouwenhorst asked Bakker to do the first inspection.

A couple of moments later, he came out of the hut. "It's huge inside," he declared. "Plenty of room for everyone. There's furniture too."

George headed inside with the commander and Vos as the other men explored the exterior.

Sure enough, tables, chairs, rugs, and beds furnished the place. George walked into the kitchen area and began to open cupboards. The sight of coffee and tea greeted him. In the lower cupboards, there were pots, pans, and crockery.

Vos walked around, as if in a daze, praising the Lord.

Without delay, Rouwenhorst set to work, organizing the men into groups to scour the plantation, to work on making tea and coffee for everyone, and to look for any medical supplies. George was put in charge of seeing that the coffee and tea were divided into equal portions. Once that was completed, Rouwenhorst's next orders came: "Vischer, take some men and see what else this plantation has to offer."

George headed outside, using his cane. Up ahead, he spotted six kampong huts. Each one was empty. As he and a few of the men explored, they found abandoned supplies in each.

This was good—all good. George paused where he stood in the center of one of the huts. "Thank you," he murmured. To whom, he didn't specify, but he felt he needed to express his gratitude.

He still wanted to be home. He and his comrades all needed medical treatment, but in this space, and in this moment, he could appreciate their good fortune.

The rumbling sounds of planes from a distance brought George back to the reality of their situation. They weren't in the clear, not by far. But they'd been granted a reprieve. He crossed to the window to see that the men outside had moved beneath palm trees, taking cover, until the Japanese bombers passed the islands.

George tried to reason with the foreboding that had crept into his chest when he thought of those planes dropping bombs on his home island. Java was most likely already occupied, so there was no reason for additional bombing. He wanted to firmly believe that his wife and children were safe in their home. He had to believe that. Or else the agony of mind would be too great.

When the sky was silent again, George headed out of the hut. He continued toward the larger hut just as Rouwenhorst called a meeting with everyone.

Once they'd all gathered inside, and the men were sampling the coffee, Rouwenhorst said, "We've been fortunate to find more supplies and food. Yet our days are numbered with such limited rations. As we wait here, Japan is taking over more and more of the East Indies. We don't know what's going on with our families, but we can hope they are safe and well." He paused and scanned the men surrounding him. "Our biggest enemy has become our festering wounds. With no medical supplies, I worry that things will get worse."

Many of the men nodded. Mulder dropped his head into his hands.

"I'm proposing a very strict rationing system," Rouwenhorst said. "We have no way of knowing how long we'll be here. The Dutch navy has probably marked us for dead, so we need to accept the fact that no purposeful rescue will be coming. And I'm sure none of us want to be captured by Japan."

A visible shudder ran through the men.

Rouwenhorst continued. "We'll stay in our smaller groups and rotate duties. We all have to be vigilant about staying out of sight. Not only from the sky, but from possible passing Japanese vessels."

All heads nodded. This had already been agreed upon, but a reminder was needed. Over the past day or so, some of the men hadn't been as quick to take cover.

"First up, we'll transfer all of our supplies near the beach to here," Rouwenhorst said, his gaze scanning the group. "We don't want any of our supplies or containers left visible."

As they set to work, and George made the trek back to the main beach, his thoughts kept plaguing him. *How long could they survive on this island? How long until the war was over?* They were surrounded by Japanese soldiers on all sides. Something had to give eventually.

The following morning, George awoke in a bed he shared with Vos. The man was snoring lightly, but that wasn't what had awakened George. He wasn't sure if his mind had ever fully shut down to sleep. He sat up in bed and shifted off, then he limped to the window that opened to a stretch of the coconut plantation. The sky had lightened with the rising sun but was still a dove gray.

Calculating quickly in his head, he knew it was Friday, March 13. They'd been missing for nearly a fortnight. George wasn't a superstitious man, and he didn't believe that Friday the thirteenth was a day of misfortunes, but he'd heard a couple of comments from the men last night about it.

Today, he decided, he'd keep extra busy with tasks to keep his mind preoccupied. It was only a date on the calendar, after all. First up, they needed to find other things to eat. Coconuts went only so far, and some of the men had been sick yesterday. One had spent all day sleeping. That didn't bode well.

George closed his eyes as a wave of dizziness passed through him. He'd just awakened, and already he wanted to sit back down. Instead, he braced a hand on the wall and ran through the rations in his mind. Should he talk to Rouwenhorst about cutting back again?

"Is it time to go on watch?" Vos murmured behind him.

George turned. The man's hair stuck up at all angles, and his beard was coming in auburn. All the men had short beards now, including George. "Almost."

Vos moved to his feet. Then he walked out of the small bedroom and into the kitchen where George assumed he'd make some coffee, or drink some coconut milk.

George's stomach growled in anticipation.

Over the past few mornings, Rouwenhorst had assigned a rotating group of men to watch the channel between the islands for native fishermen. None had been spotted yet, but George still hoped.

He found Vos in the kitchen making coffee. It was a luxury that wouldn't last long. Still, George gratefully accepted the cup offered by Vos and enjoyed every sip of the roasted flavor.

Soon, three other men joined them, including Bakker.

They trekked outside as the sun's first rays spilled across the vast horizon. The sight was beautiful, but the absolutely clear skies above foreboded a hot and languorous day. They traipsed along a path that was becoming well-worn with use to the shoreline. There, they paused beneath the edging palms. The men crouched where they stood and watched in silence.

Mornings weren't for conversation, but for reflection, and George was fine with that.

"Look," Bakker suddenly said.

George shifted his gaze. What might have appeared to be birds floating in the water were actually larger. They separated.

"Fishing boats," Bakker said.

"Are you sure?" Vos asked. "Maybe they are—"

"Fishing boats," George echoed. "Indonesians." He straightened and moved forward with his cane. "Let's signal them. Maybe we can trade or buy something."

Soon, the group of them were waving and shouting from the shoreline. Two of the fishing boats broke away from the fleet and headed directly toward the island.

"They've seen us," Vos said in a wondering tone.

George kept his cane up in the air for a few more moments, then as the fishermen neared, he lowered it. His comrades spoke varying levels of Indonesian or Malay. George knew several languages himself, but it turned out that Bakker was the most fluent, so he was elected as spokesperson.

The fishermen didn't seem all that surprised to see a ragtag group of Dutch men on the island, but George certainly wasn't going to ask them any questions about the war and thus pique their interest in his ragged group. The less these fishermen knew about them, the better.

Bakker moved to the shoreline where he could speak to the fishermen. After a short conversation, he turned to the others. "They will sell us fish and rice," Bakker said. "What money can we spare?"

In the huts, they'd found coins and had collected them all.

"I'll go and fetch money, then let the other men know of our good fortune," Vos said.

George turned back to the fishermen. With the help of Bakker communicating with them, the fishermen agreed to cook the rice and fish as well.

"They offered to take some of us to another island to get supplies," Bakker informed George.

"How many can fit?" George scanned the small fishing boats.

Bakker asked the question, and one of the fishermen held up four fingers.

"I'll go as one of them," George said.

Just then, the other men began to arrive with Rouwenhorst and Vos, who'd returned with money. After the negotiations were completed, the fishermen built fires and began to cook the fish and rice right on the shoreline.

George's stomach rumbled at the delicious scent.

When the other men found out that the fishermen had offered to take four to go get supplies, Arnoldus volunteered to be part of the group.

"We already have four," George said, looking around at the others.

Rouwenhorst frowned. "Which four volunteered?"

When George answered him, Rouwenhorst said, "You should stay back, Vischer. Your foot looks septic."

George exhaled. His foot was swollen, greenish, and painful. But he could get around with his walking stick. "I don't mind going."

Rouwenhorst shook his head. "Thank you for the offer, Vischer, but if you have to make a fast escape, you'll be doomed. We'll send Arnoldus in your place."

It was decided, then.

Vos nudged George. "You don't want to slow anyone down."

George was still trying to decide if he should take offense at the comment when it was announced that the meal was ready to eat. That was sufficient distraction.

After the fish and rice were consumed, four volunteers joined the fishermen. The men—Arnoldus, Feij, Rutgers, and Loeffen—were carrying a portion of the money Vos had divvied out.

"God speed," Vos told the men. "Don't forget which island we're on."

The volunteers laughed. The island would be imprinted on their brains for the rest of their lives. Nothing could make them forget.

George stood, leaning on his cane, with the other men as they watched the fishing boats sail away. The next time their comrades returned, they would have more supplies, and they could plan for a better future.

"Looks like rain," Bakker mused.

George lifted his chin. Dark clouds were indeed gathering, but they were some ways off. He'd be surprised if the storm reached the island at all. But if it did, they had plenty of crockery and pots lined up in the yard outside the main hut, ready to catch the rainfall.

CHAPTER FOURTEEN

"Rumors circulated that the [Japanese] had set up bordellos and needed women. My mother cut my hair and put me in my brother's clothes. Anything Dutch was forbidden. We were not even allowed to speak Dutch in public. Since we carried only Dutch names, Mom invented Chinese names for us. So I became instantly a boy with a girl's name of 'Mei Lan.'"

—GRETA KWIK, SEMARANG

MARY

Mary's feet ached despite her sturdy shoes, and she was sure that her children, mother, and sister-in-law were feeling it as well. The road tar burned hot, and she felt sorry for the refugees who didn't have shoes. Where had all of these people come from, and why did they look like they'd been refugees for months?

They were heading toward a part of the city called Tjideng. Mary knew the northwestern edge of the area to be a red-light district and wondered why Japan had chosen it. Every building they passed on the way flew the Japanese flag. It was disconcerting to see how much the city had changed in so little time. They walked past the large grassy field—Konings Plein—in the middle of the city and then came to a stretch of road that was bordered by tall rain trees. At last they had some relief from the burning sun above.

Ahead of them, a bridge spanned a drainage canal. And just beyond that, was a set of newly erected gates suspended from large black poles. Two tall flag poles had been erected on either side of the gates, proudly topped by large Japanese flags. In front of the fence connected to the gate was a row of bungalows that appeared to be deserted. To the left of the gate, Mary could see a guardhouse made of a bamboo frame and woven bamboo walls, or gedek. The roof was constructed with thatched leaves from atap palms, and the veranda in front of the guardhouse was lined with rifles.

"What have they built?" Oma murmured, walking not far from Mary.

"I don't know, Ma," Mary said in a quiet voice. It was all new to her, too.

They slowed as they reached the mass of people waiting to get inside. Japanese soldiers were going through people's belongings as they arrived at the gate. Things were being tossed aside, and there was nothing anyone could do about it. Mary took off her glasses and cleaned them. She should have brought her second pair, but had forgotten them in the rush of things.

In one of the lines, Mrs. Venema and her three daughters were detained as their belongings were searched. Mary stood in another line, a few families behind Claudia Vos and her children. When Claudia reached the front of the line, it became obvious that the guards weren't interested in searching the Vos family's luggage. No, they focused on Johan, drilling the boy with questions in Japanese.

What were they saying? What was happening?

"They're asking his age," a woman spoke behind Mary. "All boys over twelve are being held until they can be sent to a men's camp."

"Oh no," Mary breathed, as her heart climbed to her throat. Greta—or Willy—was, indeed, twelve, but she was quite petite, and it had been easy to pass her off as the ten-year-old boy the guards had obviously believed her to be.

But Johan, at age nine, was tall enough to be mistaken for an older boy.

Somehow, Johan understood what the guard was trying to ask, and he held up nine fingers.

The guards gazed at him for a moment, then let him through.

Mary's hand pressed against her chest as she tried to catch a steady breath. With the Vos family on the other side, now Mary just had to get through as well. Her pulse zipping, Mary stated her name and the names of her children in front of the guards. Then Oma and Tie gave their names.

Moments later, they walked into the enclosed settlement. If it weren't for the walls surrounding the area and the Japanese guards, it might have been another neighborhood of rows of houses. Except, there were people everywhere, hauling bags and suitcases.

Mary didn't know who'd lived in these houses beforehand, but right now, they were being overrun with new occupants.

She and her family followed a young Japanese soldier who didn't speak any Dutch. And they, of course, didn't speak any Japanese. The soldier looked barely old enough to shave. His words were sharp and brief, and they mostly communicated through gestures. So far, Mary understood that their entire family was to live in a single room.

She'd soon find out why.

Families kept piling in. One after another. The area the Japanese forces had cordoned off for the internment camp didn't have enough space for the number of people who kept arriving.

On the march, she'd seen the Slingerland family and the Van der Hurk family, but she didn't know where they had ended up. The guard led Mary and her family to a small house with a yard and fence, then ushered them toward the house. One side of the yard was dug out for a garden, although it looked as if it had been trampled recently. The house was a decent size for a family home, but not for the masses of women and children crowding inside the camp. With her family, Mary lugged their belongings up the steps of the veranda then stepped inside.

Chaos ensued, with people staking their claim to rooms or spots on the floor. Two women argued over one of the bedrooms. Tie moved quickly ahead with her single suitcase, not stopping to help Mary with the rest of their stuff. She stared at the place in disbelief. The home had probably once been functional, but the belongings had been gutted, and it was crammed with a mishmash of people and things.

"Leave the windows open," a woman called out as another woman shut the windows in the kitchen.

The second woman said something in a much quieter voice, and the first woman said, "Air and heat is better than no air at all."

"Come on, children," Mary muttered. She maneuvered their cot along the hallway until they reached a small room that might have once been a study. There was a desk and chair shoved into the corner, and two beds. A bookcase stood in the corner, and on one shelf was a worn pile of books. Otherwise, it was empty of memorabilia that might have once been stashed there. The door was missing to the study, and to all the other rooms as well. That wouldn't afford much privacy.

"Let's take it," Oma said. "There might not be anything better."

Mary entered the room, and they all set to work. Even though her hands were busy, her mind worried. At least they had given their names when they'd arrived at this place. That meant there would be a record of them, and George could find when he returned. Right?

She and Oma set up the cot. Little Georgie was already looking tired enough for a nap.

"Oh, here you are." Tie walked in and stashed her suitcase in the corner. Then she disappeared into the hallway without another word.

Mary had no idea what to expect next, so she focused on the here and now. She opened her suitcase and told everyone to unpack and settle in. Then she made up the bed for Georgie. She turned to her mother, who looked tired as well. Her fair skin had burned in the sun, and Mary guessed they were all a little sunburnt. "Ma, can you stay with him while I go find out where we can buy food for our meals?"

"Of course." Oma gathered Georgie close. His eyes were dropping, and he leaned his blond head against Oma's shoulder.

Mary hesitated, wondering whether or not to take Rita, but finally, she grasped her daughter's hand and headed out of their room. They would check out their immediate surroundings, then find out what they were supposed to be doing and helping with.

They passed by the Vos family, who'd found a portion of dining room to share with another family.

"Do you need any help?" Mary asked.

"We're fine," Claudia said, with a wave of her hand. "Thank you."

Mary nodded, then headed to the front door with Rita. They stepped onto the veranda. Johan had tied up Kells outside by the gate with a rope. Other dogs were out there, and a few people had brought cats in carriers. Mary had stayed out of the arguments of whether or not cats should be allowed in the house since some people had allergies.

Her attention was caught by a cluster of Japanese soldiers who'd gathered at the gate to the yard. They were gesturing toward a couple of boys who looked about thirteen or fourteen, not much older than the Vos children.

One of the boy's mothers was crying.

"What's going on?" Claudia asked, stepping onto the veranda too, with Johan and Greta—or Willy now—at her side.

"It looks like those boys are being separated from their mothers," Mary said.

Claudia put an arm about Johan's shoulders and pulled him closer.

Sure enough, the soldiers led away the teenaged boys, and it was then that Mary noticed the truck on the other side of the road. Several other teen boys were in the back, being guarded by Japanese soldiers.

When the crying woman and the other mother came toward the veranda, Mary asked, "What's happening? Where are your boys going?"

The woman with tears in her eyes looked up. "They're taking them to a men's camp with the other older boys. They said that our camp will be only for women, girls, and younger children."

Mary frowned at the truck as it pulled away and headed toward the gates. More families were being torn apart. The men had already been captured and sent to camps, but who knew if the boys would be in the same camps as their fathers.

Rita tugged on her hand, and Mary looked down.

"What about Johan?" Rita asked, glancing over at her friend. "Will he have to leave our camp?"

"No, Ita." Mary drew her daughter away from the grieving women. It wasn't like Mary could shield her children from what was happening around them, out in the open, but she wanted a bit of a reprieve from this hard day.

Claudia followed Mary. "Let's find out if there's a place to get food and where we're supposed to cook."

Mary couldn't imagine so many people all sharing the same kitchen in one house. There wasn't room, and food preparation would have to be done around the clock.

In every house and yard they passed, women and children worked to settle in.

Some had left bags and suitcases stacked outside against the houses because they'd run out of space inside. Despite all the shifting of lives, groups of kids ran around together as if their lives hadn't been upended in the past few hours.

Mary stopped to speak with Mrs. Slingerland and asked if she needed help with her young ones. "You take care of yourself, my dear," Mrs. Slingerland said in a silver-spoon voice, hands on her hips. "We all have our plates full. But it looks like we're a couple of houses apart."

Mrs. Van der Hurk joined them at the edge of the yard. At least the two women would be housemates. "Is this a dream or a nightmare?" Mrs. Van der Hurk commented. No one had an answer. She looked down at Rita. "Come play with Corrie any time."

Rita smiled but clung more tightly to Mary's hand. They moved on, mostly gazing about at the unbelievable situation they found themselves in. Claudia voiced several questions as they walked, but her children remained silent. Even Johan, who was usually a fountain of information or questions. His blue eyes looked about as wide as saucers as he took everything in. His sunburnt nose was close to blistering. Greta, or Willy, was naturally quiet, so her silence wasn't anything different.

"Mary!" someone called, and she turned to see Mrs. Venema.

"Where are you staying?" Mrs. Venema asked, joining them on the road. Her youngest daughter, Ina, walked out with her.

"We're both three houses that way," Mary explained. "Tie is with us too."

"Oh, that's nice your sister-in-law is close," Mrs. Venema said. "This camp is too small for all these people, yes?"

Mary couldn't agree more. "I wonder how many more people they'll allow in?"

Mrs. Venema sighed. "I've been told that the eastern boundary is the drainage canal, the northern is where the marshes are, and the southwest boundary is the railway line."

"So the camp is shaped like a triangle?" Claudia interjected.

"Correct," Mrs. Venema said. "Be grateful we're not assigned to the northwestern portion of the camp."

She didn't need to say more. All the women knew its reputation for being a red-light district.

Then Mrs. Venema peered at Greta. Her brows lifted as she put two and two together. "Haircut?"

"This is my son Willy," Claudia stated.

Greta's face flushed, and Ina stared, questions in her eyes.

"Ah, I understand," Mrs. Venema said. "I won't say a thing."

Claudia gave a stiff nod.

Mary wondered if Mrs. Venema thought Claudia had taken drastic action about her daughter, but even so, the Venema girls were older, and it would be much harder to hide their gender. To change the focus, she said, "We're going to find out what the food situation is."

"Why don't you go with them, Ina," Mrs. Venema said. "Report back here. I'll finish setting our things up."

Ina joined their group as they continued down the road. She and Greta walked toward the back, talking quietly.

Mary scanned those they passed along the way. More refugees kept coming, led by Japanese soldiers who took them to where they'd have to set up. There were no Dutch men in sight.

"Not all soldiers are Japanese," Johan said suddenly.

It was true, Mary had observed. Some Indonesians were mixed in.

"Some are Korean," Johan said. "I heard it on the radio report."

"Ah, it would make sense," Claudia said. Japan had colonized Korea in 1910, so the Koreans had been assimilated into the Japanese army.

They were nearly to the large gates at the entrance of the camp now, and Mary paused. Trucks were coming in and out, and when they did, the refugees were stopped by soldiers to let them pass. One truck was in the process of being unloaded, and the contents looked like bags of rice.

"I wonder if there's a central kitchen?" Claudia asked, echoing Mary's own question.

Someone yelled, a man's voice, and Mary looked toward the gate. A family was being separated. Older sons from their mother and younger siblings.

Before Mary could usher Rita away, one of the soldiers struck one of the boys. The mother screamed.

Mary tugged Rita along with her, back the way they'd come, back to their cramped house.

Claudia hurried right alongside them.

They were all too numb to speak about what they'd just seen.

When the houses became more familiar, Mary felt relieved to be closer. At the moment she was supremely grateful her children were young. Ina and Greta had fallen silent. When Ina broke off from the group as they reached her house, she waved, then ran off.

Even though the sun was bright and the sky a clear blue, a heaviness had settled over Mary. The reality of their situation was all around them. As they neared their assigned house, Tie hurried out and headed across the yard toward them before they reached the walkway to the veranda.

"Mary, there you are." Tie said in a rush, sweat staining her blouse. They were all hot from the day's procession and unpacking. It was now the time of afternoon when most people stayed inside, where it was cooler.

"When the siren sounds, it means we have to go to roll call," Tie said. "Our house has been assigned to a specific sector."

"Roll call?" Claudia echoed.

"The Japanese officer spoke to me—the one who speaks Dutch," Tie said, her breathing starting to calm. "They're visiting each home and giving out the instructions for roll call. It's in one hour. Where did you go?"

"We were trying to find out where and how we're eating tonight," Mary explained, not wanting to share what they'd witnessed at the front gates.

"Everything is being gathered and rationed," Tie said in a rush. "There is a central kitchen where you can pick up your rations, and food is prepared on your own. We need to turn in any food items we brought."

Mary stared. "Even the peanuts I brought to plant?"

Tie hesitated at this. "I can ask the officer, but we need to follow orders exactly. I'm not going to let our house be punished. I've been made the section leader of our sector."

She looked from Mary to Claudia. "I've already heard rumors of some women being . . ." She glanced at the children, then said, "Disciplined for insubordination."

Mary's stomach turned sour. With the children standing amongst them, she didn't ask Tie for details. They'd already seen and heard enough. "Did the officer tell you anything else about how meals will be prepared?"

"I don't know beyond what I told you," Tie said. "Right now, we need to sort through our suitcases, and I'll be inspecting the other residents' cases. All food must be collected onto the veranda before roll call."

Mary and Claudia took their children inside. The interior had become muggy with so many people inside and no breeze coming through the screened windows.

When Mary entered the shared room, she found that Georgie and Oma were both asleep on the smaller bed. It was a blessing to have them resting. Mary sorted through their suitcases and reluctantly took out any foodstuffs she'd brought. Before carrying it to the veranda though, she hid several tins beneath the larger bed where she'd stored the suitcases.

Soon, Oma stirred, and Mary updated her in quiet tones about the roll call, the food search, and how the men and boys were being separated from their families. They both looked over at Rita, who was standing in the doorless opening, watching the other families go about their business.

"I will take Rita out to the yard," Oma said, "and you rest next to Georgie while he sleeps."

"Don't go far, then, Ma," Mary said. "And if soldiers arrive, come back in here." She knew that her mother could handle herself as well as any other woman, but nothing was as it should be.

Somehow, Mary fell asleep for a short time. She woke with a start, and for half a second, she couldn't remember where she was. Then it all came back, hitting her like a mudslide. She groaned and rolled onto her side. Georgie was lying next to her, awake, his large, hazel eyes watching her.

Mary smiled and ran her fingers over his blond curls, which were slightly damp from sleeping in the humidity. "Did you sleep all right?"

He smiled back. "Hi, Mama."

He patted her cheek, and she drew him closer and breathed in his sweaty little-boy smell.

After a moment, he wriggled out of her arms.

Mary gave a soft laugh. "Should we take you to the toilet like a big boy?" Another thing she was grateful for was that Georgie was already toilet trained.

They climbed off the bed, and Mary led him through the house to find where the toilet facilities were. A line snaked along the cloistered hallway as other house residents waited their turn. Mary sighed. She supposed it would frequently be like this.

Once they were out of the toilet, Oma had returned with Rita, but before they could have a conversation, the siren went off. It was time for roll call.

The late afternoon heat was merciless as they headed out of the yard and found the sector they'd been assigned to.

Even though Mary didn't understand most of what the Japanese soldiers were saying, it was clear they were supposed to line up in rows of ten, according to designated houses. One soldier walked among them and assigned each of them a number, in order of how they stood. The numbers were in Japanese. At least Mary understood that much.

Even Georgie and Rita were expected to call out their numbers.

The officer who spoke Dutch joined the other soldiers. Mary felt immediate relief since at least she'd be able to understand him.

"Rules of the camp are as follows," the officer called out. "It is expected that all European residents, who are a conquered people, pay deference to all Nippon. You are to bow to every Japanese soldier or officer that you see. No exceptions. Punishment will be immediate. This is how you bow."

He snapped his hands to his side, his fingers stiff and straight, then he bowed at the waist. For a moment he stayed bent at an angle, then he straightened. "This will show you are respectful. We only want respectful prisoners who express humility."

Prisoners . . . the word rippled hot through Mary's body. She knew they were in an internment camp, of course. But hearing that word made it feel all that more surreal, and awful.

Mary glanced about her and saw the women nodding. They made an interesting collection of women of all ages, some wearing nicer clothing, as if they were going on holiday. Mary envied the women who had hats.

The officer said, "Roll call is called *tenko* in Japanese. This will be twice a day. You will line up in rows of ten—the same formation each morning and night. Call out your assigned number when it's your turn. Starting with *ichi, ni, san, shi, go, roku* . . ."

Mary whispered the numbers, trying to memorize them quickly. She'd need to help her children learn to say them.

They began to count off, one row at a time.

When it came to Mary's row, Tie started off the count, followed by Mary, her two children, then Oma. Claudia and her children were behind them.

Once roll call was finished, the officer paced in front of the rows and said, "In the morning, roll call will be at 8:00. You will be assigned to work groups." His gaze slid over Mary's row of women. "Older women will take care of the younger children. Everyone else will be expected to work. Evening roll call is at 5:00."

The officer paused in his walking. "You will need permission to leave the camp. There is a market outside the camp where you can shop once a week. Everything will be inspected once you return. If you miss curfew, you will be punished."

He continued to pace. "Postcards are allowed between the camps. For a postal fee."

Mary could almost hear the relief in the women around her, even though they didn't speak a word. They were all sufficiently cowed. Or maybe it was the blasted heat making them feel like they were puddles of melted wax.

Mary was happy for these women who would be able to communicate with their husbands in other camps. But what about her George? Where was he, and would she ever see him again?

CHAPTER FIFTEEN

"Discipline was very strict. Starting the next day, we found out just how tough. During roll call, a [guard] commanded us in Japanese. Nobody understood what he said. Attention! Right face! Count off! etc., all in Japanese. The first blows soon fell. It was advisable not to attempt to ward them off because they would be followed by numerous kicks and thrusts with the butt of a rifle. Blood of the first victim flowed freely and we learned the first Japanese cuss words . . ."

—FRANS J. NICOLAAS PONDER, SURABAYA CAMP

GEORGE

Four days.

It had been four days since the volunteers had left with the native fishermen. George had believed that one day away was acceptable. Two, as well. But on the third day, even Vos had started to predict the men's demise.

The dawning of the fourth day brought with it increased anxiety over the fate of their comrades. How long did it take to sail to one of the other islands? Only a few hours. How long did it take to gather supplies? A few more hours. How long would it take to return? A day at most.

Yet, it was March 17 now.

George, Vos, and Bakker were on early morning watch again, sitting in the cool sand beneath the rustling palms.

"Are those fishing boats?" Bakker said, pointing beyond the shore.

George studied the sea vessels for a moment. It wasn't a few boats, but one. "It's a prahu." The prahu was an Indonesian sailing boat. And this was the largest one George had ever seen.

The boat was headed directly for the island, so there was no use taking cover. They'd surely been spotted. Besides, there was a good chance their volunteer men were on the boat. Why else would this vessel be approaching?

"Something's not right," Vos said, his voice a murmur, but everyone heard it.

"Those aren't the same fishermen we met before," Bakker observed.

George squinted in the early morning light. "How can you tell?"

"They look like they live on the sea," Bakker continued.

Vos barked a laugh. "What, like pirates?"

No one answered, and a shudder went through George. As the prahu neared, George wondered if they should send someone to fetch Rouwenhorst and the others. This boat had at least a dozen men on it—and if there were more, the Dutch would be outnumbered. But why should that matter? George wondered at his own alarm. The Dutch weren't at war with the Indonesians . . . Yet, as the boat got closer, George could see the men well enough to presume that they would be happy to battle against anyone.

George stood stiffly next to his group of men as the Indonesians disembarked. He counted twenty-five in all. None of them resembled the group they'd met four days prior. Their rough and seaworn exteriors testified that these men spent much more time on sea than land. Besides, they were all armed with heavy bush knives. The horn handles made for a sturdy grip, and the blades were long and decisive.

"Raise your hands," George said. "To show them we aren't armed."

The men did so, and Bakker stepped forward. His hands stayed raised as he greeted the rough-looking group in their native tongue.

The Indonesians spread out, taking a defensive stance, as they studied the sunburnt Dutch men. Finally, one man replied to Bakker. Their conversation was short, and Bakker translated as he went. He told the boatmen that they were waiting for their comrades to return.

"Your comrades are in Java," one of the Indonesians said, his voice rough as he eyed Bakker.

"Have you seen them?" Bakker asked, although George heard the disbelief in his tone.

"Yes."

How did these men know the four who had volunteered?

Just then, the other Dutch men joined them on the beach. They followed suit and raised their hands as well, in a show of peace. Rouwenhorst caught George's gaze and gave him a slight nod.

This brought up their numbers to thirteen men. But they were still outnumbered and lacked any real weapons. George knew they'd lose within minutes. The Dutch might all look sturdy on their feet, but they were in various stages of weakness.

A few Indonesians who seemed to be the group's leaders fell into a vigorous conversation. Then a couple of them broke off and headed toward the beached dinghy that had been dragged to the line of palm trees.

Under his breath, Rouwenhorst murmured, "Let them have the dinghy."

George and his comrades watched in silence as the Indonesians dragged it down the beach, into the water, then loaded it on their boat.

Thankfully, the Indonesians took their leave without any further aggression. For several long moments, Rouwenhorst stood at the water's edge, his arms folded as he watched the departure of the prahu.

George headed for the first group of palms and sat in the shade. His limbs were trembling—mostly from standing so long with his hands raised, but also from the anticipation of facing a fight he couldn't win.

Bakker settled next to him. "That was close."

George couldn't agree more. "Our comrades aren't coming back, are they?"

"I don't believe so," Bakker said. "And we're now known to be here.

If two sets of fishermen found us, surely the word is out. For better or for worse."

What would stop the Indonesians from informing the Japanese military about the stranded Dutch seamen? Especially if there was a reward involved. Or what was to stop them from returning and taking them hostage?

A few meters away, Rouwenhorst paced, his brow cinched in thought.

Desperation burned white hot in George's chest. "I don't think we can stay here any longer."

At this statement, Vos walked over. "What do you mean? Where will we go?"

Rouwenhorst crossed to them, joining their group. "Vischer's right. We're sitting targets now. Too many Indonesians know our location. The Japanese army will soon if they haven't been notified already."

"But the dinghy is gone," Vos said. "Unless you have another one you've been hiding from us."

George had already considered this. The Indonesians taking the dinghy had been like a blow to the stomach. But now, they couldn't remain here day after day, hoping for rescue. It wasn't coming. He didn't know what was in Rouwenhorst's mind, but there was one solution in George's.

"We have access to two damaged lifeboats from the *Marula*," he said. "We could repair one with parts from the other."

The other men had all joined them. Rouwenhorst rubbed at the scraggly beard on his chin.

"Where would we go, though?" Vos pressed. "Where else can we be safe?"

Rouwenhorst's gaze was firm. "We can't give up on Australia yet. We still have our orders, men."

George's gaze connected with Rouwenhorst's. There was no arguing with their commanding officer. "We have sea charts that we salvaged from the lifeboats."

Rouwenhorst nodded. "Very good, Vischer. We need a plan of

action. The group that was on watch this morning will return to the hut to scour the sea charts. The rest of us will retrieve the lifeboats and bring them to this island. Today we're starting repairs. Time has run out." He looked at Jaden and Mulder. "You two will keep watch for more visiting fishermen."

Even though every word Rouwenhorst spoke was true, hearing it spoken aloud made George feel deflated. By repairing one of the lifeboats and leaving the island, they'd be giving a final farewell to their four lost comrades. They were officially giving up on them.

With half the group, George trudged back to the main hut. The day's heat had bloomed, and George was covered in perspiration by the time they stepped into the cooler interior of the hut. He was out of breath like he'd been running instead of walking.

The morning coffee had not gone very far.

Men scurried about, gathering the sea charts, then spreading them across the table. Every man in this hut had been trained on reading the maps, and most of them were familiar with the different islands— although not perfectly because there were so many.

"What about the Poeloe Pajoeng," Bakker suggested, tapping a finger to an island south of their present location.

The Poeloe Pajoeng was also called Paraplue Island, George knew. Was it currently occupied, or had the Indonesians evacuated it as well? Surely there would be shelter available and supplies left behind. At the very least, it was nearly a full day's travel and quite a distance from the Thousand Islands.

"I don't have an objection," Rouwenhorst said, scanning over the surrounding islands. "Anyone have a better idea?"

No one did, and George said, "It's not far from Java. Do we care about that?" Their families were all on Java, so was it better for them to return or keep away?

"I don't see any other choice," Vos said.

The other men murmured in agreement, so it was decided.

"We will leave on the next cloudy day," Rouwenhorst said.

Two days later, they set sail.

Thirteen men in a repaired lifeboat were once again upon the water. This time, they had more supplies with them. But it was disconcerting for George to be out on the open water once more, vulnerable to the sea's elements, even though he and the men had extra clothing items taken from the huts. They were at the mercy of fair weather or foul, native fishermen, Japanese destroyers . . . not to mention the risk of being spotted by a bomber. As long as the clouds stayed overhead, they had a chance.

Leaving at the first glimmer of dawn, they rowed as fast and steady as they could, Vos offering up frequent prayers for the clouds to stick around. They arrived at Paraplue Island nearly fifteen hours later. The sun had set, and faint pink illuminated the clouds, turning to violet as they steered their way to the shore.

Not far into the island, a lighthouse stood, though there were no signs of occupation. No lights glimmered, and no cooking fires glowed on the beach. Was the lighthouse keeper following blackout orders, or was the structure deserted?

As several of the men worked to drag the lifeboat all the way to the first line of trees, George stretched his cramped muscles. His skin felt hot and uncomfortable with the prolonged exposure to the sun that day. Perhaps they could find a freshwater pond somewhere. Before he could suggest a scouting trip, a man came walking along the beach.

His deep brown skin and grizzled beard marked him as a native islander, and he carried a long bush knife.

"Ho, there," he said in Malay. "Where are you from?"

Bakker turned to face him.

The native stopped several meters away, wariness in his gaze, but his stance was firm.

Bakker spoke for the group, being the most fluent in Malay. He explained where they were from, then added, "We're missing four men who departed with fishermen several days ago. We left the Thousand Islands because we don't trust our safety there anymore."

The native gazed at each person in turn, as if deciding whether or not he believed their story. "I am the lighthouse keeper here." He waved toward the lighthouse. "Come, I will prepare a meal for you. There is plenty."

This was the last thing George expected to hear.

Around him, his comrades were grinning.

The lighthouse keeper didn't smile back, though. He motioned for them to follow. It wasn't a hard choice to trust the man, especially since the Dutch severely outnumbered a single man.

They reached the lighthouse, and in a short time, the keeper had set out a simple meal of cooked fish, rice, and mangoes. Simple, but delicious. As they ate in the moonlight, the mood was lighter than George remembered it being since their friends had gone missing.

Rouwenhorst pressed Bakker to ask the native, "Do you have many visitors to your island, and have you heard anything of four Dutch sailors traveling with fishermen?"

At this, the lighthouse keeper set down his bowl of food. "I have heard stories, but I have not seen the men themselves."

Everyone went quiet at this information.

"Stories?" Bakker echoed.

The native folded his arms. "The stories I've heard are not good. Four Dutch men were murdered on a nearby island."

No one reacted at first. George tried to comprehend the man's words. Could they be true—could he mean *their* comrades?

"Do you know the Dutch men's names?" Rouwenhorst asked in a low rumble.

The lighthouse keeper shook his head. "No names needed. Four Dutch men on these islands are rare." He lifted a hand toward the sky. "Especially with the Japanese all around us. The Dutch are going into camps on Java. Rounded up like sheep." He clapped his palms together. "Gone. Just like that."

George wasn't fully following the man's language. Was he saying . . .

"Wait," Bakker said, then rattled off several questions.

The lighthouse keeper replied in kind.

Bakker pushed to his feet and walked the perimeter of the men, then turned and faced everyone. "Our friend here says that Dutch officers are being captured and put into prison. We had heard this about other islands outside of Java, but now it's been confirmed. Returning to Java will be a definite prison sentence. Yet hiding out on islands will only get us so far. Japanese soldiers are all around, and not everyone will be as accommodating as our new friend here."

"Reaching Australia might be impossible now, no?" George murmured to Vos, who sat next to him. "It seems Japan has infiltrated everywhere. And we'd need more supplies to make that voyage."

Mulder rose to his feet, facing the men. "How can you talk about Australia anymore? We already tried that—on a well-equipped minesweeper. We were bombed, multiple times. What makes you think we can just resupply and take off again?"

Rouwenhorst moved toward Mulder and placed a hand on his shoulder. "Mulder, sit down. We still have our original orders."

Mulder stalked away, took a seat, then buried his face in his hands.

Bakker gazed at Mulder for a moment, then said, "We're not safe on this island for much longer. Not being so near to where they executed . . ." He exhaled. "Our comrades."

Everyone went absolutely silent. George felt the weight of his comrades who'd lost their lives. Would that be the fate for them all?

The lighthouse keeper said something in rapid-fire Malay, and Bakker translated for those who didn't understand. "He recommends that we travel to Krawang and buy supplies there."

Mulder's head came up. "That's on the coast of Java."

Bakker folded his arms. "We'll have to hope there's not a concentration of Japanese troops in that area."

It was no wonder that it took a while for George to fall asleep that night. His journey was far from over, yet as he gazed at the moon overhead, he thought of Mary. If so much was already happening on Java, how was she doing? Was she sleeping well? Or was she watching the moon like he was?

The following morning, George woke with a start. The sun hadn't risen yet, but men around him were already preparing to leave the island. He rolled to his side and winced at the renewed pain in his foot. He hoped he could get medical attention in Australia, that was, if they made it there. What were the chances of surviving a sea voyage now with so much against them? Using his walking stick, he pushed to his feet, then he helped load the boat with the few things the lighthouse keeper had donated. The man himself stood a few meters off, watching the preparations.

George wondered if the native would pass along word of the Dutch seamen's visit to the island. Probably. Would it matter? They'd be long gone.

The next hours on the sea heading for Krawang proved to be a time of quiet reflection for them all. None of them had taken the news of their murdered comrades lightly. Of the twenty-four seamen on the minesweeper, eleven of them had died now. That fact was certainly sobering.

As they rowed on, George wondered if he should let his hopes lift. Everything about this voyage seemed more and more doomed. They'd been fortunate to run into the lighthouse keeper, but there were so many obstacles facing them now. Some of the men, like Vos and their commander, had claimed that God was in control of all things—in control of this situation. If that was true, were they supposed to reach Australia?

George didn't know. All they could do now was resupply, then prepare for their voyage to Australia. If they reached their destination in one piece, there they could finally assist in the Allied war effort and vindicate the lost lives of their fallen comrades.

"Hold up," Rouwenhorst said, pulling George out of his thoughts. He lifted a hand and gave the order, "Stop rowing." They were nearly to shore.

The rowers halted in their efforts and leaned forward, scanning the shoreline of Krawang.

In front of the line of trees to the left was a flag, stirring in the sea breeze. There was no mistaking the rectangle of white and the large red circle in the center.

Krawang was under Japanese occupation.

CHAPTER SIXTEEN

"Right from the start, there was a shortage of sugar
and salt. The food rations became gradually smaller and
smaller. As people became hungrier, the talk about food
increased. So an intensive exchange of food recipes ensued.
Storytelling was another popular pastime. . . . Even some
church services were allowed in Bandung camps."

—ANTON ACHERMAN, ADEK CAMP

RITA

Everyone at camp called her Ita now, just like Georgie did. She decided she liked it since she was the only Ita around.

Sometimes in the morning, before it was time for breakfast, Ita would jump on a steel covering that spanned the hole with the water meter. The jumping distracted her from her hungry stomach, and she loved the echo of the snapping noise of metal. Even when it was early in the morning, no one asked her to stop.

"Ita," Georgie called out one morning, waving from the veranda. "We're going to the kitchens."

Ita didn't need to be told twice to head out with her family and walk to the camp kitchen to get into line. Ita was hungry every day, but Mama had told her not to complain. They ate two times a day, and they had to stand in a long line at the Tjilamajah kitchen—which was the

151

kitchen for the whole camp—to get their tin bowls filled up with rice or tapioca.

Some families traded for meat at the market, and they cooked it over little fires in their yards. But most of them had to line up for the camp food. When they reached the food line, Ita's stomach was already grumbling. Sometimes the food wasn't very good, but Mama told them to eat every last bite. Even if they didn't like it. Ita's least favorite was the porridge, which was usually served at the end of each week when the food supplies ran low. Sago porridge and lumps of bread that had no taste.

Aunt Tie worked in the kitchen, and Ita wished she'd give out a little more food to her niece and nephew, but she never did. She watched everyone with her sharp muddy eyes, making sure that all the portions were equal. It didn't change if you were a child or an adult.

Ita sometimes told Mama to take some of her food to help grow the baby. Mama smiled as if she was pleased, but she always refused. At least the soldiers had let her plant a garden, and Mama said they'd have peanuts to make peanut butter.

Ita's stomach grumbled just thinking about it.

"Hush, we're almost there," Mrs. Slingerland said to her young daughter Olga, who stood in front of Ita and was whining that she was too hungry to wait anymore.

In camp, Ita heard so many whining or crying kids. Georgie wasn't like that, and he hadn't ever been. Mama called him an angel, and Ita knew she was right. Compared to these other children who gave their mothers a hard time, Georgie *was* an angel.

Ita wanted to make things easier for Mama and Oma, so she helped with Georgie all the time.

She also helped Johan with whatever chores he'd been assigned. The other day, Kells had caught rats around the house, and Ita had helped throw them in a pile on the other side of the garden. She didn't like picking up dead rats, but the job had to be done by someone.

The line shuffled forward, and soon Ita was inside the building.

There, standing over a big pot of rice, was Aunt Tie. She always seemed to be busy and didn't come into the house very much, except at night to sleep. Ita had heard some of the other ladies in their house say mean things about Aunt Tie. When Ita asked Mama about it, she'd said, "Don't repeat gossip. Your aunt is being obedient to the Japanese orders."

Weren't they all trying to be obedient? One of the women in their house had been sick two nights before and had missed morning roll call. The soldiers made Aunt Tie go back to the house and force the woman to come to roll call.

Ita scrunched up her nose at the memory of the woman being sick on the ground in front of everyone. But the soldiers still made her say her number and bow for an extra long time. Everyone at roll call had to hold their bows longer, in punishment for the woman staying home.

"What if I get sick?" Ita had whispered to Mama.

"I will carry you to roll call, then."

And Ita knew she would.

Mrs. Slingerland gave up on telling Olga to be quiet, even though the child was still whining.

Wasn't she annoying everyone? Why didn't Olga's mother care anymore? Ita looked up at her own mother, but she wasn't paying attention either. Everyone was ignoring the child.

Finally, Ita said to the young girl, "Do you know how to count?"

Olga looked over at her, then blinked slowly.

She tried again. "Can you count to five?"

Olga moved closer to her mother and clutched the edge of her skirt, but at least she had stopped whining.

"Try with me. One, two . . ."

Soon, the girl was repeating the numbers and holding up her fingers as she did so. Next, Georgie joined in, and another little girl farther up the line. In no time at all, it was their turn to get their tins filled with rice and seaweed that Ita didn't like but knew she'd have to eat. The girl smiled over at Ita before she followed her mother out of the building.

Ita smiled back. Was it so easy to stop whining and crying? Maybe it was.

She sat with her family outside the building. Most people didn't wait to walk back to their houses to eat because what if they dropped their food? And losing even a morsel or a drop to the dirt would mean less food. Besides, no one wanted to wait that long.

"That was very nice of you," Mama told Ita in a quiet voice. "Talking to Olga."

Ita felt fluttery inside. "I didn't want her to annoy everyone like she was annoying me."

Mama gave a little laugh, and Ita felt more fluttery.

"It was a very good choice," Oma said, her smile bright. "If more children were like our Ita, kind and thoughtful of everyone around them, the camp would be a happier place."

"And there'd be less crying," Ita added.

Mama's smile was soft. "Agreed. Teaching little Olga how to count reminded me that I have a present for you, Ita. I was going to wait until your birthday, but I will give it to you tonight."

A present? Excitement rushed through Ita. She didn't think she'd be getting birthday presents in a place like this. People were having to give up more and more items. Whatever the Japanese officers decided on confiscating, that's what they had to give up. One day it was pencils, another all the paper, and so on.

A woman walked past them then. Her hair looked funny and very short, like she'd tried to cut it herself.

"What happened to that woman's hair?" Ita whispered to Mama when the woman had moved on.

Mama pursed her mouth like she did when she didn't want to answer Ita's questions.

"Does she have lice?" Some kids in the next house over had lice. They had all had to cut off their hair, and no one wanted to go near them.

Mama and Oma exchanged glances, then Mama finally said, "She disobeyed a rule, and the Japanese soldiers cut off her hair as a punishment."

Ita thought about this all the way back to their house. They stopped at the yards in front of other houses, and Mama asked people how they were doing. While the women talked, Ita noticed a couple of other women with cut-off hair too. Some of them wore scarves to hide their mostly bald heads. Ita reached up to touch her bobbed hair. Her blonde locks were getting scraggly. Mama usually trimmed it, but they didn't have any scissors or anything that could be used as weapons—according to the camp rules.

Clouds moved over the sun, and the air grew thicker and muggier. Ita hoped this didn't mean it would be raining during roll call later on. When that had happened a few days ago, everyone still had to stand there, bowing, even when they were getting soaked. Ever since then, Georgie had had a runny nose.

She took her brother's hand and wished she had the energy to carry him on her back. He looked so tired, and even though they'd just eaten, Ita felt hungry again. When they reached the house and walked inside, Ita covered her mouth and nose. It smelled horrible.

"What's happened?" Oma asked one of the nearby ladies, who was changing her baby.

Maybe it was a stinky baby? Ita thought.

"The toilet is backed up," the woman said. "No one knows how to fix it, and no one wants to go ask a Japanese soldier for help."

Oma sighed. "I'll take a look. But if I can't fix it, then someone should tell one of the commanders."

"I've already informed them," Aunt Tie said, coming into the room from the kitchen area. "As soon as someone reported the problem to me at the kitchen, I told one of the commanders. But the soldiers don't have time to fix things in the houses. We're on our own."

Oma grimaced. "We can fix it." She set off toward the back of the house.

Ita looked over at Mama to see if she should go and help, too. She didn't want to, though, and Mama said nothing. So Ita followed her into their bedroom. It was stinky in there too, and Ita hoped the toilet would be fixed soon.

The wind came in through the window, and that helped a little bit. It would probably rain soon since the clouds had boiled up over them.

Ita sat on one of the beds with Georgie, and they played a counting game with things in the room.

When Oma returned, she had her shoes off and stains on her clothing. "A pipe has broken underground—someplace in the yard. We can clean out everything possible to reduce the stench, then find a new place to use the toilet."

"Where else can we go?" Mama asked. "Every house has dozens of people sharing."

"One of the women said this is happening all over the camp," Oma said. "So they are digging trenches between their yards and the road."

"Out in the open?" Mama said.

"There's not much other choice," Oma said. "We need to clean out what we can, then bury it."

Mama stood and reached for one of her oldest cotton blouses. "I'll help, Ma." Next, she turned to Ita. "Watch over Georgie. Oma and I will be working in the toilet facilities."

Ita bit her lip, but nodded. She would be fine alone with Georgie. It wasn't like they were really alone anyway. The house was full of other people. Besides, Johan and his family were nearby.

An hour or two later, Mama and Oma returned from cleaning the toilet, just before Johan arrived, skidding to a stop in in the doorway of their room.

"Have you seen Kells?" Johan asked.

The fear in Johan's eyes and the urgency in his voice reached across the small space, making Ita's heart beat double time. "No. Where did you see him last?" She tried to remember if the dog had been in the yard when they'd come back to the house that morning.

"He was roped to the fence," Johan scrubbed his fingers through his red hair. "Did you see him, Georgie?"

"No," Georgie said with a frown. "Last time I did, he was with you."

Johan rubbed his forehead. "The Japanese military is rounding up all the pets. We have to either kill them or set them free outside of the camp." His voice cut off, and his face rumpled.

Ita had never seen Johan cry before. She jumped to her feet, Mama beside her.

"We'll find him," Mama said in a rush. "Tie can tell us what to do—she can speak to the Japanese soldiers."

As if summoned, Aunt Tie appeared. "I have news."

Ita was surprised to see Aunt Tie again so soon. Maybe the news was very bad?

"News about my dog?" Johan blurted out.

Aunt Tie frowned. "I know nothing about your dog."

Johan wiped at the tears on his face. "He's missing. The Japanese soldiers said we had to give them our pets, but I can't even find Kells."

Aunt Tie waved a hand. "Someone cut all the ropes holding animals earlier—probably trying to be helpful. If your dog was smart, he went to hide."

Hearing this, Johan scurried away, his footsteps pounding their way out of the house.

"Can I go with him?" Ita asked, grabbing Mama's hand.

"Can I go, too?" Georgie asked.

Mama squeezed Ita's hand. "I'll come with you, Ita. Georgie, wait here with Oma so we know where you are."

But Aunt Tie cut in. "Wait. Before you go chasing after some mangy dog, you need to know the new orders. All Dutch flags must be turned in today. Anything like military ribbons, medals, or certificates, and all pictures of the royal family must be gathered." She held up a basket that had a few items in it already.

"I'm making the rounds. You have about ten minutes." Aunt Tie turned to leave, then paused. "There is more," she added, her eyes narrowing. "And you are the first to hear it after me since it'll be announced at roll call. There is no Sabbath day, or day of rest, at the camp. Japanese tradition doesn't include a weekly day of rest since they believe spirituality should be a part of every day. And . . . our calendar will follow the Japanese calendar, and our time zone will be the same as Tokyo."

Mama and Oma didn't really seem surprised. They nodded at Aunt Tie, who quickly left the room. Ita only cared about helping Johan find his dog. "Now can we go?"

"We need to do as Tie says first," Oma said on a sigh.

Both she and Mama opened their stored suitcases, then dug through them, searching for the newest forbidden items on the list.

"What does changing the time zone mean, Mama?" Ita asked.

Mama paused from where she searched her suitcase. "Our clocks will move ahead two hours," she said. "Instead of getting up at six in the morning, it will be like four in the morning."

"What have you found?" Aunt Tie said, coming back into their room. Her sharp gaze took in everything at once.

It hadn't felt like ten minutes, Ita thought. More like *one* minute.

Mama had pulled out a folder from her suitcase. "I have . . ." She swallowed, then started again. "George's diplomas and advancement certificates."

Aunt Tie held out her hand. "Give them over. They must be turned in. Nothing is being destroyed that I know of. These will be labeled and kept in a safe place."

Ita might be young, but she could see that Mama didn't believe Aunt Tie. Should Ita say something? She could ask Aunt Tie to let them hide the diplomas. Papa had always said that Ita's birth had brought them many blessings. Papa was promoted to third engineer, and he was given a larger salary, in addition to a marriage allowance and a child allowance. These certificates represented all of that. And now Aunt Tie wanted to take them.

Ita knew it was really the Japanese army, but Aunt Tie seemed too eager to obey them.

Ita wanted to say something, but then she remembered the woman with the shorn-off hair. Would that happen to Aunt Tie if they didn't turn in the certificates? Or maybe Mama?

"Do you have anything, Mrs. Van Benten?" Aunt Tie asked.

"Only this." Oma handed over a framed photo of Queen Wilhelmina. It had been on her dresser as long as Ita could remember.

Aunt Tie set it in her basket.

"I have something to turn in," Ita said, her voice hitching. She hadn't told Mama about everything she'd brought. Now, she moved to the floor and opened her suitcase. Inside, was a very small shirt that Oma had once made for her teddy bear. Sewn into the shirt was a Dutch flag. She'd brought it to remember her teddy bear.

Ita held it up, and Aunt Tie tucked it into a basket with all the other things. She left without another word—taking Papa's certificates and the photograph of Queen Wilhelmina with her.

"Now can we help Johan?" Ita asked, impatience in her voice, though she couldn't help it.

"Of course." Mama nodded to Oma, who nodded back.

It was their silent agreement that Oma would watch over Georgie.

Rushing out of the room, Ita hurried around the makeshift beds and bundles of clothing until she reached the front door. There, she stopped on the veranda. Johan was striding toward the door, Kells in his arms.

The dog shivered, as if he'd been swimming in a lake or a pond.

"Is he hurt?" Ita asked.

"Just scared," Johan said through gritted teeth. His blue eyes were wild, desperate. He set Kells down on the veranda, but held the dog close. "What should I do?"

At that moment, Oma came out of the house, Georgie on her hip.

Ita had never seen Oma pay much attention to the dog, but right now, she leaned over and stroked Kells' long black fur. "He's such a good dog," Oma said. "He's caught several rats in the past few days. Did you notice?"

"He's a fast dog," Johan said.

"I think . . ." Oma paused. "That the Japanese will be very happy with such a good rat catcher. Maybe we can ask for special permission."

Johan looked down at his dog, then up at Oma. "Do you think they will approve it?" His voice cracked with desperation.

Oma tapped her chin. "We can ask. Let's see, we'll talk to Tie first, then if she agrees, we'll take it up with the Japanese."

Ita saw Mama close her eyes for a second. Did Mama think Aunt Tie would turn them down?

The group of them searched out Aunt Tie, and Oma did all the talking. Aunt Tie was quiet for a long time, then finally she said, "Exactly how many rats has this dog killed?"

Johan pushed out his chest. "Four yesterday and six the day before that. I threw them out past the garden. We can go and count them all."

Aunt Tie's lips pressed together. "No need. I will report to the commander and let you know. In the meantime, keep that dog out of sight."

Johan's face broke into a grin, but it was a wobbly grin, and Ita wondered if he might start crying again. She felt like crying.

Once they were back in the house, Georgie wanted Ita to lie next to him, so she climbed onto the bed. He seemed to know that she felt worried because he curled up next to her.

Soon, Georgie fell asleep, and Mama presented a book that Ita had never seen before.

"Where did you get this?" Ita asked. It was as big as the Bible that Oma had back at home. But this book was filled with pictures and short stories.

"I traded for it. You can learn to read from this," Mama said, a smile in her voice. She settled next to Ita and turned the pages. "See here, it's a rhyme that goes with this picture."

The edge of the page was torn, but Ita didn't care. It would be fun to learn to read. As she turned more pages, she found another child's scribbles. More pages were torn, but most of the book was fine.

"Thank you, Mama," Ita said. "I will be a good reader."

Mama's smile was proud. "We are going to put together a preschool group that you can be a part of."

"Can Georgie come?" Ita asked.

"When he's a little older," Mama said. She rested her hand on her stomach, and Ita wondered if she was feeling sick.

"Is the baby all right?" Ita asked.

"Yes," Mama said. "Put your hand here, and you can feel his kicking."

Mama had told Ita she thought the baby was a boy. Ita didn't know what she thought about that. She already had a brother, so she thought maybe it would be nice to have a little sister, too. Ita let Mama guide her hand, and sure enough, she felt a small movement. "Was that your stomach?"

"It was the baby," Mama confirmed.

Someone started crying in the house somewhere—it sounded like a baby. Maybe the one Ita had seen earlier. "Will our baby cry a lot?"

Mama patted Ita's hand. "It's hard to say. But our baby will have a lot of people to help care for him, so he might not cry very much."

"I can help care for him," Ita said. "But what if it's a girl?"

"Whatever the baby is, you'll be a wonderful big sister," Mama said in her quiet voice.

Even though there was plenty of noise going on outside their room, Mama herself was always quiet when Georgie was sleeping.

Ita wondered what it would be like having another person to share their room.

The rain started outside, first a few drops, then heavier and heavier. Ita hoped that just this once, roll call would be canceled.

But a few moments later, the siren blared, signaling the roll call. Aunt Tie's voice rang out through the house, adding in her warning.

Oma rose from across the room and held out her hand to Ita.

Mama lifted the sleepy Georgie from his nap. They didn't have umbrellas or raincoats. But they, along with the rest of the house residents, headed outside.

Johan walked alongside Ita, his shoulders hunched against the driving rain. He walked barefoot, as some of the children had started doing, although Ita still wore shoes. "I hope the Japanese will let me keep my dog."

Ita might be soaking wet, and tired, and hungry, but she didn't care about any of that. She hoped the Japanese army would let Kells stay, too.

They moved into their lines as the Japanese soldiers arrived. Rain pelted down on everyone, but everyone still called out their number and bowed. Once roll call was finished and approved, the commander who spoke Dutch approached their single line. He walked with Kano, one of the Japanese guards who was friendly to the children. Mama had said he'd even treated the women fairly.

"I have approved the petition to keep your dog," the commander said, his gaze boring into Johan's bowed head.

Kano had a pleased look in his eyes. Had he helped talk the commander into this?

Ita couldn't see Johan's expression because she was bowing too, but she felt his smile as if it were her own.

"As long as he is catching rats, you can keep him," the commander continued. "You must show your house leader how many rats the dog catches each day."

Johan must have nodded because the Japanese commander and Kano moved on.

Something good *could* happen at the camp, Ita decided. Even when other things were bad or hard, this was good.

Three days later, Ita attended preschool with some of the other children in the house, including two girls named Elly and Petra. Johan was too old for preschool, and Georgie was too young. They met on the rear veranda in the shade. Ina Venema smiled at everyone, then handed out half sheets of paper. Everyone got their own pencil too. The Japanese soldiers had allowed the preschool to use pencils and paper, though both had been banned throughout the rest of the camp.

Ita was learning that the Japanese troops didn't always like what the commander ordered. When the stricter commanders weren't around, the troops would smile and try to speak to the children in a friendly way. They'd teach them some Japanese. Simple things like colors and names of things.

"I had to break the pencils in half then sharpen them," Ina explained, "or there wouldn't be enough to go around."

Ita liked Ina's smile. It was pretty and bright.

"Now," Ina said, in a teacher voice, "We will start right from the beginning, with the letter A."

This was easy, Ita decided. She already knew how to write an A. But as she wrote out the large and small letter on the paper, her pencil wobbled because of the unevenness of the veranda underneath. She didn't like the wobbly line, and she looked over at Elly's paper.

Elly had made a line but was now erasing it. With a beautiful pink eraser that looked like it had never been used. Elly continued concentrating as she wrote.

But Ita stared at the eraser. It would be nice to have a new eraser so large. She wanted to ask if she could borrow it. But Ita also knew how hard it would be to give it back, so she turned her gaze back to her own paper and wrote a new A. This one wasn't perfect either, but it was better. She would have to write very carefully no matter what. Until they could leave camp and she could get her own eraser.

CHAPTER SEVENTEEN

"When we met my father, he was a mental wreck; we barely recognized him. He kept asking to see my hands because he heard that the [Japanese] had cut off my fingers. He kept touching my hands throughout the visit. This incident took place only two to three months after he was interned. What had they done to him? That was the last time I saw my father alive."

—FEITE POSTHUMUS, CAMP 7 IN AMBARAWA

GEORGE

"We need to put distance between us and Krawang as quickly as possible," Rouwenhorst said as their group stared at the island.

George tore his gaze away from the Japanese flag anchored on the shoreline, then he changed positions with one of the rowers. It wasn't long before he was putting his might into the oars.

"Wait," Bakker said. "They're sending boats out."

George glanced over his shoulder to see a couple of fishing boats launching from the shore.

"I don't see any Japanese on the boats," Vos commented.

"They're Indonesians," Rouwenhorst said. "Perhaps they have a message for us."

Whether or not there was a message, George didn't know how wise it was to risk hanging around. But the commander insisted they wait and hear out the villagers, whose boats were now closer.

Bakker moved to the front of the lifeboat to act as spokesperson once again.

The lifeboat bobbed in the sea as the fishing boats neared. There were three Indonesians in each boat, and their lively dark eyes locked onto the Dutch men. When the first boat halted several meters away, Bakker greeted them in Malay.

After an exchange of dialogue with the fishermen, Bakker told his comrades, "There are no Japanese in Krawang right now, but they come and go." He paused, looking back at the Indonesians floating not too far from them. "They don't dare bring us anything to sell or trade—because they fear the Japanese army will find out. But if we anchor here, they'll try to help in some way tonight."

"What? Are the Indonesians now our enemies?" Mulder murmured.

Rouwenhorst threw him a sharp glance, and Mulder fell silent.

"Tell them thank you for the offer," Rouwenhorst said. "We will anchor here tonight."

The night was quick to descend, and George found he couldn't sleep when it was his turn to rest. At least they had more room here on the fifteen-person lifeboat than they'd had on the original dinghy. He gazed at the moon above, partially covered with clouds, as its glow turned everything silvery.

The quiet around him made his thoughts drift to another time, when the same silvery moon had lit the way as he and Mary walked home after their first outing together in the Netherlands. Until then, George had only caught glimpses of Mary, or spoken to her when her mother was around. These had amounted to stuttered speech on his end, and a warm smile on her end. He'd never felt tongue-tied around a woman before, but he'd also never thought a woman as pretty as Mary.

But it wasn't only that she was pretty. When he saw her, something inside of his chest expanded. He felt lighter, and his pulse raced faster. And the times he wasn't at her home, wondering what she was doing every moment, he still thought about her. A couple of his mates had teased him for becoming lost in thought.

So he'd decided to do something about it on one of his rare nights off from the evening classes he was taking to earn his A diploma as a ship's engineer.

He hadn't been exactly prepared for her to say yes, and it had been impossible to hide his surprise.

Mary had laughed. "Are you asking me to dinner as a thank you for talking my mother into giving you the room? I don't need thanks. She's been happy with your neatness and on-time rent."

George blew out a slow breath, trying to calm both his thoughts and his pulse. "I'm asking you to dinner because I want to get to know you better."

He was gratified to see a pretty blush steal across her cheeks. Was she pleased, then? Did she want to get to know him, too?

They walked to the café, and the conversation felt more stilted than George would have liked. But when Mary asked him about his KPM experiences, that was easy to talk about. So easy, that the meal was cleared by the time he finished explaining his career and future ambitions.

"I'm sorry I talked so much," George said, after taking a sip from his glass. "Tonight was supposed to be about you. I still don't know anything about you except that you light up every room you walk into."

Mary's brows raised, but there was a smile in her eyes. "You say quite remarkable things to me, George Vischer."

For some reason, he liked how she'd used his whole name. "You're a remarkable person."

Mary laughed, a warm, light sound. One that George very much enjoyed. "Perhaps you should withhold judgment until you do get to know me."

George clasped his hands on the table and leaned forward. "Then tell me everything."

Mary laughed again, then she shook her head. "Not here. I think the host wants us out of here sooner rather than later. It's quite crowded, and there are people waiting outside."

He hadn't even noticed. The tables in the café were indeed filled.

"Come," Mary continued. "I'll tell you all about myself on the walk home. We'll take the long way."

George was satisfied with that. He paid, then escorted Mary out of the café, feeling gratified when she took his arm as they began the walk back to her home.

The night air had been perfect, the moon hung low, and the stars glittered. They walked and walked, and George didn't even know where they were going half the time. Mary told him about her love for horse riding and how she'd traveled about Europe with her cousins. Then she told him about her younger years, about her alcoholic father, Adrianus Van Benten, and how she and her mother had had to strike out on their own.

George listened carefully, not wanting to miss a thing she said. Her mother had been working multiple jobs, including at a small boardinghouse for students with a café on ground floor. Mary, when still in school, helped before and after school. Every now and then her mother's alcoholic ex-husband visited and stole money out of the cash register. Once Mary had finished school, she'd found her own job. But letting the room in their house helped as well. Her voice was full of bright ambition. Mary talked about her love for sewing, embroidery, and crocheting. She even painted. "I made the rug in your room."

George slowed his step at this and looked over at her. The streetlamps made everything glow in the night. "You made the rug?"

"Yes." Her smile was bright. "It's fun. I'll show you sometime how to do it."

George planned on holding her to that promise. The more he was around Mary Van Benten, the more he wanted to be around her.

"Watch out!" Rouwenhorst called.

George's eyes popped open. He'd been in the space between half asleep and half awake, reliving memories. His eyes adjusted to the dark in time to see a boat looming above them.

George was surprised that Vos had missed the larger boat on his watch duty, but the clouds had covered up the moon and stars, offering little light.

"Brace yourselves!" Rouwenhorst shouted.

George threw himself against the side of the lifeboat as impact was made. He winced at the sound of cracking wood. Was it their boat or the other boat?

A voice from the other ship called to them.

Thankfully it was in Malay and not Japanese.

Bakker scrambled to his feet, holding onto whatever he could to keep steady in the rocking lifeboat. "We're Dutch seamen," Bakker told the skipper. "We're looking for supplies."

The skipper and Bakker spoke back and forth for a few moments, then Bakker turned to everyone, triumph on his face. "The skipper is a good Samaritan. He apologizes for running into us, and he's having his cook prepare us a meal."

This certainly intrigued George. And within the hour, a large pot of *nasi goreng* was transferred over. The dish consisted of cooked rice fried with spices and bits of meat. It had become George's favorite meal ever, and there was plenty to go around for second helpings. Even better.

Bakker asked the skipper for advice on how to get supplies, and the skipper told him to go ashore Krawang in the morning and barter there.

"No Japanese are there right now," the skipper said. "If you go ashore, the Indonesians will sell to you."

"We'll wait out the rest of the night, then," Rouwenhorst said. "Sleep if you can. We're still anchored."

George settled as low as he could in the boat, shoulder to shoulder with his comrades. A few of them fell asleep right away, if their snoring was any indication. The snoring didn't bother George though—such a small thing to be bothered about after all they'd been through the past three weeks.

It seemed that a handful of moments had passed, when conversation awakened him. He snapped his eyes open. Dawn had broken across the sky in streaks of orange and pink, and Bakker was chatting across the narrow expanse of water with the skipper of the larger boat.

The other men munched on something like biscuits—obviously sent across by the skipper. When Vos saw that George was awake, he handed one over. After eating quickly, and filling part of his always empty stomach, George said, "What are the plans?"

"We're taking Bakker and Rouwenhorst ashore to attempt some trading," Vos said. "Then we plan to travel straight to Australia."

Once the sun was up, George and his comrades rowed closer to Krawang.

Bakker and Rouwenhorst climbed out and waded to shore. Villagers were already gathered, waiting for the seamen. George watched Bakker speak with more than one native, but it seemed that no deals were being made.

When Bakker and Rouwenhorst returned to the lifeboat, the news was as expected.

"They're cowed by the Japanese," Rouwenhorst announced. "They won't sell us anything."

Defeated, they rowed away from shore toward the larger boat to report back. Bakker repeated what had happened to the skipper. Then Bakker informed everyone, "The skipper has suggested that we try another village. But it's also on the shore of Java. He'll lead us there."

Rouwenhorst took a moment to make the decision. Java had been invaded, but it seemed that most of the islands had been invaded by now. They'd never make it to Australia without supplies. Finally, the commander agreed. "We can try that—but will we run into the same issue?"

Bakker shrugged. "We have to get supplies somehow."

"Very well," Rouwenhorst said. "We'll follow the skipper."

At least they had a plan, and any forward movement was positive in George's opinion. The skipper and his crew roped the lifeboat to the larger boat and sailed the Dutch seaman to the village he'd recommended.

There was a Japanese flag flying on that shoreline, of course, but with the encouragement of the skipper, Bakker said, "We'll try our luck. It's all we can do."

So they rowed to the beach and several of the men climbed out. George got out to stretch. His foot was still painful to walk on, but he was so used to the bothersome toe that he barely paid it heed.

Indonesians gathered around Bakker and Rouwenhorst. It seemed these villagers weren't hesitant about taking their money. George found a shady spot to sit for the duration. He was again on the same island as his family, and his thoughts turned to Mary and the children until Vos settled next to him.

"Where do you think the skipper went?" Vos asked. He'd gotten a hold of a cigarette and was taking long, slow drags on it.

George had never smoked as a habit, so he wasn't tempted. "I don't know if the skipper mentioned his destination."

Vos shrugged. "I don't think he did—at least Bakker never said anything. Why did he take off so fast though? He acted like he had plenty of time at his disposal last night and this morning. But now, suddenly, he's gone."

George shifted his gaze to the sea beyond. Vos was right. The skipper's boat was nowhere in sight. Had he brought them here on purpose, then dumped them off? Why?

The answer came moments later when George heard the rumble of a truck. Maybe more than one. That in and of itself shouldn't have put him on alert, but then the Indonesians suddenly scattered, taking their goods and wares with them. Leaving the Dutch seaman virtually abandoned on the beach.

George used his walking stick to haul himself up. "What's going on?" he murmured.

"Oh no." Vos stubbed out his cigarette. "We have the wrong kind of company."

The truck came into view then, barreling out of the tree line down the beach. The tires spun the sand as the truck lumbered forward, to the exact spot where the Indonesian merchants had been a handful of moments ago.

Then a second truck came into view.

Both trucks were filled with Japanese soldiers. There was no mistaking their olive-green uniforms or their rifles. This wouldn't be a friendly visit.

George's heart felt like it had stopped, then started again with a jolt. Nothing . . . nothing could be good about this.

The Japanese soldiers poured out of the trucks, their rifles lifted and aimed right at George and his comrades. None of the Dutch were armed. Not even George's walking stick could be mistaken for any sort of a weapon.

No one seemed to move, and no one dared speak, as the Japanese soldiers approached.

Rouwenhorst stepped forward, hands up.

The other seaman followed suit. George let go of his walking stick and raised both hands. His foot pulsated with the added pressure, but he swallowed back a groan.

"Do any of us speak Japanese?" Vos whispered as the soldiers neared, their dark gazes sweeping through the Dutch, as if counting them.

A couple of the men raised their hands, including George, but no one was fluent.

As it turned out, the language barrier didn't prevent the Japanese soldiers from making clear what they intended for the Dutch to do.

Climb into the trucks.

The orders were barked in Japanese, but the motions were clear. *Move. Move. Move.*

George picked up his walking stick and pointed to his swollen foot when a soldier approached him. The Japanese said something, which was clearly *no*, so George dropped the stick again. He hobbled along with the others toward the trucks.

Where had the Indonesian merchants gone? Had the skipper deliberately brought them here, knowing they'd be taken by the Japanese army? George would probably never know. Bakker moved to his side and assisted George into the truck. The other men were quickly ushered into the bed of the truck as well.

They sat shoulder to shoulder with a couple of Japanese guards sitting across from them. The second truck was equally filled and monitored.

"Where are you taking us?" Rouwenhorst said, in Dutch. Perhaps he was hoping one of the Japanese soldiers spoke Dutch.

No such luck. The soldier closest to Rouwenhorst gave an order, which none of them could understand.

They'd find out where they were being taken when they got there.

They all knew they were on Java, but where were they being taken? There were changes all over. George spotted Japanese flags where there should have been Dutch flags. The streets were quiet, and buildings seemed abandoned. Churches, schools, places of business . . . Japanese soldiers stood sentry at street corners.

Were the Dutch people tucked safely into their homes? What about Mary and the children? Were they able to buy enough food at the markets?

The afternoon heat blazed above, but George felt numb to the scorching of his head and shoulders. His worries about his family deepened. They'd reached Batavia and passed more than one open-air market. But he hadn't seen one Dutch woman, or one Dutch child . . . no Dutch at any of the markets. Where was everyone?

The trucks continued to lumber on until they reached Tandjong Priok. The very place where they'd launched their minesweeper nearly a month ago. Now, it seemed to be some sort of Japanese command center. Vehicles and troops were everywhere. Vehicles likely confiscated, but now bearing the Japanese flag emblem. And most of the soldiers were Japanese. Once in a while, George spotted an Indonesian man wearing a Japanese uniform.

When the trucks finally stopped, George felt as if his teeth had been rattled out of his jaw. Following orders in sharp bursts of commanding language, the Dutch seamen climbed out of the trucks and were herded into a former naval headquarters building. There, they were led into an office space. Desks and chairs were pushed aside, and several mats had been scattered across the floor.

Were they to sleep there? At least there was a connecting room with a latrine—something they hadn't had access to for weeks.

The seamen crowded into the office space, taking seats on chairs. Some sat on top of the desks. George and Vos took a mat each, sprawling out their legs. They were in the heart of Japanese occupation. What was being done with naval officers? Would they be political prisoners? Used for negotiation or strategy?

Left alone, the men began to talk.

Bakker moved to one of the windows and reported on what he saw going on outside.

"We need a newspaper," Vos commented. "What's going on in the war? What kind of hold does Japan have in Java? How long will it last?"

George had all of these same questions. "What about our families?" he added.

Bakker turned from the window, his brow furrowed. "Maybe we can send letters?"

That might be too much to hope for, George decided, especially if they were truly prisoners of war.

The door to the room opened, and all conversation ceased. Two Japanese soldiers walked in, both carrying rifles. One wore a chef's hat, which looked comical, because it was askew on top of the man's head.

"I am here to take your dinner order," the soldier said in English.

Why he thought the Dutch men spoke English was anyone's guess. George knew enough of it to understand, though, and so did many of the other men.

Rouwenhorst moved to his feet from where he'd been sitting cross-legged on a mat. "We would like whatever is available. We are not picky. Something simple that is not too much trouble will be just fine."

George's stomach grumbled at the thought of having something to eat soon.

"Simple?" the man repeated. "Do you not want mixed grill with plenty of meat?"

Rouwenhorst clasped his hands together. "We would love a mixed grill," he said. "We have been many weeks without such food. Anything would be very welcome."

The soldier-chef smiled. "Very well. We will begin preparing your dinner right away." He paused. "Oh, we have water and cigarettes for you. We hear that the Dutch like smoking very much."

A few of the men chuckled. George stared in disbelief as more soldiers brought in water and cigarettes. The Dutch seamen lined up, fetched the drinks, and most of them helped themselves to the cigarettes.

Soon, the room was filled with the lazy tendrils of smoke.

Perhaps being a prisoner of war wouldn't be so terrible. If only George knew how Mary was faring.

The next hour passed in a haze, helped by the cigarette smoke. But the men only smoked one—each of them understanding the value of saving something for later. George's stomach complained, and he wondered how long it would take for the Japanese chef to cook dinner. Another hour passed, then another.

Finally, at least four hours after the chef had asked for their dinner orders, he arrived. Banging into the room with a couple of other soldiers, they brought in a pot of rice and some sort of fish stew.

George tried to hide his disappointment, as all the other men were likely doing. Food was food, and as long as it hadn't been contaminated, they'd eat it.

CHAPTER EIGHTEEN

"At night the inmates would sleep on elevated bamboo platforms,
about three feet above the muddy floor, crowded together
like sardines and placed head-to-feet. They were constantly
pestered by lice, leeches, flies, mosquitoes and fleas."

—ANDREW A. VAN DYK, CIHAPIT CAMP

GEORGE

"On your feet," someone ordered.

George opened his eyes and focused on the ceiling above. Memories crashed through him. The capture on the island, the Japanese soldiers, sleeping on a mat on the floor. All around him, his comrades were rising from their sleeping places, shuffling to the door of the room they'd been locked into.

Soft gray marked the windows to the outside, so it must be before dawn.

George shifted to his knees, wincing at the pain in his foot, more out of habit than an increase in pain. It always hurt. Always throbbed. It just was. He had no walking stick, so he hobbled to join his comrades, who'd formed a haphazard line at the door.

Vos nodded to him.

"What's happening?" George whispered.

"Bakker said something about hearing the word *Kempeitai*," Vos said. "Japanese military police."

"Are we coming back here?"

Vos shrugged.

They were marched out of the building and into a cool morning flushed with the first rays of the sun. It had rained the night before, and puddles clung to every available patch of ground that wasn't a roadway. They walked for over an hour as the sun rose. George had thought his foot was uncomfortable before—now it absolutely seethed.

The Japanese soldiers who marched them were quiet and watchful. George wondered about these young men's lives before the war, before they were conscripted into the Japanese imperial army. He was older than all of them, and it was a strange thing to be guarded over by men who were so much younger. But they were the ones with the weapons and control over Java.

"Where is everybody?" Vos murmured.

The roads were empty save for vehicles driven by Japanese soldiers. Occasionally a rickshaw passed by them, manned by an Indonesian, but no eye contact was made. The Indonesians obviously didn't want any interaction with the Dutch prisoners, or any attention from the Japanese either.

"Where are we going?"

"I don't know." George gazed at the rows of shops they walked past. Many of them were owned by Chinese people. This area of Batavia was frequently called Chinatown. But now, the place was very quiet. Almost like it had been abandoned too.

The next road they turned onto almost brought George up short.

An entire section of housing had been fenced off. It looked like someone had outlined a piece of the neighborhood and erected a wall. They slowed as they approached the gate.

Beyond the gate, George saw chaos—Japanese soldiers rushed around like ants without a queen. Trucks rattled. A Japanese voice came through a megaphone. Targets had been constructed, forming a firing range, and the report of rifle fire echoed all the way up to the clear sky. To the side of the main road leading through the camp, Dutch men and boys were crouched over bowls of food. Just sitting on the neighborhood road. Eating with their fingers.

Since George and his comrades hadn't been fed any breakfast, he could see how all formalities might be pushed aside if one was hungry enough. He'd spent the past month eating anything edible.

They were guided along the inside of the fence, then ushered into a small room that was barely large enough to fit their group. Two other men were already in there. Dutch civilians. And they looked like they'd been sitting in the room for a while. It was a couple of weeks into the war, but these two looked like they hadn't slept for a year. Their bodies were unwashed, and their clothing dingy, and their hair scraggly. In the corner sat a bucket that served as a latrine, given the stench.

George's empty stomach tightened, and he tried not to breathe through his nose.

With no explanation, the door was shut and barred from the outside.

Prison. This was the prison. And George had just been locked inside.

"Welcome to Glodok Prison," one of the civilians said, eyeing the new group of men. "Where are you from?"

George moved to the ground to sit since his foot needed some relief. Others sat, while the remaining men stood, leaning against the wall.

Rouwenhorst told the other prisoners a few basics, and George looked over. He recognized them.

"Ed? Jacques?" Eduard and Jacques were brothers, although Eduard was a long, skinny fellow, and Jacques was stocky.

"George?" Eduard said, disbelief in his tone. "I didn't recognize you."

Jacques was staring as well. "You look . . . different."

George gave a dry chuckle. "We've had a few adventures."

"You've been gone since right after the battle of the Java Sea?" Eduard asked.

"That's correct," Rouwenhorst said. "What's the news on the war-front? Are the Allies working to liberate Java?"

The two prisoners looked at each other, then Eduard refocused on Rouwenhorst. "You know nothing, do you?"

George leaned forward and blurted, "What don't we know?"

"The Royal Netherlands East Indies government surrendered on March 8," Eduard said in the silent room. "Japan not only occupies Java, but they're in control of the entire Netherlands East Indies."

"But . . ." Bakker began. "Where is everyone? What happened to the navy, the army, the civilians? The women and children?"

These were all questions currently plaguing George as well. Images of the deserted neighborhoods and abandoned shops rushed through his mind. He'd seen no Dutch women. And the Dutch men and boys he'd seen behind the fence, crouched in the dirt, now haunted his mind.

"Everyone was rounded up and put into prison camps," Jacques said in a hollow tone. "Women and children together, and men and older boys in other camps. Neighborhoods have been quartered off, and individuals assigned housing. This house is now an extension of the Glodok Prison Camp."

Eduard scoffed. "If you can call it *housing*. Dozens of men are in a single house—each lucky enough to call one corner his own."

Jacques grimaced. "I'd rather be out there, than in *here*."

"*Why* are you in here?" Bakker asked the question everyone had been thinking.

The two men looked at each other. "It seems we both had the same idea to attempt an escape while working the fields outside the walls."

Jacques folded his arms. "Our Japanese guard was in the habit of taking afternoon naps. I guess we were both too tempted to leave."

Eduard rubbed at his scraggly mop of hair. "Not that we had any-where to go, or anyone to hide us. The Japanese soldiers regularly scour houses, looking for any who might be hiding. Even the lighter-skinned Indos are brought here. Right now, pale skin will get you locked up, no matter your heritage."

"And the rest of the Indonesian men are being forced into Japanese military training," Jacques continued. "Those who refuse are being brought into the camps too."

"Camps," Rouwenhorst echoed. "How many camps are there?"

Eduard and Jacques both shrugged. "Dozens? Hundreds? We have no way of knowing."

"Do the Allies know about this?" Bakker asked.

"Another question we have no answer to," Eduard said. "If they do, it's wartime. We're occupied. End of story, for now. We'd all heard about the Japanese POW camps, and now we're living in one."

George leaned his head back against the wall. *Where is Mary?* he wondered. If what his friends were saying was true, she and the children, along with Oma, were in a camp. Was she eating food out of a bowl while sitting on a road? How was she coping with her pregnancy?

He hated being trapped here. He hated feeling so helpless. If he was to be on Java, trapped like a monkey in a cage, he wanted to be with his wife.

The prison cell grew in heat and stench as the men had no choice but to relieve themselves in the small space. The windows were open, but there was no breeze to bring respite. As the hours ticked by, the cell became hotter and more stifling.

George closed his eyes as the men discussed some of the particulars of the camp, like bowing to the Japanese soldiers, attending roll call and saying their assigned number in Japanese, learning the Japanese national anthem, being allotted jobs such as street cleaning and kitchen duty, living in cramped and unsanitary conditions . . . it was all like a terrible dream.

George knew where he was. In Glodok. In a prison. But the rest didn't seem real.

How could his wife be living like this too? How was she dealing with their young children and her aging mother? What about his sister, Tie? How was she faring?

Was Mary exhausted like he was? The conversation of the men

buzzed around him, indistinct, as he allowed his mind to wander, mostly focused on Mary. He'd known after their first date that she was the type of woman he wanted to marry. But he'd also known he needed to be patient. She needed time to warm up to the idea, to get to know him.

Mary's mother was a hardworking, devoted woman, with talents and generosity that impressed him. It was clear that Mary was much like her mother, despite any influence the character of her father had provided.

Whenever George had free time, he'd offered to help fix anything in the yard or house. Mrs. Van Benten had no trouble putting him to work and always showed her gratitude through cooking him something delicious. He got used to the lifestyle quickly, but as the date of his examination neared, he knew he'd have to say goodbye. He'd be heading to the Netherlands East Indies as a member of the KPM crew. Away from Mary. Away from the woman he'd fallen in love with.

The night before his examination he asked Mary to dinner, but he didn't want to talk in a crowded café surrounded by other people. So they walked to an out-of-the-way place, and George purchased a meal they could take with them for a sort of picnic. When they found a bench along the waterfront, the nerves hit George full force. He planned to tell Mary what his feelings were, but he had no idea if she'd reciprocate them. And what if this whole evening turned out to be a permanent goodbye?

They ate together, chatting about Mary's day and George's studying for the examination. Then Mary looked over at him and directly asked, "What are your plans after the exam? Will you set sail soon?"

This was the opening that George needed to take. He cleared his throat and said, "I leave in three days for the Netherlands East Indies."

Mary's eyes widened. "Only three days?"

George had told Mrs. Van Benten that morning but had asked her to let him tell Mary himself.

"Yes, three days," he said, his pulse zipping along. "That's why I need to tell you something important. Something that can't wait any longer."

Mary's gaze fell to her hands in her lap, and George reached out and placed a hand on top of hers.

"I don't know if this timing is very good or very bad, but I'm hoping you'll agree to marry me." Nerves thrummed through him. "I love you, Mary, and there's no one else I'd rather be with."

She lifted her eyes then, and he knew that this moment, the truth would be shown to him.

Her eyes glimmered with tears, but she was smiling.

"I don't have a home yet, or anything to my name," he said, "but I hope we can build all of that together—"

She cut him off with a kiss.

And George welcomed it with his whole heart.

A clatter made George flinch out of his daydreaming. Someone was knocking on a door. A prison door. At Glodok. George opened his eyes to see two Japanese soldiers enter. They motioned for the Dutch seamen to come with them.

Anywhere but here sounded good to George. They were led into another part of the building and made to stand before a table. Other soldiers lined the walls, their weapons pointed at the prisoners. When another Japanese man entered, it was obvious that he was a high-ranking official due to the medals on his khaki officer's uniform.

Another man, a Dutch civilian, entered as well, and stood a few feet from the commander. It turned out that he'd be the interpreter. Adjusting his glasses, he began, "Identify yourselves and state how you came to be in the village where you were picked up."

What would their own commanding officer, Captain Rouwenhorst, reveal to their enemy? George wondered.

When Rouwenhorst spoke to the interpreter, he said nothing about their mission to Australia. He only mentioned that their minesweeper had been torpedoed, and they were trying to find a safe place to land.

"You were not evading the Japanese army?" the interpreter questioned.

"It is true that we didn't want to be put into prison," Rouwenhorst said.

That was at least the partial truth, and George would have to remember Rouwenhorst's answers if he were ever to be questioned alone.

The commander seemed to accept Rouwenhorst's replies, though, because the man stood and walked among the Dutch seamen, looking each man up and down. He pointed at a few of the men, including George, and said something in Japanese.

The interpreter translated, "You men are going to the hospital."

George could have collapsed in relief. A hospital could treat his foot and the festering wounds of his comrades.

There wasn't time to say goodbye or wonder about their comrades' fate before George, Mulder, and a couple of others were led out of the building. Once again, George was struck with the atmosphere of the camp. He felt dozens of pairs of eyes upon him from the Dutch men and boys, but no one spoke to them.

He searched the eyes that connected with his, looking for answers, for information, but all he saw were more questions. He didn't recognize anyone from Laan Trivelli.

The "hospital" turned out to be a house converted into a medical center. George could see right away that it wasn't fully functional, but the doctors were Dutch so it was a relief to be able to speak to them. Still, George was careful about what he told them about the sea voyage. He also didn't mention that their destination had been Australia.

Once his foot was drained and disinfected, he was given a round of antibiotics. The doctor told him that it was way too late to stitch up the gash on his toe, so he'd have to live with the split, heart-shaped scar. That was the last thing that George was worried about.

"Can you tell me about the women's camps?" George asked the doctor. "Are they being taken care of?"

The doctor studied George for a moment. "Do you have family there?"

"My wife and two children," George said. "At least I think so. I was at sea when the camps were formed. My mother-in-law should also be with them. I don't know what's happened to my sister either." He lowered his voice. "My wife is pregnant. About five months along."

"I see," the doctor said. "There is more than one women's camp in Batavia and throughout Java. The one closest to us is called Tjideng. Sometimes we can see women from the camp traveling outside the gates. Groups of them visit the Indonesian markets."

With George's foot treated, and the possibility of seeing Mary, new hope had flooded back.

"Is there a list of names? A way to find out where my wife was taken?"

The doctor hesitated, then after a quick glance about the hospital room, he said, "The Japanese army takes excellent records. It might be possible to discover where your wife is interned."

CHAPTER NINETEEN

"My 12-year-old niece came down with jaundice and there was neither medicine nor a doctor in the camp. My mother, who cared for Maud, was advised by a fellow prisoner to feed her three head lice in the morning with *pisang mas*, a certain variety of banana. She tried the remedy, and the result was unbelievable: Maud was cured within one week."

—MATHILDE PONDER-VAN KEMPEN, GEBOG CAMP

MARY

"Tenko!" the Japanese commander called out.

"Ichi," Tie said, starting off the count for their row.

Mary spoke next, and said, "ni"—number two. Then Ita said, "san," and Georgie, "shi."

When their group had counted off, and the Japanese soldiers approved their roll call, the commander strode among the rows.

The Dutch women and children were still bent at the waist, still holding their bowed poses, until otherwise told. Mary kept her arms stiffly at her sides, even though perspiration trickled down her neck, making her itch. If someone didn't bow low enough, then roll call would start over, which only meant more hours beneath the hot sun. Something she didn't want Oma or her children to experience.

Over the past couple of months, punishments had been doled out at roll call if someone failed to bow deeply enough or if someone missed their number or if someone was found absent and the house residents didn't report it. And for so many other reasons. Interestingly enough, Mary had noticed that some of the Japanese soldiers worked to be very kind to the children in camp. This was especially true of a man named Kano, who oversaw their sector. But most soldiers regarded the adult Dutch women with disdain.

Mary and her friends at camp had discussed this more than once, and they agreed that European women were offensive to the Japanese men, in both manner and dress. And, of course, personality.

The more outspoken women had to use restraint to remain as docile as possible. Otherwise, consequences could be brutal. Women had been lectured and beaten and imprisoned—their hair shorn to shame them for disobedience.

Two rows over, one woman wore a scarf about her head. Her hair had been shorn off the week before, and Claudia had cut off a lock of her own hair so that the woman could tuck a false set of bangs into the scarf. If someone didn't know what had happened to her, they might think she still had a full head of hair.

Another bead of perspiration escaped Mary's hairline and ran along her nose, making her glasses loose on the bridge of her nose. She listened to the murmur of the Japanese soldiers as they talked about the numbers in roll call. Why it took so long, Mary didn't know. The count was always the same, morning and night.

A sigh escaped Oma behind Mary, and she tilted her head a bit to see her mother. "Are you all right?" she whispered as quietly as possible.

"I'm dizzy," Oma whispered back.

"Can you lean on me, Ma?" Mary asked.

Oma shuffled a step forward and placed a hand on the small of Mary's back. If the soldiers noticed, what would be their punishment?

Mary was worried, yes, but she also knew they were lucky in this quadrant. The Dutch-speaking commander was easier to communicate with, and the soldiers who worked beneath him were strict, but not cruel.

There was cruelty in other parts of the camp. Mary's stomach twisted to think of it. It seemed Tie was doing a stellar job of being their house leader. The Japanese commander listened to her. One example was Johan's dog. The dog seemed to know he'd been granted a reprieve and had upped his fetching skills, catching many rats.

Mary's stomach churned again. She'd heard stories of women cooking rats over unofficial fires behind their houses. Mary hoped things wouldn't come to that, but the food supply seemed to be more scant each week. There hadn't been any seaweed brought in on the latest trucks, and she couldn't remember the last time she'd had a piece of fruit.

"You may stand!" the commander called in Dutch. "New announcement."

With Oma standing upright, Mary hoped her mother felt better. Less dizzy.

The crunch of the commander's boots on the road echoed with his words. "Today you will all move houses. We have more people arriving at our camp and room needs to be made."

Mary didn't want to move houses, but maybe they'd have a bigger room? Or maybe the toilet in the new house would be working? That would make it worth it. They'd had to dig a trench for sanitation and assign work groups to clean it out each day by carrying buckets to the ditch that ran under the front gates. The mess and stench were awful. So many of them had been sick with fever, vomiting, and bloody diarrhea from dysentery. Once diagnosed, the person had to quarantine in the medical building since it was highly contagious.

Mary glanced to her side, and her gaze met Claudia's very briefly. The woman gave her a small nod. Mary knew they were thinking the same thing and both hoping that their families would be moved to the same house.

"You will take your personal belongings and suitcases," the commander continued to boom. "No furniture. That will all stay in the original house."

Mary mentally itemized their belongings. After so many things had been confiscated, she'd had little to trade at the outside markets. Once a week, the Japanese military allowed women to go to the Indonesian markets. Mary rode her bike and traded what she could, but everything was getting scarcer or more expensive. She might have to eventually trade in her bike.

Once, while on the way to the market, Claudia had suggested they make a run for it. Leave the camp and everything behind. But both women knew it wasn't an option. There was nowhere to go. Their own homes were occupied by either Japanese or Indonesians now. And where else could they take care of their children? Live in the jungled mountains and hunt for their food?

Mary was half-way through her pregnancy but she already felt like she was closer to the end. Her energy was depleted from the lack of food and decent rest. She was still hoarding an emergency supply of food— mostly in the jury-rigged false bottom of the baby pram, of all places— to be used if times grew more desperate. The peanut plants she'd planted had yet to produce.

What would it be like when she had an extra mouth to feed? The days were filled with rotating through jobs at the kitchens, visiting the medical center, knitting socks for the guards or repairing uniforms, cleaning up . . . with little to eat and much to worry about. And the nights were filled with listening to everyone else's families—the crying, the complaining, the sicknesses.

Not to mention the bed bugs. And the lice.

Half the house had lice, and Mary knew it was only a matter of time before it reached her family. Perhaps she should look forward to the move. When they were excused from roll call, the women's conversations buzzed about them, as everyone speculated where they'd have to move to.

It seemed Tie had already been given the answer, and when they reached the house, she called a meeting on the veranda. "We're moving three houses that way," she said, pointing. "We will still be in the same sector."

This was good news, Mary decided. They'd have the same Dutch-speaking commander.

"Where are the people in that house going?" Claudia asked, from someplace in the back of the group.

"Nowhere," Tie said, a deep line making a path between her brows. "They are making room for us. Like the commander said, bring your most personal belongings. There won't be room for more." She gave a half smile that wasn't much of a smile at all. "First to arrive will be the first to choose a place."

If that didn't get everyone in action, nothing else would.

Mary knew she was saying goodbye to a private room.

She rushed in with the others, gripping Georgie by the hand. Ita was with Oma. And when they reached their room, Oma said, "I will help with the children's things. You work on our suitcases."

Mary did so, and as she was adding a few more tins of food to the small stash in the baby pram, Tie came into the room. One more second and she wouldn't have seen the food.

"Hand that over," Tie said, stretching out her hand. "You know the rules. If you're caught by someone else, then you'll pay the consequences."

"They're for the children," Mary said in a low voice. She didn't want to attract the attention of any of the other house residents. "Your own niece and nephew. We've had them all this time, in case of an emergency."

Tie's jaw clamped tight, and her dark brown gaze remained steady.

"Hand them over," Oma murmured. "God will provide."

Mary wanted to argue with her mother. So far, they had eaten regularly, although everyone had lost weight. But Tie was literally taking food from children, and Mary knew she wouldn't be turning it in—but stashing it for her own use.

Mary handed over the tins. Anger kindled in her stomach, churning like a boiling pot. She was too angry to speak, so she returned to her packing, as tears burned hot in her eyes.

"Mama?" Georgie moved off the bed where he'd been watching everyone pack and looped his arm through hers. "I'm not hungry."

That dear boy . . . Mary blinked back the tears, letting the fury inside of her cool, and kissed the top of her boy's head. "All will be well, Georgie. We're together, and that's what matters." She found Ita watching her too. These children were so vulnerable, and they depended so much on her. She would protect them at all costs, even from their own aunt, if needed.

"Everyone ready?" Mary asked in a bright voice. "We'll take the cot and see if we're allowed to keep it."

By the time they reached the yard outside, most of the other women were packed up and heading to their new location. Children tagged along, carrying belongings. Mary saw Claudia and her children, and they fell into step together. Ahead of them, someone had procured a flatbed trailer on wheels, and it was loaded with belongings.

"You can add your things here, if you want," one of the women called out, motioning to Mary and Claudia.

"Oh, thank you." Mary loaded the cot and the suitcases onto the flatbed with the help of Ita. "Now, help push, children. We'll come back for the baby pram."

"I'll push the bike," Oma offered.

Everyone shuffled around, and soon Mary was pushing the flatbed, with Georgie taking position on the side. Claudia, Johan, and Willy joined in. Kells trotted alongside of them, happy to be on an adventure. Mary hoped the family could keep their dog for a good long time.

As they heaved the trailer forward, Georgie stumbled, and before anyone could stop the trailer, the back wheel went over his foot.

"Oh no," Mary gasped, reaching for him.

He gripped his foot and cried in pain. Oma left the bike and dropped to her knees.

"Let me see it, Georgie," she said over his crying. "Can you be a brave boy and let me take off your shoe?"

He nodded, his crying calming into hiccups. The boy winced as

Oma touched his foot and ankle, then her gaze met Mary's. "I'll take him to the medical center to have it looked at."

"I can, Ma," Mary said.

But Oma put a hand on her arm. "You need to figure out where we'll settle, and I think Georgie will be fine."

"Can I go with them?" Ita asked.

But Mary knew she didn't want both of her children exposed to the sick ward. "I need you to help me."

Ita nodded, biting her trembling lip.

Mary kissed Georgie before Oma loaded him onto the bike and wheeled him away.

Tie had been right. The house they'd been assigned to was already occupied. Everything was already cramped, but now, space would be cut in half. Tie commandeered a corner in the front room for herself. Claudia and her family veered toward the kitchen, and Mary headed along the main hallway. Every bedroom was filled, and the women inside didn't look happy to be accommodating more.

The last bedroom was occupied by an older woman with two young children. She'd moved their things over already, as if waiting to help out. This gave Mary a measure of hope. "We are four people, soon to be five," Mary said. "Can we share?"

"We are moving out," the older woman said. She was probably around Oma's age, but her face had much deeper lines. "I was waiting until someone who really needed the room came along, and you look like you need it."

Mary stared at the woman. "But where will you go?"

"We will manage. Come, children."

"Wait," Mary said. "What are your names?"

"My name is Hetty, and these are my grandchildren, Elly and Petra."

The girls smiled at Ita, who smiled back.

"And their mother?" Mary ventured to ask.

But the woman named Hetty glanced at the two girls, then gave a shake of her head, indicating she didn't want to say something in front of the children. Had something happened to their mother? Maybe Mary would find out later. She thanked Hetty again. Mary had found that, as a whole, most of the women were willing to help each other and share what little resources they had.

As they settled in, a woman appeared at their doorway. "I found kerosene. Does anyone in your family have lice?"

"Not right now," Mary said. "But thank you."

The woman nodded and moved on.

When Oma returned with Georgie, he was in much better spirits. Nothing had been broken, but some bruising was starting to show. Mary made him as comfortable as possible in the cot she'd set up.

Later that evening, Claudia came into the cramped quarters. She'd been working a shift in the medical center. She'd been assigned there since she'd had some nursing training before she'd married Willem. Her face was flushed in the dim lighting of the setting sun. "Come with me," she said in an urgent tone.

Mary double-checked that Ita and Georgie were occupied with Oma, then she followed Claudia into the hallway. Residents had set up along one edge of the hall, so they picked their way through until they reached the yard.

Claudia grasped Mary's hands. "One of the doctors was able to send a letter to another doctor at the Glodok prison camp for men."

Mary tightened her grip. She knew the camp. It was built behind the prison. On her way to the market, she sometimes saw the men from Glodok working in the fields, or repairing a road. They'd even marched past Tjideng before on their way to their field work. Neat rows of men overseen by the Japanese soldiers.

"Our husbands are there," Claudia said in a fierce whisper. "They're *alive*. They are in Glodok."

Mary stared at her friend as questions piled up in her mind and threatened to teeter. How . . . when . . . Her husband and Mr. Vos had been on their way to Australia. They were supposed to be helping the

Allies. They were supposed to be fighting this war. This all meant . . . "They were captured?"

"Yes, they must have been." Claudia's eyes shone with new tears. "I don't know what happened. Did they ever get out of Java in the first place? How long have they been in Glodok?"

Mary's knees felt like water, and she moved to the veranda steps, where she sat down.

Claudia joined her. "I have more news. Tomorrow is a field day, which means our husbands might be among those working in the fields."

Mary felt like she was in a dream. George was so close. It had been verified, right? Was this all real?

"You might be able to see them on your way to the market."

Mary looked over at Claudia. "We should go together."

"I'm on shift tomorrow," Claudia said, regret in her tone. "If you see Willem, though, tell him hello and that I love him."

Mary smiled at this. Her chest had expanded and her heart felt like it would soar right out. She doubted that she'd be able to talk to either of their husbands if she saw them. But, oh, how wonderful it would be to catch a glimpse.

"I will try," Mary said. "I'll do everything in my power."

Claudia laughed, although it sounded a bit like a sob too. She hugged Mary fiercely. "How will I ever sleep?"

Mary laughed too, tears in her eyes—tears of relief and hope. "How will I?"

Tomorrow, she thought . . . she might see George. Or even Willem. Maybe both. When she returned to the house, it was all she could do to keep the news to herself while the children were awake. She didn't want to give them false hope, and she wouldn't be able to answer their questions anyway.

But when all was quiet, and all the lights were out through the entire house, Mary whispered the good news to her mother. They fell asleep with their hands clasped tightly together.

The morning couldn't come soon enough, and as soon as the rising sun changed the sky from a dull gray to a lavender, Mary was up, thinking about the day.

Morning roll call had never seemed so easy. Even though they were made to bow for longer than normal since some of the rows had to be recounted, Mary didn't mind. As long as Oma was handling it all right, everything was fine. Besides, today she might see her husband.

After their meal of watery rice, Mary told Ita it was time to go to the market.

"What are we trading today?" Ita asked.

"One of my dresses," Mary said, and patted the bag slung over her shoulder with the dress inside. It was her oldest one, but even so, every bit of clothing was precious. Dresses were not practical in this place of constant work and insects.

So, with a cheerful farewell to Oma, Mary and Ita set off on the bike, Ita sitting on the rack above the back wheel and hanging onto Mary's waist. They stopped at the gate and explained their errand. The Japanese guards recorded the time and their names and their house sector.

Mary rode slowly along the road, toward the Indonesian market that was only about a kilometer from the camp. There, in the distance, was the field where the men of Glodok sometimes worked. No one was there.

Mary's heart fell. Would she have to wait longer?

Once at the market, they wandered among the stalls and merchants. There were so many things that Mary would love to trade for. Mostly the food. They paused in front of a vendor selling satay—seasoned meat grilled on skewers. Just the spicy, warm smell made her mouth water. But Mary couldn't afford much, and Ita became impatient as Mary dallied for more than an hour.

"Are you not going to get anything, Mama?"

"Of course I am." Mary moved to the booth that contained a selection of fruit. She chose a few Java plums. There was some risk that the fruit would be confiscated, and if she was allowed to keep the plums, she couldn't very well keep them for only her family. She'd have to share.

But a little fruit was better than no fruit. So, she traded her dress for six plums.

As they rode along the road back toward camp, she let Rita eat one of the plums. Mary slowed the bike when she saw men in the fields. Hope buzzed through her. Was one of the men George?

Japanese soldiers guarded the prisoners, but as Mary turned her bike off the road and headed toward the fields, no one stopped her.

"Where are we going?" Ita asked, her voice rising in pitch.

"I'm going to see if your papa is working with these men."

Ita didn't answer for a moment, but her hold tightened on Mary's waist. Then Ita called, "I see him!"

"Where?" Mary slowed the bike, and stopped, scanning the men.

Ita pointed with one arm, and sure enough . . . George was about a half dozen meters away, bent over as he tilled the ground, but there was no mistaking his profile.

Mary couldn't move. She felt like the earth was rolling beneath her feet. Her husband was here, on Java, and he was alive.

CHAPTER TWENTY

"I celebrated my seventeenth birthday in April. Bamboo fencing in Cihapit kept us inside, and there was only one gate. In the beginning, I would duck under the perimeter fence with friends to explore the outside world. We would return the same way or use a sewage culvert inside camp. We were usually loaded down with food, bacon being especially high on the wish list. But soon such escapades became very risky. Once, as we returned from a scavenging trip, the Japanese guards were waiting for us at the inlet of the culvert. I was hit on my face with a flashlight and taken to the camp jail with two of my friends."

—MARIA MCFADDEN-BEEK, CIHAPIT CAMP

RITA

"Papa!" Ita called out. She probably should be quiet so that the Japanese soldiers wouldn't get mad, but she couldn't help it.

Mama grasped her hand and tugged her close. They stood on the edge of the field, waiting for Papa to see them. Several men had looked over at them, and that's when Ita realized many of them were probably fathers too.

Then Papa lifted his head. He was still bent partway over, but as soon as he saw Ita, he straightened to his full height. Papa looked different, yet the same. His hair was longer than she remembered it, and he wore a beard. But his eyes were the very same—brown like the dark earth he was digging in.

That's when she noticed he was much thinner than she'd ever seen him. Papa had always been a strong man and could lift anything he wanted to. His broad shoulders were still wide, but his clothing was nothing Ita had ever seen him wear before. Maybe the loose shorts and soiled shirt weren't his at all.

Ita lifted her hand and waved, and Papa waved back. The smile on his face was brief and gone in a snap after he looked over at one of the Japanese guards. Then Papa set back to work. Digging up rows of dirt.

"Will the soldiers let us talk to him?" Ita asked. One soldier looked like he was half asleep as he sat against a parked truck.

"I don't know," Mama said in a quiet voice. But she didn't tug Ita away, which told her that there might be hope.

As the men worked, Ita continued to watch with her mother. From time to time, Papa would look over. He'd either smile or nod. Then he'd return to his digging. Ita's stomach grumbled. She was hungry again, and she wondered how long they'd been watching Papa work. Had it been hours or minutes? Could second mealtime be nearing? What would happen if they missed it? When the wind picked up and the clouds rolled in some time later, Ita wondered if the men would have to keep working in the rain.

Soon the soldiers' shouted orders were carried over the wind, and the men moved toward waiting trucks to take them back to their camp.

Mama's grip tightened on Ita's hand as Papa carried his shovel toward the truck, walking slower than the rest of the men. He stopped and bowed to one of the soldiers, then spoke to the Japanese man, who then looked over at Ita.

Holding her breath, Ita wondered what Papa was saying—and what language were they speaking? The soldier nodded. Papa bowed again, then he waved them over.

"Let's go." Mama hurried toward Papa.

Ita almost had to run to keep up, but it was easy to run when excited, even if she was very hungry. The other men had all climbed into the truck, but they smiled, and no one complained about the delay.

The Japanese guard watched Papa and Mama speak in quiet whispers that Ita couldn't hear, but she was happy to know her father was alive and safe. It wasn't very long before the truck started, its rumbling engine like an alarm clock signaling that time was up.

The Japanese guard said something to Papa that Ita couldn't understand. But Papa seemed to understand the Japanese, and he turned toward them with a smile. "The guard says you can come to Glodok for a visit. We can talk more."

"Truly?" Mama's voice sounded surprised.

Ita was surprised too.

But the guard indicated to Mama that she could follow their truck to the gates. Ita hurried with Mama to climb back onto the bike, and they headed after the truck. It wasn't far, or at least it didn't seem far since Ita's heart was full of excitement.

The rain hadn't started yet. With the clouds covering the sun, it was hard to guess what time it might be. Ita was so hungry she felt it had to be time for second meal . . . or later. Would Oma and Georgie worry about them if they took too long at Glodok? Would they make it back in time for roll call? Ita didn't want to be punished, but she was excited to spend more time with Papa.

Once they reached the gates, the truck drove in, and they followed on the bike. The gates closed, and another guard stopped them.

"We're with the truck," Mama explained to the guard in Dutch, pointing toward the truck that had continued driving someplace into the camp.

Where was the truck going? Weren't they supposed to keep following? Ita could see Papa's face watching them with his eyebrows pulled down. There were some other prisoners across the open area. Men and older boys. No women or younger children.

The guard replied in Japanese, and he didn't look happy. Two other guards arrived, and they began to argue with each other.

Ita wanted to run after Papa's truck, but these angry guards were blocking the way. They took Mama's bag and searched through it but didn't give it back.

Then one of them turned to Mama and began to scream at her. She tried to answer their questions, but they were speaking so fast, and they didn't want to hear any answers.

The clouds were darker, heavier, but they still held back their rain.

While the Japanese guard yelled at Mama, she kept bowing, kept trying to explain.

Mama replied in Dutch, saying she didn't understand, and she had followed the truck with her husband in it. Ita bowed too, but no one paid attention to her.

Ita wanted to yell back and tell him not to be mean to her mother. Then the guard slapped Mama so hard that her glasses fell off.

"Oh no." Ita knelt on the ground and reached for the glasses. One of the lenses had cracked. Maybe it could still be fixed?

The guard closest to her stepped on the pair of glasses before Ita could pick them up. The lenses crushed beneath his boot. Ita cried out on instinct. Why would the soldier want to break her mother's glasses?

Mama gripped Ita's shoulder and drew her up beside her. "Leave the glasses alone, Ita," she said in a firm tone.

The Dutch words seemed to make the soldier even angrier, and he slapped Mama again. She covered her face with her hands as he continued to slap at her head, her arms, and shoulders.

Ita knew she couldn't fight the men, but she wanted to protect Mama. She latched onto her mother, but all she could do was cry and stare at the diamond sparkles on the ground that used to be Mama's glasses. The guards were both yelling, their hearts full of rage, as the first one kept hitting Mama.

"Stop crying," Mama hissed, jabbing Ita with her elbow. "Stop it *now*, Ita. Keep quiet."

Ita tried. She swallowed back her tears, she squeezed her eyes shut, and she kept her mouth closed. The guards were still yelling, but finally, they stopped slapping Mama. Instead of letting them back on the bike and through the gate, they took Mama by the arm and steered her toward the command post. The other guard put his hand on Ita's shoulder and guided her behind Mama. Ita wouldn't have left her anyway.

The rain started before they stepped into a building beyond the guard post. The inside of the building was dim, and the guards led them through another door. Down the stairs they went into the dark, cut every so often by a swath of light from a strung-up lightbulb. With each step, the air grew colder until she shivered all over.

Ita had so many questions. She wanted to know if Mama was hurting. Would the guards cut her hair off? Ita wanted to know if they could still get something to eat. What would happen with the fruit that Mama had traded at the market? And where were they going?

Another door opened, and Ita and her mother were shoved inside a small room. The concrete walls and the concrete floor meant one thing—they were in jail.

Ita didn't dare ask any of her questions. It was so dark, and no matter how wide she opened her eyes, she couldn't see very much.

"Sit," Mama whispered.

Holding onto her mother, Ita bent until she was sitting on some sort of concrete ledge against the wall. There wasn't a lot of room, but it fit the both of them. Mama pulled Ita onto her lap, and she nestled close. She didn't want to cry again, but her eyes leaked with tears anyway. She kept her sniffles very quiet though.

Where had the guards gone, and what were they doing now? What would happen when they came back? Would they hit Mama again? Ita burrowed closer. "I'm sorry, Mama. I shouldn't have been so noisy."

"Nothing was your fault," Mama said, her voice sounding rough. "They don't want women and children at this camp, that's all I can guess. We need to pray that nothing worse will happen."

"Will Papa come rescue us?"

"He might not know we're here," Mama said with a sigh. "I wish I could understand more Japanese."

"Johan is trying to learn it, too. The soldiers are teaching the boys to fight Japanese style with wooden guns. They're being taught to march and sing Japanese military songs. And of course, learning their language."

"Yes," Mama whispered. "Our world has changed so much, but at least we are still together."

Ita could have argued with that. Papa was someplace else in the camp. She and Mama were in jail. And Oma and Georgie weren't with them. How was that *together*?

Instead, Ita closed her eyes against the darkness. The concrete beneath her was so cold that it made her legs ache, so she concentrated on the warmth she felt from her mother's body.

No one came. No one let them out. Ita was so hungry, but she didn't tell Mama because she was hungry too. Both of their stomachs grumbled. Was Mama's baby hungry too?

When Ita started to bounce, Mama told her about the bucket near the door and said to use it as a latrine. Ita decided she didn't like jail at all.

Finally, Ita fell asleep, and for that she was grateful.

Because when her mother nudged her awake, hours and hours must have passed—hours where she hadn't felt so hungry. Footsteps sounded outside their door, and Ita straightened, grasping for Mama's hand. Someone was coming at last.

The door opened, and yellow light spilled in. A silhouette moved in front of it, blocking most of the light. Then a man spoke. In Dutch.

Ita knew the voice. It was the Japanese commander who was in charge of their sector at Tjideng, and the one who'd visited their house once. The one who'd been nice to Johan. Someone at Glodok must have told him that they were imprisoned here.

"No women and children are allowed in this camp," the commander said. "We will escort you back to Tjideng."

Mama rose to her feet, and bowed, her trembling hand clinging to Ita's.

"We got bad information," Mama said. "Thank you for releasing us."

"If anyone asks you what happened," the commander said, "you will tell them you were punished for missing roll call."

Mama bowed again.

The door opened wider, and the commander stepped aside.

Mama tugged Ita along with her, although she didn't need any encouragement. She didn't want to stay in this cell one minute longer.

Her legs were stiff and achy, and her feet felt funny—like she was walking on sharp rocks. But she wasn't going to slow down anyone. She kept up with Mama, who walked with her head lowered. The commander walked behind them, each of his footsteps heavy with the thud of his boots.

Ita blinked in the bright sunlight as they stepped out of the building. She searched for Papa among the faces of a group of men who were working on a fence nearby, but he wasn't there. Mama's face had purple splotches on them—bruises from the guards.

"Does your face hurt?" Ita whispered. She didn't want anyone else to hear.

"Not much," Mama said.

The commander ordered them into the back of a truck, and they were on their way. Mama didn't ask what happened to her bike or her bag with the plums in it. They sat together, as the truck bounced and headed toward Tjideng. Ita felt like she'd been gone a very long time, although it had been only one night. The truck pulled into the camp, and they climbed out. Mama took ahold of Ita's arm, and they hurried toward their house. Every sound about them, soldiers giving orders, a child laughing, a baby crying, two women talking loudly . . . all blended like a screech of tropical birds.

They continued to walk, not speaking to anyone they passed. Mama's pace was slow when Ita wanted to run. Except if she ran, she'd probably fall after a few steps because she was so hungry and thirsty. Now, she wondered how she could have ever complained about porridge from the Tjilamajah kitchen. She wished they could go there now. But Mama led Ita straight to the house they lived in and shared with so many others.

Outside, sitting on the steps of the veranda were Oma and Georgie.

"Oh, my goodness." Oma rose and hurried down the steps. She met them in the yard and said only, "Come inside." No questions were asked. It seemed her grandmother knew enough without knowing anything.

But then, just before hugging her, Ita saw the worry flash across Oma's face. It made Ita realize that they'd been in a dark, cold, and bad place. What if they'd never been let go?

Mama took Georgie in her arms, and they went into the house. A few of the people stared at them. Aunt Tie was nowhere in sight. But when they reached their room, Claudia and Johan met them there. Johan surely noticed the bruises on Ita's mother—since questions mapped his face.

"What's happened to you?" Claudia asked Mama in a hushed tone.

"We saw George, and one of the guards let us follow his truck into Glodok," Mama said. "But it seems we were given bad information. They put us into the prison overnight."

Claudia pressed a hand to her chest. "Oh no!" She exhaled. "And your face?"

Mama lifted a hand to her face. Her bruising seemed even darker than it had when they'd first left the jail. "The guards slapped me, that's all. We were safe in the jail cell. Only cold and hungry."

Claudia opened her mouth as if she wanted to ask more, but then she glanced at Ita and closed her mouth again.

"Here you are." Oma had opened her suitcase and pulled out two slices of bread.

"Where did you get this?" Mama said.

Ita didn't want to ask questions. She just wanted to eat it.

"It's better I don't say," Oma said, her hazel eyes bright. "Eat up."

Ita grabbed her portion of bread and stuffed it in her mouth.

"I have something too." Johan disappeared into the hallway. Soon he returned with mushrooms. "I found these and saved them."

"You are a dear," Mama said. "You don't have to give that to us."

But Johan crouched and handed one over to Ita.

She hesitated, but when Johan kept holding it out, she finally took the mushroom. It tasted wonderful, but she knew it was because she was very hungry.

Johan kept looking at her mother's face, and the frown lines between his eyes remained. Ita hoped her mother would never be hit by the soldiers again. She was grateful they hadn't cut off her hair, though.

"Georgie," Ita said. "Should we go play with Kells?"

Georgie grinned, and Johan stood. "That's a good plan. Kells will be happy to play catch with us."

Ita wanted to leave her mother alone with Oma and Mrs. Vos. Then they could talk about whatever they needed to. And Ita could tell Johan all about her experiences. And maybe they could find more mushrooms.

CHAPTER TWENTY-ONE

"Once the Japanese allowed the American Red Cross to send food parcels. This turned out to be a great blessing for us. The contents of a cubic foot box came to be merely one snack per individual. Each person received a small cube of Spam, twenty-five raisins, a small scoop of sugar, some candy, and two cigarettes. The main benefit of this handout was that some of the boxes contained sulfa tablets. This medication saved many lives and worked wonders for treating infections and for curing dysentery patients."

—ANTON ACHERMAN, ADEK CAMP

MARY

Mary placed a hand on her belly as her other two children slept next to her in the small, cramped room. Her belly should be twice the size it was now. One might think that low weight gain during pregnancy wouldn't be something to complain about, but Mary was worried. Not just about her upcoming delivery, but worried about how she'd feed the child.

It was early August, and the baby would be born in a few weeks. She hoped that her body would produce enough milk to breastfeed the child. Infants were allowed to have milk from the kitchens, so that would also supplement. It would have to be enough.

Ita mumbled in her sleep, and Mary tried to decipher what she was saying, but it was always incoherent. Mary couldn't remember a time since coming to camp that she'd slept through the night. If it wasn't someone else in the house making enough noise to wake up Mary, it was one of her own children with needs.

There was no privacy and no sound barriers. Everyone heard everyone else and knew too many personal details. That had created a sort of numbness as the women and children moved through each day, following the same routine, with little to look forward to or anticipate.

Routine was good in this case.

It was the change in routine that was frightening. A punishment. A new rule. Another item added to the confiscation list.

Claudia and her children had managed to be in the current house again with Mary and her children, but Tie lived in another house now as the head of a different sector. She'd gained respect from the Japanese commander, and as long as she followed all his rules and handed down his orders, then peace was kept for the most part.

It was not an ideal way of life, but Mary had learned how good they had it under their commander. When other refugees were transferred to Tjideng, they shared stories about entirely deplorable living conditions and even more cramped quarters, sleeping on the ground, no medical facilities, and the frequent assault of women. "This was war" had never been an excuse that Mary could swallow down and let settle in her stomach.

There should be decency in the very fiber of humans, despite having to fight on opposite sides of an enemy line. And Mary *had* seen decency in many of the Japanese guards, even when they were following orders they didn't agree with. But she'd also seen cruelty and desperation in both the Dutch and Japanese.

A small foot, or elbow, poked Mary's stomach. Her unborn child was restless at night, when Mary had her chance to sleep. The only comfortable position was sleeping on her left side, although this lent itself to an aching left shoulder and hip from staying in that position hour after hour.

Another poke jabbed her, this one stronger. Was the child trying to do a somersault? Mary rubbed a hand over her belly and began to hum. George used to hum when she was having trouble sleeping with an active baby in her womb.

His low-tenor pitch must have been more soothing to their first two children, or maybe this third baby simply wouldn't take the bait. She continued rubbing and humming, though, wishing that George were beside her. Even in a muggy, filthy camp, it would be better with her husband. She hoped he was healthy and safe at Glodok. There'd been no chance to see him again since their encounter a little more than two months ago. Mary had been immediately banned from leaving through the gates, then the following week, the entire camp was banned. Merchants still came to the outside of the fences, and trades were made through the open spaces of the bamboo fencing. Women were trading whatever they could for hard-boiled eggs, boiled potatoes, or fried tofu and tempeh.

Ita murmured something else in her sleep. Georgie coughed a few times, then went quiet. A blessing. Mary didn't want his cough to awaken anyone else in the room.

She spent most of her waking hours praying and hoping that her children wouldn't come down with one of the dreaded illnesses that had plagued the camp, such as malaria or dysentery. Bed bugs and lice and tropical sores were nothing compared to those dangers.

The next kick was stronger, and it was almost as if the baby had stretched a leg out and held it in a flexed position. A new pain radiated from the pressure, spreading around her abdomen to her lower back.

Mary gasped as the ache deepened.

"No," she whispered. "It's too early." Maybe the contraction was innocent and not a labor one.

When it faded, she exhaled slowly. Keeping her eyes closed, she willed her body to relax, her baby to sleep, and for her own rest to come.

Less than a minute later, her eyes flew open. The pain was back. Harder and deeper than before, centered in her lower back, but encapsulating her entire abdomen. Mary breathed through it. In. Out. Her eyes squeezed shut against the tears from the pain.

As the contraction eased, she moved to her knees and crawled over the sleeping children.

"Ma," she whispered as she touched Oma's shoulder.

Her mother had never been a deep sleeper until they'd come to the camp. She was able to sleep through more and more things these days, and even took naps during the day with Georgie. Mary hadn't wanted to acknowledge that it was probably due to lack of nutrition and energy. Fruit was very rare, meat getting rarer, and seaweed happening only occasionally now.

But on this occasion, Oma's eyes flew open, and she sat up immediately. "What is it?"

"The baby," Mary said, a sob rising in her throat, because she didn't want to say the words. "The baby is coming."

For a split second, panic darted across her mother's face, then it cleared . . . into the calmness of a woman who had faced many trials in her life and had weathered them all.

"I'll wake Claudia, and she'll watch over the children. I'll go with you to the medical center," Oma whispered in a sure tone. Her gaze cut to the sheet they'd draped over the doorway. They lived in a third house now, and Mary and Claudia had secured rooms together.

"It's too soon," Mary whispered back.

Oma placed her hands on Mary's shoulders. "Babies come on their own time. If the child is meant to live, God will preserve him."

Mary nodded, although her heart felt like it had been stabbed.

A contraction hit again. This was sharper, deeper, and Mary cried out. Even through the pain sending new tears into her eyes, she hated to be noisy and wake others.

Oma alerted Claudia, who immediately agreed. "I'll be praying for you," she whispered as she held her rosary beads.

"Thank you," Mary said.

Moments later, Mary and her mother headed out of the dark house.

A Japanese guard was stationed on the road, keeping watch. Mary never knew if a soldier she encountered would be friend or foe—it was never a good idea to be outside after camp curfew. With relief, she saw that the guard was Kano.

He immediately asked what was wrong.

Oma explained that Mary was in labor, and Kano said in his careful Dutch, "I will escort you to the medical center."

It was beyond his duty, but would offer them protection and stop further questioning from any other guard they might encounter. Mary knew this was a blessing indeed.

They had to stop several times as Mary dealt with contractions so fierce she couldn't walk through them. But Kano kept his silent protection, waiting until Mary could walk again. Mary wondered about the young soldier's mother—she had raised a good man.

Once they reached the medical center, Mary was grateful that Dr. Ada Starreveld was staying through the night and could help her. Oma and the doctor helped her into a bed, and Mary tried not to think about who might have occupied the bed before her.

She was aware of little else but the pain that threatened to extinguish her own breath. All she could focus on was Oma's tight grip on her hand and her urgent words of encouragement. Dr. Starreveld took things more in stride, and then, like a thunderstorm suddenly moving on, it was over.

The cry of a newborn baby pierced the fog that had become Mary's mind.

Oma's hand stroked Mary's. "It's a boy. You have another son."

Mary saw her baby for the first time through blurry eyes. Dr. Starreveld had cut the umbilical cord and swaddled the child. Once the doctor helped Mary through personal administrations, they placed the small, warm bundle into her arms.

"He's alive?" Mary whispered, staring down at the tiny face in awe.

Oma wiped at the tears on her face. "He's alive. What will you call him?"

That wasn't a question. She and George had discussed names before . . . before everything. "Robert. We'll call him Robbie."

And then she was crying too. The pain didn't matter anymore; it had never mattered. Her son was born alive. And she would do everything in her power to make sure he thrived.

The doctor draped a clean sheet over Mary.

"Thank you," Mary whispered.

Dr. Starreveld nodded, her smile wide. "You did well." Then her smile faded a bit. "You won't be able to skip roll call in the morning, so get as much rest as you can."

"I'll watch over her if you need rest yourself, doctor," Oma said.

Dr. Starreveld's smile returned. "Thank you for that. I've grown used to napping like a cat."

When the doctor left the area, Mary asked her mother, "How will I tell George?"

Oma rested her hand briefly on her newest grandson's head. "God will provide a way to get word to him. He will be so happy."

Mary was too exhausted to offer up any more worries. For now, she would believe in her mother's words. Closing her eyes, she let sleep overtake her exhausted body. When the infant awoke, she'd need the strength to feed the child. Her last thoughts before drifting off to sleep were comprised of a simple prayer, "Please protect this new baby . . ."

When the hints of first light came, Dr. Starreveld checked over Mary and the baby, and pronounced both healthy. "You should get back to your house as soon as you feel you can walk," she said. "There is too much disease in the medical center. Make sure you nurse Robbie as long as you can. He'll need the nutrition."

Mary knew this meant she had to get more creative about maintaining her own health.

"Do you need help standing?" the doctor asked.

"I can stand," Mary said, moving to a sitting position. "And walk," she added with a grim smile. She'd be slow, but she'd make it.

It helped that the sun hadn't risen yet when she and Oma, and

Robbie, made the journey back to the house. The heat would come soon enough, but right now, the coolness was like a balm. Her steps were slow, and her pain definitely present, but as long as her baby was thriving, that was what Mary would focus on.

They crept into the house, stepped around sleeping family groups, and settled into their room. Ita's eyes popped open, and then she sat up. "You had the baby?"

Mary smiled, her throat thick with emotion as Ita scrambled over to gaze down at the sleeping infant. Ita held the child for a short time in her lap, her gaze rounded and filled with joy.

When Georgie awakened, he gave his new little brother a hug more than once.

Mary didn't know she could feel so uplifted, so complete, in these circumstances. Yes, her baby was small, but he would thrive—she'd make sure of it.

When the others awakened, everyone exclaimed over the new child.

Claudia headed out to the kitchens with her work group, leaving Mary and the baby to rest.

When she returned, she said, "Roll call will be soon. We should get an early start walking so that we aren't late."

Mary knew it would come to this. There was no way around it. Illness or childbirth weren't excuses for missing roll call. Only those confined to the medical center were exempt.

"Here, I brought your portion of breakfast," Claudia continued, presenting a small bundle of wrapped food.

"How did you get permission?"

"Tie allowed it," Claudia said. "She's in a good mood because a Red Cross delivery was made today."

The Red Cross sent supplies periodically, as mandated by the Geneva Convention, and although the Japanese soldiers went through them first, they eventually trickled down to the general camp population.

Still, Tie had made a kind gesture, Mary thought. Would this cost Tie?

"Thank you," Mary murmured. She quickly ate, then she let Claudia help her stand.

Oma said she'd bring the rest of the children when the siren sounded. This morning, she'd already gone to the camp headquarters to register Robert's name.

Mary decided that the morning's roll call was a blessing from heaven because it was short, and the counting went off without a hitch. She had bundled the baby close to her chest, and Robbie had slept the entire time. Their Japanese commander did say something surprising, though.

"In a few weeks, I will be transferred to work at another location, and Tjideng Camp will have a new commander: Captain Kenichi Sonei. You will be required to show him the utmost respect."

Mary wanted to ask if the man spoke Dutch. But she assumed they'd find out soon enough.

As they headed to their living quarters after roll call, Ita held Georgie by the hand. It was a sweet and innocent image, and it proved that even when they were surrounded by hard living conditions, tender moments still happened.

Mary spent the remainder of the day trying to rest. But women came in and out of the room all day long, exclaiming, offering advice, bringing small gifts—precious things that Mary knew most of them couldn't spare. Such as a set of cloth diapers. A small blanket. Tie had even dropped off a bar of soap. Mary rarely saw her sister-in-law now that she was in a different sector.

Claudia watched over Georgie and Ita and played games with them. Johan had built a pair of stilts with two tin cans. He'd made holes at the bottom end with a nail and a brick. He'd then run string through the holes, creating a long loop. The children would stand on the tin cans, open end down, and walk around the yard with a clattering sound.

Claudia had somehow procured a toy doctor's play set for the children to playact with. They had great fun taking turns being the patient or the doctor. Georgie had already declared he wanted to be a doctor when he grew up.

The next few weeks crawled along, and rumors passed through the camp like lightning strikes. What would the new commander be like? How would things change? Would they have more food? More work?

Their questions were answered quickly when the new camp commander arrived.

The Dutch had been instructed to stay in their roll call formations until the commander could visit each group. Mary's first impression of Captain Sonei wasn't too alarming. He was short in stature, although many of the Japanese soldiers were short to her six-foot frame. His khaki uniform was decorated with medals. His hair was buzzed short, and his narrow face sported dark brows and full lips. After they called out their numbers in Japanese, Sonei walked along the rows, hands clasped behind his back. He paused at a patch of flowering weeds on the ground. Stooping, he picked one of the flowers, then brought it to his nose.

Although Sonei was a couple rows away from Mary and her family, the nearer he grew, the more her pulse jumped and her first impression of him slipped away. If they were all puppets, the Dutch and the Japanese guards alike, Sonei was the master puppeteer, and they all danced on his string. He continued walking, the flower gripped in his fingers, as his mouth curved into a slight smile. It wasn't exactly a friendly smile, though.

Something about it made Mary's stomach churn.

When Sonei stopped in front of a child, he said something in soft Japanese. The child's eyes filled with panic—panic that had engulfed every single person the instant they caught the commander's attention—but as trained by his mother, the little boy bowed deeper.

Sonei seemed pleased with this and continued to the next row. When he stopped to gaze down at the sleeping Robbie in Mary's arms, her skin prickled. What was this man thinking? What if he spoke to her?

His smile broadened.

Still, Mary didn't relax.

Under the Java sun, the heat became hotter with each passing moment, and she didn't know how long she could keep Robbie quiet. He slept, something she'd worked hard on—keeping him on a schedule so that he'd sleep during roll call.

When the commander moved on, Mary couldn't explain the relief that shot through her.

Then Sonei asked one of his guards a question.

The guard pointed to the medical center, and Mary wondered what they were talking about. Everyone had whispered about malaria—a constant battle with so many mosquitos about.

Sonei said something else, his voice edged with flint, his face reddening, obviously displeased with the guard's answer.

The next thing Mary knew, two of the guards headed into the medical center and began hauling patients out of the building. Some of them could hardly stand. Mary recognized her friend Hilda, whose face was pale, her hair limp about her perspiring face.

Mary gasped as Captain Sonei confronted each patient, shouting at them to bow for roll call.

This much of his dialog Mary could understand. They all could.

The patients did their best to stand and hold a bow. But Hilda faltered. Her knees gave out and she sank to the ground.

Sonei was so fast to react that Mary wasn't exactly sure what had happened until two other patients hauled Hilda to her feet again and supported her standing.

Sonei struck the woman multiple times. She cried out the first time, then went silent. As the patients held her up, Mary could see the blood from Hilda's nose running down her face and soaking her shirt collar.

Everyone was always silent and tense at roll call, unless stating their number, but right now, even the wind and insects were silent.

Sonei turned away from Hilda and ordered roll call to start all over again.

CHAPTER TWENTY-TWO

※

"In Surabaya, we had to clean up and restore the heavily damaged harbor; load iron ore and other material such as rice; repair and extend the airport runway; backfill trenches; get firewood from Gresik, a small town west of Surabaya; sweep streets; clean and oil weapons; and sort out ammunition. Some guards gave us permission during our lunch break to buy sweets or tobacco and cigarettes from the numerous Indonesian vendors in the neighborhood."

—FRANS J. NICOLAAS PONDER, SURABAYA CAMP

GEORGE

The moonlight created a pale sheen across the sleeping faces of the men next to George. They were all confined to a one-by-three-meter space, which was also the only place available for keeping their personal belongings. Which didn't amount to much for George since he'd arrived at Glodok prison camp with only the sun-bleached and salt-stained clothing he'd been wearing when captured.

Not too far away from him, Vos sat up.

This happened most nights. George had trouble falling asleep, sometimes for hours, and he'd seen sleepwalkers, sleep talkers, and other men with insomnia. Vos simply sat up in his sleep as if he'd forgotten something or intended to do something, stared into nothing for a few moments.

When Vos lay back down, George released a breath.

There were dozens of men and boys in this barrack. Some of the original group of officers who'd been captured with George and imprisoned were in this camp. Some had been taken to other camps, and George wondered if he'd hear from any of them again. Reports and rumors had come in about labor camps and work crews in other Japanese-occupied countries all over Indonesia.

Here in Glodok, they were stuck in one place. Their tasks included maintaining the camp, scrounging for extra food in whatever creative ways they could come up with, whether it was finding mushrooms, catching any animal wandering into camp, repairing roads or trucks, or building runways.

The men and boys who surrounded him all had stories. All had family they were missing.

George was counting the months, no, the weeks and days. He'd gone months without seeing Mary before, when he'd been at sea. But that was knowing she was in a home with plenty of food. Now, as each week crept by, he worried more and more. Whenever he was assigned to work in the fields, he hoped to see her.

But Tjideng Camp had stopped letting prisoners leave and shop at the markets, so women weren't traveling back and forth anymore. That left the option to try to see her through the camp's bamboo fencing when he rode in the back of a truck or went on one of the marches to another work site.

Until he had a chance to see his wife again, he had to keep going.

Next to him, Eduard Gouverneur woke up. George knew Ed from the days before Japanese occupation and had been reacquainted with him on his first day in Glodok. Eduard moved to his knees and grappled his way to the rope that stretched from one end of the barracks to the other. It was a way to get out of the barracks and to the latrine without stepping on anyone in the dark. Tonight, the moon gave at least partial light, but the rope was a tried-and-true method.

Not long after, Eduard returned and fell asleep almost instantly. George was envious. His eyes remained open, and as the murky dimness of the room softened and warmed to early dawn gray, he rose from his cot. Every part of his body ached, but mostly he felt exhausted, even after resting for several hours. He nudged Vos's foot to wake him up, since he would sleep straight through the day if given the chance.

On the other side of the barracks, men were waking up, including Eduard's brother, Jacques. Their gazes connected for a brief moment, and Jacques nodded in greeting. If there was one consolation to being in this situation, it was that George had good friends in camp. Not all the men were willing to work together, and often it was each man for himself. But George's circle of friends helped each other and watched out for each other. And they would make it through together.

Yet, his thoughts strayed once again to his family. As the sun's rays cracked the violet of the horizon, he wanted to believe that today would be a day he'd see Mary. He always volunteered for any work detail outside of camp in case it afforded him the opportunity.

"Ready?" Vos asked. He was ready for the day—which amounted to putting on his shoes, changing his shirt, and making sure his cloth badge was pinned to his shirt.

George wore the same one. Camp commandant required that everyone wear a badge representing the designated job they were assigned to for the week. The kitchen staff badge was in the shape of a star. "Ready," George said.

He headed with Vos to the central kitchen, the main food source for the entire camp. Both George and Vos were on breakfast duty this week.

A rustle, then a thud sounded near the fence as they passed by, and George immediately veered toward the fence. There, a coconut had fallen into the camp from a tree that was growing on the other side of the fence. The tamarind trees had already been stripped, their fruit pods consumed before they could mature and turn sweet.

Before George could reach it, several men had come out of the barracks, half awake, and were ready to fight for the coconut. A skirmish broke out immediately. No surprise to George. It was the same with the ketapang trees that grew near the fence. If they ever dropped their nut-like fruit, fights broke out.

Vos grasped George's arm. "Let them fight over it. We can't be late."

George knew that was the case, but he was still sorry to miss out on the coconut. The shouting rose behind him, and he knew there would likely be a black eye or two as a result of the skirmish.

They continued through the camp, passing other barracks, latrines, and buildings. Men were waking up, coming out into the road, stretching, talking. A few had cigarettes. Mornings were the most peaceful time in the camp—at least the early hour before roll call. George's attention was caught by a couple of younger boys, maybe in their early teens, as they kicked around a half-inflated ball. Their morning energy was remarkable. It made George wish he could be with his own children.

"Bow," Vos hissed.

George turned his head in time to see the Japanese officer walking toward them. George joined Vos in a deep bow and hoped that it wasn't too delayed. All George could see from his bowed position was the dirt path and the officer's approaching boots.

As the guard grew closer and closer, George's mouth went dry, and he held his bow. Thankfully, the officer continued walking without questioning either of them. George had been working on expanding his Japanese, but he still had a ways to go.

The walk to the kitchen compound was silent between George and Vos. There was a constant undercurrent of tension at the camp. Even when jokes were made, or funny stories told, the tension never really lifted.

When they reached the compound that was surrounded by barbed wire and guarded by Japanese sentries, George and Vos bowed to the sentry. He checked their badges, then waved them past.

Inside the kitchen, a couple of other men had already arrived. Japanese guards were also stationed at all exits to prevent any unauthorized entries. George set to work lighting the open fireplaces in the kitchen. Soon they were a roaring blaze, which was fine on the cool mornings, but in the late afternoon, the temperature was miserable.

Moments later, Ed and Jacques entered the compound. The brothers were both assigned to the garbage detail group, and they had to help set up the meal as well.

The men didn't speak to each other, except for when necessary, and in very low tones. George had witnessed more than one beating when a man was disciplined for a conversation when he should have been focusing on work.

Ed and Jacques filled up the large drums with water, then they inserted bamboo poles through the metal rings soldered to the rims of the drums. Together, they carried them to the open fireplaces and the blazing heat.

When the water came to a boil in the drums, they'd add either rice, seaweed, tapioca, coffee, or tea. All under strict rations and orders by their superiors, of course. George had seen some of the other kitchen workers slip bits of food into seams or hidden pockets in their clothing. George hadn't attempted anything like that yet. But he didn't judge anyone for their actions. The strict rationing and the monotony of the days, combined with the constant threat of discipline or torture, changed a man.

One of the benefits, George found, of working on kitchen duty was that he didn't have to attend the morning roll call.

Sirens blared as if on cue. It was six in the morning, and if some weren't awake, they certainly would be now. No one wanted to pay the consequences for being tardy to roll call.

Today's meal was typical of most breakfasts. Called sheep's porridge, it was made of starch, diluted milk, and bits of the skin of boiled milk. Sometimes a little sugar was added when the Red Cross packages arrived.

George set to work stirring the porridge in the drums, and soon, the men ambled in for breakfast. Holding out bowls or cups, or whatever else they'd scraped together. Most of them slurped down the porridge before exiting the building.

The conversation was low, a murmur of Dutch. Information and news were shared this way since all of the internees in the camp came through the kitchen. George heard stories of men being sent to other places and countries to work on bridges or railroads, such as the Burma Railway—where the death rate was said to be high. Life was fluid here, but George didn't want to be anywhere else. The closer he was to his family's camp, the better. So, he kept his head down, did everything asked of him, and didn't take any risks. There'd already been deaths at Glodok. Men who'd arrived with illnesses. Men who'd been beaten for an infraction and weren't able to recover.

Today, there was a treat. Eggs. George's stomach growled as he handled the food that he couldn't eat more than his own ration of. Even so, as he handed out the eggs, one per person, they soon ran out. Some of the men cracked them and ate them raw. Others took them behind the kitchen where a pipe protruded, expelling steam from the cooking in the kitchen. Men placed the egg on a spoon, then held it under the steam, effectively boiling it.

Once the breakfast was served, George and Vos turned to lunch preparations. They made vats of soup that could be loaded onto the work trucks. Halfway through the day, the Japanese guards would distribute the food into the mess kits that every prisoner had to carry with him on each job.

George wanted to be assigned to one of the work crews outside. A chance to see Mary. Yet, working in the kitchen provided him protection, and it was also easier on his injured foot. It had fully healed—or at least as much as could be expected—and the pain was minimal during the day. At night, the pain caught up with him. If only he could wear more comfortable shoes. He'd been able to trade some work by helping a man replace rotted boards where he slept in the barrack for a pair of shoes that were halfway decent, but well-worn.

He glanced around without moving his head, taking in the sight of the various foot apparel worn by the men. Many had shoes, although they looked like they'd been repaired over and over. Then he had an idea. Since supplies were short, when a bike's tire went flat and couldn't be repaired, parts of the bike would be used for other things in the camp.

Maybe the rubber on the tires could be cut up and fashioned into sandals.

It might take some experimenting.

But that day, their camp commander announced that another work group had to be formed to make road repairs. Although working on road repairs could be back-breaking work, George stepped forward and bowed, offering to volunteer. He knew that the march would take them past the women's camp. And he needed every chance he could get.

Vos volunteered too, and within a half hour, they were marching in formation out of Glodok, carrying shovels, picks, or mattocks. Keeping in formation, George kept his head forward, his feet marching in unison with others. Marching was much easier now than it had been in the early weeks of living in the prison camp. Yet, after the first hundred or so meters, a dull, persistent pain began. It was hard to favor his toe, and he wasn't allowed a cane or any sort of walking stick. It was fine, though. Other men were worse off than he.

He focused on putting one foot in front of the other, moving forward, and not breaking formation, to avoid punishment. Everything had to be exact. Moving your head, placing a step, or swinging your arms at the right moment. And he took comfort in the routine and the exercise, although the back of his shirt was already soaked with perspiration. Many of the men didn't wear shirts at all, but George's skin still burned and blistered if he didn't.

His heart skipped when he realized they would indeed walk along the road outside of the Tjideng fence. They'd be so close, yet so far, so unreachable. Turning his head a little, he could see the edge of the camp less than fifty meters away. He returned his focus to front and center again, his worn shoes thudding with each step, as if echoing his heart.

Then he dared another look. They were closer still, and through the spaces between the bamboo of the fence, he could see the women clustered on the other side. The women were trying to catch a glimpse of their men through the fence openings, that was clear. Yet the men surrounding George all knew they had to keep their formation tight. He could almost feel the strain of everyone's attempt to not look over at the camp. If only he could turn his head fully, he might be able to see some of the individual faces.

"Don't slow down," Vos reminded next to him.

George hadn't slowed down, but it was as if Vos could read his mind. They'd talked about their wives and children every day. Hoping they were staying well and healthy. Hoping they were protected in their camp.

When George had seen Mary for those brief moments several months ago, he'd told her how he'd come to be at Glodok camp. He'd told her about the men they'd lost and asked her to pass on the news to their wives if they ended up in Tjideng. And he'd told her he'd do what it took to survive until they were released, and she said she'd do the same. So he was counting on that.

The morning was already scorching as they neared the Tjideng camp. Were any of the women Mary? George cut a gaze, moving his head quickly a few centimeters, then back to straight ahead again. The march continued, and he ignored his blistered feet. It wouldn't be long before they'd be too far past the camp fence to take any chances of seeing Mary.

He had to look. He'd take the risk. The Japanese guards on their march today were not lenient by any means, but they also weren't as strict as some of the others. Perhaps . . .

"George," Vos said, pushing into his thoughts. "I see Claudia."

George's chest hitched. If Claudia was at the fence, then maybe Mary was? He turned his head. Gazed for several long, heart-pounding seconds. He knew one of the guards might see him. But he kept searching faces.

There was Claudia . . . and Mary. She stood taller than most of the women, and she wore a scarf about her blonde hair. But it was definitely her. Did she have the children with her? The fence was blocking too much, and he couldn't see anything below Mary's chin.

With every ounce of control he had, he kept marching, but his head was still turned. He wanted Mary to see him. If nothing else, one shared glance would assure each other that all was well. That they were both still hanging on. She had so much more to deal with than he did. She had their children . . . and likely a baby by now.

Mary's blue eyes connected with his, and the jolt he felt went clear through him. She didn't wave or jump like some of the other women were doing. She smiled though, and George smiled back.

There was no way one of the guards hadn't noticed him by now. Who knew what the punishment would be, but George would gladly endure it. Then, Mary lifted her arms, holding up a baby for him to see.

His baby. *Their* baby.

George grinned. He wanted to shout, then run to the fence. Climb over it and embrace his wife and their new child. But his footing shifted, and George almost stumbled.

Vos stretched out an arm and steadied him. "Keep marching," he hissed.

George recovered his balance and continued marching. It had been a couple of seconds, but the image of the baby wouldn't leave his mind. Mary had delivered a son. Why George knew the baby was a boy, he couldn't say except he felt it all the way down to his sore feet.

His heart surged toward the blue sky, and his feet felt like he was walking on warm air. Whatever the next days or weeks brought, he could face them head-on now. They passed the women's camp, and George wanted to turn and run back. But he kept marching. Kept putting one foot in front of the other.

There was no reason to misstep now. He had a lot to be grateful for and a lot to live for.

He hadn't realized he was still smiling until Vos said, "Watch out."

George blinked. The nearest guard to their line was looking over at George. Immediately, he straightened his features, keeping his expression as sober and as serious as possible.

Would the guard pull him out of line? Make everyone stop? Punish him? Use him as an example in front of everyone? It happened on a daily basis. Who was George to be an exception?

The guard stared George down for a long time, and he continued to march and keep his gaze straight ahead. His stiff movements were repetitive, exacting, and in the right formation. Yet, he'd broken enough of formation when he saw Mary. His heart thumped hard as he waited for something to happen, for the punishment to come.

But the guard eventually broke his gaze, and the march continued.

George could have marched for hours, day and night, on his own elation.

Now, if only the war would end.

PART TWO

1944-1945

CHAPTER TWENTY-THREE

"We were now not allowed to cook or have running water. Every day we went to the big building and received a handful of food. In the morning we got a slice of bread which was like leather, but we could chew on it for a long time. Early every morning, and again in the afternoon, we had to stand in rows of ten people deep to bow to the captain. There was about a foot between each row. Soldiers would walk down each row, and if someone wasn't standing straight, that person got hit."

—MARIA ZEEMAN, TJIDENG CAMP

MARY

Two years.

Mary blinked against the shimmering morning heat that rose from the road beneath her chapped feet. She was bent at the waist, her head lowered, her arms full of her toddler son, Robbie. Behind her stood Ita and Georgie, holding their own bows, during the roll call.

Two years.

The passage of time seemed unfathomable. Yet, it was reality. The age of her children testified to it. Oma's age verified it. They'd been in this camp more than two years.

The Djojobojo legend had mentioned the number three in association with the length of time a hostile power would rule the Indonesian islands, but three months had long since passed. Would it be three years, then? They were nearing the two-and-a-half-year mark, as it was now June.

June 1944.

Tidbits of news came in about the progress of the war, but every forward step for the Allies seemed to be countered with a step by the Axis powers.

She'd sent notes and postcards labeled *George Vischer* to Glodok camp, but she hadn't received a reply. What did that mean? Had he received them? Some of the women in the camp received postcards coming back with the word "dead" scrawled across the original message. This hadn't happened to Mary, yet, so she held out hope.

"*Tenko!*" the commander shouted from where he stood on a pedestal.

And the counting began. No one missed roll call anymore. Not with their commander of the past twenty-one months—Captain Kenichi Sonei—a man who hadn't spared anyone from his cruelty. Sometimes, Mary believed that his own subordinates operated in fear of him. Not even the friendly and helpful soldiers like Kano and Noda could do much to soften the impact of Sonei's iron rule.

Women and children's voices called out their numbers, echoing around her, "*Ichi, ni, san, shi, go, roku . . .*"

Mary's arms ached from holding the sleeping Robbie. His thin body should be full and fleshed-out, but like the other little children in the camp, it looked more like a reed. The emergency stash of food that she'd replenished after Tie had confiscated her first cache was completely gone.

She couldn't remember the last time they'd had fruit. Most of their meals consisted of the same watery porridge, and no one was allowed to cook in houses or yards anymore.

Captain Sonei had changed up the Tjilamajah kitchen. Meals had gone from occurring twice a day to once a day, and the food portions and selections had been severely depleted.

Mary's stomach rumbled even now. Sometimes she was so hungry that she felt like she lived in another existence. She went through the motions of the day, completely numb inside and out. Once, Oma had caught Ita eating dirt right off the road. That night, when everyone else had fallen asleep, Mary had cried about it.

She'd cried about a lot of things in the first few months at camp. Even if Mary knew she could deal with whatever trial or challenge arose, her emotions still welled up inside. But then, for a time, a numbness had settled over everyone and everything. So, crying over Ita eating dirt was something unexpected. It told Mary that she still had a heart and mind that could feel pain.

In the line next to Mary, a woman sank to her knees. It was Hetty, the woman who'd given up her room to them in their second house. Hetty was shaking as she clutched her stomach and moaned.

"Get up," Mary wanted to shout, but she remained silent like everyone else.

The woman's granddaughter tried to hoist her up, but Hetty was dead weight. Her eyes were open, but they stared at nothing.

Captain Sonei's command was sharp, harsh, and finite. Hetty's granddaughters cried silently, their shoulders shaking, as two soldiers carried Hetty away. Mary could only hope that Hetty could get treatment at the medical center. That it wasn't too late.

Sonei's next orders came clear, and Mary knew most of those in their sector could understand the words. "Put her on the truck and take her to the hospital outside camp."

Mary knew there was no coming back. Anyone who was taken outside the camp, never returned. And those who died within the camp were taken outside the gates to be buried in an unknown place.

Due to the interruption, Sonei ordered roll call to begin again.

Mary swallowed back the panic climbing up her throat. She could do this. She could ignore the sizzling sun above, her clothing soaked from perspiration, her aching arms. *Ichi, ni, san, shi, go, roku . . ."* began at the far end of the rows.

"Are you all right?" Oma whispered.

Mary blinked. "Yes. Are you?"

"I think Hetty has dysentery. She was out all night at the trench, and today, I heard her vomiting."

The knot in Mary's stomach tightened. Dysentery was contagious. Under normal circumstances, it was very possible to recover from it, but without proper nutrition, many had already died from it in camp.

The row where the Venema family stood started its countdown. For the past few months, the Venema sisters had been tasked with laying out the dead bodies each day, then loading them into the coffins other women built in the camp with bamboo poles and panels made from tikor. Next, the girls loaded the coffins onto the trucks that came into the camp with food deliveries. A coffin's weight was manageable for the girls because the deceased were so thin, never weighing any more than forty kilograms. Ina, the youngest, who had been a bright, cheerful girl at fifteen was now a quiet seventeen-year-old.

The roll call continued, and Mary didn't know how she stayed on her feet. Today was no different than any other day of exertion, heat, and hunger. But for some reason, she was more exhausted than usual.

They headed to the central kitchen after roll call to stand in the long line to get their meal. If one could call it a meal. A handful of rice or a slice of dried tapioca bread was hardly sustenance. Mary's children never complained. Perhaps they were too tired, or perhaps they saw that everyone else was treated the same. To eat more meant that someone else would have even less.

Tie still worked in the central kitchen, but most days she didn't even acknowledge Mary or her children. Tie's eyes were as vacant as those of the rest of the prisoners.

Today, there was only bread. Sometimes if there were eggs, the youngest children were given them. No eggs today, though. Mary took her bread, then ushered her small family to a shady spot on the side of the building. There, they crouched and ate as slowly as possible. Bite by bite. Savoring each morsel.

And that's when Mary noticed Oma breaking off bits of her bread and handing them over to Robbie. He didn't turn down his oma's offer, but put each piece she gave him into his mouth.

Mary had no right to tell Oma what to do or not to do, but in this, Mary's heart broke a little more. Her mother had been sleeping more and more lately. Her face had thinned dramatically, and her hands trembled. She took on more than she should, often waking to soothe little Robbie in the middle of the night before Mary arose.

"Ma," Mary said in a soft voice, "you need—"

"Did you hear about Hetty?" Claudia asked, standing over them.

Johan and Greta were with her. Thinner versions of themselves, although Johan was a dozen centimeters taller now. He looked as if he'd been stretched tall without any more weight being put onto him.

"She was taken to the hospital?" Mary asked.

Claudia shook her head and sat near them, her back against the concrete wall. Johan and Greta sat cross-legged in the dirt near Ita and George.

"She didn't even make it out of the camp," Claudia said. "Poor woman."

The news should have made Mary sad, but death had become so commonplace, that it wasn't even surprising. Her bigger worry was that she might have had something contagious. "What about her granddaughters?"

"Mrs. Venema is watching out for them."

Mary wasn't surprised at Mrs. Venema's offer. It was just what the women of the camp did for each other. "I'm worried about Greta," Claudia whispered in a confidential tone.

Mary glanced over at the girl. When Captain Sonei had arrived as the new commander, he'd sent a large group of boys away to one of the men's camps. Greta was included in the group, and Claudia had had to confess that she was really a girl.

This had earned Claudia several days in jail, a shorn head, and beatings. She never said exactly what had happened, but she had bruises for weeks. Ever since then, Greta had become even more quiet. It was as if watching her mother go through something horrible had stolen the breath from Greta.

Right now, she sat with Johan, eating little bits of her bread slice.

"She has tropical sores on her upper thigh," Claudia said. "There's nothing to treat them with unless I take her to the medical center and get the chloroform powder."

Mary knew this meant there was a chance that Greta could be transported out of the camp to another location if she was too sick. No one wanted that.

"I've asked everyone I can think of for ideas," Claudia continued.

Tropical sores had become a plague the past couple of years. Mary had dealt with one herself, and it had taken weeks to clear up. "We can make a paste from leaves and grass to at least keep it covered."

Claudia pushed up the scarf she'd tied about her head and scratched above her temple. She had a deep scar there from the days she was in jail, and she also kept her hair very short. Many women were doing that because of the heat.

They both watched Greta for a moment, but the sound of an arriving truck caught their attention. Mary's heart leapt. The crates in the truck were marked with a red cross.

This meant new supplies in the camp. There wouldn't be enough for everyone, of course. Not with thousands of women and children crowded here. When they'd first arrived at the camp, there had been over two thousand women and children, and now there were more than five thousand. And the guards would pilfer through the Red Cross packages first before giving them to the house leaders, but there would be more than they had now. Maybe something could be used to treat Greta?

Claudia seemed to have the same thought. "I'm going to see if I can trade for medicine or ointment."

"What will you trade?" Mary asked. She was truly curious since they had so little.

Claudia exhaled. "My wedding ring."

Their jewelry had been confiscated long ago, but the women had been allowed to keep their wedding rings.

Mary's eyes burned with tears. It seemed she did have some emotions left. Claudia was a selfless woman. They were surrounded by women who were literally keeping their families alive through sacrifice and never-ending persistence. The nights were the worst. When the darkness covered everyone, and all the hopelessness of their situation descended in full force. Among the sounds of crying, the sounds of pain, the sounds of illness, Mary also heard the soothing words of the women comforting their children. The soft singing. The long, drawn-out fables told in whispers. The stories of people in the Bible that had faced terrible challenges.

By the time the truck stopped, everyone who'd been sitting about in groups eating, now stood. The women knew not to approach the truck, so they watched as the Japanese guards formed a half circle around the bed of the truck. The driver climbed out—an Indonesian man wearing a Japanese uniform—and after some conversation, the cargo was unloaded.

Anticipation pulsed through Mary. Would it be food? Clothing? Both? Once there had been paper and pencils in the boxes. The women were allowed to keep those, although the next day, Sonei ordered all paper and pencils to be confiscated. They'd at least had one day of their children practicing writing on real paper again. Now they were back to writing in the dirt with sticks.

Before the last crate was on the ground, Captain Sonei had arrived.

The women shrank back at his presence.

On his shoulder sat one of his pet monkeys. He kept them in a cage in the field across from the central kitchen, and they'd been trained to be vicious. Getting the attention of one of the monkeys wasn't anything anyone tried to do.

Mary ushered her children behind the growing crowd of people. There looked to be around thirty crates, more than they'd seen come into the camp in a long time.

Sonei ordered five of the crates to be taken into the building that served as headquarters, and Mary knew those would be solely for the Japanese soldiers. Then, Sonei walked away with the other guards.

The truck rumbled away, and everyone stood in the road, staring at the crates.

They'd been given no orders. The minutes ticked by, and still no one moved.

Then, one of the preteen boys who'd been a bit of a troublemaker, stepped forward with his ragtag group of friends. They tore into one of the crates. Mary noticed that Claudia was gripping Johan's shoulder to keep him in place. Mary didn't think Johan would join in with the boys anyway—he'd been given plenty of opportunities in the past but hadn't participated in any of their misdeeds.

When none of the guards came out of headquarters to stop the boys, the women joined in.

Mayhem erupted. Women, boys, and girls clawed open the crates and began ripping open packages. Arguing over items. Stealing from each other. Rice spilled on the ground, and children bent to scoop bits from the dirt, popping it right into their mouths. A woman slipped two cans under her shirt and ran.

Mary held Robbie tightly against her and called to Ita. "We need to leave right now. Bring Georgie. Come, Ma."

Oma hurried with them to the edge of the field, out of the way of everyone.

"Let's get out of here," Claudia said, joining them, her eyes wild.

Mary had seen disputes taking place when someone found a sack of spoiled food on the trash heap, but that was nothing like what was going on here. She hurried away with Claudia's family, but a high-pitched screaming brought her up short. They weren't human screams, yet. The hairs on the back of her neck stood as she turned to look.

Captain Sonei and several guards had come out of the building after all. One of them had opened the monkey cage, and the animals, caught up in the melee, were leaping through the mass of people. They'd smelled the food parcels that people had opened and were either divvy-ing up or arguing over. The monkeys attacked. Biting and screaming.

Georgie started crying, and Ita put her arm around him, as they all hurried back to the house. But before they could get into the house, Oma stumbled. She sank to her knees, breathing heavily.

"Ma?" Mary said, stopping next to her. "Are you all right?"

Oma lifted a hand and waved her off. "Just lost my balance."

"Let me help you up, Mrs. Van Benten," Claudia said, latching onto her arm.

Johan grasped Oma's other arm.

"We'll get you inside and something to drink."

Mary felt helpless as she followed the group inside. They settled Oma onto her floor mat. Johan and Ita went to get water from the pump, then returned with a couple of filled cups.

But Oma didn't want to drink. She curled on her side and wrapped her arms about her middle.

Mary handed Robbie over to Claudia, then knelt beside her mother. She placed her hand on Oma's forehead. Her skin was hot, too hot.

"You're sick," Mary said, then glanced over at Claudia.

The women shared worried looks. It was hard to tell the difference sometimes between malaria and dysentery, except for one sign. The skin went jaundiced with malaria. Oma's skin was pale, almost translucent.

"Please drink a little water if you can," Mary said, holding the cup close.

Oma lifted her head and sipped the water. Then she clutched at her stomach and moaned.

"Should I move the children's things?" Claudia asked in a quiet voice. "If she's contagious, we don't want—" She cut herself off. Words weren't needed.

"Does she need to go to the hospital?" Georgie asked in his small voice from where he watched across the room.

"I don't know yet," Mary said. But she did know. They couldn't let

Oma infect everyone if she had dysentery. Yet going to the medical center might be a death sentence in and of itself.

The minutes ticked by. A decision had to be made soon.

"We can help carry her," Claudia said. "Johan, you, and me. We'll get her there. Dr. Starreveld will watch over her. Greta, you stay here with Ita so you can let that poultice work on your leg."

Tears slipped down Mary's face, and she looked over at Ita who sat huddled with Georgie, baby Robbie on her lap. "Can you mind the children, Rietie? We need to help Oma."

Ita nodded, her arms about her little brothers.

Mary blinked against a new set of tears.

Claudia and her children stooped to help pick up Oma, but she said in a raspy voice, "I can walk. Just give me support. There's no need for the other children to come. Touching me might give them what I have."

So Johan and Greta stayed home.

As Mary and Claudia helped Oma to her feet and began the slow, laborious walk to the medical center, they stopped more than once for Oma to be sick. From a distance, Mary could see that any remnants of the Red Cross crates were completely gone. The frenzied mess had ended.

Who knew what casualties or injuries had resulted? Maybe the medical center was filled with new people with serious injuries? And Oma would be shipped outside camp.

Mary mouthed one prayer over and over as they walked. *Please spare my mother. Bring her back home to me.*

CHAPTER TWENTY-FOUR

"There were blackouts everywhere because the Japanese feared bombardments by the Allies. Through heat and cold, through rain and mud, we would march, children often getting lost. I still hear my mother's warning voice, 'Hold hands, children, hold hands!' Upon arrival, we would inevitably be locked up again in our new 'home.' Immediately divvying up the available space, the internees were desperately trying to cope with an ever-increasing crowdedness. More and more thousands of women and children would be crammed into fewer and fewer camps, resulting in unbearable living conditions."

—PIETER H. GROENEVELT, BANJUBIRU #12 CAMP

RITA

Ita perched on the edge of the gate that bordered the yard of their house. The wood was splintered and the hinges creaked as she swung back and forth, back and forth. No one bothered to tell Ita to stop swinging or to stop making so much noise, so she kept swinging as she waited for Oma to come home. Mama had said that she'd be released from the medical center that day, and she'd gone to help Oma. Couldn't Oma walk home? Wasn't she supposed to be better?

Claudia was inside the house with Georgie and Robbie. So it was just Ita, swinging on the gate, waiting for Oma. Ita sighed through her worries. The day was muggy, and the low-hanging clouds told her there would be rain soon. But there was no wind yet, and the air about her was still, as if waiting as well. She felt like she'd been at Camp Tjideng forever. Much, much longer than two years.

"Do you see her yet?" Johan asked, coming to lean against the fence.

She looked over at Johan.

He'd grown taller, and his shoulders were like sharp angles on a triangle ruler. His red hair was darker, too. It was long, nearly to his shoulders since cutting hair was a rare occurrence. She'd told him once he looked like a pirate, and he'd laughed. No one laughed much anymore.

Kells crossed the yard toward them. He could smell his owner from anywhere, and as soon as Johan appeared, the dog appeared. Kells, once a solid dog with a shiny, soft coat, was as thin as the rest of them. But he still had plenty of energy. Even now, he sat by Johan, tail thumping, ears perked, eyes alert.

Johan scratched Kells, then asked Ita, "Do you want to practice writing numbers?"

Ita didn't want to do anything, except watch and wait for Oma. But she said, "Okay."

The pair of them crouched against the fence on the dirt. The tropical grass never had a chance to grow here since there were so many people living in the house and tramping about. Maybe seventy people by now.

"Should we race to one hundred?" Johan asked.

Ita smiled at that. Everything with Johan had to be a competition or race. Even when they were starving in a prison camp. "On your mark, get set . . ."

They both shouted, "Go!" at the same time.

With her finger, Ita dragged out a number one, then smeared her hand over it and wrote number two.

Johan was faster, but Ita still kept going. If someone messed up, they had to go back three numbers. Johan kept messing up and groaning.

Ita laughed, knowing he was probably doing it on purpose so she could keep up.

"Johan!" someone called, and they both snapped their heads up.

Greta hurried into the yard, still limping from her tropical sore that was getting better now. Her clothing was little more than rags, and she wore a scarf over her shorn hair. Ita hadn't asked, or been told, why Greta had to have her hair cut off. Had she been punished by the Japanese army one night while Ita was sleeping?

Behind Greta was their friend, Ina Venema. Since both girls were on death duty, Ita stood immediately, her stomach hurting. Did they have bad news? Did Oma die after all? But they'd called Johan's name.

He was slower to stand, and by the look on his face, Ita knew he felt the same worry as she did. There was something wrong, terribly wrong.

Greta stopped in front of Johan, her chest heaving. Ina stopped too and folded her arms.

"They're killing all the dogs," Greta said, her voice trembling. "Some of them were saved like yours, but now they're killing them."

"Who—" Ita started to question, then stopped.

Johan had dropped to his knees and wrapped his arms about Kells' scruffy neck. "He's catching the rats."

Greta crouched next to her brother. "I know, but Sonei doesn't care."

Sonei was the one word in the camp that brought immediate fear into Ita's heart. Since he'd taken over the camp nearly two years ago, so many things had changed. But Johan had been allowed to keep Kells.

"I'm sorry, Johan," Greta said, her hand on her brother's shoulder. "You need to free him. Send him out of the camp. It's his only chance."

Johan lifted his face, and Ita saw his red-rimmed eyes. "I can hide him. Everyone can help me."

Greta shook her head. "Sonei knows you have the dog. Everyone does. He's going to the specific houses where they are." Her voice was sad, but determined. "You don't have a lot of time."

Johan rubbed at his eyes and straightened. Then he walked to the middle of the road and peered down both directions. Whatever he saw, he must have been convinced. He rushed back, his eyes wild, his mouth set in a straight line. Then he hoisted Kells into his arms and looked directly at Ita. "Bring a chair. I'm going to lift him over the fence."

Ita scrambled into the house and moved some things off the first chair she saw. Her chest felt tight and her head heavy. She didn't want to say goodbye to the dog, so Johan must feel ten times worse.

She carried the chair to the veranda, and Greta took it from her. "I'll carry it." She looked over at Ina. "You stay here, and if the soldiers come, tell them that Kells escaped the other day. They can search the house, and that will give us more time to get Kells over the fence."

"All right," Ina said, and sat down on the lowest step, tracing her finger through the dirt as Ita had been doing moments before, pretending she didn't know they were all about to be questioned.

Ita followed Johan and Greta around the house. They were fairly close to the fence line, but it had been reinforced with double fencing. When some women were caught trading through the original fence, they'd been punished, then a work crew had been assigned to build the second fence.

Greta set the chair against the interior fence and held the chair steady as Johan climbed atop it.

"Say goodbye, boy," Johan said, turning toward Greta and Ita.

Ita reached up and petted the dog. "Goodbye, Kells. Stay safe." She sniffled and stepped back.

Johan buried his face into the dog's fur for a long moment, until Greta urged, "Hurry, Johan."

He lifted his head, then hoisted Kells over the fence.

The dog whined and squirmed, but Johan was able to release him past the second barrier. Johan didn't climb down from the chair right away, though, because the dog had started to bark, looking up at his owner, likely confused.

"Go away, boy," Johan said in a halfhearted voice. "Get out of here."

Kells sniffed about the fence, then barked again.

"Get out of here! Run, Kells, run!" Johan's voice broke.

Ita wiped at the tears on her face.

Johan hopped off the chair, grabbed a couple of rocks, then hurled them over the fence. "Get out of here, Kells. Run!"

Finally, the dog took off.

And only then would Johan leave the fence.

Greta carried the chair in through the back door of the house, and Johan went to sit in the dirt beneath one of the trees. He buried his face in his hands, his shoulders shaking, but his cries were silent.

Ita stood a few feet away, not knowing what to do. "I'm sorry, Johan." There was nothing else she could say or do. She knew that. But the weight of Johan's pain was too much to bear alone.

She finally sat next to Johan. "He'll find you when we get out of here." Ita had no idea if that would really happen, but maybe they could dream it. "Kells is a smart dog. He'll survive out there, no problem. He's the best rat catcher at Tjideng."

Johan finally lifted his head and wiped at his face. It was streaked with dirt and tears.

"It's better this way," he said in raspy voice.

Ita frowned. "What's better this way?"

Johan turned his watery blue eyes upon her. "Next week is my twelfth birthday."

He didn't really need to say more or explain anything. Ita knew, and they all knew, that Johan would be transferred out of the camp with the next group of boys. Would he go to Glodok? Was his father still there and still alive?

Ita drew her knees up to her chest and rested her chin atop them. She missed Kells already, and she knew she'd miss Johan even more. Why couldn't this war end? They rarely heard any news about the Allies versus the Axis, and Johan would know details if anyone knew them. What was happening outside this prison camp in the rest of the world?

Johan had stopped crying, and they both sat in companionable silence, as the house crows chattered and a *tjitjak*—a gecko—scuttled about looking for insects.

"Oh, there you two are," Claudia said, coming out the back door. "Oma's home."

Ita scrambled to her feet as Claudia crossed to Johan. "Sorry, son, I heard about Kells."

Ita continued to the house while Claudia pulled her son into a hug. Ita felt like crying again, but she swallowed back the tears, wanting to be happy when she saw Oma. Once inside, she followed the narrow aisle through the hallway. People's stuff piled along both walls, but there was at least a walkway through. She arrived at their shared bedroom as Mama was helping Oma into bed.

Ita stared at her grandmother. Her hair was nearly all white, and she seemed thinner than when she'd left over a week ago.

"Ita," Oma said, looking over. "There you are."

Her voice was the same, her hazel eyes were the same, and her gentle smile was the same. Ita crossed to Oma and knelt next to the bed that her mother and little Robbie shared at night.

Oma had stretched out her hand, and Ita clasped it, feeling the protruding bones and dry skin.

"I think you've grown a few centimeters," Oma said.

She was teasing, but Ita wanted to cry, for a different reason this time. Oma looked so frail, so different, almost like she wasn't better at all.

When a tear slipped down Ita's cheek, Oma said, "Oh, my dear. Give me a hug. There's nothing to be sad about. I was well taken care of."

Ita melted into Oma's hug, and she closed her eyes. "I missed you, that's all."

Oma gave a soft chuckle, but it was more of a rasp. "I missed you, too. Now I need to hear all about what you were up to while I was gone."

Ita didn't have much to tell, and before she could say anything about Johan's dog, Japanese soldiers burst into the house.

Mama grabbed Georgie and Robbie, holding them close, and Ita nestled against Oma's side. The soldiers traipsed through the house, opening suitcases, and making plenty of racket, as they searched for the dog.

"He ran away." Johan's insistent voice could be heard from somewhere in the house.

Ita moved to her feet and walked across the bedroom.

"Stay here, Ita," Mama hissed. "Don't get in the middle of it."

So Ita hovered by the doorway. She could see down the hallway to the living room where Noda, a Korean man who was an assistant commandant to Sonei, stood, his hands behind his back, his dark eyes glaring at Johan.

For some reason, Ita felt better. Noda might be following orders, and he might be strict, but she'd also seen him treat people fairly. He wasn't out-of-control violent like Sonei.

"You can look anywhere, but he's not here," Johan said. "My dog ran away."

Noda gave a curt nod. Then he ordered the other soldiers out of the house. Once it was cleared, he turned back to the women who were huddled in their corners and spots on the floor. "We are clearing this house out immediately. This house has been marked for clearance along with five others. You'll need to find another place to live."

"Is there a house assigned to us?" Claudia asked. She was the house leader right now, and the only one authorized to question any soldiers.

Noda's gaze shifted to her. "No. You'll need to find room."

Everyone was silent until Noda left the house and crossed the yard. Then the conversations erupted. Where would they go? Where was there room?

Ita turned to look at Mama and Oma. Their expressions told her that they'd heard every word. "What are we going to do?" she asked.

"We're going to pack up," Johan said, coming into the room. His tears were dried and there was a stubborn lift to his chin. "We'll find places as far away from the gate as possible."

CHAPTER TWENTY-FIVE

"Our food rations became smaller and smaller. We cooked on our small coal hibachi-type grill and it became more difficult each day to get charcoal, cooking oil and rice. I remember collecting large snails which we found in the vicinity of the sewage and waste-water ditches. Fried in oil, they did not taste bad and provided us with much needed protein!"

—MARIA MCFADDEN-BEEK, CIHAPIT CAMP

MARY

"George, where are you?" Mary whispered to herself as she sat in the darkened front room of the new house they were living in. Through the curtainless window, the moon splashed into the house.

The moon was full tonight, and it had been hard for her to relax and fall asleep. Even with Oma back from the medical center, worries still plagued Mary. The surrounding house was mostly quiet except for the occasional cough, restless stirring, accompanied by the scuttle of the tjitjaks climbing the walls, chasing after mosquitos.

She gazed at the bright orb in the sky against the starry backdrop. Was her husband awake too? Watching the Java moon? Thinking of her? How was he faring? How was his health? When would she see him again?

Mary whispered a prayer, something she had gotten in the habit of doing lately. Morning and night. She couldn't explain it, but it helped her keep going, helped her put one more foot in front of the other, helped her forget about her own personal suffering, and turn her attention to others.

Oma wasn't doing well. Mary had to admit it to herself and prepare herself. She'd recovered from dysentery, but she was still very weak. Day after day, Mary prayed for her mother's recovery, but each night, she felt the crushing weight that Oma's body was too tired to fight anymore. Too malnourished.

Death was all around them, and three women in the house had died the week before. One had collapsed at an extra-long roll call. Another had contracted malaria. The third had been sent to punishment and never returned. Greta and Ina had told them she was among the dead a day later.

This was no way to live. No way to exist. If Mary knew there would be freedom at the end of this hell, she would push forward with stronger perseverance. But she had no way of knowing if, or when, they would be freed. How long did a war have to last? How many people had to die before countries agreed on peace terms?

She closed her eyes, staying huddled on the floor, thinking of other uncertain times in her life. They might not have been as difficult as living in this camp, but she'd had doubts before about where her future would end up. And she'd made it then. The memory of saying goodbye to George in the Netherlands, when he was her fiancé, and not knowing when she'd see him again, had been difficult.

She hadn't known how long they'd be apart—his next leave could be in months, or even a year or more.

Back then, Oma had told her to say goodbye to him at the house, but Mary couldn't watch him walk down the road and out of her sight, so she'd traveled with him to the docks. Waited the hours as the ship went through final preparations.

"Be well, Rie."

George had started calling her Rie—an affectionate term just between the two of them.

"I'm not the one sailing across the oceans," Mary had said, taking his sturdy hands in hers. She loved the way his fingers wrapped around hers, making her feel secure, safe, loved. She gazed into his brown eyes. She'd miss their golden warmth. "*You* be well."

He smiled at her, and it took everything for Mary to not cry over this farewell. She could cry plenty later on. The wind tugged at his dark hair, but it wasn't strong enough to disturb his uniform cap.

"Write to me," he said, leaning close.

"Of course." Although they both knew that it would take weeks and months for them to receive any sort of letters from each other. "Here." She fished out a letter from her pocket. "I've written a letter for you to read tomorrow."

George chuckled. Then he pocketed the envelope. "I hope you wrote a lot of sweet words."

He certainly had the talent for making her blush. "Well, you *are* my fiancé. I'm allowed a few sweet words."

He grinned at this and then he kissed her. Other farewells were taking place around them, out in public, but Mary didn't pay attention to anyone else. She didn't know when she'd next see her George, or when she'd be able to look into his warm brown eyes, or be wrapped up in his arms.

When they did part, Mary stayed at the docks long after the ship had departed. Wondering how she'd manage the next days, even the next hour, knowing that she was separated from George for the foreseeable future. Maybe she'd write him a letter every day.

"Mama?"

Mary felt the brush of a small, warm hand on her arm. She wiped at her cheeks—not realizing that she'd been crying at her memories, then she turned to see Georgie. His eyes were wide and luminous in the dark. She hoped she hadn't awakened him, but she always welcomed him in her arms. He nestled into her lap, and she pulled him close. He'd long since grown out of the toddler stage and should be in school, learning numbers and letters. He should be eating regular meals and playing catch with his father.

Instead, he was a thin boy who still took naps every day because his energy level was so low. His gentle soul had seen and been through so much. What would Georgie be like as a man? Would he always have this haunted look in his eyes?

Tears, unbidden, pricked her eyes. She blinked them away because tears didn't do any good. They only stung her throat and made her chest ache and her head throb.

"What's wrong, Mama?" Georgie whispered.

Always the perceptive child, he was. "I'm watching the pretty moon," Mary whispered back. "And thinking of how much I love you, my darling."

Georgie's little arms tightened around her neck. "I love you too, Mama."

The sweetest words Mary had ever heard. And, come what may, they would be enough.

She closed her eyes, content in this quiet moment with her son. They were few and far between with so many people in the house, always surrounding her.

When the siren went off, a jolt went through Mary's body. At one time, sirens in the middle of the night, signaling a bomb raid, had been common. But here, at Tjideng Camp, a siren meant roll call.

How was that possible? Had the siren malfunctioned?

People around her stirred, waking up to the blaring noise.

"What's going on?" Claudia asked from across the room.

Johan stood and picked his way to the front door, then opened it wide. Claudia followed him.

Through the doorway, what Mary saw was unmistakable. Japanese soldiers were approaching the house. People across the road were coming out of their houses en masse.

Claudia stepped out onto the veranda, received instructions from one of the Japanese soldiers, then came back to the doorway. "Roll call!" she called out. "Everyone get up!"

The movements around Mary, that had been slow and bewildered, now turned frantic as people pulled on clothing, found their shoes—for those who had them—and headed outside.

"Georgie, help Ita push the pram outside with Robbie," Mary told him, then she moved to help her mother.

"Ma," Mary said, nudging her mother. How was the woman sleeping through the siren?

Oma opened her eyes, peering at Mary in confusion. "What's . . . happening?"

"It's roll call," Mary said. "It's the middle of the night, but at least there's a full moon so we can find our way."

The electricity to the houses had been shut off weeks ago, and so they could only see by moonlight after dark.

Oma was slow to move, despite Mary's urging her on. They were nearly the last ones out of the house, and by the time they reached the field where they stood with their sector, Mary's skin was damp with perspiration. Mostly from panic. But they'd made it before the counting began.

Robbie was wide awake in the pram, so Mary whispered for him to keep quiet as she lifted him out. At least he seemed to understand that much.

As they all held their bowed positions, Mary heard Captain Sonei's sharp words at the far end of the rows of people. Someone cried out, and Mary closed her eyes at the sounds that followed. A woman was being punished for whatever infraction Sonei had decided she'd committed. It was hard to believe that moments before, the woman had been asleep. They were all living and walking through a nightmare.

Finally, the woman's cries cut off, and even though Mary felt sorry for the woman's pain, she was grateful for the silence, as listening to her cries was torturous for everyone.

"Tenko!"

Mary would be happy for a time when she never had to hear that word again.

The counting began, row after row. Sonei kept stopping the roll call though, and barking out orders in Japanese, which Mary now understood. People weren't bowing deeply enough. People weren't speaking their numbers clearly enough. Sonei was on a mission of torture.

When the roll call made its way to Mary's row, she called out her number and Robbie's. She listened to Ita and George speak, loud and clear, as they'd been trained to do. Oma's voice was a rasp, though, and Sonei moved through the row until he was standing right next to her.

Please don't hurt her, Mary pled in her heart. *Please don't touch Ma.*

Sonei said something about not understanding Oma's number. She repeated it.

Sonei laughed. Then he spoke in rapid Japanese to one of his soldiers.

Tension gripped Mary. Would they beat Oma?

Sonei's boots stomped past Mary, away from Oma, and for a few seconds, she breathed freely.

"Tenko!" Sonei bellowed.

They were starting over. From the beginning.

Even though it was well after midnight, for the next several hours, Sonei played this cat and mouse game. Starting roll call over. Again and again. Finding a cause to punish a woman. He left the children alone, thankfully. It had been that way since the beginning. The women were punished, the children left alone. If a child committed an infraction, their mother would pay for it.

When it next came to Oma's turn, Sonei didn't target her, but moved on. Four women collapsed. No one was allowed to help them. None of the soldiers administered to them or carried them to the medical center. Tears pooled in Mary's eyes, and she bit down on her trembling lips. Would this nightmare of a night ever end?

It did.

But only after the black sky shifted to the color of iron, and the birds began their wakeup calls. And only after flies landed on the four fallen women. A sign of death.

Only then was roll call over, and the women and children allowed to return to their houses. Exhausted and sick and demoralized.

As they walked slowly back to the house among the crowd of women, Mary clutched Robbie close, though holding him for more than six hours had taken its toll on her. Ita held Georgie's hand firmly, and her other hand grasped Oma's. Mother's steps were slow, unsteady.

It was a sight that Mary knew would be imprinted on her mind forever. Her little girl, helping her brother and grandmother after a long night of terror. In this moment, humanity still existed. Among the muddy dirt, the pulsing fear, the new and old bruises, the empty stomachs . . . compassion still bloomed. Now if it would spread to the rest of the world.

As her small family settled on the floor to sleep for maybe an hour until the day's work crews started and the only meal of the day was served from the kitchen, Mary went into the yard with a tin can to find anything from nature that was edible. Oma needed nourishment, and soon. She wouldn't make it much longer if she didn't have sustenance.

Some of the kids from the house would collect snails in the early morning, then boil them and add them to their rice ration. Mary found a few snails, then added grass. She'd cook that too.

But when Mary returned to the house, Claudia met her at the door.

"Your mother . . ." she said in a worried whisper. "She's not doing well."

Mary hurried into the house. The children were all asleep, and Oma was lying down, too. It appeared that she was sleeping, except her eyes were open and her breathing sounded labored.

"Ma?" Mary set aside the tin can that she'd gathered the snails in. "What's wrong? Are you in pain?"

Oma didn't answer. Not even her eyes shifted to Mary.

She placed a hand on her mother's forehead. It was hot, too hot.

"Ma." Mary bent closer. "Can you drink something? Eat something? I'll make some tea."

Claudia appeared at her side and handed over a cup with water in it. She must have gone to the pump, because the water in the house had been shut off. Broken pipes that no one had been able to fix yet.

Mary took it gratefully. She wrapped a hand around the back of Oma's head and lifted her a bit. "Here, drink this, Ma."

But there was no response.

Mary laid her back down and set the cup to the side. She touched Oma's hands and found them cold to the touch. "What should we do?" Mary whispered to Claudia. "Carry her to the medical center?"

Claudia reached out and smoothed the white hair from Oma's forehead. "I can fetch Johan and Greta to help."

They both knew it had been a miracle for Oma to return from the medical center in the first place. If they brought her back, what would happen? There were limited treatments and medications. Serious cases were sent outside the camp in a truck. Never to be seen again.

"I don't know," Mary said. "I've had an awful feeling about Mother for days."

Claudia grimaced.

The two women huddled around Oma, watching her breathe.

The air had turned warm and muggy with the rising sun when Oma took a long, shuddering breath, then fell silent.

"Ma?" Mary said. "Ma!" She shook Oma's shoulder, but there was no movement, no response, and no more breathing.

Mary stared at the still form that had once housed her mother's vibrant soul and personality. Oma had come to Java to help Mary with the children and they'd formed a stronger bond. For the past several years, she'd been part of the family's daily life. She'd helped raise her grandchildren, and they all adored her.

She'd made life more bearable at Tjideng Camp.

And now her light was gone. Just like that.

Was it the dysentery? The six-hour-roll call? Or the months upon months of despondency and malnutrition?

All of them . . . this Mary knew deep inside. Her mother was seventy years old. By some accounts, she'd lived a long life. By Mary's account, it wasn't long enough.

"What is the date?" Mary said, her voice choking on tears.

"July 11."

July 11, 1944. A day Mary would never forget. She pulled one of Oma's hands close and gazed down at her face. Oma had closed her eyes, and she looked as if she could be sleeping. Except that her face was peaceful, serene, as if all cares had been lifted.

Had she felt pain? Had she known she was going to die? The thoughts brought tears to Mary's eyes. If only Oma could have held on until the war was over, then she could have recovered her full health. They could have been a family again, reunited with George.

All of that was impossible now.

"Mama?"

Oh no. Ita was awake, and Mary would have to tell her the news. She wiped at her eyes and drew in a shaky breath.

"Why are you crying, Mama?"

Had she been crying aloud? She turned to look at Ita. Her daughter was kneeling on her bedroll, her blonde hair matted and wild about her face, dirt streaks on her cheeks, and dirt beneath her fingernails. Something that Mary hardly noticed anymore. All children looked the same at Tjideng.

But in the early morning light, Mary saw her only daughter with clear eyes. Ita was strong, resilient, nearly a grown-up already at just seven years old. She could be relied on, and she would thrive no matter the setbacks.

Mary held out her hand. "Come here, Rietie."

Ita scrambled to Mary, and they clasped hands.

"I'm crying because Oma went to heaven this morning. She's in a better place, so we should be happy for her, but I'm sad too because I'll miss her."

Ita looked over at Oma. She didn't speak for a moment. Then she reached out, slowly, and touched Oma's hand. She wrapped her smaller fingers around the boney ones of her grandmother.

"Goodbye, Oma," Ita whispered.

Tears flooded Mary's eyes again, and she didn't know who reached for the other first. But they held each other for a long moment, letting their tears fall.

"Georgie is going to miss her so much," Ita whispered after a while. "Will they take her away in a truck?"

Mary's stomach twisted at the thought, but there was only one answer. "Yes. They'll bury her outside the camp. But her soul is no longer in her body."

Ita nodded against Mary's side. "I know. Her body doesn't look the same anymore."

"You're right." The still form only resembled the woman who'd been her mother.

Ita began to quietly hum, and Mary recognized it as a hymn that Oma frequently hummed to the children at night. Mary joined in. Even without words, her voice cracked. Their voices stayed quiet, and no one around them who was still sleeping seemed to be disturbed. Breakfast was about an hour away, and Mary knew that no one would sleep through breakfast. After the song concluded, Mary wiped fresh tears from her face. Remarkably, she felt peaceful. Almost calm. Definitely resigned. Her mother's earthly suffering was over, although she'd be dearly missed every moment of every day.

Mary looked around and saw Claudia waiting on the other side of the room, her hands clasped in her lap.

"Can you help me?" Mary asked in a quiet voice.

"I will help you carry her to the medical center," Claudia said.

It was what Mary needed to do. Take her mother's body to where it would be joined with others who died that day. In the afternoon, Greta and Ina's work crew would load the bodies onto a truck that would take them outside the camp and bury them. Where, exactly, Mary didn't know. But she'd find out.

For now, it was better to move her mother while Robbie and Georgie were sleeping.

Ita drew away as if she knew what needed to take place too. "I'll watch my brothers."

"Thank you," Mary whispered. Her voice felt stuck.

Ita turned to Oma one more time, then leaned forward and kissed her cheek.

Mary's heart ached so much that it was painful. But it was time to act. She'd grieve later. Claudia woke up Johan and Greta, and between the four of them, they carried Oma's body outside.

The guard on duty in the street in front of their house was Kano. He strode over, and his mouth pinched when he saw who they were carrying. "I will help."

Mary and Claudia walked alongside the group as Kano, Johan, and Greta carried Oma to the medical center. As they passed by others, no one spoke to them, but their dull eyes said it all—they understood the pain.

Once they reached the medical center, Kano directed them to where to set her body. Other bodies had already been collected or dropped off. A group of women had been tasked to make coffins each day, and there was talk that they might run out of materials to continue their work in a few weeks' time. So Mary was grateful that her mother would at least have a coffin. Still, she tried not to internalize the fact that she'd be leaving Oma in such a way.

They informed Dr. Starreveld so that Oma's name would be recorded: Maria Van Benten-Zwaan.

As they walked away from the medical center, Mary said, "Thank you, everyone, for your help."

Johan and Greta only nodded.

Tie came out of the kitchens just then, her boney frame more gaunt than the last time Mary had seen her. Tie's eyes darted from Mary to the medical center. "Is it Oma?"

Mary paused in the road. Tie had never been close to Oma, but there was still a family connection. "Yes, she's gone."

Tie didn't say anything for a moment, then she exhaled. "Sorry for your loss." Without waiting for any answer, she headed toward the kitchen again.

Mary knew that they were all coping in their own way in this camp, but for her, staying close to her family and friends was what made each day bearable.

She didn't have time to dwell on Tie much longer, though, because the main gates opened, letting in a truck. It was strange that deliveries would come this early. The monkeys in the cages by the gates awakened and began jumping around and gawking at the truck. One of the monkeys started chattering in a high-pitched squeal. The driver stopped the truck not far from them, and on the other side of the road, Captain Sonei came out of one of the buildings.

Mary felt sick. No one wanted to be in the line of sight of Sonei, and now, here she was with Claudia and her children. There was nowhere to escape to, nothing to hide behind without getting noticed.

All the surrounding women and children in the area bowed low as Sonei strode toward the truck. Then they scurried away to be anywhere but near the captain. The problem was that no matter the direction Mary moved, it would attract attention. So after their bows, they remained in place, watching and waiting.

Then, Claudia gasped.

Mary looked down the road to see Japanese soldiers leading boys toward the truck.

Boys who were Johan's age or younger.

Some of them were carrying suitcases with belongings, others were empty-handed. About a third wore shoes, but the rest were barefoot. A handful didn't even have shirts on.

Mary knew Claudia had known this day would come, but the reality of it happing to their Johan was agonizing. Claudia grasped Johan's arm and drew him behind her. Mary didn't blame her friend. Of course, Johan wasn't really concealed, because he was taller than his mother.

Some of the boys being led by the soldiers were part of the ruffian gang that always stirred up trouble. Rumors were that they didn't even live with their families, but banded together and camped. Thankfully, Johan had steered clear of them.

Sonei talked to the Japanese soldiers, then motioned toward the truck. In moments, the boys were climbing in and crowding together. There had to be almost two dozen of them. A ways down the road, a woman came running, crying, calling after her son.

One of the guards approached her, his rifle aimed straight at her.

She stopped then, not daring to go any closer. She sank to her knees and collapsed into a crying heap.

Mary grabbed for Claudia's hand and squeezed.

"Maybe they will go to Glodok where our husbands are," Mary whispered, swallowing hard to keep the wobble out of her voice. "They'll be taken care of. They probably have better food anyway, with all that farming they do."

Tears streamed down Claudia's face.

At that moment, Sonei turned in their direction. He pointed right at Johan.

It was done. The time they'd all dreaded for more than two years was happening.

Johan stepped around his mother, but before he could move away, Claudia and Greta gave him a fierce hug. It was brief, which was a good thing. No one wanted to aggravate the captain who'd made them all stand for a six-hour roll call in the middle of the night.

Did the man ever sleep?

Johan moved forward, his steps quick yet slow at the same time. Mary blinked at the tears in her eyes, watching the boy who'd been a beloved neighbor and friend to her children walk toward the truck. He spoke to a soldier, who seemed to be making a record of each name.

Then, with a final glance at his mother, Johan climbed into the truck.

A few other boys followed, then it was as if Johan was swallowed up by the sea of gangly teen boys. Gone from view, just like that.

When the truck started up, the sound jolted through Mary, much like the siren had hours before. The monkeys in the cage by the gate screeched at the truck as it rumbled past. The gates swung open, and Mary and Claudia and Greta stood in a cluster, gripping each other's hands, as they watched the boys being driven away from their mothers.

Anger and disgust shot through Mary, hot and fast. Nothing about separating families, husbands from wives, sons from mothers, was good or justifiable. Her heart hurt for Johan being taken from his mother and sister. Maybe he'd be at Glodok—not too far away, and Mary could only hope that Vos and George were still alive.

A line began to form at the central kitchen. Breakfast would be served soon. If one could even call a handful of rice any sort of meal. The woman who'd been chasing after her son was still bent over in the middle of the road. She hadn't moved, but she appeared to still be breathing. Was it possible to die of a broken heart?

For a brief instant, Mary thought she needed to hurry to the house and tell Oma and the children to come get in line for their food. But Oma wasn't here any longer. Her body would be transported out of the camp by this afternoon.

Everything had changed again with Oma's death. And now her children would also grieve over Johan being taken out of camp. If today was this hard, what would tomorrow bring?

CHAPTER TWENTY-SIX

"In February 1945, the oldest boys at Tjideng, expected to turn twelve in the following few months, were transferred to camp Baros 6 in Tjimahi near Bandung. I was one of the one hundred boys affected. The experience of forced separation from one's mother during already very trying circumstances indeed was profoundly traumatic. We were apportioned over four small homes, each with a leader and deputy leader to look after us. Although our meals too were inadequate and living circumstances were unpleasant, we were comparatively better off and reasonably well looked after at Tjimahi."

—RALPH OCKERSE, TJIMAHI CAMP

RITA

"This is how we can remember Oma," Mama had said yesterday when they'd stood over a small garden area where they'd planted a kamboja flower.

Ita had come back to the same spot this morning before breakfast and roll call and before the summer sun made everything too hot. She gazed at the new flowering plant and its small white petals and yellow center. Had it already grown? And how did Mama think that growing a plant would help them remember Oma? Ita couldn't believe Oma was gone. She'd been sick but had gotten better but now this. The awful all-night roll call had probably made Oma sick again.

Ita knew Oma was old—seventy years old—which was older than a lot of the people in the camp. But Oma had always been strong and could do anything the younger women could do. Ita sat with a thump on some stubbly grass. She'd cried a lot yesterday, and it felt like she'd cried out everything in her body. If Oma could die, then what about the rest of her family? Maybe they weren't as strong as Ita had thought.

She rested her chin on her knees and watched a tjitjak dart through the grass, then move past Oma's plant. Ita didn't want anyone or anything touching the plant. She moved to her knees, dug out some dirt, and created a mound around the plant. Maybe that would help keep out any extra insects. At least the ones that couldn't fly.

Ita found a nearby stick and made a circle around the mound, then she wrote the name *Oma* in the dirt in front of the mound. She could spell a lot of words now, and she'd even taught Georgie to spell. He was a fast learner.

She scooted back and started writing numbers at the edge of the dirt in quick succession. It was faster with a stick, she found, something she wanted to inform Johan about. But he was no longer here. Some of her crying yesterday had been about Johan leaving too. There hadn't been any goodbyes between them.

When Mama told her he'd left in a truck with the other boys, Ita felt like sneaking out of the camp and running to find him. She could sneak him back in, and he could live somewhere in the trees.

But maybe . . . maybe he was at Glodok? With Papa and Mr. Vos? Maybe that's where Kells had run away to? And now they were all together.

At least Johan was still alive.

Oma wasn't.

Ita decided she could be happy about Johan going to Glodok. He would help their fathers, and when the war was over, they could all move back into their houses.

"Ita," Greta said, coming to stand over where Ita crouched by the garden. "Can you keep good care of these for Johan while he's gone? Maybe you can teach Georgie."

Ita looked up at Greta. Her hair was longer now, but she still looked a lot like her brother. Did she miss him a lot? Did her stomach ache as much as Ita's did when she thought of Oma and Johan both gone?

Greta held up two ropes that were connected to two tin cans. They were the stilts Johan had made. They'd had fun balancing on them, then learning to walk, then finally running. Most of the time, though, they'd fallen over laughing.

Now, seeing the tin cans in Greta's hands proved that Johan really had been transferred out of camp.

Ita set down her stick and took the ropes from Greta. "Sure, I'll keep them safe. Have you learned to use them?"

"A little," Greta said, her shy smile appearing. "I'm not as good as you and Johan though."

It was kind of amazing to be better at something than a teenaged girl. "It's not too hard," Ita said. "You push with your feet at the same time you pull up on the ropes."

"Can you show me?" Greta asked.

Her bright blue eyes were so much like Johan's. A pang moved through Ita's chest at the realization.

"All right," Ita agreed, although she was sure that Greta could've figured it out on her own with practice. She set the tin cans in front of her feet, then lifted the ropes. Stepping onto the cans, she swayed a bit to get her balance. Then she started walking.

"You can't keep your feet close together, and you have to take small steps."

Greta nodded. "That makes sense."

"Here, you try them." Ita stepped off the cans and helped Greta line them up in front of her.

Ita had been right. It didn't take long for Greta to get the hang of walking on the cans. She laughed whenever she lost her balance. Ita laughed too. It felt strange to laugh the day after she'd cried so much.

Greta got off the tin cans and handed them back. "Thanks for teaching me. I'm glad you and Johan were such good friends."

Tears spilled onto Greta's cheeks, surprising Ita. Well, maybe she shouldn't be surprised. Greta must miss her brother. Ita wouldn't like it if Georgie or Robbie were taken out of camp. Would the war last that long, so that she'd lose her brothers too?

On impulse, Ita stepped forward to hug Greta.

She had to do such hard things on her work crew. Had she been the one to help put Oma into the truck too?

Greta hugged her back, then wiped at her eyes. "Do you want to learn to play hopscotch later on?" Greta suddenly asked. "Ina and I play it together when we can."

Ita had seen the game, but it was always played by the older girls. "All right." Her smile pushed through. "That would be fun."

Then it was time to hurry to the house. Her heart felt lighter now. Most of the people she loved were still with her at the camp. She would keep good care of the flowering plant, and she would keep learning and helping her brothers. That would make Oma happy from wherever she was in heaven.

Inside the house, everyone was getting dressed and ready for the day.

Mrs. Vos sat in a corner, working on her sewing, her mouth set in a tight line, her eyes swollen and red. Ita knew she was sad about Johan and Oma. But she also knew that the women in the camp needed to stay on top of their work assignments so Captain Sonei wouldn't become upset. Mrs. Vos and Mama had been tasked with mending uniforms for the Japanese soldiers. It was an important job, and only certain women were asked to do it.

Mama caught Ita's eyes from their tiny section of the house and anxiously waved her over. "You need to tell me where you're going," Mama said. Mama hadn't combed her hair yet, and it hung about her face, limp. Her eyes were red-rimmed, and it made Ita miss Oma again.

"I was in the garden," Ita answered.

Mama's gaze dropped to the dirt on Ita's hands. They never really got clean enough, so dirt was just part of what they had to put up with.

"Now that Oma is not with us anymore, you need to stay close." Mama exhaled, her eyes closing for a second. She looked older, or had Ita not noticed it because of Oma's age?

Behind her, Georgie and Robbie were still sleeping. Were they sick? They were usually awake by now.

"I will stay close," Ita promised. "Are Georgie and Robbie sick?"

Mama's eyes opened at that, and she looked over at the brothers. "I don't think so."

Ita moved to her bed roll and slipped the tin can stilts underneath so that they would be out of sight of other curious children.

"Are those from Johan?" Mama asked in a quiet, tired voice.

"Greta gave them to me," Ita explained.

Mama hadn't dressed yet, and Ita was about to ask her if she should fetch water from the pump, when Mama said, "Can you go to the kitchen and fetch the milk for Robbie before roll call?"

Ita straightened. She'd been asked to get the milk a handful of times. The Tjilamajah kitchen gave out milk for the babies, but the camp residents had to get there before roll call or else it would be gone for the day. Ita found her cup and hurried out of the house. The distance wasn't far, but she didn't want to take too long.

Inside the kitchen, she held out the cup to get the milk from one of the kitchen crew. The color of the milk was more blue than white, and Ita wondered if it was watered down. She wouldn't taste it though— every drop would be for Robbie. As she came out of the kitchen, a woman started screaming across the street. A Japanese guard stood over her, shouting about how she'd broken a rule.

Not a day went by that Ita didn't hear someone screaming, but this was right in front of her. The woman was crouched in the dirt, and the Japanese guard began to bludgeon her.

Ita's heart nearly stopped. Panic climbed up her throat. She didn't want to be here. She didn't want to watch the poor woman. No one was doing anything about it because no one could.

Ita began to run around the nearest house, so she could avoid the road for a little longer. She ran as fast as she could, holding back sobs that seemed to claw at her chest. Before she knew it, some of the milk had spilled.

"Oh no," she wailed. If Robbie didn't get all of his milk, he might get too weak, then he'd get sick like other babies.

Ita kept running, but she couldn't stop the sobs. By the time she reached the house, half the original milk was in the cup. Mama would be so upset, Ita knew it.

She wiped at her face and walked into the house. Mama rose and crossed to her. She peered at Ita. "Are you all right?"

Ita's throat was too tight to speak. She could only nod.

Mama looked into the cup, saw that there was only half the milk, but didn't say anything about it. She didn't get mad or ask what happened. She simply lifted Robbie from the pram and gave him the milk.

Ita sat down with a thump. Breathing in, breathing out. She tried to forget the screaming woman, but even if she shut her eyes, she knew she wouldn't.

Then the siren went off.

Roll call must be early.

Those in the house who were still sleeping woke up, and the activity went into a frenzy.

Ita was already dressed, so she nudged Georgie awake and helped him dress. Mama was ready by the time they were. But she was moving so slowly, and her eyes looked so tired. Then Ita noticed that her mom was sweating. It would be a hot day, but it wasn't hot quite yet.

"Mama," Ita said. "Are *you* sick?"

Mama didn't answer. She just continued to usher Robbie and Georgie along as they walked to the field for roll call. Robbie whined to be carried, but Ita intervened. "I'll give you a piggyback ride."

So, she did. Robbie was hard to carry when she was so hungry, but

Ita didn't mind. She knew that Oma would be happy at how much she was helping her mother.

When they got to the field, Ita handed Robbie off to her mother, and they all stood in their rows. Their rows had to shift numbers because Oma and Johan were gone. Ita bowed and closed her eyes. She almost always closed her eyes because she didn't want to see the mean Captain Sonei. She didn't want to hear his voice either, but she couldn't cover up her ears. There would be trouble.

She was mad that he'd made Johan leave the camp. It seemed that boys were being forced to leave every day, but more people were coming into the camp too, always making it more crowded.

Sonei started the roll call, and in what seemed to be a miracle, it only lasted an hour. Then they were dismissed for breakfast. As they walked back to the house to get their tins for breakfast, Ita heard Mama and Mrs. Vos talking about the hospital.

"What are they talking about?" Ita asked Greta.

The teenager's eyes cut to Ita, and she said, "Sonei made an announcement. The medical center will be cleared out today, and everyone there will be sent to the hospital outside of camp."

Ita scrunched her nose. She knew that no one ever came back from the hospital, at least to their camp.

"Does the hospital have room for everyone?" Ita asked.

Greta gave a shrug, but her eyes looked sad. Ita wished she could talk about this with Johan.

Mama kept wiping at her face, her hands still shaky.

Ita's stomach felt like a knot of worry—a feeling worse than being hungry. "I think my mama is sick," she told Greta.

Greta looked behind them. Mama was carrying Robbie, and Georgie walked next to Mrs. Vos.

"She looks tired," Greta said. "Maybe she's sad about your grandmother."

"She's sweating."

"We're all sweating."

Ita knew this was true, but even if Mama was very sad, there was still something else wrong. Maybe her mother didn't want to say she was sick because the medical center was being cleared out?

Ita moved to her mother's side. "I'll take Robbie."

Mama didn't even protest and handed over the toddler.

"Let's see if you can walk like a big boy," Ita said.

He shimmied out of her arms, and Ita took his small hand in hers. Together, they walked the rest of the way.

When they reached their house, Ita's gaze bugged in surprise at a group of people with bags and suitcases standing in their yard. They weren't people Ita recognized, so what were they doing here? Did everyone have to move houses again? As they neared, they heard the Korean guard named Noda giving instructions. Ita kept her hold tight on Robbie's hand.

Greta translated for Ita since she knew the language better than most. "They're making the camp smaller, so these people have to move into our house."

There were at least fifteen new people. Ita didn't know how it would be possible to fit more people. Would they sleep standing up? "The camp should be bigger, not smaller," Ita whispered to Greta at the same time Claudia questioned Noda.

Everyone held their breath. It could be dangerous to question a soldier's orders or actions. Ita had seen a woman beaten once for asking Captain Sonei a question. But Noda was different. He was more willing than many of the other guards to speak to the women and answer questions.

When Noda answered, Greta explained to Ita, "If the camp is smaller, than Sonei thinks it will be safer. And if he sends away the people who are sick, then they won't die at Tjideng, and Sonei's reports to Tokyo will look better."

Ita tried to process all of this, but the only conclusion she came up with was that Captain Sonei was heartless. She'd heard her mother and other women talk about how the soldiers from Japan were only doing what they must—serving their country in a time of war—and that many of them knew there wasn't any reason to be cruel to each other.

Yet, Ita had witnessed cruelty every day because of what Captain Sonei commanded. Before he came, life had been strict, and food had been rationed. But now, everything was much worse, and Sonei's orders didn't make sense.

Ita led Robbie into the house, where everyone worked to rearrange their things, making room for the new residents. No one complained. What was the use? Besides, complaining took energy that they didn't have. Their morning meal was on everyone's mind, and soon they were walking to the central kitchen.

Mama had been quiet this whole time, and she was still sweating. Maybe eating would help her. But she didn't seem any better after they'd eaten their portions of tasteless porridge.

As they walked back to the house, they had to pass the medical center. A crowd was gathered in front of the building, and a line of soldiers was making sure the crowd stayed back some distance.

Sick people were being ushered or carried out. Some were too weak to stand, so they sat on the ground or even lay down on the dirt. The soldiers forbid bystanders from helping the sick people as they crumpled under the hot sun, waiting for a bus or truck to come and pick them up.

"Can I go with my daughter?" a woman asked from the crowd, pressing forward to the front.

The soldier closest to her turned and waved her off, barking orders in Japanese.

The woman sank to her knees, crying. A couple of people tried to comfort her, but she kept on crying. Other women and children were crying too.

"What are they saying?" Ita asked Greta.

"Only those who are sick are being taken out of the camp. No mothers can leave with their sick children, and no children can leave with their sick mothers."

267

Ita wiped at the perspiration on her face. She wasn't sick, but she felt sick watching the crying mothers and the crying children.

More and more people crowded in, but no one was arguing with the soldiers. They all knew better than that.

Greta grabbed Ita's arm. "We should get out of here." She jerked a nod to where Mama and Claudia stood, with tears running down their faces.

Ita moved through the crowd with Greta, holding onto her arm, until they reached their mothers.

"You need to leave," Greta told her mother, her tone fierce and determined. "There's nothing any of you can do here to help anyone, unless you want to join my work crew."

A shiver raced over Ita at the thought of having to join the work crew full of teen girls that had to take care of the dead bodies.

Claudia wiped at her tears, then looked at her daughter. "We'll leave." She reached for Georgie's hand to help Mama, who was keeping Robbie close.

Their ragtag group split off from the crowd and walked back to their house. Greta walked with them. With everything upended at camp, Ita didn't know what the day would bring.

Mama said she had to lie down for a little bit. She was shivering, even though it wasn't cold. Mrs. Vos excused herself to join the mending crew, and without saying anything, Greta left to report to the medical center with the Venema sisters.

"Watch your brothers," Mrs. Vos said. "And try to get your mother to drink water throughout the day. We want to keep her away from the medical center today if possible. Tomorrow might be better." Her brows were pinched together so there was a deep line on her forehead.

"What's wrong with her?" Ita asked in a small voice.

Mrs. Vos hesitated. Was the news bad?

"I think it's malaria," Mrs. Vos said at last. "See how her skin is yellowish?"

Ita didn't know to look for that. But she knew that sometimes people died of malaria—she'd heard Greta talk about it before.

Something inside of Ita felt numb, and it grew and grew, until her whole body tingled. Mama couldn't be sick, and she couldn't die. Then Ita would have no one.

She didn't even realize that tears were falling.

"Your mother is young and strong," Mrs. Vos said, bending close and patting Ita on the shoulder. "Malaria is something she can recover from."

Ita wanted to believe her. She had to.

"I'll be back as soon as I can to check on things."

After Mrs. Vos left, Ita pulled out the doctor kit that she and Georgie sometimes played with. She put Georgie in charge of playing with Robbie on her bedroll. It might not last very long, but maybe Robbie would take a nap soon.

She turned back to Mama, whose eyes were closed. Ita didn't know if she was sleeping. She got one of Robbie's shirts wet and put it on Mama's forehead. Something she'd seen Mama do before.

Mrs. Venema stopped to check on Mama before leaving the house. Kneeling beside her, she placed a poultice on Mama's forehead. "This is made from tamarind and will draw out the fever. If anyone notices your mother absent from the street sweeping crew, I'll tell the soldiers that she is sick, but not until after the trucks have left the camp. We don't want her on those trucks."

Ita's tight throat hurt. It was up to her to help Mama get better. There was no one else.

CHAPTER TWENTY-SEVEN

"[For] three months we were put on a real starvation diet
of one cup of starch, made from tapioca flour, per day. This
concoction makes excellent glue but becomes watery when
salt is added. Many died during that time. The first ones to pass
on were the big guys, those who were used to large meals.
They were buried in shallow graves because we, the grave
diggers, did not have the strength to dig deeper graves."

—HENDRICK B. BABTIST, RAWAHSENENG CAMP

MARY

Mary gazed at the moon in the sky as it filled the room with silvery light. It was a new year now—1945—but no one had stayed up to celebrate. Would anyone even wish each other happy new year in the morning? She had little idea of how the war was progressing. They received only scraps of information in the camp, and it always had to be spoken of in hushed tones.

She'd heard something about a battle they were calling the Ardennes Offensive, in which the Allies had been fighting the Germans for weeks. Word had also reached them that Paris had been liberated—months ago. That had to be good news, right? Were they seeing the end of the war? Would she see her husband again soon?

Mary was more than happy to say goodbye to 1944. She'd finally recovered from malaria, but she was one of the lucky ones. Having survived such an ordeal, her mind had been on George almost nonstop these past months. Was he still at Glodok? Was he well, or had he contracted a fatal disease like so many others had? She knew the chances he was still at Glodok were slim. Men were being sent on work crews and shipped to other Axis-powered nations to rebuild infrastructure that had been destroyed by Allied bombs.

Inside Tjideng Camp, the months continued to pass and nothing improved. It was hard to imagine life outside the camp any longer. Would it ever end? She heard a child cry, and on instinct, she turned to look. She knew it wasn't one of her children, but still, her mother's heart went on alert.

The child in question was shushed by his mother, and the house fell silent again. Although it was never completely silent. Her gaze slid to her own sleeping children. Robbie slept in between Ita and Georgie. They were tangled up together, lost in their dreams.

Mary had never thought she'd be raising her children in such a manner, without George, and without Oma. Missing Oma had become a new burden in her life. Mary had always been grateful for her mother's assistance, but now that she was gone, a gaping hole had been left.

Mary honestly didn't know how she carried on day after day. She'd labored on various crews—repairing the gedek and kawat walls that were topped with coils of barbed wire, washing linens for the medical center, sweeping the streets, working in the kitchen . . . Mary had done it all. And Ita had cared for her brothers whenever Mary was on shift.

Some of the older women in the house helped out with the children who were too young for work crews, but Ita carried the brunt of helping with her own brothers. Mary released a sigh. If only she could find a way to care for Ita better. But there were no other options in this camp.

When work shifts ended for the day, Ita spent a lot of time with Greta and Ina. They'd become fast friends, even though Ita was so much younger than both of them. It did Mary's heart good to see the three girls playing hopscotch and other games together. The children didn't dare play in the roads anymore, so all games were confined to the area behind the houses or the side yards.

As the night wore on, Mary finally reached the stage past exhaustion where she could sleep. And as she closed her eyes in relief, her thoughts turned to the early years with George.

In the months after she'd said goodbye to him—her fiancé—at the docks in the Netherlands, she'd experienced a profound sense of loneliness. But his letters helped. Oh, the letters!

They came in batches. And she'd even wondered at first if he was writing more than she was. One night she started in on a newly arrived stack.

Marry me, he wrote in the first. *Today.*

She laughed at his boldness, then tears filled her eyes.

The next letter was filled with details about his travels and duties. All interesting, but she skimmed to the personal stuff to read first and to savor. *I miss you more than I thought possible. I'm waiting impatiently for word of an extended leave. When I should be focused on my tasks, I'm thinking of how long we have to wait to marry.*

She cherished every word and knew she'd be reading them over and over. Opening the next letter, she read the first few lines, then her breath stalled.

One of my mates has married his fiancée by proxy. This is enabling his new wife to travel to the NEI where they are going to set up house. The NEI is my home port right now, and I thought . . .

Mary's heart raced as she continued reading. How would it all work? Could she really marry by proxy, and then what? Travel by herself to join her new husband? Warmth spread through her as she thought of the possibilities. She'd have to leave her mother behind. Yet, her mother was always telling her to live her own life. To follow her heart and look for new opportunities. Traveling to the Netherlands East Indies would definitely fit all of those ideas.

The letter continued, with details explaining how Mary needed to set it up. As she read and reread the letter, she grew more excited about the idea. She'd run it past her mother, of course, but marrying George sooner rather than later became more and more appealing.

She hurried out of her bedroom to where her mother was working in the kitchen. Emotions charged through her, so she simply handed over the letter to be read.

"Are you truly considering this?" her mother asked, looking up from the letter, her hazel eyes wide.

"It's all a jumble in my mind, but . . ." Mary touched her fingers to her neck. "I want to do it. I don't know why, but I do."

Her mother gave a small laugh. "Well, you're in love, and you're missing him, and . . ."

Mary waited, hoping that Ma would be supportive. It was going to be hard even if she was.

"You're young and have your whole life ahead of you . . . " Ma set the letter aside, her eyes watering. "Marriage by proxy is perfectly acceptable. I can't believe my daughter is going to be a married woman."

Mary couldn't believe it either. Her mind spun with what the next steps would be. She needed to make an appointment at the justice court. She needed to find someone to stand in—well, that was easy—her cousin Jo Pennenberg would do it. She needed to book passage to the Netherlands East Indies. Nerves thrummed in her stomach. She'd traveled throughout Europe, but she hadn't crossed oceans before. What would she pack? More importantly, what would she leave behind?

The next time she saw George, he'd be her husband.

She turned the letter over and started to make a list.

Mother had disappeared for a moment, and when she reappeared, she carried a white dress and veil.

Mary recognized it immediately as her mother's wedding dress. The bodice was flounced, and the skirt would reach to the floor on a shorter woman.

"Wear this," Ma said, holding up the dress, a bright smile on her face.

"Even during a proxy wedding?"

Ma gave a firm nod. "Yes, after all, it will be your wedding day."

Would there be wedding bells?

Before Mary could imagine the bells, the roll call siren blared, jerking her awake. Hours had passed.

She was grateful for the extra sleep, but more grateful that her work crew was an afternoon one this week—cleaning out the sewage trenches. They had to do it bucket by bucket, and it was awful. Then they carried the buckets to the ditch by the main gate that transported the sludge under the gedek wall. The camp's swelled population had long ago overloaded the systems, and there were no working pipes or electricity in the houses.

Mary numbly went through the movements of preparing her family for roll call. Ita and Georgie were mostly self-sufficient, and Robbie knew the routine well enough. He was two and a half and had spent his entire life in a prisoner-of-war camp. He knew nothing else and nothing better.

As they headed outside, they found that a crowd had gathered on the road. Was there roll call or not?

Down the road a ways, Sonei stood with his other officers. It seemed that roll call would be right on the road.

After the sector of women and children formed their rows, Sonei walked among the rows, listening to the numbers. Still, after all this time, and hundreds of roll calls, perspiration broke out on Mary's brow.

To her left, she could see Claudia and Greta standing in their own row. Greta wore what looked to be tea towels stitched together to create a shirt and skirt. More and more, the women had to be creative since the clothing they'd arrived in had long since deteriorated.

Mary said her number, then listened for her children's crisp voices. When their row was completed, Mary exhaled in relief. Fortunately, they only had to go through one roll call, and at the end, Sonei made an announcement in Japanese.

Mary didn't understand every word, but she got the gist of it. No longer would there be slow lines at the kitchen. Each house would send two people to carry back the food for the entire house. Then it would be divided among the house residents. Mary tried to think through the logistics of it, but it was hard to see how it would work. Once they were dismissed from roll call, Mary approached Claudia.

"Do we have anything to carry food with to support the entire house of people?" Mary asked Claudia.

"Buckets?"

"We can send two people," Mary said. "How many buckets can they carry?"

Claudia looked perplexed. Then Mrs. Venema joined them. "What about the bathtub? It's not being used anyway."

Well, it was, for someone's bed.

A woman from a different house overheard them. "That might be our only option, too."

The idea ran through the crowd of women, and soon, everyone was heading back to their houses to see how hard it would be to uproot the bathtubs.

Greta and Ina were chosen as the first pair from their house to fetch breakfast. The tub was almost too heavy for them to carry between them, but neither girl complained. Mary had no idea how any of this would work, but Claudia ordered everyone to fetch their bowls or cups so they'd be ready by the time Greta and Ina returned.

When the girls came into view with the tub, the women and children clambered off the veranda. "Wait," Claudia demanded.

Everyone listened to her since she was the house leader.

For that, Mary was grateful.

"You will line up in order of your roll call number," Claudia continued.

It might have been chaos if Claudia hadn't demanded order, but by the time the girls entered the yard, carefully balancing the tub between them, everyone stood in line.

Claudia assigned two women to calculate portions and serve, while she oversaw the process.

Today the food was seaweed cooked into rice. No one complained, but several women nitpicked if someone's portion seemed larger than another person's. There were over a hundred to feed, after all.

Mary took her portion after making sure her children had theirs. As they sat apart from the group at the edge of the yard to eat, one woman began reading her Bible aloud. Everyone in the house was used to the woman's habits and eccentricities, and reading Bible verses aloud was something she did nearly every night. They had all given up arguing with her or telling her to stop.

Not everyone in the camp was religious. In fact, some women were atheist.

Mary didn't mind the Bible reading, but she did wish the woman would choose a wider variety of verses to read. She mostly stuck to the book of Revelations. This, of course, made Mary think of the Djojobojo legend. It had been nearly three years since they'd been put into this camp.

The meal was over quickly, even though Mary and her children had eaten as slowly as possible. Well, Robbie always ate quickly no matter what.

With the decrease in food supply, everyone was taking siestas between work shifts. Mary had little trouble falling asleep for a nap. It was only at night that her thoughts wouldn't turn off. But now, with what little energy the food gave them, it was time to wash their clothing. Mary and her children didn't have much, but she still wanted them all as clean as possible.

"Come," she said. "It's bath time."

Ita went into the house to fetch the tin bucket the children would stand in while Mary poured water over them. The water that collected into the bucket would then be used to wash out their extra set of clothing. They were rotating between a handful of clothing pieces for each person.

Ita came out of the house with the tin bucket, then headed to the water pump where she fetched the water. They found a grassy area in the yard and set down the bucket. Then Mary poured water over each child as they stood in the bucket.

When it was his turn, Robbie laughed as the water trickled down his body. He clapped his hands together and said, "More, more, more."

Mary smiled at the sweet child's playfulness. She cleaned herself last, then they changed from their wet clothing to dry clothing and finished washing out the wet clothing. It was time-consuming, but Mary always felt better, more human, after.

It was a small thing, but it had become a saving grace.

CHAPTER TWENTY-EIGHT

"What sticks in my mind about the entire internment exercise was the endless waiting—waiting for food, waiting for the end of the war, waiting for appèl [roll call] and waiting for the Americans."

—CHRISTINE VAN STARCKENBORGH, TJIDENG CAMP

RITA

The first sign that things were changing started with the shipment of brown beans that arrived in the month of May, 1945. Ita laughed to see how excited the women in the house were about the news. There were smiles and laughter, and everything felt light and hopeful.

Mrs. Vos reported to everyone. "The kitchen is trying to stretch out the supply of beans. They are making the beans into a paste, then adding it to the bread."

The bread in the camp could hardly be called bread. It was sticky and gray, but from the very beginning Mama had told Ita to never turn down any food. Ita never did.

When she first tasted the bean paste in the sticky bread, she decided it was definitely an improvement. Sitting not far from them were Mrs. Vos and Greta. Ita wondered why Greta wasn't laughing or smiling like all of the other girls. In fact, her eyes looked worried.

"Greta looks sad," Ita told her mother.

Mama looked up from where she was helping Georgie write the alphabet in the dirt. Her gaze moved to Greta, then back to Ita.

"Her job is very difficult."

That was true, but this was something different, Ita was sure of it. The next chance she had to talk to Greta, Ita sat on the edge of the veranda next to her. "Are you not happy about the beans arriving at camp? Some people think there will be more shipments."

Greta pursed her lips.

"What's wrong? Is there bad news?"

Greta looked about to see if others were listening. "The word will get out soon enough, so I guess I can tell you. My mother knows, and she has probably told your mother, too."

Ita nodded for her friend to continue. It took a little more effort to find out information from Greta. Johan had always just volunteered it.

"The Japanese soldiers are stockpiling the rice," Greta said. "For themselves. That's why there's less food than before."

Ita felt a flash of anger shoot through her. This seemed extra cruel. "Why?" But did there have to be a reason?

"The rice harvests have failed and . . ." Greta lowered her voice to a whisper. "There are rumors that Japan is being heavily bombed by the Allies. The Japanese are afraid that the Allies are coming to Java."

Ita blinked at this news. "What will happen to all the Japanese guards if the Allies come to Java?"

"They will have to go back to Japan."

"And we'll be free?"

Greta nodded, but she didn't look happy. She picked at the slivers of wood sticking up from the veranda floor.

"We can go back home, then." Excitement grew within Ita. What would it be like to be home again? With a real bed? Food? Clothing? She'd have her teddy bear again. She might have grown out of playing with such toys, but her teddy bear would always have an honored spot in her bedroom.

"We may not have homes anymore," Greta said in a soft voice. "There are other people living in them by now, and besides . . ."

Ita frowned. She'd considered that, of course, and had heard people talk about it. But with the war over, everyone would go back to where they had come from, right?

"The Indonesians want independence from the Dutch," Greta said.

These were ideas that Ita knew had been in the newspapers before the war. But Greta's words sent a new wave of foreboding through Ita. She didn't fully understand, but she knew it meant one thing. The Dutch wouldn't have homes any longer on Java. And that included Ita and her family.

"What are we going to do if the war ends?" she asked, feeling her throat tighten.

"The war will end," Greta said with some authority. "But the Dutch will face a new battle."

"In another war?"

Greta shrugged at this. "It will be up to the queen."

Ita wondered, though, about how a queen on the other side of the world could stop the Indonesians from fighting for independence when all the Dutch people were in prison camps, malnourished, weak, and just trying to get through each day alive.

"Do you think we'll see our fathers again?" Ita asked—a question she'd thought about a lot but didn't dare bring up with Mama. In asking Greta, she was referring to Johan too.

Greta continued to pick at the wood splinters. "Our fathers are strong men. They survived the bombing of the minesweeper, five days on a raft with no food, and being stranded on an island."

Yes, she was right. Ita would focus on that. What else could she do?

"There is some good news for us, though," Greta said. "Tomorrow, a shipment of duck eggs will be coming in."

Duck eggs had never been a normal food item for Ita's family, but she knew that Mama would have them all eat their share. Protein that wasn't snails would be welcome.

Most days, Ita would go to the gate with some of the other children and watch the trucks coming and going. The trucks came different times each day, and that's when the meal preparation would start. They brought in food and then took out the makeshift caskets a rotating crew of women had built from almost nothing. Some days, when supplies were unavailable, just bodies would be loaded on. A year or two ago, Ita would have hated to watch caskets being loaded by the teen girls into the backs of the trucks, but now, it was something to cut into the boredom of the day.

During one such afternoon, Ita sat with Georgie as they watched a truck lumber through the main gate. As per usual, the driver was an Indonesian man working for Japan. Everyone worked for Japan.

Ita stiffened when the truck stopped and she saw a Japanese soldier, who had been sitting in the back, stand up. It was Captain Sonei. There was no mistaking his uniform. Why was he in the truck?

The children and other women sitting on the edge of the road immediately stood and bowed before the commander.

Sonei shouted something in Japanese, then he moved to the cab of the truck and banged on the roof. He told the driver to turn the truck around and leave the camp. Ita understood that much. But she had no idea why it was happening.

She, along with the other children, watched the truck leave.

Workers came out of the kitchen and stared after the truck as well. It stopped just outside the gate, and Captain Sonei climbed off again. Then he walked through the gate toward the stunned crowd of people.

Next, he waved the truck to come back into the camp.

Relief shot through Ita. The food was back. But instead of stopping and unloading the supplies, the driver moved forward a short distance, then turned around and drove out of the camp again. What was going on? Ita had no answers for the questions being asked around her. Work crews had stopped their tasks, and everyone was heading toward the gates to find out what was happening. Ita gripped Georgie's hand, keeping him close, as the crowds swelled around them.

"There you are," Mama said, finding Ita in the crowd. Robbie was with her. "What's going on?"

"The captain's sent the food truck out of the camp twice now. I don't know why."

Then Sonei spoke through a megaphone, ordering a meeting with the house leaders.

Ita watched as Mrs. Vos joined the group of women. Ita couldn't hear everything the captain said, but by the expressions on the leaders' faces, she knew it wasn't good news.

When the leaders hurried back to the main part of the crowd, the word came.

The driver of the truck hadn't been respected; none of the women had bowed to him. Even though he was Indonesian, he was considered an employee of the emperor of Japan. As punishment, Sonei would cut off the food to the camp for three days. No one would eat. Not even the food already in the kitchen. Starting today. With a tremulous voice, Mrs. Vos directed a team of girls to go into the kitchen and bring out all of the remaining food. Then she ordered another group of girls to start digging trenches where the food would be buried.

Ita tightened her hold on Georgie's hand. Both women and children around her had started crying. The girls who were carrying out the food had tears on their faces. The girls digging trenches looked as solemn as if they were digging their own graves. Ita's stomach twisted and twisted. Not only was she hungry, but watching the food that she should have been able to eat being buried—even if her portion would've been miniscule—was torturous.

But Captain Sonei wasn't done. He joined the girls at the trench and began to stomp on the dumped-out bread with his boots. He kicked dirt over the bread, making it inedible if it wasn't already before.

Even though people around her were crying, Ita just stared in silence at the captain. His face was red from exertion, and perspiration soaked the collar of his uniform.

The expressions of the other Japanese guards were blank and didn't show any emotion. Maybe they disapproved? If they did, there was nothing any of them could do about it. Ita spotted Kano in the group. His jaw was clenched, his eyes forward, his body motionless.

Next, Captain Sonei headed into the kitchens, muttering and sometimes shouting things Ita didn't understand. He kicked over the drums filled with porridge and soups that would have fed thousands of people in a few hours. Ita gasped as the liquid spread across the ground, mixing with dirt and turning into mud.

It was too much. Seeing all the destruction made her feel like she was going to vomit. But she couldn't lose what little nutrition her body had in it. Next to her, Georgie had started crying. Ita knelt beside her brother and pulled him into a hug so that his face was turned away from the terrifying captain.

When the captain began to hurl bricks, one of them cracked and broke the electric clock that hung on the wall. The kitchen staff wouldn't know what time had been allotted to them for meal preparations any longer.

Captain Sonei stomped out of the kitchen, and after a guard handed him a megaphone, he announced in a breezy tone that everyone was forbidden from entering the kitchen. It was officially closed.

The silence that followed might as well have been a funeral.

No one spoke, no one moved, until a woman began to cry.

Only then did Mama usher Ita and her brothers along the street. Even with the pulse of fear making its way through all of them, Mama was already making a plan. "We will regularly drink water and rest as much as possible."

Right now, Ita thought, she was hungry—as she had been for months and years now—but what would it be like to have no food?

"And," Mama continued, this time in a hushed voice. "I have a few emergency items we can eat tomorrow."

Tomorrow felt so very far away, but Ita was grateful for her mother's planning. Did the other women have emergency food stashes too? Maybe the three days wouldn't be so horrible.

When they reached their house, Mama talked to Kano, asking him if Sonei would keep his three-day promise. Or if there was anything the other guards could do to help. Kano's eyes were sad when he said, "There is nothing we can do. Sonei will have to change his own mind."

Once they walked into the house, they found chaos. Women were upturning beds, clothing piles, and other items, searching for any scraps. Children were crying. One woman shouted at her child to be quiet.

Mama pursed her lips and gathered Ita and her brothers into their small bedroom. She quietly hummed as she organized some of their things that had been searched through, as if she hadn't been bothered at all.

A little while later, she went out to find rusty nails.

"What's that for?" Georgie asked when she returned with a collection of nails.

"The nails will give us iron when we boil them in water," Mama said, then added them to boiling water that Claudia had prepared.

Ita sipped slowly. There wasn't much taste, but it was better than nothing.

The night was long, even though most people were sleeping. Children throughout the house cried about feeling hungry. Mothers tried to soothe their children, but the crying continued, starting up from another child as soon as one had stopped.

Ita kept her eyes closed and pressed her hands against her stomach as she curled on her side. The pressure helped to ease some of the gnawing pain. Thankfully, Georgie and Robbie were sleeping, although Ita was sure that Mama wasn't.

When Mama rose from her bedroll and sat with her knees pulled up, gazing out the window at the moon, Ita rose too. Usually, Mama would have told her to go back to sleep, but tonight, Mama wrapped an arm about her and pulled her close. Ita rested her head on Mama's shoulder.

"Sometimes I wonder if Papa is watching the moon at the same time," Mama whispered. "If he can't sleep and he's awake too."

Ita liked it when Mama talked about Papa. It made him feel closer, like he wasn't so far away, and it hadn't been so long since she'd seen him. And it also helped to look at Mama's picture of him every so often just to remind herself what he looked like and that she really did have a papa out there somewhere.

"Do you think he has a captain as mean as Sonei?" Ita asked quietly.

"No one is as mean as Sonei," Mama said with a surprisingly firm voice.

That meant that Papa's camp hadn't been forced to bury their food when their captain was angry. "Greta said that the Allies are bombing Japan now."

"Yes, I've heard that too," Mama said. "War is awful. The destruction is senseless. I don't want anyone to be bombed, but I don't see how else the war will end."

Ita didn't see either. Maybe when one of the sides ran out of soldiers and commanders? Maybe when Captain Sonei was an old man? That would mean that Ita would live in this camp forever and ever.

Mama didn't say much else, and eventually, Ita's exhaustion surpassed the pain in her stomach, and she was able to sleep.

The next day, Ita didn't want to get out of her bed. She didn't want to move. Moving made her stomach remember that there was nothing to fill it. But in the middle of the sweltering afternoon, Mama pressed a few bits of lentils into Ita's hand. "Eat these when no one is looking at you," she whispered.

Tears sprung to her eyes, and immediately her mouth was watering. She turned to her other side, then quickly put the lentils into her mouth. She closed her eyes, savoring the taste, then she slowly chewed. After she swallowed, she kept her eyes closed, focusing on the food settling in her stomach. Filling her up.

But it didn't fill her up. A morsel of lentils didn't have the power to do that. It did, however, give her some hope.

Ita turned back over. Georgie was also lying down, chewing his own lentils.

"Where did Mama find the food?" he whispered to her.

Ita didn't know, but Mama had heard and answered quietly, "The medical staff handed out bread and lentils from their emergency supplies this morning. I was lucky to get anything." Her gaze shifted away.

Ita moved to sit up. "Did everyone get something?"

Mama shook her head. "No. There wasn't enough, but at least Captain Sonei didn't see what happened. He issued a new order though."

Ita didn't like the sound of that.

"No one is allowed to have a cooking fire in their yards. If one is discovered, food will be withheld for an entire week."

No one wanted that to happen.

The women around them got creative for the next two days, though, by putting a little salt in a cup of water.

Ita thought the fourth day would never come, but finally they heard the megaphones blaring throughout camp, ordering the food carriers to come to the kitchen. Claudia assigned two teenagers, including Greta, to take the tub to the kitchen, and everyone crowded in the yard and on the veranda to wait.

If Ita had had any energy, she would have gone onto the road to watch. The wait was long, nearly an hour, Ita guessed.

When Greta and the other teenager returned with the tub full of mixed rice and porridge, there was a smile on Greta's face.

Ita smiled too, but she soon learned that her friend's smile wasn't because of the kitchen being open again. Ita saw her speaking to her mother, gesturing with excitement.

"What's the good news?" Ita asked, knowing she was being nosy, but no one hushed her.

Greta turned her excited eyes on Ita. "Captain Sonei is being transferred to another assignment. He's leaving our camp soon."

Some of the women close enough to hear let out gasps.

Mrs. Vos smiled too. "Can it be true?" She clasped her hands and pressed them against her chest.

"We are not allowed to celebrate or look happy," Greta said, but her smile remained.

Then Ita thought of a new complication. "Who will replace him, though? Will it be someone who's meaner?"

"The rumor is that it will be someone better," Greta said.

Ita didn't know what to believe. Good news had filtered through the camp before, and good things hadn't happened. Was this another rumor that Greta was desperate to believe in?

But the rice and porridge that day was the best thing that Ita had ever tasted at camp.

After Ita had eaten, she remained on the veranda, not moving. Many of the women and children went back into the house to lie down. With the meals starting again, the jobs would begin too, and roll call.

Ita wanted to let the new food settle in her stomach, then turn into strength and energy for the rest of her body.

Over the next two days, Captain Sonei didn't leave, but the rumors grew and grew, until during morning roll call on the third day, one of Sonei's assistants showed up wearing an officer's uniform. And the sword hanging at his side looked new and polished until it gleamed in the sun. It was obvious that a Japanese soldier named Ohara had been promoted. Was this the true sign that Sonei would be leaving?

Finally, Ita allowed some hope to enter her heart.

When Sonei paraded Lieutenant Sakai, another one of his assistants, before the women at roll call, Ita paid attention to every movement and word.

"We will celebrate the promotion of Lieutenant Sakai to captain with a feast," Sonei told everyone through his blaring megaphone.

None of the women cheered or shouted hooray, but Ita could feel their emotions running through her, joining with her own. Sonei ordered the slaughter of two piglets for their feast, which of course, none of the women or children took part in. But Ita was happy that the Japanese soldiers were celebrating—it meant that Sonei would really be leaving.

As the approaching twilight finally cooled off the heat of the day, Ita heard Mama talking to Mrs. Vos.

"I'll believe it when he's gone and doesn't come back," Mama said.

Mrs. Vos folded her arms about her middle. "I agree, but the women a few houses down are celebrating with music. I'm afraid if they're caught, Sonei will change his mind just so that he can keep giving out punishments."

If Ita went onto the veranda, she could hear the faint strains of music coming down the road. She didn't dare go any closer. Someone was playing a violin, then other women sang songs. As much as Ita wanted to hear it, she didn't want to be part of any punishments should they be caught.

She pulled her knees to her chest and rested her chin atop her knees. Someone laughed inside the house. The conversation that floated around the veranda was light. It felt like hope. It felt like someday, the war would end. Someday, Ita would go home.

CHAPTER TWENTY-NINE

"Each person had his own routine for eating his ration. Some just gobbled it all up, others savored it slowly and chewed forever on what was chewable, and still others ate what was warm and saved the bread, or part of it, for later as I did."

—K. A. PETER VAN BERKUM, DE WIJK CAMP

MARY

Mary bent over the socks she was knitting for the soldiers. She didn't mind the work. It let her sit down as well as watch over her children, although Ita and Georgie were very independent. Robbie sat next to her, turning the pages of Ita's large story book. Somehow, despite all the times items had been confiscated in camp, her family had been able to hold on to the book.

"I heard that Ina's older sister has dysentery," Claudia said from across the room, where she was also knitting.

Mary stalled in her knitting. "Oh no."

Claudia nodded.

There was nothing to be said. Nothing to be done. Not really. They could only wait and hope.

"I'm going to take a short nap," Claudia said with a yawn. "Wake me if needed."

Mary nodded. She wasn't surprised that within minutes Claudia was sound asleep. Even though Mary had such a good friend in Claudia, and friendships with several other women at the camp, she felt lonely without Oma, who'd been gone more than a year now.

Life in the camp had changed so much in the past few months. Mostly because Sonei was finally gone. For the second time. The first time, he'd been gone only a few days. Then he'd returned in a drunken rage, and when he'd discovered that some of the women had started trading for goods through the bamboo fence, he'd punished them by taking their wedding rings. The last things they possessed. The women were beaten and their heads shaved. The entire camp's food was destroyed again.

But now, with Sonei gone for good, they'd had relative peace for weeks—at least as much peace as possible while still living half-starved in a prison camp. Red Cross packages were arriving with more frequency, and they were now able to keep most of what came in on the trucks, dividing the supplies by household.

On one recent day, a whole group of postcards had arrived in Tjideng. There was nothing for Mary and nothing for Claudia, but Mary had been glad to see others rejoicing.

Of course, some of the letters had not been happy. Several of the friends she'd made in camp had received terrible news about their husbands and sons and were grieving losses that had happened months ago, unbeknownst to them. Mary tried not think of what would happen to her heart if such a postcard came to announce George's death. To hold out hope for so long, to endure so much, and then to receive a knife to the heart.

In addition, dysentery had swept through the camp like a wildfire. In July, more than fifty people were transported out of camp to recover. Mary wondered if they'd ever return. Now, a couple of weeks into August, four or five people were dying daily. One of the doctors had also become sick, and the teenaged girls were busier than ever with their task of transporting dead bodies.

The medical staff had run out of treatments for dysentery, so finding blood in the contents of a child's defecation was terrifying, often meaning death was only days away. The contagious disease wouldn't let up. It was impossible for Mary to keep her children separated from each other, but she worked hard to keep them separated from others.

Noises floated in from outside, conversations, laughter . . . a rare sound that had started to happen only after Sonei's departure. Several people were sleeping inside the house, so when someone started crying outside, Mary plainly heard. With Sonei gone, she knew it wasn't because of a beating. It was likely bad news, either about a family member's illness, or a death announced through a postcard.

Mary continued the rhythm of her stitching. She'd become so used to illness, news of death, and other setbacks, that sometimes she felt numb to it all. Sure, she'd comforted her friends, but inside, she dreaded the news for herself. Did this make her coldhearted? It was almost as if she couldn't feel deeply anymore, not deep sorrow, not true joy; she just existed. Her children existed, and of course she loved them with everything she had, but they were her last threads of humanity.

Last night, she'd dreamed that the war had ended. She and her family had returned to their home. Nothing had been touched. Nothing had been changed. George was in the front yard, kneeling down and changing a bike tire. She couldn't see his face, but it was him. She wanted to greet him, hug him, but instead she walked into the house to check if there was food. She opened every cupboard and every drawer.

The shelves teemed with food, but it was all food from the Red Cross. Tins of flour, sardines, wafers, coffee, sugar . . . Then she searched for her hidden jewelry box in the garden so that she could go to the market and buy fresh vegetables and fruit.

While she was still digging in the dream's garden, she'd woken up to the sound of the sirens.

Roll call went much faster now without Captain Sonei. They weren't made to stand for extra hours in the hot sun. They still had to bow, they still had to count, but there were no punishments for women who fainted or sank to their knees.

Sick women or children weren't forced out of the medical center to attend roll call. They were allowed to stay in their sick beds.

Still, so many more people were getting sick and dying. Mostly of dysentery. Other ailments and diseases included jaundice, typhoid, edema, pellagra, beriberi, and malaria. She'd had her own bout of malaria that she'd thankfully survived.

Now, they were getting more food trucked in, but it seemed everyone was hungrier. The women dug through the trash to find any scrap of rotted food or discarded bits of bread. They were catching insects and bugs that hadn't been eaten by the tjitjaks, then cooking them over fires in the yards.

The Japanese soldiers didn't stop them. Not with Sonei gone for good.

All of this, Mary observed from afar. She didn't search through the trash, but she did collect anything that was growing and edible. Her children knew to eat whatever she fed them without any complaints.

Once, Mary saw Kano leave a couple of tins of sardines where Ita and Georgie were playing on the veranda. He only told them to, "Give it to your mother," and then, without any other explanation, had walked away. Mary knew the tins must have been food from his own Red Cross package.

The front door opened, then closed. Mary didn't even look up from her knitting. Not until two dusty, cracked feet stopped in front of her, crossing her line of vision.

"Mama's asleep?"

Mary lifted her gaze to see Greta. Her hair was short because she'd cut off the braid she'd grown the past two years in camp in order to make a wig for a woman whose head had been shorn. Her chest heaved as if she'd been running. But she might have just been exhausted from so much work.

Mary glanced at Claudia, who was curled on her side atop her bed roll. "Only for a few moments."

Greta crossed to her mother, then nudged her awake.

Mary was about to admonish the girl—Claudia needed sleep—that was plain.

But something in Greta's eyes kept Mary silent. The girl often found out news before anyone else in the house because she was always working by the gates.

Claudia's eyes snapped open, her expression immediately alert. "What's happened?"

"There's news of powerful bombs that have killed thousands of Japanese, maybe hundreds of thousands," Greta said in a fierce voice.

Mary's hands stilled as she listened.

Claudia rubbed at her eyes.

No one wanted more death, but no one wanted the war to continue either.

"The Japanese will never give up," Claudia said in an equally fierce tone. "They're ingrained with loyalty to their emperor. Death is more honorable than surrender."

Claudia was right, Mary decided. Yet, a glimmer of hope had sprung up in Mary's breast, and she didn't have the heart to tamp it down. They'd been in this camp for three and a half years. Maybe the end really was in sight.

When Greta left the house, Claudia looked over at Mary with tired eyes.

The woman had changed so much over the years, but Mary knew what she saw in her longtime friend was only a reflection of herself. Her gaunt face, her angular limbs, her scarred legs and arms from tropical sores, her ankles swollen with edema, her stubby and cracked nails. But in Claudia's eyes, there was still fire . . . the will to live. For weeks, months, years, whatever it took to taste freedom again.

"Happy birthday," Claudia said in a gentle tone.

Mary smiled. "Thank you." The response was automatic, but the emotions settled heavy on her shoulders. It was August 16, 1945, her fortieth birthday. How many more birthdays would she have in this camp?

What about her children? Robbie knew no other life, and Georgie couldn't remember anything different.

When she finished knitting the last set of socks, Mary rose to her feet. As if by silent, mutual agreement, she and Claudia headed outside with Robbie. Ita and Georgie were in the yard, playing a game with some of the other children. It was some sort of a cricket game, but there was no ball, so they were hitting sticks in the air, trying to get them to sail across the road.

The house they lived in butted up against the fence parallel to the railroad that ran across the dike.

Out of habit, everyone turned to watch the train as it snaked by. They could see the top of it, and sometimes they could see the passengers through the open windows—all Indonesian civilians or Japanese troops.

Mary's heart stalled when she saw that the train was full of Indonesians, and several of them were leaning out the window, staring straight into their camp.

"The war is over!" one of them shouted in Malay.

No, several of them were shouting the same thing.

"The war has ended!"

"Japan has surrendered!"

Mary didn't move for a long time after the train had passed. Maybe it had been a dream. Maybe she was still sleeping in a cocoon of heat inside the house, and her mind was playing tricks on her.

"Did you hear that?" Claudia said, coming to stand next to her. "Can it be true?"

Without looking at her friend, Mary said, "I heard it. Are you part of my dream now?"

A strange laugh escaped Claudia, and Mary turned then. Claudia's eyes were red with tears and her chin trembled. "Is the war really over? Or could a train full of Javanese civilians be playing a cruel game?"

Mary released a thready breath that caught in her throat. A lump formed, and her chest went tight. Her dream last night . . . and then this . . .

She reached for Claudia's arm and held on tight because she didn't know if her knees would hold her up.

Claudia turned fully toward Mary, the tears streaking her cheeks.

Mary didn't even know she could cry anymore, but a sob surged deep within her. And then she was hugging Claudia, holding on tight, as if she could squeeze the words of those on the train into reality. How sweet were the words, how exquisite the news, but somehow it was full of pain and grief as well. For all that had changed, for all that had been lost, for all those who'd died. Millions upon millions.

But right now, Mary would hold her friend tightly and they'd cry together.

Around them, the news was spreading, the conversations growing. Women cheered, women cried, children ran around shouting.

No one knew what would happen in the next hour, or the next day, but they would bask in the light that had broken through years of darkness and despair.

Over the next days, everyone was talking, speculating, and asking questions of each other.

The Korean guard Noda didn't know any more than the prisoners. He'd heard the same rumors, but orders hadn't come from the Japanese government of what the liberation steps would be. Kano didn't know anything more than the prisoners either. The routine remained except that roll call was only in the evenings now, instead of twice a day. The food supply was better, and rice rations doubled, but people were still dying, because they had trouble digesting any richer foods.

There was talk of sneaking into the military office and turning on the one radio in camp. But no one dared when it came down to it. Even with Captain Sonei gone for weeks, the fear he'd instilled in the women remained.

Another week passed, and small changes happened, but nothing that was entirely unusual. The Japanese guards stopped asking for socks to be knitted and uniforms to be repaired, so Mary had more idle time.

One afternoon, while Mary was catching flies with her children, after the sewer ditch crew had finished their daily task, Claudia came hurrying toward them. "There's been a meeting called with all the house leaders."

Mary straightened. Meetings with house leaders usually meant more restrictions or an issuance of punishment. "Do you have any idea what it will be about?"

Claudia shook her head at the same time that Tie could be seen striding down the road in her long skirt—which she'd started wearing after being given more and more authority among the house leaders.

Tie raised a hand in greeting but didn't stop to speak to anyone, or speculate. That was her way. She'd kept her distance for years.

After Claudia hurried away, Mary took the children inside the house. They'd wait for news there. She didn't want to congregate near the gate to hear whatever Lieutenant Sakai was going to say. If there were punishments doled out, Mary didn't want her children to be witness to them.

She tamped down her curiosity, which was mostly anxiety anyway, as she waited. Ita asked if she could join the other children near the gate, but Mary told her no.

So they waited. And wondered.

When Claudia finally returned, she called a house meeting. Mary tried to read the woman's expression. She was smiling. A rare thing.

That meant the news could only be good, right?

"Ladies," Claudia began. "Lieutenant Sakai has posted a bulletin to the notice board. It states that the war is over as officially declared by Emperor Hirohito. Japan has surrendered to the Allies, and we are to wait at this camp until the Allied armies arrive to relocate us."

Mary's hands shook as she pulled her children closer. This was real. This was happening. Women threw out questions, many of them the same ones that Mary might have asked if she weren't focused on finding the bulletin. She had to see the words herself.

CHAPTER THIRTY

"There was no law and order. Native bands used to roam the streets looking for white people or anybody else they did not like. We then huddled and listened to their shouting and the hollow clangs their sharpened bamboo sticks made when hitting a metal pole, and we relaxed only after they had passed the house."

—GRETA KWIK, SEMARANG

RITA

Ita shifted closer to the notice board, moving between the women who'd crowded around to read the announcement. She'd checked the notice board daily ever since the British Red Cross had started posting the names of those who had died. Papa was never on the lists. At least, not yet.

But this notice was written in English—a language that Ita didn't read or write.

"Who can read English?" one woman asked.

"I can." Someone volunteered, and Ita was surprised to see it was Aunt Tie. The woman never visited, and Mama had stopped taking them on visits to see her. Whenever Ita saw her aunt around the camp, Aunt Tie would say hello, but she would never ask after any of them.

Aunt Tie took her position at the front of the gathered group. Her voice was loud enough she didn't need one of those megaphones that the Japanese soldiers used.

After repeated requests by the Allies to stop the war, His Majesty Emperor Hirohito has ordered the cessation of hostilities. As a result, the status of the internees has been brought to an end on the understanding that their release from captivity will await the arrival of representatives from the Allied armies. The date of this arrival is not yet known.

For military political reasons you have been brought together here and that is why you have suffered the difficulties of the war; henceforth your circumstances will improve. Until the formal capitulation, the Japanese army will remain responsible for the maintenance of peace and order in the camps. In response to this requirement the existing regulations will remain in force. Now that the war has ended the provision of food will improve.

Money belonging to internees can be utilized to purchase necessary goods. The moneys taken into custody by the Nipponese authorities will be shortly returned.

General Nagano,

Commander Nipponese 16th Army, Jakarta,

22 August 2605

"Mama," Ita said in a quiet voice. "What does all of that mean?"

Her mother rested a hand on her shoulder. "The war is over, Rietie."

She'd heard this stated over and over, but what did that *mean*? "Do we get to go home?"

Mama's lips pressed together, and she steered Ita out of the crowd. When they stopped under a scraggly palm tree, Mama said, "There is nowhere for us to go yet. Our homes are occupied. Besides, we need to find your father, and the Vos family needs to find their father and Johan."

Ita hoped that Johan would come back to their camp, then she could tell him everything that had happened since he'd left. Would he remember her? Or would he be too old to care about a young girl?

"Will Papa come here from Glodok?"

"I don't know that," Mama said. "He may have been transferred somewhere else."

Aunt Tie came to stand beside them. "If he's not at Glodok, he's probably dead," she announced with an edge to her words.

Mama puffed out a breath as if she was annoyed.

"But there are ladies who are going to work on reuniting families through the Red Cross," Aunt Tie continued in her bossy voice. "Lieutenant Sakai is allowing them to use one of the offices."

"They can find Papa, then," Ita burst out. "Or *we* can go find *him*. Glodok isn't so far."

"No one's going anywhere," Aunt Tie said. "Haven't you told her anything, Mary? She's not a child anymore—none of these children are." Without adding anything more, she strode off.

Ita wasn't sure why Aunt Tie spoke sharply to Mama. The two women never seemed to like each other. "What does she mean? I thought the war was over."

"The *world* war is over," Mama said in a quiet voice.

Ita wondered why there were tears in Mama's eyes. Weren't they supposed to be happy about all of this? Was Mama getting sick again?

Mama cleared her throat. "You might as well know. Some children have probably been told already. The Indonesians have declared their independence from the Dutch."

Ita wrinkled her brow. Greta had said something about this too, but if the world war was over, did that change more things?

Before she could determine exactly what this meant, Mama said, "This means, because we are Dutch, we are safer inside the camp walls.

The Japanese guards are going to protect us from the Indonesian rebel groups who want all Dutch people to leave the islands."

Ita nodded slowly, although she wasn't sure why the Japanese guards who'd been their enemies were now having to protect them from people who used to be friends. Maybe they weren't all friends like Ita had thought? She still remembered Kemala, Anja, Dea, and Bima. They would always be her friends, right?

"So that's why we can't go back to our house?"

"Yes," Mama said on a sigh. "Not only is another family living there, but we aren't safe to travel in the open. Groups of rebels are rising up and taking back everything on the islands. The Dutch have become their new enemies."

Ita didn't know what it felt like to be Indonesian and have your islands taken over by Dutch colonists. But she did know what it felt like to be put into a prison camp and ruled over by a different kind of people. She didn't really blame the Indonesians for wanting to rule their own country again, but she knew this probably wasn't something she should say to other adults.

It did mean one terrible thing for her, though. Ita no longer had a home. Anywhere.

Mrs. Vos joined them, walking up with Greta. "We're collecting all red, white, and blue material. We're having a flag-making party since the war is over now."

They all headed to the house to search for materials. They lived in a house that was close to the gate, which meant they heard all the news before others farther back in the camp. Ita wondered, though, if displaying flags would be a good thing if the Indonesians wanted the Dutch people to leave their islands.

The mood was happy when they arrived at their house. This was unusual because one family was always crying over the news of a dead father or brother or son. There was no crying right now, though.

Women and older children had gathered into sewing groups. Blue, red, and white seemed to be the only colors she could see. She'd been told the war was over, and seeing these women busy sewing Dutch flags, sent hope through Ita. Maybe this was all truly real.

Then the megaphone sounded on their street. Mrs. Vos hurried out so that she'd get all the instructions. It seemed that even with the war over, and Japan surrendering, the Japanese guards at the camp were still making decisions.

"Lieutenant Sakai has ordered all flag making to stop," the orders came loud and clear so that Ita had no problem deciphering them. "No flag making, and no singing of the Dutch national anthem. Those who are caught will be severely punished."

The women making the flags groaned in disappointment.

Arguments broke out. Some of the women thought it was a smart idea—they were doing this in too much haste. One woman said, "The Japanese can't tell us what to do anymore."

Another woman argued back, "They still have the weapons and control of the food supply. This is a minor thing to stop."

Mrs. Vos came into the house then and held up her hands, her signal for everyone to be quiet and listen. "We must be patient. There is a new government on Java, and it's no longer Dutch. We don't want to antagonize the Indonesian rebel groups that roam the villages. We don't know if the world powers will recognize their declaration of independence, but we must keep order until we know what our next steps are."

Ita frowned. She didn't know what "antagonize" meant, but she'd ask Mama. Or Greta.

The women continued to murmur and mutter, but they put away their pieces of fabric. This made Ita feel better. She hated the punishments. Since Sonei had left, there hadn't been the punishments that made the women scream and shout with pain. She didn't want any of that to return.

Greta came into the house. Everyone looked at her because she frequently had news that she would share. The women wanted to know why Sakai was forbidding them from making flags and why he was threatening punishments.

But Greta held up her hand for quiet, just like her mother did to call for attention.

"The food trucks are getting stopped and looted by the Indonesian rebel groups," Greta said. "So the trucks will be coming during the middle of the night, but there will be no time to load the dead bodies. This means that we will need to dig mass graves for the dead."

The women didn't respond for a moment. Ita didn't know numbers, but Greta had told her more people were dying per day now than before, even with more food available. The overeating of foods they weren't used to was causing just as many problems as starvation had. They were so close to freedom! And now they wouldn't get to be buried in a proper cemetery?

The joy of the news of the war ending and everyone making flags had suddenly left the room. The harsh reality of their lives in this prison camp continued.

"Lieutenant Sakai is no better than Captain Sonei," one woman cried out.

Greta set her hands on her hips. "Look outside the gates if you have to," she said in a fierce tone.

Ita had never heard Greta sound angry like this.

"There are rebel groups roaming the area who are attacking anything that has to do with the Dutch people. Do you want the bodies of our loved ones desecrated?"

Ita moved closer to Mama, who was staring at Greta, horror in her eyes.

"I know it's hard to believe, but the Japanese army is protecting us now," Greta continued, her usually soft voice commanding. "If the Japanese leave, then we are without protection. Some of us can barely run, let alone fight against a mob of Indonesian rebels who haven't been starving for almost four years."

Heads started to nod.

The megaphone sounded outside, and Mrs. Vos hurried onto the veranda again. This time the announcement was rapid, short. She was back inside in moments.

"Everyone, listen," Mrs. Vos said, her voice trembling.

Was she crying?

Ita nestled against her mother. What more bad news could there be?

"Allied troops are coming to the camp to help protect us." Her eyes gleamed bright. "And there are Dutch prisoners among them. Some of them might be our men."

Ita watched women and children scramble to their feet. They hurried out to go watch by the gates.

But Ita didn't move. She didn't want to go wait and watch. It would get her hopes up too much.

Mama slipped an arm about her. "If Papa is among the men, we will know soon enough."

Georgie moved to the battered suitcase that held their precious few belongings. He pulled out the picture of their father and stared at it. Ita's eyes brimmed with tears. If she was worried about not recognizing Papa, then Georgie was even more worried.

He looked over at her with his beautiful hazel eyes.

"If you want to go to the gate, then I'll go too," she told her brother, even though he hadn't asked.

Georgie wiped at his cheeks, then nodded.

Ita hoped that her little brother's heart wouldn't be broken.

Mama was smiling though. How could she smile? What if Papa was lost to them forever?

"Come, we'll all go together." She scooped Robbie in her arms, then Ita and Georgie followed her out of the house.

The roads were abuzz with conversation among women, children playing their games, and smells of people cooking things in their yards. All things that had been suppressed by Captain Sonei.

Yet, they were still hungry, they were still dying, and they were still prisoners.

Ita crossed the yard slowly since she didn't want to hurry just to feel disappointed.

She and Georgie perched on the sagging fence beneath the shade of a palm tree. From here, they had a view of most of the gate, but they kept out of the crowds of people. A breeze ruffled through their hair—the kind that cooled their sticky bodies when sitting in the shade.

A couple of trucks were heading toward the gates, driven by Allied soldiers, and behind those trucks men trudged along. They didn't look like soldiers though—not with their worn and dirty clothing, scraggly hair, and thin bodies. Instead, they looked steps away from lying down in their own graves.

When the gates opened, the trucks drove in, sending up plumes of dust that swirled in the wind. The men and boys in their rags entered the camp, then stopped after the gates shut, waiting for instruction. The trucks lumbered to a stop, and the Allied soldiers climbed out.

Lieutenant Sakai greeted them, and conversations that Ita couldn't hear went back and forth.

Ita examined the faces of the men and boys she could see from her position.

"Is one of them Papa?" Georgie asked, hope in his little voice.

"I don't know," Ita said. "I can't see him."

Mama said nothing from where she leaned against the fence, holding onto Robbie.

A woman started screaming, crying really, but it wasn't the cry of pain that Ita had heard so often. She was shouting a name over and over.

"Willem! Willem!"

It was then that Ita realized Mrs. Vos was the woman pushing through the others, crying out for . . . her husband.

"Mama," Ita whispered. "It's Mr. Vos." His red hair was still red, but he looked more like a scarecrow in a storybook than a man.

Her heart thumped. Was Johan . . .?

Mr. Vos strode toward his wife.

It seemed that Lieutenant Sakai was going to allow the men to greet their families. No one stopped Mrs. Vos, and no one stopped her husband.

Another person moved out of the line of men. A different man. This one with red hair too, although it was darker.

"Johan!" Georgie yelled.

Was it really . . . Ita gasped as Johan joined his mother. Greta was there too, in a tangle of arms and sobs, hugging each other.

More reunions happened, and Ita lost sight of the Vos family because people were moving all about now. Looking, seeking, calling out.

"George," Mama whispered at the same time that Ita saw a man walking toward them.

He might be thinner, but his walk was the same. A walk that Ita recognized, that she knew, that belonged to her father. But was he her father? She squinted against the glare of the sun and the brightness of the blue sky.

Mama had straightened, and with Robbie still in her arms, she began to walk toward the man.

It *was* Papa.

The realization shivered through Ita's body, all the way to her toes. He was alive, and he was here, at Tjideng Camp.

"Papa!" she cried out, but it was only a rasp. Her throat was so tight that her voice had stopped working.

Georgie's hand found hers, clutching tight. "Is that Papa?" he asked, hope widening his eyes.

Ita's tears started, and she could only nod *yes*, over and over. Papa wore ill-fitting, patched-up khaki shorts, a shirt with no sleeves, and sandals that looked like he'd made them from bicycle tires.

Mama reached him first, and Papa cradled Robbie's face. With tears on his cheeks, he bent forward and kissed Robbie on the forehead. Then he hugged Mama, Robbie nestled between them. They hugged so tightly that Ita wondered if they would ever come apart. Hand in hand with Georgie, she met her parents in the road. All of the other reunions, all of the other instructions between the Allies and Japan, were blown away on the wind.

Papa broke away from Mama.

Tears made trails along his face, and he took Robbie in his arms and kissed him over and over.

Robbie's face had gone red, and he wasn't sure what to make of the dark-haired, golden-skinned stranger that was his father. But then Papa saw Ita and Georgie. She wondered if they had changed as much as he had changed. What did Papa see in them?

He crouched and held out his arms.

Ita tugged Georgie with her, who broke out into a grin.

"Papa!" he shouted, connecting the man with the picture he'd memorized.

Then, Ita was in Papa's arms. He didn't smell of the starched cotton and pine that she remembered. He smelled of war: mud and sweat and blood. His voice was the same, though, and his brown eyes . . . they were the same too. A scar like a tiny ant trail followed one of his cheekbones, and his hair was cut funny.

But it was him. His voice, his eyes, and the love she could feel—were all the same.

Papa was here. At last. Nothing else mattered right now.

CHAPTER THIRTY-ONE

"Following August 21, all internees were requested to assemble at the lawn near the front gate. Our camp leader informed all of us that on August 15, the Japanese had officially capitulated and the war was over. Also, Schotel impressed upon us that we had to stay within the campground boundaries because it simply had become too dangerous to leave camp. Large numbers of fanatic Indonesian *pemuda* (young man) had turned unruly following Sukarno's proclamation of Indonesia's independence. They became a serious threat to the Dutch colonialists, whom they attacked at every opportunity."

—RALPH OCKERSE, TJIMAHI CAMP

GEORGE

George and Vos had fallen into a routine. After a day spent working throughout the Tjideng camp, which consisted of clearing sewage ditches and garbage, George would head to the medical center to see if any help was needed there. Most times, Vos came along.

It was nearly dusk, and the day's heat had finally faded to a dull swelter. Anytime the sun wasn't directly overhead, things became bearable.

As they walked to the medical center, they passed by a group of young men.

"Where are you headed?" George asked. He'd been told of the gangs of boys that had stirred up trouble at Tjideng. He didn't want to see that happen again.

"We're collecting wood for cooking fires," one young man said. "Starting with the interior gedek wall toward the back of the camp."

George didn't like the idea, not at all. They were all stuck together in this camp for a reason. "I'd caution you against destroying the bamboo fence that's protecting us." Even as he spoke, he knew the young men would do as they pleased. He had no authority over them, and times had changed. Which meant, it was every man for himself most days. George had experienced plenty of that at Glodok.

He and Vos trudged to the medical center. George's nose wrinkled as they passed the fresher burial pits. The entire camp stank. With no sewer system for years, and poor cleanliness, it was no wonder. He didn't imagine other camps throughout the rest of the islands had been much better, but having so many thousands crammed into such tight housing, only amplified it here. Disease and infections were rampant among the women and children—the elderly had had the worst of it. George had been sorry to hear about Oma's passing. On one hand, he was grateful her suffering was over, but on the other hand, she was missed so much by his family.

The quiet of the morning was interrupted as two women, along with their children, hurried past George and Vos.

George did a double take. One of them looked like his sister, Tie, but it wasn't her after all. Their reunion had been brief when he'd first arrived, and it was clear that Tie had gone through experiences she didn't want to talk about. She was as skinny as Mary—all the women were. Her stiff personality had grown even more distant than it had been before the war.

"Where are they taking their children so quickly?" Vos asked, breaking into George's thoughts.

"I have no idea."

They watched the group continue to the front gates and bow to the guard. They exchanged some words, and after a moment, the guard opened the gate and let them through.

George stared after the group. "What just happened?" He strode to the guard who'd finished closing the gate again. "Where are those women going? They won't be safe out there."

The Japanese guard gave a shrug. "The war is over. We can't force anyone to stay inside."

"But how will they survive out there?"

"Not our problem." The guard waved a hand. "They want to go, then that's their decision."

Vos set a hand on George's shoulder. "We can't order everyone about."

George knew this, of course, but there had to be more order. More information given out to those in the camp. They needed to understand.

Over the past few weeks, local Indonesian townsfolk had brought gifts of food to Tjideng. With so much need and demand, it wasn't enough to pass out to everyone. But the sentiment was a turning point. Some of those who arrived were former servants looking for their employers, wanting to return to their jobs and lives from before the war.

Unfortunately, none of the Dutch were in a position to rehire their former employees.

George moved away from the gate, feeling deflated. Vos was right. They couldn't force anyone to stay in the camp, but still he worried about the women traveling without protection. He walked with Vos to the medical building, where they met with a doctor at the entrance to find out what needed doing.

Then he heard a shout from somewhere outside. Turning, George saw the women running back toward the gates. The confused Japanese guard opened them.

Beyond the women, coming up Laan Trivelli, was a crowd of youths and men. They were waving red and white flags, shouting and chanting words that George couldn't yet decipher as they beat tongtongs. And

. . . they carried weapons. The men were armed with golok swords and ratjangs.

The women and their children slipped through the gate, and the guard locked it. Other residents and guards came out of the houses and buildings to see what was going on.

The crowd of rebels neared, shouting and screaming.

"What are they saying?" Dr. Starreveld asked.

"I don't know," Vos replied. "But they're out for blood."

"We need to arm ourselves," Dr. Starreveld continued, her voice a measure of calm in the erupting panic beyond the gate. "The Japanese are the ones with the weapons, though."

George's skin crawled. Men lived in Tjideng camp now, but they were recovering from years of malnourishment. This rebel group was strong and healthy and filled with vengeful anger.

More guards lined the gates, the Japanese bringing out their bayonets. That would help, but George knew they were outnumbered and outmanned.

There must have been enough of a defense at the front gate to deter the rebel group, who marched along the railway embankment on the other side of the wall.

"They're tearing down the walls!" someone shouted.

Panicked words shot through the crowd, and those who'd come out of their houses ran back in. To hide? To find something to fight back with?

The sun had fully set, and darkness would soon be upon them. "Someone needs to tell Sakai," George said. His gaze connected with Vos first, then the doctor.

The doctors in the camp had a lot more sway with the Lieutenant. "I'll go ask him for a revolver," Dr. Starreveld said. "Maybe shooting it in the air will scare them away."

George swallowed, his throat feeling like it was on fire. An all-out battle with this rebel group would result only in tragedy for the Dutch.

"We'll meet you at the fence," George said, determined to find something to fight with and join the Dutch men creating a barrier between the fence and the camp.

All George could come up with was a knife from the medical center, and he and Vos charged toward the group who'd gathered. Most of the men carried shovels and pieces of wood. It turned out, his weapon was one of the better ones.

The interior fence still held, but it would be only a matter of minutes before the exterior fence fell. The rebel group's screams filled the night with fear as they continuously beat tongtongs.

"Look," Vos hissed, nudging George.

Dr. Starreveld was running toward them, and behind her, a group of Japanese guards, carrying rifles. They took position at the wall, and the guard named Kano lifted a rifle and shot into the night sky. This was followed by another series of rifle shots by more Japanese guards.

The drumming of the tongtongs stopped. The chanting of the rebels turned to panicked questions.

Kano fired, setting off another round by the other Japanese guards.

Voices outside the walls called to each other to run, and then the voices faded. The Dutch and the Japanese stood together, listening, and waiting. Had the group left for good? At least the rebels now knew that there were weapons inside the camp.

After nearly an hour of standing around, discussing their options, George headed back to his house. Something had to change. His family was not safe here. They were like sitting ducks.

George knew he wouldn't sleep that night.

"What happened?" Mary asked as soon as he entered their shared room.

Since the children were already asleep, he told her in whispered words the events of the night. She nestled close and linked hands as he explained the danger outside the walls. "We need to find a way out of here," he said, against her hair.

Mary kept her hair short, but it was thin, regardless. Everything about her was thin, and even though George knew he didn't look much better, it hurt him deep inside to see his wife and children suffering from the ravages of years of malnutrition.

"Aren't we safer inside these walls?" Mary asked.

"I thought so, until tonight." George squeezed her fingers. Like his hands, hers were rough, calloused, her nails brittle. "There has to be a better way to live until we can get off this island."

Mary nodded against his shoulder, and he looked over at their sleeping children.

The reunion with his family had been beautiful, yet bittersweet. Seeing his son Robbie had brought such a joy and relief. And Ita and Georgie—having grown up so much—not only in stature but in intelligence.

But his children were all so thin, their skin crusted with scabs and littered with scars, their eyes hollows of trepidation and anxiety. Georgie was such a quiet boy, though helpful and obedient to his mother. Robbie stuck to George every chance possible. And Rita . . . the sight of her thin arms and thin legs had nearly broken his heart when he saw her. She was Mary's right-hand helper, and he marveled at how independent and smart she was.

And Mary . . . her no-nonsense personality had become quieter. She ducked her head a lot, and she avoided answering some of his questions. Sometimes she seemed to tune out when he was speaking. It was as if she went someplace else in her mind for a few moments.

Eventually Mary fell asleep, but George remained awake, turning possibilities over in his mind. As the dawn-gray sky turned a pale lavender, George wasn't sure if he'd come up with a solution of how to get his family out of this over-crowded, disease-infested camp.

But right now, Mary was nestled against him in sleep. Robbie was curled up on his other side. It had taken a handful of days to really gain Robbie's trust, but lately the toddler followed him everywhere. George didn't mind at all. Being with his wife and children was the most important thing.

They could face what they had to, and it would be together.

Everyone in the crowded house still slept, gaining every minute of rest that they could before another day of work began. At least they were working for the betterment of their situation, instead of following interminable orders with no end in sight. And at least George's family had a roof over their heads. Many of the newly reunited families were camping in the yards outside.

Day after day, he and the other men repaired sewer lines, water lines, and electrical hookups. And day after day, they ate the meager offerings that had been trucked in. Over the years of imprisonment, George had sometimes wondered if death was a blessing for those who fell victim. Struggling each day physically and mentally and emotionally had taken its toll on all of them. Yet, having good friends at Glodok had helped tremendously. Kept him going. Unfortunately, Jacques and Ed had both succumbed to malaria. There were simply not enough medical supplies to treat every diseased person.

Because of the loss of his friends, he was more determined to live a life outside of war. To make the best of what came next. To provide for his family. Which was why he wanted to get them out of Tjideng.

George had thought Glodok was a prisoners' nightmare, but this place was atrocious.

Mary had told him a few things, but mostly she didn't want to talk about the past. Not even the immediate past. The aftermath of the abuse and deprivation these women and children had suffered was plain for all to see.

The day that Johan had arrived in Glodok had been a day of both joy and grief. Willem had been thrilled to see his son again, but he knew his wife needed their boy's help more. Johan had told them about the terror of the man, Captain Sonei. He'd also told them about the other guards who were afraid of Sonei and followed his orders with no other choice.

Vos prayed night and day, aloud, and with quite a bit of fervency, for the war to end. For the Dutch to be freed. For their women to be freed.

George would never claim to be a praying man, but his heart beat to the rhythm of Vos's words.

"You're awake?" Mary spoke in a sleepy voice, stirring next to him. "Did you sleep at all?"

"I'm not sure." George had closed his eyes, and time had passed, but he wasn't sure if he'd truly slept. "We can't stay here."

Mary rose to a sitting position and peered at him. Her blonde hair tumbled about her face, and her cheeks had filled out a little more. With the Allies dropping parachutes of food containers, the available nutrition had improved. But there was still a long way to go. "Where will we go, George? The islands are overrun with civil unrest."

"I've been talking to Willem about the possibility of moving closer to one of the bases the Allies are occupying. It will give us the protection we need until we can get out of Java."

At this, Mary sighed. "Where will we go after that?"

He knew the question wasn't general. They'd be shipped to the motherland—the Netherlands. Another war-torn country trying to recover from Nazi occupation. But in the Netherlands, they wouldn't be the target of genocide.

The queen of Holland would have her hands full with the influx of refugees that would be seeking repatriation soon. "I don't know yet, but we'll stay together no matter what. I'll find work wherever I can. I'm sure there are a lot of rebuilding projects."

They both fell silent for a moment. The window had lightened with the approaching sunrise, but everyone else in the house still slept. It was the brief space where they could have some privacy, which wasn't really privacy at all.

"Things are working here again," Mary said. "The toilets, the plumbing, the water, the electricity. It's so much better than it was."

George turned and took Mary into his arms. "It's a step forward, but inside the camp, we're just five out of thousands of people. If we can get a place close to the Allied base, then we'll have a chance to get on one of the first ships out. I'm going to offer my services. Maybe that will earn us a quicker way out."

Mary nodded against his chest, and he pulled her closer. "What if it doesn't work? Will we be worse off?"

"If we don't take a risk, then we'll never know," George said. "At Glodok, we found the hidden getaway vehicles that the Japanese soldiers had ready in case the Allies arrived. We took the pistols they'd concealed in the trucks, and we stripped the tires."

Mary lifted her head. "How did you hide everything?"

George smiled. "We didn't. Not exactly. We used the tire rubber for our shoes and the leather from the seats for jackets. I hid one of the pistols in the false bottom I created in my clogs."

Mary stifled a gasp. "You paraded all of that in front of the soldiers?"

"They were none the wiser," George said. "We took out the batteries of the vehicles and the radio components. Vos kept a radio transistor hidden in the bamboo yoke he used to carry buckets of water. Of course, the raid couldn't remain secret forever. Eventually, the Japanese military discovered what we'd done, but they never found the pistols or who'd done the raiding. Kept the soldiers on their toes."

"George, I can't believe you did all that."

He kissed the top of her head. "I'd do just about anything to keep my family safe." The room began to lighten as the sun crested the horizon, and people throughout the house stirred. Their privacy had ended.

George headed out of the house. He wanted to talk to Dr. Starreveld at the medical center. Find out how she'd talked Lieutenant Sakai into sending guards with the rifles.

As if he were on the same time schedule, Vos appeared in the yard too. They walked together to the medical center.

Dr. Starreveld was already there—not surprising to George. The medical staff seemed to work at all hours. George was happy to help on his off hours. In return for this extra work, they found favor with the doctors and nurses. Something that might come in handy if one of their family members became ill. It was a trick that George had learned at

Glodok. He treated all the Japanese soldiers with equanimity. Yes, they were strict and doled out punishments to those who broke the rules, but most of them were just trying to get through the war too. Serving their country, staying loyal to their emperor. Following orders.

It was men like Captain Sonei who deserved imprisonment or execution. George had the feeling that once the Allies heard about the atrocities the man had committed and forced those under his command to commit, he would be tried in a war crimes court.

The thought brought the smallest bit of satisfaction to George's mind, although he'd rather the atrocities hadn't happened at all.

"How did you get Sakai to send troops to the fence?" George asked.

"I spoke to Sakai directly. I reminded him of his orders to protect the Dutch. But instead of doing it himself, he ordered his men to load ammunition into their rifles. I think he knew that displaying a few bayonets at the gate hadn't worked."

George nodded.

"Mr. Vischer," Dr. Starreveld continued. "The Japanese military gave us back our radios. And this morning, it was announced that housing was being made available in some of the neighborhoods near the former NEI naval base, which is now under Allied control."

George had one question. "Can we head out on the next truck?"

"You'll have to clear it with Sakai," she said. "You're free to leave, of course, but leaving on a truck might be another issue after what happened last night."

George thanked the doctor and headed toward the commander's office. He would wait all day if he had to in order to get an audience with the man. Vos settled in the dirt next to George, leaning against the wall.

Neither man had to speak. They were both good at waiting. It's what they'd been doing for over three years.

Finally, Sakai allowed a meeting, and George gave a formal bow, then began his appeal.

"The overcrowding here is getting worse," he said after thanking the man for hearing his case. "We're taking our families out of the camp, but we wanted to get permission to ride out on one of the trucks—as far as it will go. There will be no special location. We need a head start since we don't have money for a train."

He didn't want to take a train anyway. Not if the rebel groups were looking for more targets.

Sakai, sitting at his battered desk, his fingers steepled in front of him, took a long moment to respond.

Then, finally, he dipped his chin. "You will go out on the food truck this afternoon." He looked over at one of his guards. "Check the records to see if the belongings of the Vischer and Vos families have been returned. If they haven't, return them right away."

The guard bowed.

George and Vos both bowed.

George couldn't believe his luck. The truck would cut down their traveling time and offer them protection as well. He could only hope it would get them close enough to the naval base that they could walk the rest of the way before dark.

He hurried back to the house where Mary was preparing the children for the morning. Ita was self-sufficient, and she was like a mother hen to her younger brothers. George was impressed while at the same time sad that he'd missed the last years with his children.

"Mary," he said, settling next to her, and keeping his voice low. He told her what he'd arranged, then cautioned her to be discreet about their packing.

Mary blinked rapidly, and her smile appeared. "Truly?" She drew in a deep breath. "Will we be safe?"

"We can't stay here," George said. "Dysentery is running rampant again. More and more freed prisoners are arriving to seek shelter inside the walls. If we're close to the Allied naval base, I can work on getting us on one of the first ships out. But I can't do that from here."

Mary wiped at her eyes. "We will go, then."

George didn't know if Mary's tears were because she was happy or overwhelmed. Maybe she was both. He grasped her calloused hand. "I won't let anything happen to you and the children, or my sister. We'll get off this island and start a new life."

In her eyes, he saw the trust there. A trust he intended to always earn.

CHAPTER THIRTY-TWO

"About [this] camp life I'd rather not write. It would spoil this first letter and I am also determined to forget about this crazy period as soon as possible. The future interests me more. I have made a thousand and one plans, but they remain dreams."

—BOUDEWIJN A. J. VAN OORT SR., TJIMAHI CAMP

RITA

Ita sat with her knees pulled up, wedged between Johan and Georgie, as they rode in the back of a food truck. Greta sat on the other side of Johan. Across from them, the adults sat, swaying against each other with the truck's movement. Robbie sat on Papa's lap. Everyone had been told to stay low and not lift their heads above the sides of the wood railing that edged the open bed. Aunt Tie hadn't come with them. She'd told Papa that she was going to work at the camp until the ship was ready.

"Where are we going again?" Georgie asked for the fourth or fifth time.

Ita knew he was just tired. She was tired too. They'd been driving for what felt like forever, and the wind and sun and sights had been exciting at first, but now her stomach hurt with all the jostling.

Johan was the one who answered in a patient tone. His voice had deepened during his absence from Tjideng, and he had stubbly red whiskers on his chin. "Our fathers are going to find us a place to live close

319

to the naval base. The Allies are there now, and they can help us get on a ship."

Georgie absorbed the information. "But we're not coming back to Tjideng?"

Ita felt the shudder ripple through Johan.

"No," he said in a firm voice. "Even with the Bersiap going on, we have to find another place to live so we can escape the diseased housing."

Ita had heard the word *Bersiap* more than once, and was beginning to understand that it was the word the Dutch were using to describe the Indonesian National Revolution. Johan had told her all about what had happened last night with the rebel mob tearing down the fence. Mama had made her stay inside until Papa returned. Ita had thought they'd be safe in a camp with walls and the Japanese army to protect them. But last night had shown them how open to attack Tjideng was. Would they be safe in another location?

Her brother easily accepted Johan's answer.

Ita was glad they'd left Tjideng, but it felt a bit like she was dreaming. Maybe she'd wake up in a few hours and learn they hadn't left at all. When the truck had pulled out of the camp, she'd hoped that everything she was seeing would be for the last time—the central kitchen, the monkey cage, the guardhouse, Captain Sonei's house, the concrete bridge . . . Mama and Mrs. Vos had both cried after the gates closed behind them, and the truck drove along Laan Trivelli with its tall shady trees and houses with wide verandas.

Ita's heart rate had kicked up a notch when they'd neared their old home. It looked different somehow, even though it was the same. The yard seemed vast, her favorite mango tree giant, and the house larger than Ita remembered. Had she really lived in a place with so many rooms and so much space with only her family?

The house was also sad. As if it missed the days before the war. When there had been laughter and music and cooking and . . . life. The streets were quiet. Maybe because it was the middle of the afternoon and people were sleeping through the hottest part of the day.

What had happened to Kemala, Anja, Dea, and Bima?

Ita thought back to the moment they'd actually stopped right in front of the house.

"Mary," Papa had said in a quiet voice. "We're near the house. We could stop and look for your jewelry box."

Mama stared at him. "It's not safe to stop. Besides, our house is occupied, and we can't expect—"

"If we see trouble, we don't stop," Papa said. "I want you to have something from our lives before all of this." He waved a hand.

After a long moment, Mama gave a short nod.

Papa moved to the window that separated the driver from everyone else and spoke to the man in Malay. In moments, the truck had stopped in front of the old house.

Mama climbed out of the truck, Papa following. Mr. Vos went with them as well.

"We need to hurry," Papa said. "The sooner we are gone, the better."

Ita had craned her neck to watch her parents and Mr. Vos dig with their hands in the area that used to be a garden. It was overrun with other plants now. They started a few different holes, until Mama finally held up a box covered in dirt. Ita smiled at the triumph on Mama's face, but she was still nervous about someone trying to stop them. Were there rebels in this neighborhood?

No one came out of the other houses. But it felt like they were being watched all the same.

Papa and Mr. Vos quickly filled in the other holes, as Mama hurried back to the truck, brushing dirt from the metal box as she went. When Papa and Mr. Vos reached the truck and climbed in, the driver wasted no time in stepping on the gas pedal.

And they were off again.

After Mama cleaned off most of the dirt, she opened the box. She didn't show everyone the contents, but her smile said it all. She had her jewelry back.

Now, long after they'd passed their old house, Ita was still wondering about who lived there. Was her teddy bear still on her bed? And had they watched Mama dig in what used to be a garden?

Georgie had fallen asleep again, his head on Ita's shoulder. At first, he'd gazed about, looking at everything in wonder, asking question after question. Robbie didn't seem as entranced with the change in scenery and activity. He was content to be sitting on Papa's lap.

Occasionally, they would see the trains that ran parallel to the roads. Taking a train would have been much faster, but Papa had said that the trains weren't safe. Ita didn't understand why. Dutch people had arrived on the trains that came into the camp.

She smoothed her new skirt over her knees and picked at a thread on the seam. Well, the skirt wasn't new exactly. It had come in one of those Red Cross donation boxes. Everyone had sorted through the boxes, finding what would mostly fit them. There hadn't been time to try things on before choosing what to keep, so Ita's clothes might not fit, but at least they weren't falling apart like her old ones had.

Suddenly the truck slowed, then took a quick turn onto a smaller road that was bumpy with rocks.

"Where are we going?" Mrs. Vos asked, her tone sharp. She peered over the side of the truck. Papa shifted to the back window of the cab. There wasn't even a window, only an opening.

He spoke Malay to the driver, and Ita realized she'd forgotten most of the Malay words she'd known before.

When Papa turned back to the family, he said, "The train up ahead has been stopped by a rebel group." His eyes narrowed, and he looked over at Mr. Vos.

Something silent passed between them. Ita didn't know what was happening, but a hard pit formed in her stomach. It was something bad, that she was sure of. She was grateful to the driver of their truck for taking a detour. If she'd had something to give him as a thank you, she would. But their suitcases held only personal belongings. At least Japan had given back Papa's certificates that they'd taken from Mama when they'd first arrived at camp.

Ita had even gotten back her teddy bear's shirt with the flag on it. She would never see that teddy bear again, but since Oma had sewn the shirt, Ita would always keep it.

As the truck continued bumping along, Johan turned to look over the side, through the wooden slats.

"Keep your eyes on each other," Mr. Vos said, his voice sounding worried. "You don't need to see what's happening, son."

Johan obeyed, but Ita could feel the tension coming from him. What was happening? She wouldn't look, but she was still curious. Mama and Mrs. Vos had their eyes closed, but Greta stared down at her hands, which were gripped tightly in her lap.

"What are they doing?" Ita whispered so that just Johan could hear.

Some things about him might have changed, but he still was always willing to answer any of her questions. "At camp there were rumors that the Dutch people are being forced off trains." He paused. "And they're shooting them."

Ita's stomach lurched. This was bad, very bad.

Her father had been smart to get them a ride on this truck instead. They didn't have money for a train anyway, but what if they'd found tickets?

Ita felt sorry for the people on the train. Were there kids like her? In the camp, the Japanese soldiers had always been nice to the children. If a child broke a rule, their mother would be punished, not the child. But did the rebel groups spare children? What would happen to the children without their parents?

She had so many questions, but she couldn't ask Johan all of them now. And she didn't want to ask any of the adults. At least not here, not right now.

The truck driver must have been shaken up over the train incident because he told Papa he was going to continue past his route and take them all the way to the naval base. When they arrived, it was nearly dark, so Ita could only see groups of buildings. No one was in the streets.

The Bersiap activities included a natural curfew—at least that's what

Johan said. He'd told her that the rebel groups were more active at night, when they could target a few people at a time.

Ita tried not to think of rebels attacking her family. They didn't have any weapons to defend themselves. She would fight, though. She'd protect Georgie and Robbie no matter what.

When the truck finally stopped, Ita was glad to get out of her cramped position. Papa helped her out of the truck, then he turned to help everyone else. Mrs. Vos insisted on giving the truck driver a piece of her jewelry she'd gotten back at camp, but he refused it.

"Karma will repay me and you."

The truck lumbered off, and the two families were left to stand on a quiet street in the dark.

"Come," Papa said. "We'll inquire at the headquarters building. Someone will be on guard."

As they walked along, Johan's stride slowed to Ita's.

She shivered, not from cold, but from dreading what might happen next.

"We're in Allied territory now," he said. "We'll be much safer."

Ita wanted to believe his words. He hadn't been wrong about anything else.

They found a place to sleep after Papa knocked on several doors at the naval base. They were led into a large room that had no beds. Ita wasn't picky anyway. She lay on the hard floor next to her family and listened as everyone settled in.

She wanted to sleep, she really did, but the silence was so strange. There were no crying babies or mothers hushing their children, no people coughing up sickness or going in and out to use the sewage trench, no one talking in their sleep . . . the silence made Ita wish there was some noise, somewhere.

Ita was awakened when someone knocked on the door of the room they'd been put in. It startled her at first because there had been no doors in Tjideng, and no one knocked for anything. The sun was up though, and everyone else in the two families was already awake.

Mr. Vos opened the door, and two men in blue uniforms walked in. Ita knew the men weren't Dutch because they were healthy, clean, and wearing British uniforms.

One of them knew some Dutch, but Mr. Vos knew better English. After a couple of minutes, Papa turned to everyone. "The Allies have invited the Dutch children and their families to go to a lunch party and tour the American warship in the harbor."

Ita didn't know what to think. The words *lunch* and *party* weren't something she'd experienced in years. She wasn't going to say no, and neither was anyone else. Both families headed down to the harbor, a place Papa called Tandjong Priok.

Papa said the last time he'd seen the harbor was the night he'd left Java with a group of naval officers.

The ship was so large that Ita nearly lost her balance as she tilted her head to see the whole thing. Music played, and aboard there were already families with children. And the lunch . . . Ita didn't know what to look at first. Fruits, vegetables, egg rolls, and bread. Real bread. Not the gray sticky kind made from tapioca. This bread was light and airy, and there was butter.

Everyone was smiling. Everyone was laughing. She heard a new word—*Yankee*—referring to the American sailors.

There were swings and games for the children. Papa and Mama stood together, holding hands. The tired lines about their faces had softened. Robbie had a lollipop in his mouth, and Ita knew it was his first taste of candy.

As the sea breeze tugged at her hair, and the laughter of children surrounded her, Ita decided that *all would be well*. Just as Mama had said.

CHAPTER THIRTY-THREE

"The Gurkhas, having arrived in the country only a few hours earlier,
stood staring at the scene in silence. They were used to fighting
between men: a war against children was something new for them."

—BOUDEWIJN VAN OORT, TJIDENG CAMP

RITA

From the bedroom window, Ita watched the men below, loading into military trucks. The Gurkha soldiers had arrived. Papa had said they were from India and served in the British Army. Ita was fascinated by their dark khaki uniforms, wide-brimmed hats, and long rifles.

They'd been living in the small house Ita's parents were renting near Tandjong Priok for three months. Well, it was a room, really. The Vos family had rented another room in the house. Papa had them all on the waiting list for the first ship to transport the Dutch out of Java. He'd volunteered to be an engineer on any ship that would take his family.

Papa and Mr. Vos came and went, but everyone else stayed in the house or the yard. Papa said that no one was to go anywhere unless one of the men was with them. During the days, the streets were busy with all sorts of people. Allied soldiers and sailors. Indonesian merchants doing a brisk business with the Europeans and Eurasians who'd congregated there. And now military groups, such as the Gurkhas and the Seaforth Highlanders, were arriving from all over the world.

"They're here to protect the Dutch since the rebels are getting stronger," Johan said, walking into the room. His hair had been cut short recently and it made him look younger.

Ita returned her gaze to the window. "Where are they going?"

"They'll be divvied out among the camps."

At first, the Japanese soldiers had orders to stay and protect the Dutch people in the camps. They had even fought the *pemuda*—the Indonesian rebels—and driven them from the city of Bandung so it could be turned over to the British. But now, their orders were coming to an end. Allied leadership had arrived in Java in late September, and Lieutenant General Sir Philip Christison accepted the formal surrender of the Japanese troops on Java and was now overseeing their disarmament and repatriation. Papa had told Ita this meant the Japanese soldiers were leaving. British troops had arrived at the camps on the island as part of something called RAPWI, the Recovery of Allied Prisoners of War and Internees. But reports on the radio made it sound like the Dutch people on the entire island, and other islands as well, were still in danger. So more soldiers were coming to Java.

Johan listened to the radio at all hours in the bedroom he shared with his parents and Greta.

Ita wondered if the radio was ever turned off.

That's how she'd learned that four Japanese soldiers had been killed by Indonesians in downtown Batavia. Two more were killed in the outskirts of the city along with an Indo. She thought of the soldiers like Kano and Noda at Tjideng, who'd been kind and helpful even when they'd had harsh orders.

Watching the Gurkhas reminded Ita of the time she'd watched the Japanese army arrive on Laan Trivelli. Both signaled change in the country. Both signaled the start of a new war.

"The Japanese are being sent back to Japan," Johan explained. "That's why these other groups are arriving to help with security until all of the Dutch can leave."

Ita was pleased to tell Johan that she already knew this information.

"Papa told me about General Christison trying to restore order, but he doesn't want to make things worse."

Johan nodded at this. "I think you're now smarter than any kid I know."

A smile tugged at Ita's mouth. "How long before we can leave?"

"I don't know," Johan said while watching the troops finish loading into the trucks. The engines started up. "But I hope it's soon."

The radio droned from the other room, and Greta must have turned up the volume, because Ita heard the next report clearly.

"Due to the ongoing boycott of European customers at pasars throughout the islands," the newscaster said, "local refusal to take money that has been distributed by the Red Cross, and the recent killings of European citizens and Japanese soldiers in Batavia and throughout Java, the Royal Air Force is currently facilitating the evacuation of British Commonwealth and American citizens."

Ita frowned at this. When the newscaster switched to a different report, she asked Johan, "What about the Dutch?"

Johan gave a half laugh. "Very good question, Ita. It seems we will be the last to leave. We're likely going to be waiting for the ships to drop off the Americans and British, then come back for us."

Ita leaned her head against the glass of the window. It was warm with the morning sun. For the moment, the neighborhood seemed so peaceful and quiet, even though Ita had heard news reports about a battle that resulted when the Japanese soldiers tried to force the merchants at the pasars to sell to European customers. The outcome was more killings of Europeans and Japanese.

The news switched again. "The Seaforth Highlanders have replaced the Japanese guards completely at Tjideng camp. Lieutenant Sakai and his men are the next to be repatriated to their own country."

Ita looked at Johan. He was nodding slowly, as if this is what he'd expected.

"What was it like at Glodok?" Ita asked in a quiet voice. She didn't mind Greta overhearing if she happened to come in. The adults were downstairs, preparing a meal—everyone rotated turns. And Georgie and Robbie were taking naps. Georgie was probably too old to take naps, but he'd seemed to struggle the most with gaining weight since they'd left camp. The brightness of his eyes had faded, although his smile was still angelic.

Johan leaned against the window frame, looking past her. "Our fathers watched out for me. There were a lot of good men there, watching over the boys who were motherless. But there were the bad apples as well. Punishments were liberally given if anyone broke the rules. There are things I wish I'd never seen, and hope that someday I'll forget."

Johan wasn't usually this personal with her, but she could tell he didn't want to give her specific stories. Maybe another time he would. But she did like how he talked to her like an adult. He never ignored her questions.

His blue gaze settled on her. "We have to move forward, Ita. We can't live in the past."

Ita had been told this by her parents, too, whenever she asked a question about Papa's camp or something she remembered about Tjideng. She didn't know if it was a good thing to forget the past, though. "I don't know if I can forget."

Johan slipped his hands into the pockets of his baggy shorts that were held up by a belt. With a sigh, he said, "When we sail out of Java, I intend to leave all the memories behind. Every day will be a new day with potential for good. The internment camp doesn't deserve any more of my thoughts and time."

Ita furrowed her brow. She understood why Johan wanted to forget the past. She could see the scars on his arms, his legs, one above his left eyebrow. She didn't think those were from Tjideng where the children were protected and the mothers punished instead.

Johan had been through things he would stay silent about.

Sometimes, on nights she couldn't sleep, Ita had heard her parents' whispered words. Papa asking Mama questions, and Mama either refusing to answer or saying things that were only good. Not that there was much good that had happened in the last three and a half years, but there were small moments of triumph. Papa whispered stories about Glodok camp and the way he and his friends would sometimes mess up their work assignments on purpose. A runway laid by prisoners had crumbled a time or two, and the Japanese would have to build it themselves. When Papa and his comrades were supposed to help fix broken-down trucks, they'd often leave something wrong so that the trucks would break down again. Ita liked to think of her Papa fighting the war his own way, even when he was a prisoner of war.

"I'm going to tell my story," Ita said. "Someday. Maybe when I'm grown with children or grandchildren of my own. But I don't want my experiences to be forgotten."

Johan's smile was sad, and he turned toward the window again. A tear skated down his cheek, and he didn't bother wiping it away. "Write your story, then, Ita. Tell the world about what the Dutch faced. Our failures, our triumphs, our pains, and our joys."

Ita felt like crying, too. She didn't know why. Someday, she determined, someday she'd write everything down.

That thought carried her through the next days and weeks as her questions were diverted by her parents, and the news on Java grew worse. The rebels were in full control of utilities, and the food supply was being compromised. Staying on Java would mean either starvation or death at the hands of a mob.

Johan had been right about one thing—the Dutch were the last Europeans civilians to leave the islands. Papa secured a position on the first ship available to the Dutch, the British troopship *Staffordshire*. He would be one of several supervisors over the evacuees. He'd been in training for five days when, finally, the captain of the ship determined they were ready to load the evacuees.

Time had been crawling for months, for years, and suddenly, on a December day in 1945, a canvas-topped military truck pulled up in front of their house.

Ita looked about their rented bedroom for the last time—her

temporary home. She'd only miss it as a place where her family had been able to heal together and get to know Papa again. But now it was time to move on.

"Hurry, Ita," Mama called.

Mama's voice was stronger now. Her color healthy. Her cheeks filled out. Her hair brighter and thicker.

Ita joined the two families at the door as they waited for an armed guard to escort them out.

Now, even in daylight, there had been attacks on the Dutch. Snipers didn't wait until dark. No one was safe, anywhere.

They followed the guard outside, crossed the yard, and climbed into the back of the truck. "Stay low at all times!" the guard warned them.

His warning didn't need to be stated twice.

Ita had listened to plenty of news reports with Johan. She knew about the snipers, the executions, and how the mobs didn't care if you were a man, woman, or child.

Now, Ita lay down in the truck, Georgie nestled beside her.

"Are you scared, Ita?" Georgie whispered.

Ita could say no, but she was sure that Georgie could hear the frantic pace of her heartbeat. "I'm scared," she whispered back. "But we're to-gether, and that's all that matters."

"I'm scared too," Georgie said.

Ita didn't know that the truck ride would take so long—or maybe it just seemed very long. She heard guns firing from time to time. Once the truck swerved sharply. Then it came to an abrupt stop.

The driver told everyone to get out immediately. They'd have to walk the rest of the way to the ship.

Papa protested, but the armed guard was already unloading their suitcases.

"Stay together," Papa said with a grim expression after the truck turned around and went back the way it had driven. "We're going to run. If something drops, do not stop." He looked at Ita. "Hold onto Johan."

She reached for Johan's hand, and he gripped hers tight.

Then to Mama, Papa said, "You've got Robbie? I've got Georgie."

And they ran.

Ita's stomach hurt as they sprinted toward the waiting ship. Other Dutch people were heading in the same direction. Some walking. Others running. A line of armed guards stood in front of the gangplank, with a narrow opening to let the Dutch through.

But several meters in front of Ita, a man stumbled and fell. She thought he'd tripped until she saw the blood on his back.

Johan's grip on her tightened, and he steered her around the man. "Keep running," he said through heaving breaths. "Don't look back, Ita."

She obeyed, but her vision blurred with tears. Her legs were so tired. Her stomach wanted to empty itself. And her heart felt like it was trying to jump out of her chest.

They reached the line of guards, and everyone ran through the opening and hurried up the gangplank. Papa waited until everyone had gone through, then he brought up the rear.

Ita's shins burned, her thighs ached, and she couldn't catch her breath.

Someone fired a rifle. It sounded really close. Ita would have ducked, but Johan's grip was holding her up.

Then they were on the ship, and sailors ushered them to the far side, away from the shore. Ita felt bad for the man who'd been shot just before reaching the ship. Seconds away from freedom.

"Down the stairs," someone shouted in Dutch.

It was repeated again.

Ita followed her mother and Robbie, descending below deck into the dimness.

Voices echoed off the walls, from people in front of them, and people coming in behind them. There was no way to escape the train of people moving down the stairs. The scent was musty, stale, and sharp all at once. It smelled of wood and grease and sweat.

One sailor led the Vos family down another corridor. And Ita's family was led to a cabin that barely fit a single bunkbed. Papa said something about getting hammocks ready for the other passengers to sleep in the cargo holds, and then he left with the sailors. Leaving Ita with Mama and her brothers. Mama didn't waste time in making decisions. "Ita, you and Georgie will be on the top bunk. Robbie and I will share the bottom bunk."

"What about Papa?" Georgie asked.

"He will sleep on a different schedule," Mama said. "He has a lot of responsibility now."

Ita was only too delighted to climb onto the top bunk then help Georgie up. They perched on their high post and looked out the porthole at the grays and blues of the sea and sky.

"What's that?" Georgie asked, pointing out the porthole, where beyond was another smaller ship.

"That's a minesweeper," Mama said, coming to stand near them and looking out the porthole. Robbie was busy checking out his new bunk. "It's going to sail in front of our ship and scan for sea mines."

All Ita could think about was that they were finally leaving Java, yet their ship could still be blown to pieces. She shivered and folded her arms.

Mama patted her leg. "We're together, Rietie," she said in a soft voice. "All will be well."

"I know," Ita said. But did she really know? She had to believe it, because what else could she believe in to help her not feel so afraid?

Only after the ship left the harbor did Mama allow them to climb the stairs to the open deck. Ita's stomach felt like it was slowly turning upside down, and Mama said that the fresh air would help.

Maybe it did, but mostly Ita tried to ignore the jumble inside.

Greta came over to Ita with Ina Venema. A handful of families they knew from Tjideng, including the Venemas, were on board. The three girls immediately fell into conversation to catch up on the past few months. Then Aunt Tie approached them. Ita hadn't known she'd be on this ship, and she was sure that Papa had something to do with it.

"Where's George?" she asked Mama without looking her in the eyes.

"He's below making arrangements for everyone's accommodations. He's in charge of the women and children."

Aunt Tie tutted. She had gained a little weight back, but she was as erect as ever in her Red Cross charity clothing of a skirt that was still too big at the waist and a well-washed cotton shirt of blue and white stripes.

Then, Aunt Tie walked off without another word.

Mama steered Greta, Ita, and the boys toward the rest of the Vos family, where they stood at the rail, gazing at Tandjong Priok harbor. A crowd of people remained at the harbor, and even from a distance, Ita recognized them as Dutch refugees.

"What are they doing?" Ita asked when she reached Johan's side.

"They were trying to get on the ship, but there's no room," Johan said. "It's overcrowded already. You're lucky to have a cabin."

Ita looked up at him. His red hair blew in the brisk wind. Clouds had gathered above, stormy and gray. It would rain soon, and Ita wondered what it would be like to be floating in a sea when there was water above and below.

"Where is your family sleeping?"

"We have a cabin, too," Johan said. "But you should see the cargo holds. They're full of people, hammocks, and belongings." He grimaced. "No privacy. Not much different than the camps."

Yet, the ship was vastly different. Their former enemy wasn't calling them to roll call. They would have better food—that was one answer Georgie had already secured from a sailor. The people could sleep in hammocks and bunks. There was no dirt. No mosquitos. No insects. No monkeys. No screaming, beaten women. No Captain Sonei.

Papa joined them at the rail and gave a report to Mama about organizing the families that had arrived. Most of them were women and children—families who had lost husbands during the war. They would be traveling to Singapore, then changing to the Dutch troopship *New*

Amsterdam. They'd be joining about four thousand British troops who were leaving Burma and heading to England.

"I'm worried about disease," Papa said in a quiet voice to Mama.

Mama kept her gaze on the harbor that was getting farther and farther away. "There are medical supplies on the ship, yes?"

"Yes," Papa said. "But we have thousands aboard. A single illness will spread like a brushfire."

Mama sighed. Robbie was clinging to her hand. Georgie gripped the rail with both hands, staring at one of the minesweepers as if he were memorizing each part.

Greta had joined her mother, and Mr. Vos stood a few feet apart from everyone, his gaze locked on the water churning below.

Ita redirected her gaze back to the water and the harbor beyond. Everyone on this ship was a survivor. Everyone had experienced inhumanity. The cost of war. This Ita had witnessed firsthand.

"I've changed my mind." Johan rested his elbows on the railing, so that they were the same height. "I don't want to forget the last four years, either. I'm going to write down my experiences when we get to the Netherlands. People need to know what happened on Java during the war."

Ita felt a smile grow on her face. Not because Johan's story would be a happy one, but because she agreed. They shouldn't keep silent. Maybe her parents would, and his parents would, but she and Johan would tell their stories so that their children and grandchildren would know that humanity would always rise above the rubble of lost dreams, hatred, and prejudice.

Ita and her family were living proof.

AFTERMATH

George Vischer's concerns about disease on the ship turned out to be correct. There were thousands of women and children aboard the ship bound for the Netherlands, many still suffering the aftereffects of years of malnutrition. Disease ran rampant. Measles broke out on the ship, and most of the children caught it, including Ita and her two younger brothers. Any illness was devastating to the malnourished children and their mothers. Mary, at almost six feet tall, weighed only eighty-nine pounds when the family finally arrived in Rotterdam. And the three Vischer children were desperately ill by the journey's end.

Ita recounts a terrifying experience with Georgie on the ship. Everyone in the family had been seasick, including Georgie. One day, he stood on the washbasin in order to reach the porthole and vomit out of it. Mary, in her own sick daze, dozed off just as he was climbing up. When she next opened her eyes, Georgie was gone, and the porthole window still open. In a panic, Mary shouted to Rita—asking if she'd seen anything. They ran down the stuffy corridors, calling for Georgie. When they reached the toilets, there was one stall door closed . . . with sweet Georgie inside. "Yes, Mama, I'm here," he replied to their panicked query.

The Dutch troopship *New Amsterdam* took the refugees from Singapore to the port at Southampton, England. On the stop at Aqaba, Jordan, they were allowed to go on shore, where they were given donated clothing, but it was not sufficient for the winter they were about to face in Europe. They arrived in Southampton on New Year's Day, 1946. The women and children had to be transferred to another ship to take them to Rotterdam. Rita remembers having to be carried by her father across the dock in Southampton because she was too weak to walk.

She also remembers the harbors of Rotterdam and Amsterdam as being completely destroyed. The Netherlands had taken the brunt of Allied and Axis airspace battles. Europe's freezing temperatures proved to be fatal for many of the sick children, and some of them contracted pneumonia.

The family at last arrived in Holland and traveled to their Aunt Mary and Uncle Jan's house in Aleidesstraat. Amazingly enough, their house had survived the bombing. But because the three children were quite ill, they were quickly taken and admitted to a small navy hospital—a converted house in the small town of Doorn. At the hospital, doctors gave Mary and George devastating news. Rita, Georgie, and Robbie all had double pneumonia, and none of them were likely to survive.

With medicine and healthy food, however, Rita and Robbie *did* survive the illness. But sweet, young Georgie succumbed to pneumonia on February 1, 1946, just a few weeks shy of his seventh birthday. Mary told Rita more than once that she believed Georgie was too good for this world—that if it weren't for his sweet, angelic nature, she might not have made it through the challenges of a prison camp.

After Georgie's death, the Vischer family spent the next years rebuilding their lives in the Netherlands. The family secured a place to rent, the fourth floor of a house in Rotterdam, and George worked for the country's naval ministry in the housing and ground department. Two more children, Emy and Erik, were born to the family. In 1948, the navy released George and he returned to duty with KPM as second engineer and qualified chief.

The family lived five years in the Netherlands. George accepted a position as second engineer with the royal Java China Paket Vaart Maatschappij (The Royal Interocean Lines). While on his first route, he found accommodations for his family in Umkomaas, one and a half hours south of Durban, South Africa. So, in March 1951, the Vischer family relocated once again.

In 1964, as chief engineer of the *MS Ruys,* George received knighthood for both peace and wartime contributions to the Netherlands. Queen Juliana, who had succeeded her mother, Queen Wilhelmina, conferred the honors.

Rita spent the rest of her teenage years in South Africa and met her husband Bob Elliott when she was nineteen. They eventually married and had four children. Each of Rita and Bob's children married and emigrated to the United States. In 2002, at the age of sixty-five—and now a widow for seven years—Rita joined her children in the States.

AFTERWORD

BY MARIE (RITA) VISCHER ELLIOTT

August 1, 2022

One of the thoughts I've contemplated over the years has been how incredible it is that there were people, including myself, who actually survived these awful conditions. What was the secret to surviving a concentration camp—an inherent strong constitution, the will or instinct to survive, the fear of death, courage, or a mass of people standing together and determined to beat the enemy by surviving?

In my case, it could possibly have been my mother's strong willpower to keep her children alive at all costs. I could sense it and feel it! Even Georgie survived, although his body did succumb later, as a result of illness after our arrival in the Netherlands. As Georgie exhaled his final breaths, he stretched out his arms, and said, "Oma, ik kom," meaning "Oma, I'm coming."

I learned that the human race is very resilient and adaptable, but life itself is fragile. We should not take it for granted.

"Food, glorious food," Oliver Twist said. Our sentiments entirely! My father's expression was: "It doesn't have to be nice, as long as there is a LOT of it!" Of course, by the time the war ended, our stomachs had shrunk so much that we could only eat a little.

I heard a friend once say about me, "Mary doesn't leave any food on her plate." Only then did I realize that this was very true. My children knew that what they dished up, they had to eat, and it was NOT going into the trash! I still try very hard to cook or freeze perishables before they expire. And it still hurts to throw food away.

What do I remember most from the war years? Living with constant fear, seeing the bombs fall, getting into our waterlogged and miserable dungeon of a bomb shelter and then fearing we could get bombed anyway. Seeing the Japanese army arrive, and the beatings and screaming of the enemy. My very dear mother being beaten up, the constant hunger and hurt stomach, and being locked up in a prison. Then later the fear of being shot by the rebel Indonesians. After safely arriving on board the ship, fear still followed me as I worried about being blown to pieces by the many sea mines that could explode. Such terrible trauma for a child or any children to endure.

I remember our arrival in Europe, when I was so sick that my father had to carry me off the ship. Later seeing my parents grieve over the loss of their son Georgie.

There were, of course, a few happy moments. Our baby brother Robbie's arrival in the camp, and friends helping Mother survive her illness. Little acts of kindness of friends and people. Seeing my father one day, and learning that he was still alive after the war. Later stopping at Aqaba for clothing and the experience of sailing through the Suez Canal, which was still intact as it had been of benefit to Japan to keep it open.

These experiences in my extreme childhood made an indelible imprint on my being. Nothing is more important to me than my family and extended family everywhere and my friends all over the world. I love being with my children and their families, fifteen grandchildren, and one great-grandson. I find great pleasure also in spending time with my friends. I care very little about material "things" and wealth. Although I do like nice things, I am not at all attached to them. It has made me always very appreciative and grateful for a kindness shown me and a smile or handshake given me. Even though I grew up quickly, I still enjoy the little and simple things life has to offer, such as walking in the beauty of nature, and listening to the stillness thereof! Riding a carousel, swinging, dancing, going down a slide, and stomping through heaps of fallen leaves—I still enjoy all of this in my senior years.

Our family never spoke about the war ever again. It was a closed book. My parents said: "Forget and Forgive." In later years, I did ask my mother some questions I had about various details, some she answered and others not. I've never wanted to watch a war movie or any movie that had shootings in it, and I've never wanted to read a book about war, or concentration camps either.

My parents had the joy of extending our family by two more children born after the war, a sister Emy and a brother Erik. Years later, after we moved to South Africa, I was greatly blessed to find a wonderful husband, Bob Elliott, who passed away at age sixty-one. We have four amazing children—Paul, Warren, Dean, and Sasha—who are a great joy to me. Recently, my sister Emy shared with me that, growing up, I would ignore any questions she asked me about the war. And so she eventually gave up asking. I found that interesting, as I had no idea I was doing this. Now, in later life, I have been able to speak about it more often, hence the book!

There are no winners in a war. We all face hard things in our lives, some of those things may feel insurmountable. In those moments, I've learned that happiness comes from within, it cannot be found elsewhere. Most importantly, I have come to believe what my sweet oma and wonderful mother lived by—that this life is not the end. God is real, and I've learned to put my trust in Him.

This story is for my grandchildren: Landon, Khaya, Hamish, Caleb, Malachi, Tosca, Noah, Jared, Ceanne, Justin, Hayden, Brendan, Serenity, Lucas, Samantha, and my great-grandson Harlem, and a great-granddaughter on the way. Remember to be grateful always and that your Heavenly Father loves you.

MARIA VAN BENTEN-ZWAAN

July 7, 1874–July 11, 1944
Kamp, Batavia, Indonesia
Place of Burial: Semarang, Central Java, Indonesia

MARIA VAN BENTEN-ZWAAN (OMA)

GEORGE AND MARY VISCHER

GEORGIE AND RITA VISCHER

ROBERT (ROBBIE) VISCHER

BLOK V.	No.	No.	NAME		F/M	AGE	
	1		Verhaart	J.A.	F.	44	
	2		Verhaart	P.	M.	14	
	3		Bodderij	D.	F.	39	
	4		Bodderij	A.	M.	14	
	5		Bodderij	C.F.	F.	9	
	6		Muthert	E.A.C.	F.	42	
	7		Tuynman	H.N.M.	F.	36	
	8		Landzaad	W.H.	F.	41	
	9		Rademaker	G.	F.	36	
	10		Wente	B.J.J.	F.	47	
	11		Radsma	J.	F.	48	
	12		Radsma	J.	F.	16	
	13		Denker	N.	F.	50	
	14		Denker	H.J.E.	F.	23	
	15		Denker	W.	F.	19	
	16		Denker	C.J.F.	F.	18	
	17		Nelson	A.M.M.	F.	48	
	18		Ermeling	A.W.C.	F.	51	
	19		van Leur	J.	F.	53	
	20		Scheltema	A.	F.	47	
	21		Scheltema	L.H.	F.	18	
	22		Scheltema	J.H.	M.	16	
	23		Hennink	S.	F.	49	
	24		Hennink	A.E.	F.	19	
	25		Hennink	H.C.	M.	16	
	26		Hennink	J.M.	M.	10	
	27		Haselhoff	C.A.	F.	45	
	28		Haselhoff	R.	M.	13	
	29		Haselhoff	H.	F.	12	
	30		van Benten	M.	F.	69	
	31		Jansen	D.	F.	30	
	32		Vischer	M.J.	F.	38	
	33		Vischer	M.B.	F.	6	
	34		Vischer	G.	M.	4	
	35		Vischer	R.R.J.	M.	1	
	36		Poppe	J.C.C.	F.	38	
	37		Poppe	A.J.J.	M.	14	
	38		Poppe	C.C.	M.	13	
	39		Key	M.C.W.	F.	41	
	40		Key	J.	M.	16	
	41		Key	F.	M.	14	
	42		Key	H.	M.	8	
	43		Lüschen	E.J.	F.	39	
	44		Visser	J.	F.	31	
	45		van Tijn	F.	F.	35	
	46		van Tijn	J.	M.	5	
	47		van Tijn	Ph.	M.	2	
	48		Zwart	M.	F.	66	
	49		Duin	J.	M.	15	
	50		v. Pel	D.	M.	39	
	51		Wouters	C.	F.	41	
	52		Wouters	M.J.	M.	10	
	53		Wouters	K.D.	M.	8	
	54		Purner	S.	F.	35	
	55		Engelen	A.	F.	32	
	56		Engelen	J.E.M.	F.	3	
	57		Engelen	P.B.	M.	1	
	58		Lodders	D.	F.	32	
	59		Lodders	B.	F.	4	
	60		Versteegh	J.M.	F.	37	

TJIDENG CAMP ROSTER

宣　誓

下名ハ抑留者トシテ爪哇軍抑留所ニ保護抑
セラルルニ付テハ軍抑留所諸規則命令ニ違
セス且ツ逃走セサルコトヲ会能ナル神ノ名
於テ茲ニ宣誓ス

　　昭和十九年　月　日
但シ各人署名ハ別冊名簿ニ依ル

SOERAT SOEMPAH.

Jang bertanda tangan dibawah ini kami orang tahanan (Jokoorjoosjo),
jang akan di tahan dan dilindoongkan di dalam Tempat Tahanan Djawa
(Djawa Goen Jokoorjoosjo), maka kami orang tahanan bersoempah atas nama
Toehan jang Maha Kooasa, bahwa kami tidak sekali kali melanggar atas peronta
dan atoeran^2 segala galanja jang telah di tetapkan oleh jang berkoeasa
Tempat Tahanan (Goen Jokoerjoesjo) serta tidak melerikan diri kemana mana.

2604

Tanda tangan masing^2
di lampirkan
menoeroet Bookoe
nama daftaran berikoe.

SWORN DECLARATION.

We, the undersigned, protected and interned in
a Java Internment Camp, declare on oath, in the name of
Almighty God, that, whatever the circumstances, we shall
Commander of the said Camp, and that we shall not attempt
to escape therefrom.

2604

SIGNATURES to be appended in
an annexed list in the same
order as in the Internee Files.

TJIDENG CAMP SWORN DECLARATION

CHAPTER NOTES

CHAPTER 1

In December 1941, after the bombing of Pearl Harbor, the Royal Netherlands Indies Army was mobilized, and all male Dutch citizens in the archipelago, ages eighteen and up, were recruited into the military. Younger Dutch teenagers in the Netherlands East Indies (NEI) were asked to volunteer for civilian defense entities, such as the fire departments, the air defense services, radio and telephone stations, and at the harbors and airports, unloading supplies (*The Defining Years*, 71). Over the next few days, blackouts, curfews, and air raid sirens were all put into use (*Tjideng Reunion*, 122). By Christmas, Allied forces, including Australian, British, and American, began arriving in the major cities of the NEI (*The Defining Years*, 72).

CHAPTER 2

In mid-December, 1941, the Malay language press began to publish a series about the Djojobojo legends. A popular prediction warned that the Javanese people (natives to the island of Java) would be ruled by a light-skinned people for three centuries. Then, those "people of the white buffalo" would be driven away by "a yellow-skinned people" coming from the north, who would only occupy the island for "the lifetime of a rooster"—which is three years. The prophecy went on to say that a new leader would appear and herald a "period of independence and progress" (*Tjideng Reunion*, 124).

CHAPTER 3

Wafer-shaped pieces of rubber were issued in order to prevent con-cussions. People would take them into their bomb shelters, then clench the wafers between their teeth as bombs dropped (*The Defining Years*, 162). In her memoir, *Lost Childhood*, Annelex Hofstra Layson recalled that her family received rubber beaded necklaces. When the airplanes flew over their bomb shelter, they would chew on the rubber to produce saliva and then swallow the saliva. Swallowing would help prevent their eardrums from bursting (22).

CHAPTER 4

Once the Battle of the Java Sea was lost, the island of Java was open to Japanese invasion, and attacks occurred in several places at once. British Prime Minister Winston Churchill ordered members of the British Royal Air Force (RAF) stationed on Java to "arm themselves and make for the hills." There, the RAF were to engage in guerilla warfare "in a force to be known as the Blue Army" (*The Defining Years*, 44).

As Japan invaded the NEI and began rounding up Dutch citizens, native Indonesians watched with a mix of interest and fear. Animosity between the Dutch and Indonesians had existed on and off since 1796, when the government of the Netherlands had taken control of the ar-chipelago. Historically, the Dutch government had used violence to squelch Indonesian protests on many occasions. And some groups of Indonesians believed they'd suffered more than they'd gained from the Dutch modernization of their homeland (see https://foreignpolicy .com/2020/08/10/dutch-colonial-history-indonesia-villains-victims).

CHAPTER 5

George Vischer and his crewmates on the *Endeh* were not the only sailors and soldiers hoping to reach Australia in order to avoid cap-ture and become a part of the Allied forces in Australia. Willem H. Maaskamp, who was seventeen years old when the Java Sea fell to Japan, wrote that his brother Fred, a decorated pilot in the NEI Air Force, was "ordered to fly to Australia since the Allied forces needed experienced airmen as instructors." Fred was declared missing in action shortly after leaving and later declared dead (*The Defining Years*, 73).

Annelex Hofstra Layson's father, a pilot in the Dutch navy, was also sent to Australia, in the hope that there he would be safe from capture and could join the Allied movement. Like Fred Maaskamp, Annelex's father never made it to Australia. His plane was shot down over the ocean (*Lost Childhood*, 22–23).

CHAPTER 6

George Vischer wrote about his experiences on the Java Sea in a series of articles titled "Fight for Survival against Japs in the Java Sea," which was published in *The Moth Magazine* in 1990 (https://www.moth .org.za/). His articles are a detailed account of his experiences on the Auxiliary Minesweeper *Endeh*. Although Vos is a fictional character, all of the other men on the minesweeper were real, and their experiences follow true events. Marie (Rita) Vischer recalled that the bullet that grazed her father's boot left an indent at the top of his big toe that was visible for the rest of his life.

CHAPTER 7

Nearly every morning in early 1942, when the skies were clear of clouds, the air raid sirens went off. Afternoon thunderstorms frequently chased air raid threats away in the later part of the day. With the Allied Java Air Command having access to only eighty-six planes, and the Japanese military with over 340 modern aircraft, the odds were in Japan's favor. The skies above Java Island became a hotspot of clashing Japanese bombers and Dutch Hawk fighters (*Tjideng Reunion*, 131–32).

On Monday, March 2, 1942, newspaper headlines read: "The Battle for Java Has Started." A counterattack by the Allies had been planned, but it soon failed since Japanese forces were prepared with naval fire power and torpedoes. Even the Red Cross couldn't find a place to set up in Batavia. Cities were restricting the flow of refugees because space was running out quickly (*Tjideng Reunion*, 135–37).

Once Japan invaded Java, troops arrived, making their way into

towns and establishing command centers. Many historical accounts re-
call rows of Japanese troops marching into towns. Greta Kwik remembers watching Japanese soldiers enter her mountain town of Ambarawa
when she was nine years old: "They had flapping neck pieces hanging
from the back of their *kepis*, and bedrolls, canteens, guns and other
things on their backs. Someone carried the Japanese flag in front of the
sweating men" (*The Defining Years*, 215).

Throughout this novel, I've included foods either described to me
by Marie Vischer, or by a man named Vilas Yang—an Indonesian who
is originally from Java, but now lives in Utah. Vilas said that common
foods people ate for meals on Java include pecel, gado-gado, soto, sate,
nasi kuning, nasi campur, nasi putih, and rawon. Many of the meals
would be accompanied by vegetables, peanuts, hard-boiled eggs, fried-
shrimp krupuk, boiled potatoes, fried tofu, tempeh, nasi goreng, bahmi
goreng, and lontong.

CHAPTER 8

George Vischer wrote, "Our life jackets were filled with kapok, and
soon became heavy and less buoyant. We therefore removed the jackets
by day, tied them to our heads so as to give them a chance to drain and
dry out, and then put them on again at night. We took it in turns to go
into the dinghy to paddle or bail" (*The Moth Magazine*, March 1990, 5).

On Wednesday, March 4, 1942, George said his crew had their first
meal since leaving the *Endeh* the Sunday before. This meal for seventeen
men consisted of a divided coconut and its milk, which amounted to
about a three-centimeter square per person (*The Moth Magazine*, March
1990, 5). Marie Vischer told me that this was just like her father's personality: "He would have made sure the portions were exact and that
everyone received his share."

CHAPTER 9

George Vischer recounted that the surviving group had two paddles, life jackets, and three coconuts as they set off on their dinghy in
a southerly direction. They knew that a small error in judgment would

make them miss their destination—the Thousand Islands (*The Moth Magazine*, March 1990, 5). They decided to aim for the Thousand Islands because they knew the NEI had evacuated the islands to prevent lights or fires acting as beacons to the Japanese invasion. Besides, the islands contained coconut plantations, and the men could survive on those until they were rescued. The days passed, and George estimated they arrived at the first island at about 15:00 hours on Friday, March 6. The first order of business was performed by First Class Seaman Bakker, who was one of the fittest, climbing to the top of the coconut trees and tossing down coconuts (*The Moth Magazine*, April 1990, 5).

CHAPTER 10

By March 1942, regular programming on the radio had stopped. Music played, interrupted every hour by an announcement by General Hein Ter Poorten. When the ceasefire was declared, Ter Poorten advised that everyone had "nothing to fear and should remain calm and carry on as normal" (*Tjideng Reunion*, 139). But the fact that most of the indigenous population of Indonesia—which outnumbered the European population by a factor of one hundred to one—had sided with the Japanese cause, made the Dutch people's living situations more precarious (*Tjideng Reunion*, 141).

Japanese people had been living and working in the NEI for years, so when the invasion happened, some Japanese were already in place to take on official military duties. Rita la Fontaine-de Clercq Zubli was twelve years old when Japanese troops arrived in her town of Jambi, Sumatra. She remembers a former shop owner from town arriving at her home. The high-ranking Japanese officer spoke fluent Dutch, and he informed her family to pack their belongings and official documents, as they needed to register at the police station. Zubli eventually followed a plan concocted by her parish priest as a means of protection; she cut her very long hair short and adopted the life of a boy (*The Defining Years*, 197–98).

Other young women acted similarly. I based the character of Greta Vos, for example, on the real Greta Kwik, who wrote about her experiences in the essay collection *The Defining Years of the Dutch East Indies, 1942–1949*. Although Kwik was never interned in a camp, she wrote that rumors of Japanese bordellos needing more women were circulating the area, so her mother cut Greta's hair short and made her wear her brother's clothing. Mrs. Kwik even gave her children Chinese names so that they wouldn't be targeted as being Dutch (215). Some women reported wearing unattractive clothing and not wearing makeup so they wouldn't attract unwanted attention from a Japanese commander, who they feared "would pursue her and eventually take her as his mistress against her will" (*The Defining Years,* 119).

CHAPTER 11

Discovering a lifeboat from the *Marula* was both a blessing and a sobering reminder of the Dutch navy's losses. George wrote, "Although the lifeboat was badly damaged, her inventory was 100% intact. Her stores included ship's biscuits, tins of condensed milk, 12 bottles of Scotch, sea charts, tools, oars, lamps, masts, sails, etc." The supplies would prove lifesaving to the stranded men (*The Moth Magazine*, April 1990, 5).

Another joyous find was discovering a small pondok, or bamboo hut, with additional supplies inside. When the group found "a freshwater pond or well at the back," George wrote, "we were so happy at our findings that we jumped into this pond and swam and washed, making it completely useless for drinking" (*The Moth Magazine*, April 1990, 5). Soon they found another shelter in the form of a completely furnished bamboo hut, including six Kampong huts nearby. Inside, supplies such as coffee, tea, pans, pots, and crockery had been left behind *(ibid)*.

CHAPTER 12

The ten Japanese demands were printed in newspapers and announced on the radio, comprising of "relinquishment of all arms, self internment of all military personnel, delivery to the Japanese command of all dead Japanese troops, imprisoned Japanese people and goods formerly belonging to Japanese citizens" (*Tjideng Reunion*, 141–142). Other

demands included stopping "destruction of military equipment, buildings, roads," and to cease "all communication with the external world,"
and finally, "to co-operate with an orderly transition of power to the
Japanese authorities" (142).

By August 1942, more detailed rules were posted throughout many
towns, announcing the expectation that "all European residents, being
members of a conquered people, exhibit deference to *dai* Nippon, and in
particular the Nipponese army."

Europeans were informed that, among other things:

"Provocative behaviour is unacceptable. . . .

"It is permitted to leave your residence, but only for essential purposes, such as food purchases, doctor visits, etc. One must, moreover,
behave properly, not spreading rumors, and they should not transgress
the rules of good living. . . .

"Everywhere outside of the home, it is mandatory to express humility when meeting a member of the Nipponese army, regardless of rank.
This is done by bowing" (*Tjideng Reunion,* 171–72).

CHAPTER 13

The injuries and illnesses suffered by the survivors of the *Endeh* went
untreated for weeks. And without medical supplies, the men's wounds
turned septic. For George, however, this proved to be a blessing in dis-
guise, as his offer to accompany the fishermen who arrived on March
13, 1942, was turned down on account of his wounded foot (*The Moth
Magazine,* April 1990, 5).

CHAPTER 14

When the Japanese army began rounding up European civilians
and taking them to camps, it was under the pretense that they were
sending unprotected women and children into "protected areas" since so
many men were away fighting. Camps were often located in undesirable
parts of town, a tactic the refugees immediately recognized as a "bad
omen" (*Tjideng Reunion,* 175). Tjideng, for example was near a red-light
district. Refugees traveling to Tjideng would have reached the concrete

bridge that spanned the Tjideng canal, then waited in a line to enter the camp. Just weeks prior, the "protection camp" had been a regular neighborhood. A high gedek wall topped with kawat now ran the perimeter of the neighborhood. Lookout towers and a bamboo guardhouse, complete with a rack of rifles, sat at the camp's entrance (340). The boundaries of the camp were triangular, consisting of the Tjideng kali canal on the east, the marsh on the north, and the railway on the southwest (353).

In the camps throughout Indonesia, the first roll call of the day was usually held around 6:00 a.m., and the camp would be awakened by sirens or trumpet blasts. Prisoners assembled in groups either in the street at a designated spot on their "neighborhood" block, or in an open space elsewhere in the camp. Roll calls typically lasted an hour, but sometimes went on for much longer. During roll call, the prisoners lined up in rows, held their bows—unless called to attention—then counted off as instructed, in Japanese. Errors meant that the counting would start all over again, elongating the instruction to remain bent over in a bow, no matter the weather conditions (*The Defining Years*, 21–22).

In her memoir *Dutch Girl from Jakarta*, Maria Zeeman detailed her experience in Tjideng from 1942 to 1946. At first, conditions weren't great, but they were allowed to leave the camp once a week to shop at the market. "Then, all of a sudden, the soldiers closed the gates and put a double fence around the camp" (23). The women were no longer allowed to communicate with outsiders who came to the fences and, if they were caught doing so, received swift punishment (ibid).

CHAPTER 15

George Vischer and his crew waited several days for the return of their comrades who'd volunteered to go with the fishermen in search of more supplies. On March 17, 1942, when a prahu arrived with twenty-five Indonesian natives, the Dutch crew was informed that their friends who'd volunteered had returned to Java. The crew was suspicious of this claim and, as described in this chapter, they chose to leave the island for their own safety. They repaired the damaged lifeboat from the *Marula* and made their escape to Poeloe Pajoeng, also called Paraplue Island, where they learned from the lighthouse keeper that the four volunteers had been murdered on a nearby island (*The Moth Magazine*, May 1990, 9).

CHAPTER 16

Mary Vischer brought along peanuts to Tjideng Camp, which she was able to plant in a little garden during their early months there. Almost everything of value was confiscated during their time at the camp. But the Japanese military was oddly structured in their methods. Marie (Rita) told me, "If it was the day for confiscating pencils, and the Japanese saw a pen lying on the floor, they would not take it that particular day, even though pens had been confiscated previously."

As the weeks and months progressed, the food situation became more dismal. Marie said, "In the beginning, we received a little rice and seaweed and bread made from starch (or tapioca). You could see through it, and it was hard as a rock. We were only able to chop little pieces at a time and soak it to eat it. My mother made us eat everything we got, no matter how awful it was. The bread and seaweed didn't last very long, and thereafter we ate one dessert spoon of rice."

As the camp became increasingly crowded, problems with the sewage system occurred daily, quickly going from bad to worse. Eventually, the situation was beyond repair, and ditches were built to accommodate the women and children. Stepping over sewer ditches filled with a cesspool of human waste became common (*Tjideng Reunion*, 342). Internees were assigned rotating chores, one of which was cleaning out these ditches. According to Ralph Ockerse and Evelijn Blaney, a brother and sister who lived in Tjideng Camp, "Frequently, cesspools required attention when these began to overflow and had to be emptied with a can or similar container. The occupants at Tjideng had to take turns to do this by the assignment of people to *corvees* (chores). . . . In fact, there was an overwhelming amount of work that daily needed to be done in Tjideng without further delay, which, under the circumstances, no one else but the internees were responsible for to get it done" (*Our Childhood in the Former Colonial Dutch East Indies*, 139–40).

On March 27, 1942, by declaration of the Japanese emperor, the date was changed to March 27, 2602. This was because, "by Japanese reckoning, their civilization . . . was some six hundred years older than Western civilization as defined by the onset of the Christian era. The Japanese did not bother changing the calendar any further, and so, aside from the year, all other date references remained the same" (*Tjideng Reunion*, 152).

Japan also declared that the NEI would begin operating on Tokyo time, which was two hours ahead. The shift caused distress for those inside and outside the camps: "In the tropics the sun normally rises and sets around six o'clock in the morning and evening with hardly any twilight.

"Henceforth the sun would rise at four thirty in the morning and set at four thirty in the evening, a curious disruption causing widespread confusion, especially for the Indonesian workers" (ibid).

When the Dutch were funneled into the internment camps, many of them brought their pets. Unfortunately, they ended up being forced to let their pets go, or have them destroyed (*The Defining Years*, 15).

There were a few exceptions, and Johan's experience with his dog is based on a real dog named Keesey, a black retriever who belonged to Andrew van Dyk. Andrew's family brought Keesey with them to the Cihapit camp. "As soon as the order to eliminate pets was issued, we hastily approached the all-Dutch women's camp staff to plead our cause to retain him. We had difficulties keeping rats from infesting our overcrowded living quarters, and Keesey was an excellent rat catcher. The Japanese camp commandant had a Japanese doctor evaluate the petition, examine the dog, and advise him on the matter. The end result was that we were permitted to keep Keesey, for a while at least. However, I was to show the camp leader, a Dutch woman, a weekly quota of rats caught" (*The Defining Years*, 16).

Marie (Rita) Vischer was on the cusp of starting school when her family was sent to Tjideng Camp. Her mother had to get creative, and she was able to procure an old nursery rhyme book. "My pride and joy," Rita said, "was a thick book with rhymes and short stories, the size of a large Bible. It had torn pages and scribbles in it but I absolutely treasured it!" In addition, a preschool group was put together in the early months of internment that Rita was able to join.

CHAPTER 17

The account of the *Endeh* crew receiving help from a skipper who made them a large pot of nashi goreng and directed them to a village on Java follows George's telling from *The Moth Magazine* (May 1990, 9).

Ironically, the Dutchmen were first taken to a location at their former naval station at Tandjong Priok, which was now under the control of Japanese soldiers. "We were not treated badly by the Japanese troops," George remembered. "We were given food, drink and cigarettes." Then, the following day, they "were taken to the Kempetai in Batavia and, after interrogation, put in a cell in the Glodok prison with two civilians" (ibid).

CHAPTER 18

It was at Glodok prison camp that George and his crew learned the extent of what had happened in the three weeks they'd been at sea or stranded on islands. In short, they learned that the Battle of Java Sea had been badly lost by the Allies and that the Japanese troops had made their way onto the main island of Java almost immediately. Only one week later, on March 8, 1942, the Royal Dutch East Indies government had formally surrendered. Japan officially occupied the NEI and had begun rounding up everyone with Allied connections: the Dutch, British, American, and French. Men in military service were taken first, followed by the eventual rounding up of everyone else, including women and children (*The Defining Years*, 73).

CHAPTER 19

In this chapter, Mary reflects on the surprising kindness of a number of soldiers in the camp, particularly that of a Japanese soldier named Kano. Although his character is fictional, he is based on another Kano, a real soldier who worked in the Ambarawa camp and watched out for a boy named Feite Posthumus. Kano took Feite to visit his ill mother in the hospital a time or two and showed Feite kindness when his mother passed away. Feite wrote that Kano took care to watch out for many of the boys. At one time, "Kano showed up . . . passing along little notes to and from parents in other camps. He kept these notes inside his very ugly [Japanese] baseball cap, an ideal hiding place" (*The Defining Years,* 179, 181).

Not every soldier under Captain Sonei's command agreed with his methods of punishment. One of the Korean guards, Noda, was said to have thought that Sonei was a sick and disturbed man. I've added the character of Noda to the story since he's named in *Tjideng Reunion* (376).

Many of the stories from the internment camps mention how kind the Japanese guards were to the younger children. Annelex Hofstra Layson recalled, "We spent nearly three years at Halmaheira. In all that time we got to know the personalities of our guards. They weren't all mean. The younger ones were sometimes more lenient—especially to us kids—than the older ones. We even came to think of one, a watchman whose post was near our hut, as our friend. He didn't get so upset with us if we forgot to bow or how to say something in Japanese exactly right" (*Lost Childhood,* 67–68).

CHAPTER 20

When Annelex Hofstra Layson was reunited with her thirteen-year-old brother Jack, he told her about his experiences in one of the men's prison camps. The boys there "had been given wooden guns and were being trained to fight for the glory of the Japanese emperor. They had been taught to march in the Japanese style, to sing Japanese military songs, and to obey orders without questioning them" (*Lost Childhood,* 86–87).

CHAPTER 21

As mandated by the Geneva Convention, the internment camps periodically received Red Cross supplies, although the items didn't always trickle down to the prisoners. Annelex Hofstra Layson remembered, "Red Cross days were exciting days. There was never anywhere near enough clothes to go around and rarely was anything a perfect fit, but any 'new' piece of clothing was cause for celebration. It is impossible to describe the thrill of seeing the Red Cross trucks arrive" (*Lost Childhood*, 63).

While Johan is a fictional character, the story of him building a pair of stilts with two tin cans is based on true accounts. The children made holes at the bottom end of tin cans with a nail and a brick, then ran string through the holes, creating a long loop. The children would stand on the cans, open end down, and walk around the yard with a clattering sound (*Tjideng Reunion*, 378).

Siblings Ralph Ockerse and Evelijn Blaney, who spent the last sixteen months of their internment at Tjideng Camp, called it "by far the worst experience" of the camps they'd been in (*Our Childhood*, 123). At the beginning of the war years, Tjideng Camp housed 2,600 internees, but by August 1945, more than 10,300 women and children lived at the camp. The siblings distinctly remember roll calls held on Laan Trivelli, which ran through the camp, at 8:00 in the morning and 5:00 in the evening (123–24).

They also described "three occasions when Sonei ordered punishment roll calls that lasted for hours on end. Each roll call coincided with a full moon. . . . One after another, people would collapse as dehydration set in. No one was allowed to attend to those lying in place on the street. Doing so would invite severe punishment. Many among those assembled were barefoot, and when the tar-covered street had begun to soften, blisters developed on the soles of their feet" (*Our Childhood*, 128–29).

CHAPTER 22

Living conditions were very cramped throughout the internment camps. The refugees and newcomers were simply crowded into existing houses and structures. A family was lucky if they got a room to themselves. Barracks previously belonging to the KNIL (Royal Netherlands-Indies Army) were converted into units for the POWs, such as George Vischer at Glodok. Many internees had to sleep next to each other, side by side, and head to feet, in an approximately three-by-six-foot space (*The Defining Years*, 17).

In many of the internment camps throughout the NEI, camp

members had to wear designated cloth or metal badges pinned to their shirts or shorts that showed what job they were assigned—such as garbage collecting duty or kitchen duty. Failure to wear a badge would result in punishment (*The Defining Years*, 20–21).

Throughout the islands' internment camps, prisoners became creative when foraging for food. Siblings Ralph Ockerse and Evelijn Blaney recounted, "During stormy nights, luck had it when, on occasion, a coconut would drop inside the fence. One could clearly hear it come down as it rustled through the leaves and landed with a thud. On such occasions, many of the women residing in the rooms facing the fence would jump out of the bed and race outside to try to find and get it. Regrettably, this sometimes led to disputes or quarrels and gradually reflected a deterioration of human behavior" (*Our Childhood*, 115–16). Another tree that produced edible fruit was the *ketapan*, which "produces an edible nut embedded within its fleshy fruit. At times, a *ketapan* fruit would drop just inside the fence, which triggered a similar race to recover it" (116).

The experiences of George Vischer working at the prison kitchen in Glodok are patterned after Andrew A. Van Dyk's explanation of how most camps worked. Daily routines for kitchen staff usually started around four in the morning. Large, 44-gallon drums were filled with water and installed above the fireplaces. Water was boiled to prepare tapioca, rice, vegetables, coffee, or tea—all dependent on those items being available (*The Defining Years*, 20–21).

The description of the men cooking eggs at Glodok is taken from Ockerse and Blaney's experience: "To boil [eggs], we had to go through a lot of inconvenience. Through the outside front wall of the kitchen protruded a pipe coming down alongside the wall to just above the ground level from which excess steam vented from meals prepared in the kitchen. Sometimes, [we] would stand in very long lines to take our turn to boil our two eggs, held on a spoon in the stream trickling out" (*Our Childhood*, 115).

Details about the men from Glodok prison who were allowed out of camp to be on work crews are based on Van Dyk's experiences: "Each of the inmates carried only a mess kit, consisting of empty tins which were used for soup or porridge and tea. Additionally, they had with them a self-made spoon, fork, and knife, and either a real water bottle or a length of bamboo cut so that one end remained closed. They marched along in shreds of clothing, wearing diverse headgear and footwear. Most of them had native clogs or walked barefooted. On their shoulders they carried shovels, picks, mattocks, and other pieces of equipment to perform work on the roads, in the fields, or in the hills" (*The Defining Years*, 22).

Mealtime for the work crews came from a Japanese truck that delivered "either soup or gruel into their mess kits. This was augmented by one or two pieces of boiled sweet potato, and finally a cup of tea was slopped into the inmate's drinking cup" (*The Defining Years*, 23).

Throughout the internment camps in Indonesia, internees used every resource available to them. For the purposes of this book, I drew from Ockerse and Blaney's account of their mother making sandals from pieces of wood, then fastening the wood to the foot with a strap made from the rubber tire of a bicycle (*Our Childhood*, 117–18).

CHAPTER 23

No news was good news was a frequent mantra at Tjideng Camp. Postcards were allowed to be sent between camps, although they weren't always received or replied to. "The most common way of learning that a loved one in another camp had died was having a postcard come back to the sender with a curt message 'dead' written on it in pencil, and an upside down *tjap* (stamp) on it" (*Tjideng Reunion*, 357).

A house next to the medical clinic at Tjideng was reserved for a morgue. Each day, teen girls who'd been assigned to the task of pall-bearers, would transport coffins to the delivery truck that had brought in food to the camp. In the early days of the camp, prisoners were allowed to travel to the cemetery with their loved ones for the interment, but Captain Sonei put a stop to that. Eventually the delivery of coffins stopped, and instead, a truckload of bamboo poles and *tikars*—mats used for bedding—were delivered to the camp. Five women at Tjideng volunteered to make the new coffins from the bamboo poles and *tikar* panels (*Tjideng Reunion*, 359–60).

Tropical sores became a plague throughout internment camps due to lack of medical supplies. Maria Zeeman, who spent the war years at Tjideng Camp, said, "I got a sore on my leg. It got worse and worse, and it was so painful and stank to high heaven. . . . and all anyone could do was try to keep it clean any way they could in that awful place. Oh, my goodness, I wished I could just lay there and never get up. . . . I was in such agony. . . . Many others died or lost their limbs. But my mother and Fransje never gave up. They saved my life" (*Dutch Girl from Jakarta*, 26–27).

Siblings Ralph Ockerse and Evelijn Blaney wrote about Commander Sonei's pet monkeys, which were used to harass the internees at Tjideng Camp. "At the corner of Tjilamajaweg and Tjioejoengweg, opposite to the central kitchen on that field, was a large cage where several monkeys were kept. Those monkeys were the pride of Camp Commander Sonei. . . . On one occasion, for inexplicable reasons, Sonei sadistically released the monkeys that immediately proceeded to mount an attack and viciously bit any internee that happened to be in their path. Most of the victims bit by the monkeys did get seriously ill" (*Our Childhood*, 131–32).

CHAPTER 24

Marie Vischer told me about the many noises children would make in camp, perhaps as a distraction or for simple entertainment: "At one of the houses, I used to jump on the steel plate over the hole with the water meter. I loved the noise it made and also the jumping. Always thought someone would come out to stop the noise, but no one ever did! Also, we had a creaking gate somewhere which I used to swing on and loved the noise. Again, no one came out to stop me! I suppose they felt some child was happy in their misery!"

Moving and condensing space inside the camps, especially at Tjideng Camp, was a common occurrence. Those who lived closer to the main gate were happy to move into a house farther away, since the "de poort"—main gate—was where so many of Captain Sonei's atrocities took place. "All morning long people were forced to gather their stuff and to find another spot in another overcrowded house, where you have to push people out of the way to get a small space. We've gone through this almost every week—I had to move twice and each time I lost things" (*Tjideng Reunion,* 352).

Meals began to deteriorate as the war progressed, and at Tjideng Camp, Rita remembered how the milk had been diluted, making it a transparent bluish tint (see also *Our Childhood,* 130).

CHAPTER 25

While at Tjideng Camp, Jeroen Brouwers said that he knew all about death before he learned to read. With so much death happening around him, he learned to attach no emotion to it, "no fear, no sorrow, no revulsion. A person who was dead was rolled into a rush mat and taken away on a handcart. Her possessions, especially if they included a crumb or grain of food, were fought over, and the place she vacated would be 'tchopped' even before the corpse was removed" (*Sunken Red,* 48).

The ruffian gang of boys in this chapter is based on an account from Ralph Ockerse and Evelijn Blaney, who wrote, "Throughout the camp, one could hear the daily yelling contests between mothers and their children, initiated in utter desperation by the frustrated mothers who had lost complete control over their older children. This had especially become alarming of a fairly sizable group of boys who had turned eleven years of age and become the oldest males at Tjideng by late 1944. These boys felt that they were now 'in charge.' They persistently challenged and arranged fights among the eleven-year-old boys to establish supremacy and crown the one with authority and dominance over all others" (*Our Childhood,* 133).

Ralph Ockerse steered clear of the group, even though he was challenged multiple times. In January 1945, the Japanese authority at Tjideng decided that the oldest boys would be transferred to an all-male camp. This included the boys who were aged eleven, which was considered twelve by the Japanese calendar. The Japanese rationale was "that at eleven, the boys posed a potential sexual threat to female internees" (*Our Childhood,* 134). Along with one hundred other eleven-year-old boys from Tjideng, Ralph Ockerse was transferred to a camp in Tjimahi.

CHAPTER 26

The medical center at Tjideng Camp was an improvised hospital, run by four or five doctors and a team of nurses. Medical supplies were very limited, or nonexistent, and there was only so much that could be done for the very ill. Captain Sonei ordered the hospital to be cleared out and dying patients to be transferred out of camp more than once, since he had to report deaths to headquarters in Tokyo and didn't want a black mark on his name. Sick mothers were separated from their children and sick children were taken away from their mothers (*Tjideng Reunion*, 348).

At the internment camps throughout Indonesia, work crews were assigned to the internees. Each house was organized by the house leader. "Work parties were needed to clear the septic tank with a bucket and carry the contents to the ditch by the roadside and then to move the septic sludge along the ditch to where it disappeared under the gedek by the side of the main gate" (*Tjideng Reunion*, 355–356). Younger children were used mostly for this task. The older girls were assigned coffin duty as pallbearers since they were the strongest group. Other work parties fixed the gedek and kawat walls, another team swept streets, another worked washing linens for the hospital, and others were on kitchen duty (356).

CHAPTER 27

As the months in the internment camps dragged on, clothing became bedraggled. Internees who were transferred from other camps into Tjideng arrived with next to nothing. Arguments broke out over clotheslines as people accused each other of stealing pieces of clothing. "Any piece of cloth, no matter how ragged, had become a potential bartering item for food or a means of maintaining a minimal sense of decorum and modesty in our dress. Tea towels had to serve as clothing when other garments had worn out" (*Tjideng Reunion*, 357).

The woman shouting out Bible verses to internees is based on Boudewijn Van Oort's account of a woman who had sewn a Bible into her coat and smuggled it into the camp. She would read verses out loud to any internees who'd listen and, like the woman here, she favored verses in the Book of Revelations (*Tjideng Reunion,* 356).

I also relied on Boudewijn for details about washing clothing and bodies in camp: "Washing took a considerable effort, for whatever supply of water was available had to be carefully recycled. The usual ritual was for my mother to pour water into a small tin bath, placed on what was left of the lawn, wash me first, and then use the same water to wash herself and, finally, our clothes" (361).

CHAPTER 28

For several years, Java had experienced a food shortage due to failed rice crops and the cessation of inter-island trade. "Aggravating this situation was the decision made by the Japanese authorities on May 3, 1945, to stockpile rice for the anticipated final showdown with Allied forces on Java" (*Tjideng Reunion,* 362). So when a shipment of brown beans arrived at Tjideng Camp, the kitchen staff worked to stretch out the supply. They "hollowed out the loaves of sticky, unpalatable bread, mixed the crumbs with brown beans and used this as filling for the bread shell" (363).

Later that month, a shipment of duck eggs arrived, and there would be enough for one egg to be split among three people. Some would trade the eggs for gula Djawa, "a brown sticky confection made from palm sugar. A number of children had developed acetone poisoning from lack of sugar, and a craving for sugar was a widespread phenomenon" (*Tjideng Reunion,* 364).

Boiling up during these months was the drive for Indonesian independence from the Netherlands, and a commission was established in Batavia to lay the groundwork (*Tjideng Reunion,* 366). These increased political and war tensions compounded Captain Sonei's cruelty. One way in which he displayed particular cruelty at the time was by withholding and destroying food. The incident in this chapter occurred on a Tuesday in June 1945 exactly as described: Sonei hid in the back of a bread truck and noticed that the internees weren't bowing to the Indonesian driver. He ordered the truck to leave the camp, had it return, and then sent it away again. He then decreed that no food would be had for three days and that all food currently in the camp should be destroyed. "He stomped up and down on the bread in the ditches to make sure it was indeed inedible and then, beside himself with rage, entered the kitchens, kicking over the drums so that the soup and porridge being prepared for ten thousand mouths oozed over the ground to turn into mud" (*Tjideng Reunion*, 367).

Fortunately, later that month, Sonei was promoted and appointed "by the Japanese military to assume the position of head of the office for all prisoner of war concentration camps on Java" (*Our Childhood*, 129). After Sonei left camp, a Lieutenant Sakai took charge, and the Japanese troops celebrated the change in command with a feast consisting of two piglets. The internees celebrated in other ways, including a musical soiree where "Mrs. t'Hoen gave a short violin recital followed by the singing of some chansons by Greta Beuk and Crince le Roy" (*Tjideng Reunion*, 371).

CHAPTER 29

Once Captain Sonei left Tjideng Camp, the children began to play in the streets. They invented many games with sticks and yarn spools. They also played hopscotch with stones and created stilts from tins (*Tjideng Reunion*, 378). Siblings Ralph Ockerse and Evelijn Blaney remember playing marbles, spinning the tops, and an Indonesian game called *gatrik* "which involved various ways of hitting a smaller with a larger stick" (*Our Childhood*, 126).

In Japan, the philosophy of fighting to the death rather than surrendering was strong, dating back to the twelfth century and enshrined in the Bushido Code. "It became the official philosophy of education for Japanese of all classes until the post-World War II period" (*The Defining Years*, 159).

A welcome change after Sonei left was that Japanese guards began paying the women thirty-five cents to knit socks. It was required, however, that the socks be thirty-five centimeters long. "The women soon discovered that the thirty-five-centimetre standard sock could be achieved faster and with less effort if a shorter product was soaked in water and then stretched with the help of a brick, providing as well a small surplus of cotton" (*Tjideng Reunion*, 379).

Mary Vischer's dream about the war ending comes from a personal interview with Marie (Rita). She told me that "On the night of the 15th of August, Mom dreamed that the war was over. And the next day, August 16th, on her birthday, a train came by on the railroad tracks elevated by a dike, along one side of the camp's fence, so we could see it going by. Javanese were shouting and hanging out of the train, saying that the war had ended. We had no contact with the outside world at all and had no idea that Europe was already free."

As depicted in this chapter, four to five people were still dying each day in camp, despite the war being over (*Tjideng Camp*, 381). Jeroen Brouwers, who spent time at Tjideng Camp, recalled, "I saw dead women every day: their legs gave out during the prolonged roll calls in the hammering heat in the kampulan square (the roll call square); they fell forward or backward or sideways while on work detail; they did not get up when it grew light in the morning, or they sat down or lay down in the middle of the day, closed their eyes and turned out to be dead" (*Sunken Red*, 48).

I took some details about life in Tjideng on the days leading up to and right after the end of the war from Boudewijn Van Oort. According to Van Oort, August 23, 1945, started out as any other day. His mother rose early to join the kitchen staff, and breakfast consisted of starchy tapioca porridge, dished out from bathtubs to each house. Since the end of war announcement, rice rations had increased due to approval by Lt. Sakai. Roll call, since Sonei's departure, had switched to only once a day. That afternoon, the vegetable truck arrived with food to be delivered, and carried out coffins on the way back through the gate. Then later in the afternoon, Sakai sent for the house leaders. No one thought anything was too amiss until the house leaders called the residents of their houses together for an announcement. "There will be no more appèl [roll call]," a house leader announced. "Lieutenant Sakai's formal announcement can be found in the camp office. I believe it says the war is over, but we must stay in the camp until the Allies arrive" (*Tjideng Reunion*,

392). The announcement was a statement written in English and tacked to the notice board (393).

CHAPTER 30

In celebration of the end of the war, Dutch internees began to cobble together any cloth they could of red, white, or blue, in order to stitch flags. Creating Dutch flags would boost morale and give the ailing prisoners new hope. Train loads of people began arriving at Tjideng Camp, with nowhere else to go since their homes had been taken over by Indonesians. Fortunately, more food was coming in, and the Red Cross was able to increase its presence (*Tjideng Reunion,* 396). Lieutenant Sakai approved space in his office for some of the Dutch women to work on updating the Tjideng Camp resident list so that families could work toward reunification (395). In addition, Sakai ordered the belongings of the internees to be returned to each of them (399). But when Sakai found out about the Dutch flags being made, he put a stop to it, so that the rebellion uprisings wouldn't see flags flying above the camp (396).

CHAPTER 31

As the food supply to the camps increased after the war, the demand for firewood increased, and that was obtained by internees breaking down the gedek fencing (*Tjideng Reunion,* 401). The problem with this was that the broken fencing made the internees more exposed to the rebellion groups. Some women simply walked out of the camp, and no one stopped them. They decided that the risk on the outside was better than staying confined in the camp, endlessly waiting. During this time, Indos, who were a mix of Indonesian and European descent, so they hadn't been interned, arrived at the camp, bringing gifts of food. Some of them sought out former employers or friends or relatives (ibid).

Marie Vischer told me about two of her father's close friends, Eduard and Jacques Gouverneur. The Gouverneur brothers were Dutch, although their names were French. Both brothers were in the internment camp with George and both passed away from disease before the war ended. When Marie's brother Erik was born in in 1948, he was named after his father and brother and the Gouverneur brothers: Erik George Eduard Jacques.

By September 1945, the Indonesian rebellion for independence had taken firm hold throughout Java. Europeans were warned to stay inside camps or travel with an armed escort if they had to go into the streets. The Allies had arrived at Tandjong Priok, but liberation would still take months of work (*Tjideng Reunion*, 417). The Japanese guards that had remained behind turned into the protectors of the Dutch, and they set to work cleaning up the camps as well, including cleaning out sewage ditches and clearing garbage from streets. A truck stocked with petroleum stoves was delivered to Tjideng Camp, and the women were then able to begin cooking for themselves (418).

On the night of September 18, 1945, a rebel group of Indonesian men and youth attached Tjideng Camp. They marched up Laan Trivelli, armed with goloks and rantjangs, waving their red and white flags, while screaming for independence. As they beat their tongtongs, they began to tear down the bamboo walls around the camp (419). One of the medical doctors asked to borrow Sakai's revolver, and with a few threatening shots, the mob was dispersed (420).

During these weeks, Dutch men began arriving at Tjideng, seeking out their loved ones. Sometimes, the journey to the camp was more dangerous than the previous three years of being interned, as they were now at risk of being captured and tortured by the rebels (421).

CHAPTER 32

When British soldiers finally arrived to offer protection to the Dutch internees, they were still vastly outnumbered: it was a few dozen against thousands of rebel Indonesians. The solution was temporary at best. Protests were happening all over Java, and even the armed platoon of sailors from *HMS Cumberland* could only stand and watch. Security was precarious. Despite the arrival of Allied forces, camp cleanup, the additional food, and the reuniting of families, the dreams of being able to return to their island homes and resume their lives had vanished for the

Dutch. They would have to be repatriated to another country (*Tjideng Reunion*, 420).

Details of the party on an American warship in Tandjong Priok harbor come from several sources, including my interviews with Marie (Rita). "I remember there being music and some swings and we were given candy," she told me. "I know it was American as I heard the words *Yanks*, and *Yankees*, referring to the American sailors. We ran around the ship, crazily and so happy to be free." The sailors provided lunch to the visitors of their ship and gave out rolls that weren't as hard as rocks (*Tjideng Reunion*, 418).

CHAPTER 33

With Allied armies stretched thin across the globe, involved in rescue and humanitarian work, the British sent the Gurkhas and Seaforth Highlanders to Tandjong Priok. Since Java was effectively controlled by the nationalists, the Allied forces had a precarious job to extradite Dutch and European citizens from the islands (*Tjideng Reunion*, 422–23).

As described in the chapter, the Vischer family was able to get out on the first ship transporting Dutch citizens. Marie (Rita) Vischer told me, "My dad was able to get us on the first ship out and the Dutch authorities made him in charge of all the women and children on the ship *Staffordshire*. I remember getting on an army truck with canvas over the top with armed guards and hearing shooting with bullets flying everywhere. Again, I was petrified and did not think we would get to the ship alive. Occasionally I went to lie flat on the truck floor, as I was extremely scared and didn't want to be shot. For some reason the truck dropped us off quite a long way from the ship. We had to run to the gangway and up the gangway away from the snipers while the guards had their guns ready."

CONCLUDING HISTORICAL NOTE

Who was Captain Kenichi Sonei? Boudewijn Van Oort explained that Kenichi Sonei was a captain in the Imperial Japanese army. He was born in Japan and served in China before arriving in Java as a member of the 16th Army. In September 1942, Sonei was assigned to oversee several prison camps in Batavia, and he soon became notorious for his brutal punishments and lunatic-type actions. In early 1944, Sonei was reassigned to take over the supervision of several women's prison camps, which included Tjideng Camp, where his reign of terror continued. After the war, Captain Sonei was tried for war crimes in Batavia, and convicted on September 2, 1946, as a class B war criminal. He was executed December 7, 1946. An English transcript of the trial is available at https://www.boudewynvanoort.com/wp-content/uploads/2021/11/Sonei-Trial.pdf.

Boudewijn Van Oort, who translated the trial transcript and lived in Tjideng as a young boy, has written extensively on the camp and maintains a web site with more information about his and others' experiences. It can be accessed at https://www.boudewynvanoort.com/.

Early in the war, Japan opposed the Indonesians gaining independence from the Dutch because it wanted to keep control over the mineral wealth of the archipelago. But in 1945 that changed when Japan realized they were about to lose the war to Western powers, and Japan supported the Indonesians in their declaration for independence from the Dutch.

By the end of 1945, the Dutch were in no position to maintain their stance in the Indies after nearly four years of living in concentration camps, because during this same time, their mother country was rebuilding after Nazi occupation.

After the atomic bombs were dropped on Japan, the Japanese government capitulated, and Indonesia declared its independence from the Dutch. Yet, it still took the Netherlands four more years to realize they were fighting a losing battle in the newly established Indonesia. The Netherlands finally capitulated in 1949. "By 1948, the situation was seen as untenable and loud voices within the United States and the United Nations began to call for an end to Dutch involvement in Indonesia. In 1949, a final agreement was brokered between the Netherlands and the newly formed United States of Indonesia which transferred sovereignty to the Indonesian government and ceded the claims of the Dutch over the ceded territory" ("Dutch Disaster in Indonesia").

Officers and crew of the *Endeh* who were killed in action:

Marine Steam Service (Msd) Officer Second Class, Lieutenant P. Hooft

Third Engineer Government Navy, Lieutenant Third Class G. M. Jules Eduard Van Wijnmalen

Recruit Quartermaster Jan Joost Ter Pelkwijk

Sailor First Class Cornelius Chatelain

Sailor First Class Jacobus Jens

Recruit Sailor Adelbert Wilhem August Pesch

Sailor Third Class Jacobus Franciscus Franken

Officers and crew of the *Endeh* who were kidnapped and killed in the Thousand Islands:

Lieutenant Commander Second Class Menno Jans Arnoldus

Second Officer Government Navy, Lieutenant Third Class Hendrik Rutgers

Third Officer Government Navy, Lieutenant Third Class Dirk Pieter Cornelis Feij

Recruit Sailor Ferdinand Christiaan Loeffen

List of contributors to *The Defining Years of the Dutch East Indies, 1942–1949: Survivors' Accounts of Japanese Invasion and Enslavement of Europeans and the Revolution That Created Free Indonesia:*

Edited by Jan A. Krancher

Contributors: Frans J. Nicolaas Ponder, Willem Wanrooy, Arthur Stock, Anton Acherman, Johannes Vandenbroek, William H. Maaskamp, Denis Dutrieux, Mathilde Ponder-Van Kempen, Barend A.

Van Nooten, Willy Riemersma-Philippi, Maria McFadden-Beek, Karel Senior, Hendrik B. Babtist, Pieter Groenevelt, Jan Vos, Feite Posthumus, K. A. Peter Van Berkum, Rita la Fontaine-de Clercq Zubli, Greta Kwik, Gerda Dikman-Van den Broek, J. Alexandra Humphrey-Spier, Amani J. Fliers-Hoeke, Joyce F. Kater-Hoeke

SELECTED BIBLIOGRAPHY

Brouwers, Jeroen, and Adrienne Dixon. *Sunken Red*. New York City: New Amsterdam Books, 1992.

Krancher, Jan A., ed. *The Defining Years of the Dutch East Indies, 1942–1949: Survivors' Accounts of Japanese Invasion and Enslavement of Europeans and the Revolution That Created Free Indonesia*. Jefferson, NC: McFarland, 2003.

Layson, Annelex Hofstra and Herman J. Viola. *Lost Childhood: My Life in a Japanese Prison Camp during World War II*. National Geographic, 2008.

Ockerse, Ralph, and Evelijn Blaney. *Our Childhood in the Former Colonial Dutch East Indies: Recollections before and during Our Wartime Internment by the Japanese*. Xlibris, 2011.

Piper, Grant. "Dutch Disaster in Indonesia." *Medium*, Exploring History, 12 September 2020, https://medium.com/exploring-history/dutch-disaster-in-indonesia-a5a59d9fe533.

Van Oort, Boudewijn. *Tjideng Reunion: A Memoir of World War II on Java*. Seaside Press, 2013.

Vischer, George. "Fight for Survival Against Japs in the Java Sea." *The Moth Magazine*. March 1990, 1–5, https://www.moth.org.za/.

Vischer, George. "Fight for Survival Against Japs in the Java Sea." *The Moth Magazine*. April 1990, 5–9, https://www.moth.org.za/.

Vischer, George. "Fight for Survival Against Japs in the Java Sea." *The Moth Magazine*. May 1990, 9, https://www.moth.org.za/.

Zeeman, Maria. *Dutch Girl from Jakarta: From Indonesian Concentration Camp to Freedom*. Los Angeles: Los Nietos Press Downey, 2019.

DISCUSSION QUESTIONS

1. Before reading this book, did you know about the Dutch experience during WWII on Java Island? If not, what surprised you?

2. Ironically, Japanese individuals were interned throughout the US during WWII, and Europeans were interned by Japan throughout the Indonesian archipelago. Why or why not is sequestering a specific race of people during a world war a good idea?

3. In both the Dutch and the Japanese, we see various characters, some who are extremists and others who have soft hearts no matter the situation. How do you think you'd act, or hope you'd act, if forced to experience destitution and the desperation that a war brings?

4. Even though Rita was quite young when she was interned with her family, war has a way of giving everyone a hard dose of reality. What sort of characteristics showed Rita's maturity far beyond her years?

5. It seems typical for those who've experienced traumas such as a war-torn situation, to not speak about what they've gone through. This was the case for Rita's mother and father after they returned to the Netherlands. Why do you think they didn't want to share their experiences as Rita and Robbie got older or when they had more children?

6. Rita said that her brother Georgie rarely gave her mother, Mary, any trouble, and he was always bringing comfort to her. Why do you think this was Georgie's personality, and why do you think some boys like Johan didn't join the troublemakers in camp?

7. Since George Vischer was so isolated from his family during the war, and also went through a terrible experience on the Java Sea, why

do you think he continued working for a shipping company that took him from his family for long stretches and put him back on the ocean?

8. Mary copes with her family's internment by staying as busy as possible, as well as focusing on taking care of her children and mother. Can you relate to her insight here: "She'd become so used to illness, news of death, and other setbacks, that sometimes she felt numb to it all."

9. At the end of the book, Johan and Rita agree to keep telling their stories. They don't want to forget what happened to them. Do you think it's sometimes better to forget an experience, or more important to share what you've gone through?

10. In Rita's afterword, she said, "There are no winners in a war. We all face hard things in our lives, some of those things may feel insurmountable. In those moments, I've learned that happiness comes from within, it cannot be found elsewhere." What helps you endure challenges and keep moving forward in life?

ACKNOWLEDGMENTS

Writing the story of Marie Vischer Elliott and her family was an honor and an experience I'll never forget. I'm grateful for Marie's willingness to share her journey with me, for it makes my life's journey all the richer. I've been able to meet one of Marie's good friends, and her grandson, Hamish, as well. I hope to meet more of the family.

I'm grateful to my publisher for their support of my writing—it really does take a team to bring this book into your hands. Many thanks to Chris Schoebinger who spearheaded this project from day one to completion. There are many behind-the-scenes people who work on my behalf, and I'd like to especially thank Heidi Gordon, Lisa Mangum, Derk Koldewyn, Ilise Levine, Troy Butcher, Callie Hansen, Alison Palmer, and editor extraordinaire, Janna DeVore.

Presubmission, I consulted with Vilas Yang for details about Java Island. My niece Cassidy Clegg typed up my annotations from several research books. My sister Julianne Clegg and author Julie Wright read the first draft (sorry!) and gave excellent feedback. Although my sister did say she was "stressed the whole time." My literary agent Ann Leslie Tuttle, who I'm grateful to have as a publishing associate, as always, sent along insightful comments. Thanks as well to Liz Hansen for sharing her experiences of living in Indonesia. Additional thanks go to author friends Jen Geigle Johnson and Rebecca Connolly for acting as daily sounding boards.

My family has been a major support of my writing career. Thank you to my parents, Kent and Gayle Brown, and my father-in-law, Lester

Moore. And of course, thanks to my husband, Chris, our children, Kaelin, Kara, Dana, and Rose, and our grandson Ezra.

In addition to listing my research sources in the chapter notes and bibliography, I'd like to thank the men and women who courageously recorded their stories of survival: Ralph Ockerse, Evelijn Blaney, Jan A. Krancher and the many people he brought together in his compilation, Boudewijn Van Oort, Jeroen Brouwers, Annelex Hofstra Layson, Maria Zeeman, and of course George Vischer. I know there are many more stories to read, and my research will never truly be finished. Everyone's story is unique and discovering the history of the war years in the Indonesian archipelago provides an even more complete picture of our pasts.